60

FARRAR
STRAUS
GIROUX

ALSO BY SIMONETTA AGNELLO HORNBY

The Almond Picker

THE MARCHESA

THE MARCHESA

Simonetta Agnello Hornby

Translated from the Italian by Alastair McEwen

Farrar, Straus and Giroux

New York

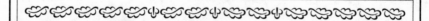

Farrar, Straus and Giroux
19 Union Square West, New York 10003

Copyright © 2004 by Giangiacomo Feltrinelli Editore Milano
Translation copyright © 2007 by Alastair McEwen
All rights reserved
Distributed in Canada by Douglas & McIntyre Ltd.
Printed in the United States of America
Originally published in 2004 by Giangiacomo Feltrinelli Editore, Italy, as *La Zia Marchesa*
Published in the United States by Farrar, Straus and Giroux
First American edition, 2007

Library of Congress Cataloging-in-Publication Data
Agnello Hornby, Simonetta.
  [Zia marchesa. English]
  The marchesa / Simonetta Agnello Hornby ; translated from the Italian by
Alastair McEwen.
    p. cm.
  ISBN-13: 978-0-374-18245-8 (hardcover : alk. paper)
  ISBN-10: 0-374-18245-0 (hardcover : alk. paper)
  I. McEwen, Alastair.   II. Title.

PQ4861.G567Z3313 2007
853'.92—dc22

                                                      2006030400

Designed by Jonathan D. Lippincott

www.fsgbooks.com

1 3 5 7 9 10 8 6 4 2

To the Hornbini
born and to be born,
and to their great-grandmother

Expect nothing that does not come from yourself.

—Luigi Pirandello (from the guest book of Baroness Maria Giudice)

Cast of Characters

Baron Stefano Safamita di Muralisci, married to
Caterina Lattuca, and his family

Guglielmo, widower, married to Maria Stella Mufuleto di Meusa
   Caterina, married to her uncle Domenico
Assunta, house nun
Domenico, married to his niece Caterina
   Stefano, marries Filomena Carcarozzo
      Caterina, Guglielmo, and other children
   Costanza, marries the Marchese Pietro Patella di Sabbiamena
   Giacomo, marries Adelaide Lattuca
      ten surviving children
Carolina, widow of Baron Antonio Arrassa dello Scravaglio
   Gesuela, Stefano, and other children
Teresa, married to Cavaliere Mariano Lo Vallo
   Paolo (wife Eleonora) and other children
Vanna, married to Baron Giovanni Ramazza di Limuna
   Maria Carolina, Ignazio, Ferdinando, Vincenzo, and other children
      Alfonsina, marries Cavaliere Cesare Calliasalata
Maria Anna, married to Count Alessandro Pertusi di Trasi
   Giuseppe (daughter Giovanna)
   Stefano (son Sandro, marries Maria Teresa)

Maria Antonia, marries Senator Iero Bentivoglio di Piscitelli
   six other children

Relatives and friends of the Safamitas

Count Antonio Safamita di Vasciterre and his wife, Illuminata
Count Gioacchino Moschitta di Acere and his wife, Orsolina
Senator Don Baldo Bentivoglio di Piscitelli
   Iero, marries Maria Antonia Trasi
Baron Francesco Vuttichina di Orata, a cousin of Count Pertusi di Trasi
Baron Pasquale Almerico and his wife, Mariangela
Cavaliere Bartolomeo Lattuca, father of Giacomo Safamita's wife,
   Adelaide

Priests to the Safamita household

Father Gaspare Sedita
Father Matteo Puma
Father Tommaso Ingaggiato

The Safamita household staff

MAJORDOMOS
   Calogero Giordano, in Castle Sarentini
   Filippo Leccasarda, in Safamita House
   Antonino Cicero, in Palazzo Safamita

GOVERNESSES
   Mademoiselle Annie Besser
   Madame Else von Schuden

COACHMEN
   Vito Pelonero, to Baron Guglielmo
   Paolo Mercurio, to Baron Domenico

VALETS AND PERSONAL MAIDS
  Gaetano Cucurullo, to Baron Guglielmo
  Gaspare Quagliata, to Baron Domenico
  Peppinella Radica and Santuzza Diodato, to Donna Assunta
  Nora Aiutamicristo, to Baroness Caterina
  Maddalena Lisca, to Costanza as a child
  Rosa Nascimbene, to Costanza as an adult

WET NURSES
  Amalia Cuffaro, to Costanza; née Belice, married to Diego Cuffaro
      son Giovannino
  Rosa Vinciguerra, to Stefano
  Maria Caponetto, to Giacomo

ELDERLY FEMALE RETAINERS
  Maria Teccapiglia, once maid to Baroness Maria Stella, widow of
      Gaetano Tignuso
  Annuzza la Cirara, house seamstress

KITCHEN STAFF
  head cook
  Lina Munnizza, assistant cook

People of Sarentini and district

Carmelo and Titta Cuffaro
Pina Pissuta, midwife
Celestina Vita, midwife
Melchiorre Tuttolomondo, married to Teodora Gaetano and Clotilde
Carmine Belice, Amalia's brother
    Pinuzza and other children
Teresina Pastanova, Prince Chisicussi's kept woman and former
    mistress of the Marchese Sabbiamena

The staff at Malivinnitti

Pepi Tignuso, a mafioso
  son Lillo
Gaspare and Mimmo Tignuso, Pepi's nephews, sons of the late
  Gaetano Tignuso and Maria Teccapiglia

The Sabbiamena household staff

Baldassare Cacopardo, valet to the Marchese Sabbiamena
Carmelo Galifi, majordomo of Sabbiamena House in Cacaci
Agostino Porrazzo, majordomo of Palazzo Sabbiamena in Palermo
Assunta Sucameli, a maid
Rura Fecarotta, a maid
Antonio, the Marchese Sabbiamena's bastard son

Marchese Pietro Sabbiamena's relatives

Prince Gaetano Virrina di Chisicussi, an uncle
  son Alvaro
Baroness Annina Finocchiaro di Lannificchiati, an aunt

Others

The Italian prefect Ermenegildo Calloni

PART ONE

"God ministers to old and young alike."

December 1898
On the Montagnazza, Amalia Cuffaro, wet nurse to Costanza
Safamita, chats with her niece Pinuzza Belice as she braids her hair.

Amalia Cuffaro finished spoon-feeding Pinuzza with the pap made from dry bread and goat's milk. Using a corner of the napkin tied round Pinuzza's neck, she wiped her mouth and chin—Pinuzza dribbled and would often spit out the food, even the things she was fond of—then gave the napkin a good shake and flicked off the bread that Pinuzza had spat onto her shoulder. The ants were lying in wait: the most populous colony had settled inside the hollow stone where the big water jug stood; from there they would emerge in compact formation to head for all the manna that fell from on high every morning.

Disheartened, Amalia was lost in thought: a lot of bread and milk was thrown away in the household, where the only thing they had in abundance was hunger; they were bad ants—warlike, with big bodies and reddish heads, the kind that bite—and bold enough to climb up onto the chair to which Pinuzza was strapped. They would run all over her, their bites leaving her skin covered in red spots. Sometimes Amalia even found them inside the poor dear's mouth. Pinuzza could not defend herself, and Amalia would have to stick her fingers into the girl's mouth to rid her of the audacious little creatures.

Still supple despite her years, Amalia straightened up in the middle of the cave, legs apart, ready to renew her stubborn, endless battle against the ants. She bent down and ran her arm between her legs to grasp the back hem of her skirts; on straightening again, she pulled the cloth forwards and tucked it into her waistband, turning her skirt into a pair of baggy, Oriental-style pantaloons. Then she took the short palmetto leaves that served her as a brush and got down to work, making sure that her skirts didn't trail on the ground, lest even one of the horrible insects climb on her. She swept carefully, throwing the columns of ants into disarray as they converged on Pinuzza's chair from every corner of the cave. She pushed the little heap of rubbish swarming with maddened ants onto the tiny ledge at the entry, and finally, with a last swipe of her brush, she sent it over the precipice—dust, bread crumbs, ants, and all.

After the premature death of her mistress, Amalia had refused to join her son, Giovannino, in America and had returned to her family. Her younger brother, Carmine Belice, took her in out of a sense of duty, but reluctantly; after the death of her parents-in-law and Giovannino's departure, Amalia had squandered her wages and even the property given to her by the Safamita family, and she came back to the Belice household as poor as she had left it to marry Diego Cuffaro forty years before. There was no room for Amalia in the Belice home—a hovel in which eight people lived and slept crammed together, along with the hens, the goat, and the donkey—so her brother had found for her and his daughter, Pinuzza, a cave on the Montagnazza, where there was no landlord. Moreover, as he would say to scandalmongers and to the merely curious, a doctor had suggested that the fresh air and sunshine would be good for Pinuzza's health.

On that part of the Sicilian coast, there is a white marl cliff standing about six hundred and fifty feet high and about six miles long, and its slopes contain a wealth of natural crevices and caves. In places this cliff protrudes into the sea like a promontory, and in others it retreats, curving back inland to form little beaches and coves. In one of these stood Riporto, the fishing village nearest to Sarentini, where Carmine Belice and his family lived. Since time immemorial the indigenous population had taken refuge in the natural caves of the Montagnazza—the local name for the cliff—enlarging them and digging out new ones when they had to hide from marauding Barbary pirates or Turkish corsairs. Access to the caves was impossible for those who didn't know them; in fact, only a few renegades had ever managed to reach them and carry off Christians doomed to Turkish slavery. Then these enemy attacks petered out, and by the mid-eighteenth century pirate incursions had become a thing of the past.

As people grew poorer and poorer, the caves were repopulated and inhabited by fugitives, criminals on the run, and young men bent on dodging the detested military service imposed by Italy's newly united government. In the caves on the lower, more accessible levels, a small colony of poor wretches, invalids, outcasts, and birds of passage took up residence. They dug out precipitous, treacherous flights of steps which the rain made smooth and even destroyed with implacable regularity, turning them into dangerous slides. In some areas the mouths of the caves had been widened in apparent symmetry and could be reached only by narrow access passageways that ran along the edge of the sheer drop.

From the sea, this part of the Montagnazza appeared to sailors by day like the undulating white façade of an immensely long building; in the evening, after sunset, when the oil lamps were burning, it looked like a fat, phosphorescent worm. The rest of the cliff curved southwards, then plunged steeply into the sea. Indomitable, it granted refuge to seagulls and, in spring and summer, served as a resting place for migrant birds. Lashed by wind and rain in winter, dazzling and almost incandescent under the summer sun, it was always most beautiful. It reminded Amalia of an immense, gleaming mass of sheep's milk curds, trembling and smooth, freshly removed from the mould by the shepherd.

Aunt and niece lived in one of these caves, the only one in the third row, almost immediately beneath the flat cliff top. The monotony of their days was relieved by weekly visits from Carmine Belice or from Pinuzza's brothers, who would bring food and firewood. It was a hard life, but Amalia was grateful to have escaped from her brother's hovel, where she could no longer bear to live after so many years spent in the palatial mansions of the aristocracy. Amalia loved solitude and nature, and on the Montagnazza she had these in abundance, while Pinuzza was a constant and agreeable companion. Amalia even managed to earn some money by mending clothes for the women below, which they passed up and down in a basket attached to a rope, and so she could indulge in her only luxury: Revalenza Arabica, a restorative powder to which she ascribed every property imaginable.

As for Pinuzza, the Montagnazza was an improvement over Riporto. Her father and her three brothers had lowered her down to the cave; they had wrapped her in a blanket folded into a kind of cradle and bound like a cocoon at the end of a thick rope, which two of her brothers wound around their bodies and then fed out little by little as the third brother bore Pinuzza down the face of the Montagnazza, hanging on to the spikes fixed here and there to the marl to guide his burden and keep the sharp outcrops from hurting his sister. Thus had Pinuzza moved from confinement in the hovel, damp and almost devoid of light, to confinement in the cave. But there, tended by her aunt in the healthful fresh air and the warmth of the sun, she was restored to better health.

Pinuzza was awaiting the ritual daily grooming. She was fourteen. Despite her infirmity, she cherished hopes and desires like any other young girl and looked forward to the pleasure of feeling neat and tidy. Amalia cleaned her mouth once again, wiping away the drool with a damp cloth, then lifted her chair and put it down carefully at the mouth of the cave.

Before Pinuzza there was sea and sky, nothing else. The winter sun was pleasantly warm. "Today I'm going to delouse you and redo your braids," said her aunt, and Pinuzza smiled. Her tormented and twisted little body had but one ornament: a head of thick, glossy black hair. Amalia took a large bone comb whose handle was embellished with mother-of-pearl decorations and began to comb the nits from Pinuzza's hair, using the part with fine teeth. She parted her niece's hair with nimble fingers, light and sure, as if the locks of the plump braids were bobbins and she were making pillow lace. It was a moment of particular intimacy for both of them: Amalia would go back over her fondest memories, and her talk would begin to flow freely. Pinuzza listened to her entranced.

"When the marchesa was a lass she didn't like having her hair done. It took hours to persuade her. And you couldn't blame her neither, because her hair was all tangles, not like yours, which is manageable and straight. Only when I sat her at the window with the sea before us in the distance, only then could I do her hair proper."

"Why?" asked Pinuzza.

"She had special hair, she did. But it wasn't fine, for all the blood of barons that ran in her veins: it was wiry as horsehair and curly as unpicked wool, so the more you smoothed it down the more it would curl. You couldn't keep it in order, and it even escaped from braids. But what a wonderful colour! As a little girl she had hair red as gold; the noonday sun it was. As she grew up it got darker and darker, like lumps of sulphur among the rocks; and when she became a woman it went the dark red of the sunset, with coppery highlights. When the sun shone on her head, her braids would gleam like the coals in a flatiron."

"She must have been beautiful, and she must have had lots of sweethearts," said Pinuzza, sighing.

"But she didn't. People didn't like her, for she was very different. They'd stop on the street and stare at her when she went by in her carriage, and they'd cross their fingers to ward off bad luck: people who are different aren't liked. I don't understand why, but that's the way it is." Amalia broke off, the glossy locks of Pinuzza's hair taut between her fingers, her gaze lost in the distance.

"Did she like her hair, or not?"

Amalia began braiding again, slowly. "Do you know, I've no idea! I loved her like a daughter and I served her to the last, but there are lots of things about her I don't know. The fact is, she was different from everyone—from the Safamita family, from the other nobles, from folk like us . . ." Amalia realised she was digressing; this was a conversation she often held with herself.

"But did she like being different from everyone else?" insisted Pinuzza.

"The nobility are different from everyone else in any case, and that can't be anything but a pleasure for them. First of all, they're never poor or hungry and they do as they please, and then . . . Of course, she liked being rich all right . . . But looking different brought her only misfortune and sadness: people took her for a creature of the Devil. Once they even threw stones at her."

"Do you know how she felt inside when they threw stones at her?"

Amalia had talked too much, and without thinking. Her sister-in-law had told her that when Pinuzza was a little girl she had put her at the door to get some fresh air while she tidied the house. Later she found the girl covered in blood: the local children had picked on her. After that Pinuzza had not seen the sunlight.

Amalia replied briefly. "She felt bad inside, but she forgave them. They were ignorant youngsters, and she had a big heart. A heart of gold like her hair, though the others couldn't have cared less about that."

"I would've had them thrashed, that lot, had the soles of their feet beaten until they couldn't walk. That would've taught them!" Pinuzza became agitated and raised her voice. "They threw stones at me, too, the way they do with dogs, only I couldn't hide, and I curse them now as I cursed them then."

Amalia hurriedly finished the braid and draped it over Pinuzza's shoulder, leaving it to hang down over her breast, so that her niece could admire it, glossy and tidy.

As Pinuzza was happily toying with it, she asked suddenly, "What did her mother say about it?"

"About what?" Amalia didn't like talking about Baroness Safamita.

"About her daughter's hair, and her being different."

"Nothing, what was she supposed to say? She was her daughter."

"You mean your marchesa was special for her mother, too, when she was born and her mother saw she was so different, or what?"

"Of course she was. But let's go inside now, it's hot in the sun," Amalia replied hastily.

Pinuzza rested in a niche in the cave wall, on a straw mattress. Amalia went back outside. It was midday. She stood looking at the sea, gleaming and flat as a board. There were no boats at that hour; silence reigned supreme. The memory of Costanza Safamita's birth came back to her, vivid and painful, casting a shadow over her heart and her eyes.

2

"Coughs, smoke, and loving sighs: these three things you can't disguise."

The wet nurse's first encounter with Costanza Safamita

Huddled in a corner of the large room, almost hidden by a screen, Amalia watched the comings and goings of the women, and the bustling of the midwives. She was horrified by the pains of the woman in the throes of labour and at the same time fascinated by the opulence of the baroness's bedroom.

Given that Baroness Safamita was in the seventh month of her pregnancy, donna Titta Cuffaro, Amalia's mother-in-law, had brought her that afternoon to the mansion house to arrange for her move into the baron's household, where she would await the birth of the child she would breast-feed. Sitting in the little kitchen where the scullions worked, Amalia listened entranced to the chatter of the serving women as they shelled a mountain of late peas piled on a marble work top. Lina Munnizza, the assistant cook, divided her time between the stove and the table, where she stood carefully selecting the smallest, sweetest peas for the young baron's table, which the head cook would prepare in his own fashion. The other peas, the big, hard floury ones, would be served to the household staff lightly sautéed in olive oil with a little green onion and garlic. Amalia's mouth was watering; they had offered her some empty peapods: her mother-in-law would be well pleased with this gift. She was looking forward to going home, her thoughts on Giovannino and the tasty broth she would prepare that evening.

But fate decreed otherwise: don Filippo Leccasarda, the majordomo, summoned her to his office, where donna Titta was waiting for her with Giovannino. She was to go into service immediately, don Filippo informed her laconically: the moment of farewell had suddenly arrived. Everything happened as if in a dream. The hushed atmosphere of that singular house soothed the emotions and smoothed out the rough edges. Clinging to her breast, Giovannino had fallen asleep as he suckled. Nora Aiutamicristo, the baroness's personal maid, came to them with an order: the young baron wished to reassure his wife in labour that the child about to be born would find instant nourishment, so he wanted the wet nurse to be taken into her presence on the main floor. The farewells were rapid: Giovannino slept on in his grandmother's arms, and now he belonged to the Cuffaro family alone; Amalia had become a member of the Safamita household and would remain in its service for as long as the masters pleased.

Nora Aiutamicristo led Amalia up the service stairs, through rooms, corridors, and parlours. Overwhelmed by the giltwork of the furnishings, the glitter of crystal chandeliers, the painted ceilings, the deep-piled carpets, and the sumptuous tapestries, she struggled to keep up with Nora's rapid pace.

"We are coming to the baroness's bedroom."

"Where does the young baron sleep?" asked Amalia curiously.

"Nobles each have their own personal rooms, those for the wife and those for the husband, then they do as they wish between themselves." Nora turned round with a severe look. "Let me give you some sisterly advice: you don't ask questions in the Safamita household. Bear that in mind, if you want to stay here."

Amalia said no more, but she did not forget this. In silence, they made their way along a corridor as wide as a gallery, furnished with chairs and small, narrow tables. Nora stopped in front of a large door. She put her ear to it, then knocked gently and without waiting for a reply opened it, gesturing at Amalia to go in.

Amalia saw herself again, just turned eighteen, alone and insecure, walking into the room with little steps: it was immense, big as a sacristy, the furniture dark and imposing. The baroness's table had been placed in front of the balcony, where it could catch the dusty reddish light of the dying day; she could not take her eyes off that huge table surrounded by women, who formed a screen around the baroness. Pina Pissuta, the midwife, was bent over the woman in labour, while the others bustled about. Then the midwife straightened up and turned to Amalia; she extended an arm in her direction with the palm open towards her. Amalia obeyed and stopped where she was, in the middle of the room. A cry. Then the sound of many voices. She could sense the reproving looks of two maids: she wished the ground would swallow her up, make her disappear, and carry her back home to her son; even the thought of her husband was not entirely disagreeable. Looking up, she saw that she was right underneath a chandelier whose bronze arms branched out and upwards, menacing as an upended spider. She murmured a charm against ill luck; she felt faint. Pina Pissuta had left the group of women and was coming towards her. In the same autocratic manner as before, she told Amalia to keep out of the way, pointing at the nook assigned to her: she would be summoned when the time was right.

Amalia was left there for hours, relegated to the corner, almost forgotten. She in turn forgot home and son and, numbed, didn't notice that milk was oozing from her nipples, wetting her bodice, now stained by two large damp rings. The other midwife brought her back to reality. "Wash her carefully," she said, hastily handing Amalia the newborn baby girl wrapped in a cloth, and then returned to the table where Pina Pissuta was dealing with the mother, who was having difficulties. Beside Amalia stood a little table adapted to serve as a changing top, with lots of enamel basins and towels, cloths, nappy pins, swaddling clothes, a little blouse, a frock, a bonnet, gloves, a jacket, bibs, shoes, and a small basket with the first necessities. In the half-light, Amalia slowly removed the clots stuck to the baby's skin, using cotton wads soaked beforehand in warm water with a dash of rose water and then well squeezed. She washed the baby's hands and carefully tried to remove the slimy mucus that still stuck to her hair.

Intent as she was on washing the baby—she fitted perfectly in the hollow of Amalia's hand—pouring lukewarm water over her head with tender, solemn movements, as if she were at a baptismal font, Amalia didn't notice the arrival of Baroness Carolina Scravaglio, or the gleaming light of the candlesticks that she had ordered brought closer. She was staring intensely at the creature to whom she would devote the next two years of her life or maybe more; waves of tenderness welled up within her like mild labour pains, and a powerful love for the baby girl grew in her. In the candlelight she discovered the rich red colour of the baby's hair as she gradually dried it with a muslin cloth. She looked up and exclaimed, "This is a really special baroness. She has hair red as the sun. Happy the man who will marry her; look how plump and firm her flesh is. She's really long, too, the biggest seven-month baby in the world!" She wrapped the baby in a shawl and clasped her to her bosom.

Amalia still remembered the words with which she had had the audacity to address the young baron when he presented himself, standing with his legs apart, before her: "Would your lordship like to hold his daughter?" She had forgotten that you don't give newborn babies to men to hold, that only women handle them, yet the young baron took that red-haired daughter of his and held her close, looking at her like a lover.

Amalia dried a tear—the memory of Costanza in her father's arms always moved her.

3

"Good luck and male children."

Costanza Safamita is born in the mansion in Sarentini, 22 May 1859.

In her bedroom, the baroness lay on a dinner table that had been decked out like an altar, draped with woollen blankets, oilcloth, and sheets of the finest cotton with closely embroidered borders; her legs, raised and supported by pillows, were decorously covered with a sheet. The footmen had hastily carried her from the small dining room that afternoon, when the baroness's waters had broken as she was taking lunch with her aunt and sister-in-law Baroness Carolina Arassa dello Scravaglio.

The room was all abuzz. The women of the house were comforting the exhausted mother, slumped on the pillows piled behind her shoulders and head: she looked as if she were about to doze off. The voices were muted as if by enchantment.

Pina Pissuta, the family's midwife, assisted by her niece and apprentice, Filomena Battaria, and by Celestina Vita, also a midwife, was at work at the end of the table. Motionless as statues, three maids held up oil lamps while the others silently carried out Pina Pissuta's orders. Amalia Cuffaro, the wet nurse to the baby about to be born, had been relegated to a corner of the room and there she stayed, motionless, on a stool, as if she were part of the new baby's layette.

The baroness was in full labour. Pina Pissuta examined the dilation in the light of the lamp skilfully directed by her niece: she could glimpse the baby's cranium. She laid her right hand on the baroness's warm belly; the contractions were intensifying, but she wasn't moaning. Pina sighed. The baroness was suffering: a poorly dilated vagina. Certain women were fated to be no good at bearing children; it happened among the wealthy, too. The Safamitas knew this but had given the baroness no peace, stubbornly persisting after the death of her firstborn son in their determination to have heirs to their riches. She had borne Stefano seven years before—a real miracle—but that had been followed by other miscarriages, frequent and painful. Pina had done what she shouldn't have done: two years earlier, she had dared to suggest to the young baron that he give up trying to have more children; she had told him that other husbands took care to avoid pregnancies for the sake of their wives' health, yet they had their gratifications, and plenty of them! The young baron hadn't liked this talk, but perhaps because she had chosen the right moment he didn't seem to take offense. He curtly replied that certain half measures were fine for women like her, but not for his baroness. Then the young baron, who had slept with Pina often enough in the past, this one time had gone all the way with her.

The final expulsive contractions were coming. Pale and soaked in sweat, the baroness tried to pull herself up by leaning against two women; her arms clenching theirs, her nails almost sunk in their flesh, she was groaning but stayed bent forwards to see. A last thrust, another effort, then a deep, raucous cry: the head had emerged. Pina Pissuta straightened up with ferret-like speed, as if she wanted to fortify herself before the final struggle, then bent down again, using her elbow to push back the lock of hair that had fallen over her forehead, and got back to work with total concentration; for good reason she was thought to be the best midwife in the area. She held the little head in her hands; working in harmony with the mother's thrusts, she helped the child to complete the metamorphosis from foetus to baby. There—she had come out. Pina Pissuta held the newborn in her arms. Perfect.

"A baby girl is born to the baroness!" she exclaimed loudly, to make herself heard in the antechamber where the baron and the young baron were waiting together with their sister and the nuns. She shook the newborn baby to open her lungs, and the child wailed. She seemed in perfect health. Pina handed her to Celestina, to cut and tie up the umbilical cord, pierce her ears, and give her a thorough check, and returned to look after the baroness, who was stretched out on the table, weeping.

"I don't want a girl. It should have been a boy—no, no, no . . ."

Celestina went up to her with the baby in her arms, swaddled in a cloth. The baroness gave her a weary, sullen glance, pushed her away with her arm, and covered her eyes with one hand. She was sobbing. She doesn't even want to expel the placenta, thought Pina Pissuta. She seems sadder now than when they came out dead on her. The nobility are really strange folk, but I would never have expected this from her. A little lass has been born healthy and alive, but her mother is weeping and doesn't want her. None of the maids dared comfort the baroness; silent and dismayed, they watched the midwives bustling around her and then one by one slipped off with some excuse: some to fill up the jugs with hot water, others to take the soiled sheets to the laundry, and others again to tell the household staff of the good news and to gossip.

Baroness Scravaglio, leaving her maid with the young nuns, entered the room. Her niece and sister-in-law was now repeating mechanically, "No, no, I don't want a girl," raising her voice every time she had the strength to do so.

"Caterina, you already have a son. It's lovely to have a girl—daughters are always there when you need them," Baroness Scravaglio said to her. But Caterina was paying her no heed and, vexed, had turned away on her side, so instead she went up to the wet nurse, who was busy looking after the newborn baby. "Well, she's no beauty," the baroness said to herself.

"She looks like an albino monkey—blotchy skin, hair all over her shoulders and her face, too, and all that hair . . . horrible."

In the half-light one couldn't see the colour of the child's hair. Baroness Scravaglio ordered more candles to be brought. Two maids came running, each with a five-branched candlestick. Erect and haughty, the baroness towered over the wet nurse, her gaze full of disgust at the baby's head of flaming red hair. The wet nurse noticed this. She awkwardly murmured some compliment to Baroness Scravaglio, then, forgetful of her position, blurted out, "What are you looking at? Leave us two alone!"

Baroness Scravaglio moved away; then she stopped at one end of the table, gazing disconcertedly at the mother. The young baroness was yelling: she was refusing to follow the midwives' instructions, and Pina Pissuta had to force her to expel the placenta by dint of massage and vigorous pressure on her belly.

"Ever since Mimì married his niece, they've all gone mad in this house, including the wet nurse!" Baroness Scravaglio said to herself, and, turning on her heel, returned to the antechamber without bidding anyone goodbye.

The young nuns specially invited by Donna Assunta Safamita to implore the protection of the Virgin Mary over mother and baby had been left alone in the antechamber. Gauche and awkward, they sat on the edges of their armchairs, visibly distressed. They startled every time the baroness screamed. Their virginal modesty was shocked by the mystery of birth, and they were also being exposed to unknown, strong language, which made them feel defiled. Baroness Scravaglio barely glanced at them as she hurriedly crossed the antechamber on her way to the green drawing room where her brothers had taken refuge, far from the scene of the birth.

"She's got red hair, and she seems healthy," she announced. "But whoever had red hair in the Safamita family?"

Guglielmo, the elder brother, asked, "How's my little girl?"

Domenico kept repeating, as if he were talking to himself, "My Caterina is really suffering this time." He bent over in his armchair and held his head between his hands.

"I certainly wasn't expecting a redhead. No redheads have ever been born in the Safamita family," said his sister. Standing there in the middle of the room, she demanded a reply.

"You've always been a fool, Carolina, and ignorant, too," said Guglielmo coldly. "In the house in Palermo there's a portrait of an ancestor with red hair." He got to his feet. "I'm going to see how Caterina's doing, and to meet my first granddaughter."

Voraciously attached to the wet nurse's breast, Costanza was suckling. Her grandfather Guglielmo Safamita, Baron Muralisci, watched her, sunk in his own thoughts. Then he lightly stroked her little hand and headed towards his daughter. Caterina was resting, exhausted, beneath the canopy of the big bed. "Do you want to see her?" he asked tenderly. The new mother opened her eyes. "No, no, it should have been a boy." She started to weep again, and her father left the room.

Domenico Safamita went straight to the newborn baby, who was still suckling but now only for comfort. He stood, legs apart, firmly planted, his hands entwined behind his back. The women still at work in the room stopped to watch, protected by the half-light. The wet nurse detached the baby from her breast, leaving it uncovered, white and swollen, the nipple dark and full. Entirely without embarrassment, she proffered the newborn baby to the young baron, holding her up in her well-turned arms, bare to above the elbow. The baron took the baby into his big, manly hands. He looked at her intently, holding her tightly, away from his body, as if she were some little animal, his eyes fixed on the snubby little face. He settled her on his right arm, clutched her close to his chest, and went up to his wife with slow steps: "Love of my life, what a beautiful daughter you have given me! Look at her." And he sat down beside Caterina on the edge of the bed, lowering his arm to give her a better look at the baby.

The baroness turned her head away with a sudden movement. "She's a girl. I don't want her, she should have been a boy," she murmured.

"Turn round." Cold and detached, the young baron assumed the imperious tone of the Safamitas. "Look at her," he insisted. "This daughter you have given me is mine, do you understand? She is my daughter. I love her, and you must love her, too. Do you understand?" He was speaking in a low voice so that he could not be heard by the maids, who were backed against the wall, timorous and embarrassed but all ears.

Slowly the baron lifted up the baby, bending over her slightly. His long beard and moustache brushed the child, concealing her from the gaze of the others as he covered her cheeks with little kisses. He laid her down on the bed beside her mother, drawing a silk sheet over her. Then he got to his feet and stood there looking at them, one beside the other. Finally, he bent over and kissed his wife. Caterina's dry lips were pursed and wouldn't open; he had to thrust his tongue forcefully between them. They kissed each other passionately. The maids were used to seeing this, but not the other women. Celestina and the wet nurse looked on in embarrassment. Heedless, the couple carried on kissing. The baby girl seemed shoved to the edge of the bed.

At that very moment the baron came back into the room, and his arrival put an end to the scene.

4

"Of wealth and sanctity believe but half."

In Castle Sarentini, Donna Assunta Safamita prays with her "house nuns."

Of the medieval Castle Sarentini very little remained, so heavily had it been reconstructed over the centuries; it was a big building, still pompously called "the castle." Clad in plaster that was faintly pink and surrounded by tree-filled gardens, it towered almost benignly, like the pale cherry of a green marzipan cassata, atop the hill on whose slopes the village of Sarentini had sprung up in the seventeenth century. And thus it dominated and inspired the respect of the town below.

It had been built on the highest of the hills that broke away in clusters from the mountains of the interior and sloped down towards the coast, dividing the fertile lands of the Sarentini district into two valleys. One valley undulated down and then flattened out at the sea, barely notched by the bed of the river Tinto, which by now was almost dry: the old watercourse could be recognised by the canebrakes flourishing in the stony riverbed like a thirsty green snake. The other valley, wider, dark, and generous, broadened out into wheat fields before it was closed off by the mountains of the hinterland.

Donna Assunta Safamita had gone to ground in the small drawing room of Castle Sarentini, surrounded by her women, as soon as she heard that Caterina was in labour. She had refused to go to Safamita House out of a sense of repugnance and modesty no different from that of the nuns, and she participated in the event at a distance, reciting Rosaries and propitiatory prayers. Donna Assunta sat in her armchair; the other women—huddled on hard chairs, in a circle, each with rosary in hand, overcome and anxious—were reeling off the beads, repeating litanies, brief prayers, and even rhymes about saints real and apocryphal.

Such choral devotions filled the days of these ladies—elderly widows and women resigned to spinsterhood—and they were a source of comfort. But with the passing of the hours the vocal praying took on an anxious, almost hysterical tone. The women exchanged frightened looks, mumbled, and filled the pauses with sighs in order to get their breath before murmuring sotto voce—fearing Donna Assunta's disapproval, "Poor lass," "Who knows how she's suffering," "Still no news," "Let's hope the baby will live," "Children, what a cross to bear."

Donna Assunta was still tenacious and bossy, her fifty-odd years notwithstanding: when she began to intone the Paternoster, her voice weary but firm, she was instantly followed by the muttering of her mystical and obedient companions. Only the heaving of the starched white bands of the bonnet over her shoulders and robust bosom betrayed her emotion: every so often she would turn her gaze to the door, hoping that someone would announce the good news of the birth of another son and further guarantee of the continuance of the Safamita line. She, too, had always been anxious about that marriage—forbidden by the Church and, what's more, a mismatch in her view; but she had to admit that it had proved to be a happy union and would have been even more so had it not been marred by Caterina's difficulty in bringing her many pregnancies to term. *Hallowed be Thy name.* She was thinking of her niece's unhappy destiny. An only child, Caterina had spent her infancy in the castle without the company of other children and with constant worries over her sick mother. *Thy will be done.* Left a widower, Guglielmo had not wanted to remarry and, morbidly attached to his daughter, had refused to send her to the convent school in Palermo with her cousins. Donna Assunta's niece had lived a solitary life, tutored by Mademoiselle Besser, a foreigner and a Protestant—two good reasons for arousing Assunta's suspicions—until she conceived a passion for her uncle. And then Caterina had left no stone unturned until he gave up his bachelor life, his travels, and his friends in Palermo to stay in Sarentini, bewitched by his niece. She had always been strange, this taciturn girl who preferred solitude, reading, and music to the company of other women. As a child, she had been obsessed with tortoises, and her father had allowed them to infest the terrace, which they ruled. After her marriage, she always stayed at home alone and was reluctant to receive guests; it seemed that she was fulfilled only by the company of her husband and later by that of Stefano, her one living son. Yet she was an obedient wife, a good mistress of the house, and an irreproachable mother. Still, Assunta perceived that something wasn't right. She felt that Caterina was distant; there was a certain *je ne sais quoi* about her, something impenetrable, obscure, almost tragic. *Lead us not into temptation and deliver us from evil.*

"Amen" intoned the other women, and they went back to their Ave Marias.

5

"He who solves his problem lives to fight another day."

A conversation dense with allusions between the Safamita brothers

It was late at night, and it was cool in the green drawing room at Safamita House. Carolina Scravaglio had finally gone to bed, but not before declaring melodramatically that it was up to her, as the eldest sister and a married woman, to stand in for her sister-in-law the dear departed Maria Stella: she would stay on at the mansion house to look after Caterina. The brothers were left alone, to their evident relief. They were united by a profound, undisguised intolerance of Carolina. Drained by the emotions of the day, they smoked in silence, each immersed in his own thoughts.

Domenico Safamita was cold. He felt like having a little fire. He wakened Gaspare, dozing on a stool behind the door, who trotted off to rouse some of the other servants. Rather smelly from the warm sweat of first sleep, their livery dishevelled, their shirts hanging down over hastily donned breeches, two footmen knelt in front of the fireplace and busied themselves before the bored and indifferent gaze of their masters. Domenico lit another cigar, stretched himself out in his armchair, and raised his head. The smoke rose in the room, lit first by the candlelight and then gradually paling as it was swallowed up in the darkness of the high painted ceiling.

Eyes lowered, Guglielmo glanced idly at the flames. With deep, slow breaths he inhaled the aroma of the olive branches crackling in the fireplace.

"I don't want Carolina sleeping here tomorrow, too," said Domenico. "Would you put her up in the castle?"

"But she's here to be with Caterina." Guglielmo didn't like the idea of having to play host to his intolerable sister, who was also said to have become a kleptomaniac.

"She doesn't want her around," Domenico said defensively.

"Is anything missing?"

"She hasn't stolen anything so far as I know. I ordered her maid to keep an eye on her."

"She's no thief . . . it's an illness. Of course I'll put her up at the castle. She's my sister." After a brief pause he added, "And yours, too."

"I know, but Caterina needs peace and quiet. Carolina talks a lot, and it's often nonsense. Today she told me a complicated story. I'm afraid she's taken things from her friends and is in trouble. Perhaps someone is put out with her and is blackmailing her or wishes her ill. I don't know . . . the fact is, she's fearful about something."

"She's talked to me about these suspicions—more than once." Guglielmo went back to looking at the fire: long, swaying, sensual tongues of flame issued from the logs like snakes, pursuing one another before vanishing up the chimney.

Domenico gave the embers a poke and contemplated the flames—long, red. "Who was it?" he asked point-blank.

"This baby is alive." Guglielmo didn't take his eyes off the flames, not for an instant.

"Did you have anything to do with it?" insisted his brother.

"Yes and no," replied the baron, imperturbable.

"What does that mean?" Domenico's voice came as if dredged up from his guts.

"It means what it means. Caterina does as she pleases and as she thinks fit. I am only her father, not her husband. It is for you to give her orders. She always listens to you." They were rivals once more.

"He has to go," said Domenico.

"I've already seen to that," replied Guglielmo, looking him straight in the eye.

"When?"

"He's my man." The baron wanted to keep matters confidential.

"Did you know?" Domenico was chewing nervously on his cigar.

"I wasn't sure of it."

"And now? Are you sure?"

"I've seen the baby, and you have, too." Guglielmo's look was sombre and fierce.

"She's a redhead," said Domenico.

"Indeed," replied his brother. He took the cigar box, offered one to Domenico, who grunted "No, thanks" between clenched teeth, and lit one for himself.

"What about our sisters?" Domenico asked suddenly.

"What do you expect from those idiots? Assunta will be happy if you ask her to be the godmother, which is her due in place of our mother, God rest her soul. As for the others, they don't count." Guglielmo got to his feet and rapidly changed the subject. "Do you know that Carolina wants a loan?" At fifty-seven he was still a handsome man, elegant and agile, with thick hair and only a tinge of grey in his beard. He looked at his younger brother and was moved by his undisguised dismay. Deep dismay.

He forgot the rivalries past and present, the perennial conflicts that Domenico's mere presence aroused in him—his ally and rival, his only daughter's husband and lover. He felt sorry for him. On one side of the fireplace hung a portrait of their father, Stefano Safamita; the background of the painting showed Villa la Camusa, the family's summer residence just outside the town, where he had no longer wanted to set foot after his wife's death. Sad thoughts of the past resurfaced. He walked about the drawing room and then, reluctantly and with some embarrassment, went up to his brother's armchair and laid his gnarled hand on his shoulder, a rare gesture of solidarity for a Safamita; they were a family little inclined to effusiveness and extremely reserved.

"We two, grandfather and father, will have to look after this baby if Caterina doesn't want anything to do with her. Safamita blood runs in her veins and she must be rich, like her brother Stefano. I'm going to bed. You do the same, Mimì," he said finally, using the almost forgotten pet name for his younger brother. And he went out without giving Domenico a further glance.

In the carriage, during the brief trip to the castle, the baron asked Gaetano Cucurullo if he had carried out his orders.

"Yes, your lordship," replied his trusted valet. "I sent word to the manager of the Corbotta. He'll come tomorrow evening, and I told don Antonino Cicero to call for Ciappa, the master painter."

"Good," said Guglielmo, pleased. Then he added, "I like my granddaughter, Costanza, a redhead like the daughter of the blessed Giuseppe. This is a good sign, Tano. A little girl was just what was needed in the Safamita family."

That night the baron slept peacefully and did not dream. But his brother remained awake. At dawn he went into his wife's room; he found her sleeping quietly, on her back, her chestnut hair flowing over the pillow like a halo. He stretched out beside her, on the lace coverlet, fully dressed, and explored her with his gaze for the umpteenth time: small face, thin lips, the slightly aquiline Safamita nose, soft smooth skin . . . he loved her as she was—the ardent child who had chosen him as her husband when she was eight years old. He desired her. He took a curl of her hair between his fingers, toying with it but being careful not to wake her. Then he laid his head on the pillow and fell into a deep sleep.

First thing in the morning, the maids went into the green drawing room to clean. Still burning in the fireplace were some pieces of gilded, polished wood, horsehair stuffing, scraps of damask: in one of his fits of rage the young baron had smashed a chair. This time, perhaps to celebrate in his own way the birth of his daughter, Costanza, he had also decided to burn it, rather than leave the majordomo with the task of having it fixed.

In the afternoon, in the pantry, the maids cleaned the vegetables for that evening's dinner and, in the absence of the menservants, they talked at length and freely. At first they couldn't understand a thing, then they concluded that the young baron had broken the chair out of disappointment at the birth of a daughter.

6

"When the tree falls, every man runs to make firewood."

Sarentini buzzes with gossip following the birth of Costanza Safamita
and forgets the king's death, but not the past.

The gossip began that very evening, rumours which slithered all around town until the Safamita family, with their legendary munificence, quelled them on the occasion of Costanza's baptism, albeit only temporarily.

The news of the birth of a daughter to the young Baron Safamita spread through Sarentini in a flash, confirming, as if there were any need, that the rumour mill always trumps orthodox channels of communication. The town crier, whose task was to inform people, with an accompanying roll of drums, of the death of the unloved King Ferdinando II, in the distant palace of Caserta, and of the ascension to the throne of Francesco II, found that this news aroused scant interest and no sorrow among the people. On the other hand, the busybodies gave the man no peace about the Safamita household; in low voices they asked him repeatedly for news, which he dispensed with the dignity appropriate to his station.

People gossiped even more than was proper. Of course, there was plenty to gossip about concerning that arrogant family, which at the beginning of the century had left Palermo for Sarentini following Baron Stefano Muralisci's marriage to Caterina Lattuca, a bourgeois heiress. The Safamitas had proved to be grasping and haughty; they had reinforced their squads of private guards, employed ruthless field overseers and watchmen, reconstructed and all but fortified their farms, and behaved as if they were sovereign rulers of their lands, even of the town itself. Having taken up residence in the castle of the Princes Arcuneri, barons of Sarentini, who had been absentee landlords for generations and were by then impoverished, the Safamitas had spared no expense in enlarging it. They could all have lived there comfortably, but the young baron decided to have a grandiose mansion house built where he could live with his niece, whom he had married after persuading the bishop to issue a dispensation from the prohibition of marriage between close blood relatives. It was known that she had become infatuated with her uncle and had seduced him. But money does not wash away sins, and everyone, rich and poor alike, must sooner or later pay the reckoning: this dreadful red-haired daughter, like no daughter who had ever been seen in the memory of Sarentini, now bore witness to her mother's shame. But there was worse: the mother had rejected the child. Rumour had it that at her birth the mother had behaved like a madwoman and had not even taken the baby in her arms. The young nuns from the Convent of the Carmine had plenty to say about this. On the pretext of buying sweets and biscuits, people went to the convent wheel to listen through the zinc grille as the sister dispenser repeated what the innocent young nuns had said after being called to Safamita House to pray for the birth. In her customary calm, sweet lilt, the sister said the novices were still atremble over the obscene cries of the baroness, who had clearly been seized by the Devil during labour, and over her desperation after the birth, as if she were disgusted by her own flesh and blood.

But it wasn't only outsiders who were talking about the features of the newborn girl and the welcome her mother gave her. Even Baroness Scravaglio spoke of her sister-in-law's appalling behaviour. Caterina Safamita bore the mark of evil and it was necessary to find an exorcist, or to fall back on the old and effective methods of witchcraft to save her and all the Safamitas.

Nor did the people of Sarentini spare the young baron: he was haughty, stubbornly determined to outdo his brother in luxury and wealth, and, of course, devoured by his unhealthy passion for his niece. God's punishment had been visited upon him, causing all the children they conceived together to die except that one son—and the boy was not above criticism, either, though to voice it would have been unwise—and now he was landed with a red-haired daughter with bovine eyes and a yellowish face blotched with freckles.

That very few people had seen her, that Costanza was a normal baby girl with red hair and a fair complexion, was conveniently ignored. Soon Costanza Safamita's ugliness was sanctioned; it became a byword in people's conversations and was handed down to subsequent generations.

"A red mane is the Devil's bane." The old sayings have a lot of truth in them.

7

"Hardships and ease are yours if you please."

*Amalia Cuffaro remembers her marriage and the conception of her son,
thanks to the intervention of her mother-in-law and of Saint John Beheaded.*

The steamship slipped placidly over the sea, no longer rough but not yet clear or uniformly smooth and far from its usual bright blue. Ruffled by small, foamy waves, its creased taffeta surface was divided into broad horizontal stripes of light blues, greens, and greys, while the outermost streaks were almost purple: the residual effects of a storm. The ship ploughed across the streaks of colour on its way to the open sea, its prow pointed at the horizon, its long whitish wake fanning out behind. Black smoke from its funnel rose straight up, paling as it blended with the dark sky. At a respectful distance, two fishing smacks under half sail cautiously proceeded in its wake, their trawl nets dragging behind them. The sky was a mass of leaden clouds, no longer piled high but arrayed in thick, wide layers in various shades of grey—from a pale, almost shining hue to an oppressive darkness that seemed ready to become lashing rain again.

The air was bracing. Amalia and Pinuzza stayed outside to escape the penetrating stench in the cave, saturated by the damp that oozed from the porous white stone, dripped down the walls in large teardrops, and fell from the roof in fat beads.

Motionless on their chairs and well wrapped up—they had put on all the clothes they owned—they drew in deep gulps of fresh air, their eyes fixed on the sea. During the raging storm, Pinuzza had been silent, frightened by the thunder and huddled in the alcove that served her as chair, table, and bed. Now, in the open, she couldn't stop asking questions.

"Where's that big ship going?"

"To an island far away."

"How do you know?"

"Don Paolo told me."

"And will it go to New York from there?"

"I don't know."

"Would you like to go to New York to see Giovannino?"

"Of course."

"So why don't you?"

"Because I'm here with you."

"What's that got to do with it? He's your son, and he needs you. If you want to, you should go, and I'll go back to town."

"I haven't seen him since he was eighteen."

"Why did he go away?"

"To work. That is the fate of all us poor folk."

"But why didn't you go with him?"

"So as not to leave the marchesa."

"You loved her more than your own son."

"No, differently. I loved both of them."

"She wasn't your kin like Giovannino, but you stayed with . . ." Pinuzza left the phrase in midair and fell silent.

The ship, now only a fleck of black stubble, was about to disappear, about to plunge lightly beyond the line of the horizon, in free but safe fall onto another, enormous sea—the one that led to the distant land where Giovannino lived, thought Amalia, who found it hard to believe what don Paolo had told her: that the world was round as a dove's egg. For her, the sea was like a fountain with many basins, on which leaves floated and slipped down from one pool to the next, infinitely.

"But how did you end up with the marchesa? Did a witch put a spell on you?" Pinuzza went on.

"Let's go back inside. It's late, and you'll catch cold." Amalia's tone was gentle but firm. The ship had vanished. The fishing smacks were returning to shore. Amalia took the blanket off her lap, laid it carefully on the chair, and lifted Pinuzza up.

Clinging to each other to keep warm—the blankets were soaked with damp—they had a hard time getting to sleep that night. Pinuzza was shivering, huddled up, her curved back pressing against her aunt's bosom and belly like a gigantic foetus; finally they fell asleep. As she drowsed, Amalia had visions and nightmares.

Until her marriage, Amalia had lived in a hovel that clung to the sides of the hill on which Castle Sarentini stood. Baron Stefano Safamita had offered this place to Amalia's father, a member of the Lattuca household and a good baker, when he'd been blinded by glaucoma and fired by the bakery owner. The youngest daughter and her father's favourite, Amalia served him as a guide. They loved each other very much and were so close they seemed glued together. It was a hard life but not an unhappy one. Amalia and her elder sister were not destined to find husbands, because there wasn't enough money to provide dowries for all the daughters, but Amalia wasn't worried: she was happy to remain at home with her family.

Instead she got married when she was barely fourteen. Donna Titta Cuffaro wanted her for her only son, Diego, and she expected neither dowry nor trousseau. "I'll take her just as she comes, with only the clothes she has on her back!" she declared. This future mother-in-law struck Amalia as menacing; she understood that donna Titta had chosen her because a less unfortunate family would not have given a daughter's hand in marriage to someone like Diego, all crooked and twisted, weak in mind and body.

The Cuffaros had seen far better times. In the past their tavern had been frequented by English soldiers, who drank a lot and paid on the nail. Don Diego Cuffaro, donna Titta's father-in-law, certain that the English occupation of Sicily was destined to endure and thinking himself clever, had struck a deal with a tenant farmer to buy wine at a fixed price for a long period, bypassing the usual middlemen. But, as luck would have it, after the defeat of the French in 1815 the English army—all seventeen thousand of them, and seventeen is a number of ill omen, as everyone in Sicily knows—left the island never to return. The price of grape must fell, and the contract brought ruin upon the family. The Cuffaros tried to negotiate better terms, but this wasn't possible, and not from meanness on the farmer's part. He would have helped them, but he wasn't in a position to do so: he had to answer to "others," who were quite prepared to kill all of them as a warning.

Amalia remembered the family's dismay at the barrels of wine they had to buy at each vintage. There were a great many of them, and no room for them in the back shop; they filled the house, which was already full of unsold wine from the previous year that wasn't even good for making vinegar. They would have been swamped by debts if they hadn't supplemented the family income by serving as a clearinghouse for confidential messages and smuggled goods. Mother and daughter-in-law saw to these activities while the menfolk sat outside, on guard.

In her innocence, Amalia still didn't know that she was destined to become a source of income for the Cuffaros, who were planning to put her in service as a wet nurse to a rich family that would keep her for as long as possible; they would use the wet nurse's wardrobe and wages in a final attempt to get the wine contract redeemed. Nor was that all. The Cuffaros feared, and with reason, that Diego might be unable to make her pregnant, and they had come up with a nefarious stratagem if that were to be the case.

The marriage was not consummated on the wedding night, and not for lack of goodwill on the part of the newlyweds. The sheets that Amalia had to hang outside the door on the following day were stained with the blood of some old hens that had been butchered to make the broth for the wedding breakfast: her old hag of a mother-in-law had set it aside deliberately; she had thought of everything. A thrill of disgust made Amalia shudder. Right at the decisive moment—when matters must be concluded—Diego hadn't come up to scratch, and he'd thrown himself down on the blanket that served as sheet and mattress, grumbling, sweating—and defeated. Donna Titta, who made her son tell her everything, suggested that they try in the afternoons, when Diego was stronger. Amalia came to abhor these afternoon couplings which her mother-in-law insisted on. The shameless woman would take up a position behind the curtain that separated their pallet from the rest of the room, where they lived together with the donkey, and direct her son, yelling, "Stick it in, Diego, stick it in! Count to ten! Stick it in, get it in, and you'll manage to do it inside! Careful, Diego!" She would even push the curtain aside and poke her head in to make sure he was obeying her orders.

After two years of marriage, and finally making sense of the vague hints her in-laws let drop, Amalia understood their diabolical plan: if Diego could not make it, then his father would step in. Amalia remembered her disquiet at the way don Carmelo looked at her, and the way his slimy pawing became more and more forward and repulsive. Frightened and unable even to help her, Diego—who was a blockhead but who loved her—suffered this in silence; his mother noticed and was distressed but said nothing to her husband.

In a last, desperate attempt, donna Titta appealed to Saint John the Baptist—or San Giovanni Decollato, Saint John Beheaded, as the islanders called him—to whom she recited a powerful charm. She told Amalia the story of the charm many times, boasting that she had been behind the birth of Giovannino and that therefore the baby was doubly hers. Overcoming her fear, she had gone by night to obey the orders of the wise woman who said that any charm addressed to Saint John Beheaded had to be intoned out loud by the supplicant alone, in secret, in the darkness of a cavern outside the town—a cavern filled with the pungent stench of bat droppings, a place that only the desperate spirits who haunted it could find good.

Donna Titta's account was so vivid that Amalia could almost see the scene: there she was in the huge cave, surrounded by bats fluttering about and brushing her shoulders, until, maddened by the odour of human hair, they dived at her head to grab some of it and tear it out with their hooked talons. But donna Titta was protected by a shawl bound tightly under her chin, and though she was frightened and deafened by their squeaking, she was undaunted, with the strength that faith and mother love arouse. She remained standing, planted squarely on her feet like a stone giant, and in a firm voice repeated correctly all the verses of the exorcism.

And so, thanks to his mother, Diego finally succeeded and in October 1858 Giovannino was born: San Giovanni Decollato deserved to have the child bear his name instead of his grandfather's. Amalia was seventeen. Donna Titta took on the role of mother as soon as Giovannino emerged from the womb, and it was then that she told Amalia brutally that they had destined her to become a wet nurse. Amalia begged them not to take Giovannino from her, but even Diego took their side, as if she no longer counted for anything, and she had to give in. "This boy is a Cuffaro, he belongs to me, and I'll raise him as I please," her mother-in-law told her, victory stamped on her face. Even the midwife—who was still in the house, half drunk with the wine they'd offered her—paled at such wickedness. Thereafter donna Titta acted as the mother, while chores in the house and in the tavern fell to Amalia. The innocent baby Giovannino grew handsome and strong. Whenever donna Titta gave him to his mother at feeding time, fat tears would roll down Amalia's cheeks and onto her breasts, trickling over her nipples and slipping between the baby's lips. Giovannino was raised on milk and tears.

It was almost morning, and the pink light of dawn was filtering through cracks in the stones. Amalia no longer felt cold. Clinging to Pinuzza, she cried her eyes out, then fell into an uneasy sleep.

8

"A red mane is the Devil's bane."

Costanza Safamita's baptism and don Paolo Mercurio's insatiable curiosity

The orders given by the Safamita brothers were clear: no expense was to be spared; it had to be a baptismal celebration that no guest, indeed the entire town, would ever forget. And so it was: it was talked about for a long time in the province and even in Palermo, and not only because of the pomp and the abundant feast.

The only person who didn't enjoy it was unfortunately the baroness, or so rumour had it. After the birth of the redheaded baby she never left her rooms and received no visitors. Sad and silent, Caterina Safamita lay on her bed in the shadows, with only the slightest chink in the curtains, enough to let in light so that her maid could look after her. A stone pillow was placed on her belly to flatten it and her bosom bound tightly to prevent the onset of lactation.

She found even the company of her beloved Stefano distressing. As for the baby Costanza, whom she saw in the mornings and evenings in her husband's presence and on his request, her rejection was total: from the day of her birth her mother never held the child in her arms.

Her sisters-in-law Carolina Scravaglio and Donna Assunta took advantage of the situation to take control of things. Each for her own reasons—a desire to outdo her arrogant niece and sister-in-law in Carolina's case, gratitude for having been chosen as godmother on Assunta's part—plunged enthusiastically into the unhoped-for task, which also created an agreeable opportunity to renew the bonds of affection between them. Often, during those days, the two sisters recalled their happy childhood in the castle and laughed together at little things as they had done in the old days.

This serene activity had a beneficial effect on Baroness Scravaglio's strange affliction. She stopped stealing, apart from one regrettable occasion when don Filippo Leccasarda had to get Rosa Vinciguerra, a maid of whom the baroness was particularly fond, to help him persuade the lady to remove from her hair the six silver spoons she had stuck into her chignon, creating a bizarre fanlike headdress like the one that wet nurses wore; she believed that the others, like her, could not see them.

The day before the baptism Donna Assunta ordered twelve large potted jasmine shrubs to be taken from the castle greenhouses. For the people of Sarentini this was an unexpected but most pleasant event, a delight for the senses and a foretaste of what was to come the next day.

Early in the morning the two main gates of the castle were thrown open simultaneously, and from the broad avenues of the gardens a convoy of multicoloured carts made their way down towards the young baron's mansion house, each laden with a large tub of jasmine, bound and wrapped as if the contents were glass and not earthenware. The luxuriant, glossy plants were as tall as a man, with their long branches in full bloom as if it were already summer, folded in on themselves to form perfect ovals. The tubs had been generously watered to keep the potting soil compact; the grateful plants gave off profuse gusts of their delicate scent, sweet and fresh, which intensified as the roots gradually absorbed the water. The carters moved their loads forwards carefully, aware of their effect. The intense scent of jasmine swept away the stink of manure on the filthy streets, spread through the alleyways intersecting the main road, drifted down into courtyards and up to terraces, found its way into houses through chinks in the window frames and under doors, like an intoxicating, sweet, invisible mist. Women, old people, and children looked on from balconies and windows, groups of passersby slipped into the doorways to make way for the carts or hugged the walls of the houses, motionless as the statues of saints.

Decked out in full regalia for the occasion, the mules proceeded, as the coachmen, proud and alert in the green livery of the Safamitas, slowed their pace. The guards at Safamita House were waiting for them, lined up in ranks at the entry, ready to unload the carts.

"There's a nice smell," said one fellow, hugging the wall of the mansion house.

"It's the smell of power," said a voice near him.

"It's not for the likes of us. We have to make do with smelling it from a distance, no more than that," added don Paolo Mercurio, and he slipped away.

For Costanza Safamita's baptism in Safamita House, the cupboard-altar was taken from the red drawing room where it usually stood, serenely incognito—tall, imposing, and austere in its inlaid casing. Now, its doors wide open, it stood majestically in the main salon. It had been polished from top to bottom; even the giltwork and the little cupids on the inside had been touched up by a gilder brought in specially from Palermo. Finally an altar and only an altar, it flaunted its beauty almost wantonly: all the silver, enamel, mirrors, precious woods, inlays of hard stone, and sculptures drew the observer's eye to the antique crucifix of pure gold— a languid and delicate Christ, almost feminine, set against a background of sky-blue, green, and pink enamelwork—purchased in France by the young baron.

The scent of the jasmine bushes, arranged in a semicircle on either side of the altar, saturated the room.

The baptism was attended only by the Safamitas and their relatives, the baroness's two maids, and the wet nurse. Gaspare Quagliata, the young baron's valet, acted as altar boy. In order to officiate, Father Sedita, the old priest to the Safamita household, had braved the journey from the monastery of Grottavacante, to which he had withdrawn in his old age. He was assisted by Father Puma. The ceremony was intimate and brief out of respect for the baroness, who had been weakened by the birth and was still indisposed. Hidden in the lacework of her christening dress, Costanza dozed off in the proud arms of her wet nurse. Amalia, with all the freshness of her eighteen years and decked out in the wet nurse's traditional gold and coral jewellery, wore in her chignon the engraved brass pins and tall combs, spread out like an open fan, that were a sign of her position.

Count Antonio Safamita di Vasciterre, the young baron's first cousin and head of the family, had come specially from Palermo with his wife, to act as godfather together with the godmother, Donna Assunta. When the ceremony began, Costanza was placed in her godmother's arms—an arrangement not to her liking, for she began to bawl and wriggle, red spots blotching her milk-white skin as she thrashed about in her swaddling clothes like a little fish trapped in a net. She didn't calm down until she was handed back to the wet nurse.

Caterina Safamita, on her husband's arm, was visibly in distress. At one point she almost fainted, and right after the service she withdrew to her room. The Safamitas stayed on for a while in the mansion house, where they partook of refreshments with the domestic staff. Then, preceded by the baron, they set off in their glossy summer carriages for the thanksgiving mass at the main church, leaving mother and daughter behind.

On the occasion of celebrations and festivities, the Safamita family were in the habit of inviting their hired hands and staff, with their families, as well as the common folk who had dealings with them—in short, all Sarentini—to join them. With punctilious pride Guglielmo and Domenico Safamita kept up this legacy from feudal times, which was on the wane among most of Sicily's aristocracy. Thus they had let it be known through the usual indirect channels that the thanksgiving mass would be held in the main church and that townspeople wishing to take part were welcome.

The bells pealed out for the mass. Everyone set off for the church, filling the square. The baron and his grandson Stefano, standing at the main entrance, looked like father and son: the same distant look, the same pale complexion, the same dignified bearing. Stefano instinctively and naturally imitated his grandfather, showing none of the impatience or boredom that might have been expected from a boy of seven. They stayed under the portico till the last moment, welcoming all the guests, families, and townspeople, using the same reserved courtesy to thank whoever offered felicitations—some with a handshake, others with a nod, according to their social rank—and behaving, as the gossips later had it, not only with the assurance and boldness of the biggest landowners in the area, which is exactly what they were, but as if even the church belonged to them. This, too, was not far from the truth, because their ancestors the Lattucas had built it and the Safamita family paid for its upkeep.

The dean officiated, assisted by Father Puma and under the weary but benevolent gaze of Father Sedita, sunk back in the little armchair specially brought to the church for him at the young baron's command. Guests and townspeople thronged the central and lateral naves. The organist was accompanied by a violinist called in from Palermo for the occasion; the nuns from the Convent of Portulano sang like angels.

During the mass, the castle staff set up in the square a public reception for all the congregation and anyone else who wanted to take part. Under the blooming oleanders that grew close to the parapet on the verge of the steep crag, at the foot of which the vast panorama of the interior opened up, stood four fine painted carts laden with all manner of good things—the mules still in their full regalia, the coachmen in their finest livery. Footmen from the castle, ramrod stiff and motionless beside the carts, carried silver trays embellished with the family coat of arms and piled with bread rings, marzipan sweets, pink sugared almonds, nougat, and pale-pink sugar candy, all of the finest quality. As soon as the baron appeared at the portico, the ranks of liveried servants moved as one, making their way into the midst of the throng to offer the refreshments. They circulated round the square as if it were a drawing room in Safamita House, stopping in front of everyone—poor, in rags, or noble as he might be—offering sweets. Other footmen walked about with trays of lemonade, grenadine, and little glasses of *zammù*, anise-flavoured liqueur with water. It seemed like the miracle of the loaves and fishes: the more people ate and drank, the more biscuits and drinks appeared on the silver trays. The Safamitas and their guests accepted the good wishes of the people and boarded their coaches to return to the castle. The people of Sarentini who had attended the mass and the reception were more than satisfied.

The baron had also organized the real christening party at Castle Sarentini, to which he had invited a few local worthies and a sizable group of relatives and friends who came from the neighbouring towns and from Palermo. Lunch was taken on the terrace, and the Safamita brothers' two cooks outdid themselves in the quantity and quality of the food served. The fine weather—not too hot, bright, serene—permitted the guests to stroll through the castle gardens and admire them. The Safamitas loved plants; apart from traditional varieties of flowers and shrubs there were also rare ones, all luxuriant and well tended. In the afternoon, the baron's coach arrived and proceeded slowly along the wide driveway that ran through the garden and came to a stop at the round terrace alongside the marble basin. The wet nurse descended with Costanza. They were soon surrounded by the guests, who were curious to see the strange creature with their own eyes.

The Safamita brothers played host, stopping to talk with everyone in turn, but keeping well away from each other. The baron seemed very happy, as if he were the one who had had a daughter. He was even talkative—he who in the salons usually kept silent. Domenico Safamita seemed pensive—perhaps he was worried about his wife's health—but when he talked about the new baby his face lit up.

Count Vasciterre and his wife, Illuminata, were seated beside Donna Assunta, as was right and proper: less wealthy than their cousins, they had come as honoured guests and were treated accordingly. The count summoned Stefano, who was about to go to boarding school in Palermo: "Your name is Safamita, and you mustn't forget it, just as you didn't today in church," he said. "We respect the common people and we expect to be respected by them," he continued amiably as Donna Assunta looked on complacently. Then he started telling the boy old stories about the family, extolling their loyalty to the crown. Some members of the provincial bourgeoisie, curious and a little embarrassed, having declined Donna Assunta's offer to sit on the empty seats, stood by listening. Farther away, small groups of noblemen and women were all ears—not to know the history of the Safamita family but to glean some element good for gossip and criticism. Antonio Safamita, who was actually well liked—or maybe precisely for this reason—was not exempt from gossip.

"First of all, remember that you are of ancient stock, and then that you are Sicilian. We are faithful to the Holy Mother Church, and we shall stay that way, and the Kingdom of the Two Sicilies must endure, and it shall endure." Then, with an ironic smile, the count added for the benefit of the others, "Yes, indeed, it shall endure, even though these days some people have forgotten the meaning of the word 'loyalty.'" Stefano listened in silence, concealing his boredom like an adult: these counsels were the same as his grandfather's.

"We have always served the Holy Mother Church, as is borne out by honours received over the centuries. We Safamitas do not think of money. Remember that you have a Christian soul!" The count nodded in Father Puma's direction and received in return a grimace that might have been a half smile.

Baron Francesco Vuttichina di Orata, a cousin of Count Alessandro Pertuso di Trasi, one of the baron's brothers-in-law, whispered to the person next to him, "He hasn't the courage to say that they beat their breasts in church in exchange for a nice little position in the Holy Inquisition— handed down from father to son. It put food on the table for generations of Safamitas. Holy love, my foot! They winkled that cash out of the Tribunal of the Holy Office!"

"Right," replied Baldo Bentivoglio di Piscitelli, a known separatist and now, it was rumoured, a Carbonaro. "Call it *holy*. And the Bourbons kept the *Holy* Inquisition going," he said, "in order to keep thousands of useless people in work."

"I'm not sure about that," broke in Count Gioacchino Moschitta di Acere. "Heresy should be combatted, and that's needed nowadays!"

"It was useful, useful," said Orata, "perhaps. But it was a historical absurdity, and it had to be abolished."

"The world was a different place a hundred years ago," added Acere.

As Bentivoglio wandered off, Orata added in a low voice, "Baldo thinks he's clever, thanks to certain friendships he cultivates. He doesn't even know how to behave like a gentleman." The others nodded imperceptibly, so as not to take sides with the outspoken Orata—Bentivoglio was a rich, ambitious aristocrat, and who could tell which way the wind would blow in the future?—though they wanted to encourage him to talk. Orata gave them what they wanted: "Lord, Lord . . . we all know whom his father, Prince Piscitelli, married so as to get out of debt—a small-town bourgeois woman! You're born a gentleman, you don't become one. We'll have to wait for generations to come before we get back to having all four quarterings of nobility."

This declaration was met with emphatic nods, knowing looks, and titters: they were agreed, conscious of their ascendancy.

Don Paolo Mercurio was homesick for Palermo and the festivities of the nobility that the young baron had assiduously attended in his youth; he and the other coachmen had enjoyed observing them furtively. Now he lurked at a window on the second floor, watching the guests and trying to guess what they were talking about from their expressions and gestures; in any case he already knew, since their talk was always the same.

The guests had instinctively formed into separate groups without realising they had, the way farmyard animals do. But the merging and separating was done according to social class, wealth, and provenance, and this was deliberate. The bearing of the aristocrats had its own inborn elegance. The men strutted about slowly, with studied indolence; to some of the ladies they would make an imperceptible bow, with others they would kiss their hands ostentatiously, according to what message was to be conveyed. Among themselves they used a dialectic of gesture and deportment: erect, with arms folded when they were in agreement, with hands in pockets when they felt relaxed and at ease, stroking beard and moustache when they wanted it understood that they were thinking—all in accordance with a rigid etiquette that had become part of everyday life and was thus natural to them. The ladies, adorned in jewels, moved about with the same airy ease that marked their constant chatter.

The guests from Palermo, disdaining the company of provincials, kept to themselves, with men and women occasionally mingling. They reverted to salon rituals: veiled criticism of the hosts, more explicit comments about the others, and the usual gossip they fed on as their daily bread.

To don Paolo, looking down on them, the ladies' crinolines in their pale spring colours were like the jellyfish that sometimes, when the sea was calm as a millpond, floated to the surface and drifted around the ships, bobbing to the caress of the waves, languid and beautiful but ready to strike, just like those women with their knack for stinging ripostes.

The bourgeois guests chatted among themselves, stiff in their Sunday best, strictly divided by family unit and gender, their eyes darting, their ears open, ready to pick up and remember everything about this rare occasion when the Safamitas treated them on an equal footing—from the beauty of the gardens to the titles and the elegance of the aristocrats who were present. The women were awkward and prim, especially the elderly ones. The younger women, who had gone to boarding schools with aristocrats, behaved with a kind of contrived nonchalance that betrayed an elusive hint of something rustic and demure, which don Paolo liked very much.

The incipient changes in Sicilian society were reflected in the splendour of the jewels worn by these bourgeois ladies, almost on a par with those of the noblewomen, and by the looks that a few impoverished aristocratic dowry-hunters unobtrusively cast in the direction of the heiresses. And now that the euphoria of lunch and the sated fatigue of digestion had passed, the men's serious faces and the movements of their hands indicated that the time had come to get down to business.

Don Paolo scanned the terrace, with its vivid flooring of zigzag green and white tiles. Footmen were carrying away dirty plates and glasses; others, standing behind the laden tables at each end of the terrace, were still waiting to serve. He recognised Father Puma's corpulent figure hidden behind the trunks of the wisteria beneath the canopy, next to the refreshments table. He, too, was observing the guests.

Nothing of the priest about him, thought don Paolo, who like his master did not think highly of Father Puma or of the clergy in general.

Father Puma had spotted that hiding place just as he was on the point of leaving and had grasped the opportunity to gaze unseen on the face of the young baron, directing at him all the scorn and rancour he usually had to conceal under feigned respect and deference. Fuming, he brooded over the slights and wrongs he had suffered, an effort that made his saliva run, so that he had to take a sip of wine from time to time to slake his burning thirst.

Why did he treat me like that in front of everyone today? I was good enough to celebrate Stefano's baptism, but not the one for this hairy little redhead, oh no. Father Puma isn't good enough. He wanted to humiliate me in public for faults that are not mine, as if I had something to do with this girl, who is ugly in the bargain. People are talking, putting two and two together. He wants to destroy me, he wants me a slave in chains, he knows I must put up with everything, I can't do without them. It would serve him right if I put a curse, the evil eye, on him and his daughter, but she is her mother's daughter, and I cannot, I cannot . . .

It's his fault that I'm not the dean here. Since he came back to Sarentini he has done nothing but thwart me, oppose me, deride me. This is how the nobles amuse themselves, cruelly misusing those who can't talk back because they depend on them. He barely says hello, he humiliates me. He thanks me with gritted teeth, and only when he has to; at his table he relegates me to the worst seat, and he denies me access to the baroness. Love, my foot! He took her for her dowry! That poor girl has done nothing but suffer, and she daren't even speak of it in the confessional, she's so afraid of him. For her, only for her, I submit to his scorn, as long as I can go to the mansion house to remind her that I, Father Puma, am here for her and for Stefano. I, I who gave blood for the Safamitas and who never tire of praying for them, I who ask only for the chance to help that unhappy woman.

Purple with rage and the wine he'd swilled down, Father Puma felt he would burst. He went off, failing to bid farewell to his hosts—the first time he had insulted the Safamitas. That, too, passed unnoticed.

Don Paolo leaned against the shutter. His legs were getting tired and his vision was blurred, but he didn't want to miss the show.

It was sunset. Long shadows fell across the terrace. Guests were still slowly moving about, passing from one group to another, breaking up and coming together again like so many snails escaped from a basket. Timid and uncertain at first, they slither around and then, with slow determination, pile up on top of one another in heaps, only to separate again as if by enchantment; the first to move off leaves a gleaming, slimy trail that the others obediently slide along, one by one. The guests gradually converged at the balustrade and lowered their voices: nobles and bourgeois, shoulder to shoulder, contemplating the sunset. The azure sky was streaked with long, delicate, rosy brush marks on the horizon. An almost transparent moon peeped out from behind the trees. The sea, expectant, glittered in the distance: the sun had swollen into a fiery ball and was now setting in a crimson glory that spread across the horizon. Slowly and solemnly, the streaks rose up and expanded into broad iridescent bands—from vermilion to carmine, from magenta to violet—that caressed the timid light of the first stars. The sweet, heavy scent of pretty-by-night flooded the terrace.

Don Paolo Mercurio sighed and went back to the stables.

9

"Think, old tree, of when you were a seedling."

Costanza Safamita's first three years

Until she was three, it can be said that Costanza Safamita's life was much like that of the other little girls of her class and station. In the autumn of 1860 her little brother, Giacomo, was born. Wherever the family was—the town houses or, in summer, the country houses—she lived in her rooms, close to those of her brothers.

Three people looked after her: her wet nurse, who remained in service after she was weaned; Maddalena Lisca, her maid; and Madame Else von Schuden—this last, elderly by now, having stayed on with the Safamitas after Stefano's departure for boarding school. As a young woman Madame had been an opera singer, and she taught the baroness new songs and sonatas. Now she became fond of the little girl and asked if she might teach her French, which thus became Costanza's second language, after Sicilian.

Caterina Safamita had gradually recovered from her melancholy after Costanza's birth, but she continued to show no interest in her unwanted daughter. She was reluctant to play with the child or even to hold her in her arms; when the wet nurse brought Costanza to her room, she couldn't wait to send her away. Her husband and the domestic staff thought this was a passing phase, but it wasn't. Caterina was an instinctive person and she would have liked to enjoy this baby; she almost convinced herself that her husband might be right, that love for Costanza would come to her—or, at least, she hoped so.

Stefano, who had resigned himself to his mother's recurrent miscarriages and no longer hoped for a brother or sister, accepted Costanza with enthusiasm and grew very fond of her; he used to sit next to the wet nurse to look at his little sister, and he would lull her to sleep, cradling her in his arms and singing nursery rhymes to her. Demonstrating his indifference to the respective roles of male and female, as well as a precociously rebellious nonconformism, Stefano also wanted to learn how to swaddle Costanza and dress her—in short, to look after her—activities that were considered women's work. This was a source of consternation among the servants, but it did not bother his father or his grandfather. Certain that Stefano would soon demonstrate his masculinity, and unconcerned about other people's opinions, they suspected that Stefano's interest in his sister had to do with the fact that he, too, appreciated the wet nurse's opulent curves. But Caterina Safamita grew jealous: first she tried to estrange Stefano from his sister, then she decided to indulge him and she would join him in Costanza's rooms to be close to him. Thus it was that, thanks to Stefano, Costanza discovered her mother and became tenaciously attached to her. But Caterina still did not love her. The mere sight of the child aroused in her an intolerable distress, and when Stefano left for boarding school she went back to ignoring her.

At sixteen months, Costanza was already walking and talking. She greeted Giacomo's birth with joy and curiosity. She didn't understand why her mother was no longer well disposed to her, and she sensed her aversion. When she saw her mother with Giacomo she would try to stay with her, but Caterina ordered the wet nurse to take her away. Costanza would be in despair.

The wet nurse didn't know what to do; there was no one to turn to to help get the baroness to see a little sense. She decided to take the little girl to the domestic quarters more often, far from her mother and her brother. There, Costanza got to know not only the staff but also workers and artisans, barbers, surveyors, shopkeepers, and clerks—men who in some way depended on the Safamitas for their livelihood. These men felt that it was important to keep up the ancient relationship of familiarity and vassalage—almost a right—and to know the children of their feudal lord, their future masters. In Costanza's case they were also prompted by curiosity, for there was much talk about the young baron's red-haired daughter, and they commented freely on her looks, careless of the fact that she might hear them.

Costanza grew to become a healthy little girl, tall and slim. She had a long, slender neck and a small face; a fair, almost transparent complexion, covered with freckles; a small, snub nose; big eyes of two different colours—both were hazel, but one had blue-grey flecks—fringed by long, straw-coloured lashes; and a mane of thick, tight, unruly, flame-red curls that would escape from braids, ribbons, hairpins, and hair grips to form an aura around her face, enhancing her paleness. She was different from everyone, as if she were of another world, another race.

Don Paolo Mercurio, personal coachman to the household for more than twenty years, like his father and his father before him—so he knew the entire family—said there had been redheads in the Safamita family in the past. The blessed Giuseppe Safamita—a devout man captured by Barbary pirates and then ransomed by the Archconfraternity for the Redemption of Christians in Palermo—had also had a red-haired daughter, who died young. He had seen a painting of her in the town house in Palermo.

That was enough to still the wagging tongues among the servants, but not the ferocious and explicit comments of others. Some went further, and derided the family as well as the little girl, confident that the wet nurse would not report this chatter to the masters. Amalia was sure that Costanza understood she was being mocked, because she refused to speak to these men; she would hide her face with her hands, gesturing for them to be sent away, and she didn't want them to touch her.

One day, while Costanza was playing with her grandfather on the terrace of the castle, Amalia ended up telling the baron of her worries, at which point he bombarded her with questions and finally made her explain things in minute detail, ordering her to report on everything that people were saying. He intended to see to the protection of his granddaughter, and he was as good as his word. Amalia told him exactly what had been said, and in the fullness of time the guilty ones were sent elsewhere or even dismissed, with no mercy and no explanations. No one ever knew the real reason.

10

"Better the devil you know than the devil you don't."

Pepi Tignuso travels by coach.
Events preceding the birth of Giacomo Safamita

It was in the early days of May 1860. Domenico Safamita was preparing to go to bed when suddenly there came an insistent knocking at the door. Don Filippo Leccasarda pushed the door open, causing don Gaspare to collide with it. The majordomo was out of breath: "Excuse me, my lord. The lord baron sends word that he wants to see you at the castle: the field overseer of Malivinnitti is coming." Gaspare handed the young baron the jacket he had just taken off, and in less than no time the pair were in the coach en route to the castle.

Domenico found his brother in the entrance hall, leaning against an internal door; Pepi Tignuso was standing diagonally opposite, wiping the sweat from his brow with a crumpled handkerchief. The young baron made a sketchy greeting, raising his eyebrows slightly and muttering, "Sorry about the delay."

"Pepi has just come from Malivinnitti," explained his brother. "They're bringing him some water." Turning to the field overseer, he added, "I want the young baron to hear this. He must know that I have bequeathed Malivinnitti to his daughter, Costanza."

"*Voscenza benadica,*" stammered Pepi as he gulped down the water from the glass offered him by Gaetano Cucurrullo. It was the age-old formula addressed by servant to master: "Bless me, milord. I needed a drop of cool water. I've spent the day on horseback."

"Well?" asked the baron in a commanding tone.

Pepi Tignuso was a shrewd and trustworthy field overseer: he followed the baron's valet with his eyes, waiting for him to leave before he spoke. "Your lordship knows I'm your man. I've done everything for the Safamitas, out of respect for you, and this you know."

"What has happened?"

"Nothing has happened yet, but what is going to happen is a truly big thing, and very terrible. I'm a field overseer, and when your lordship is not at Malivinnitti I do as you've instructed me, to please you. This time I don't know what to do. Your lordship must command me."

Domenico Safamita leaned against the entryway, his eyes flashing, ready to have his say as soon as his elder brother gave him a sign: the family hierarchy had to be visibly respected in the presence of under-lings. Pepi was the same age as he—as boys they had played together at Malivinnitti—yet the overseer looked like an old man, and Domenico had never seen him so worried. His hair, flattened by the constant use of his beret, fell in locks over his sweaty brow, which was divided into two horizontal strata. The skin on the upper part was pale and tender, while the rest of his face, including the heavy drooping eyelids, was burnt dark by the sun. His face was the colour of terra-cotta, wrinkled, tough, soaked in a blend of dust and sweat. He stank. It wasn't easy for him to stand straight on his bandy legs, but he did his best.

"Your lordship knows I keep my eyes and ears open on all sides, so that I may serve you. There's no need to ask me for names—they're all trusted men. But a shipload of armed revolutionaries is arriving from the mainland. They're special, this bunch. They have the gift of gab, and our boys forget their duty and follow them. They could charm the hind legs off a donkey, this lot could. I know they want to talk first of all with the poor folk, the field hands, the peasants—in other words, they've come to make revolution round our way. I'm told they're looking for places where they can eat and sleep and so on. They've set their sights on Malivinnitti—we have everything they need, and plenty of it, too." Sipping more water, Pepi eyed them: the Safamitas were inscrutable.

"No one knows Malivinnitti better than I do. I was born there, so I know every peasant and every field hand by name, and I know all about them. Outsiders have never come to Malivinnitti since the Tignuso fam-ily has been there, always at your service. But these men are a shady bunch, and they want to come to us. I went round the wheat fields: there's not much green. The Russell's wheat is taller than my mare and ready for reaping. It must be watched: it'll scorch soon. We have to think of the harvest and we need field hands for it. But if those who're talking to me are right—and too many people are talking to me, your lordship must believe me—the peasants and field hands are joining these bare-faced scoundrels. They won't listen to me, and maybe there *won't* be a harvest at Malivinnitti this year.

"Your lordship knows that since last month there have been uprisings here and there, not only in Palermo but in the countryside. It's like when the ground rumbles before an earthquake. This ship is bringing us the earthquake—revolution. And this time the people from outside are using the only word that everyone understands, both peasants and townfolk. 'Freedom,' 'independence,' 'constitution' are words they don't understand. But as soon as they're off the boat this lot starts saying, 'Land, there's land for all of you. Come with us.' And when they hear 'land' our poor devils follow them and think of nothing else. Pepi Tignuso's word of honour, I'm ashamed to say it, but I have no power against this evil brood of revolutionaries. Hands for the harvest at Malivinnitti cannot be found, alive or dead."

"Get to the point."

"These robbers want to come to Malivinnitti to steal and destroy. I can't maintain order, not even if your lordship sends me all your guards . . . We have to think this over."

"Then let's think it over, Pepi."

"They want to make revolution, and Malivinnitti isn't the right place to do it. They want information and men to arm; they'll take bread, straw, a piece of cheese, and then go elsewhere. If we don't give them these things, they'll just take them without so much as a thank-you and then destroy everything. Your lordship may say, 'Pepi, let's wait, the ship is still at sea.' But if it doesn't happen this time it'll happen the next time. And people have had their fill of the Bourbons."

Pepi looked the baron in the eye and went on with deliberate slowness. "There are two other things we can do. One is to send out word that if they ask for our help we'll listen and then decide. Let's hope this will calm down the workers. Though I don't know if we can save ourselves from the others—the armed bands of desperadoes who are roaming the countryside and belong to no one. All they need is an uprising and they'll fall on us. There's no reasoning with them.

"The second way is different. If what I've heard is correct, we must stockpile grain and water right away and give out information whenever we have to. We can say that the Safamitas don't want to make difficulties but don't want to take sides, either. That's the only way to be sure these thieving revolutionaries won't start sleeping and eating in your lordship's house at Malivinnitti, or here in the castle."

"Are things this serious?" asked the baron.

"Yes, indeed they are. I've talked with the overseers of other masters at other holdings. For some of them a revolution would be useful. But I am your man and I wish you well . . . we can think about this. No one must touch Malivinnitti, for it belongs to the young baroness."

Pepi had finished. He shot a knowing look at the two brothers and leaned against a marble column, averting his eyes to give them an opportunity to communicate in silence, unobserved.

The baron looked at his brother, who slowly lowered his eyes.

"Pepi, do as you must. But remember, not a word about our political position. The king is still king," said Guglielmo Safamita.

The overseer straightened up again. "At your orders, your lordship, and thank you for your trust."

"On one condition, Pepi," added Domenico. "I wish to take my daughter to the harvest this year, and everything must be in order by then."

"Don't worry, your lordship, I'll do what I can."

The three men stood in silence, sensing the importance of the decision. Pepi Tignuso looked around. He had never before set foot in the main floor of the castle; the baron always used to receive him in his offices, as he did with all the others. The large, unadorned room was dominated by a big rectangular table on which stood two five-armed candelabra and an enormous silver tray; in the corners, white marble busts of pensive men sat atop green marble columns. It looked like a funeral chamber, and all that was missing was the deceased.

"Your excellencies must forgive me, but I must get back to Malivinnitti right away. There's a lot to do, and I haven't slept since yesterday. I'm exhausted. May I ask your permission to have someone bring me an unused coach for two or three hours, so I can sleep in it for a bit?"

"Speak to Gaetano."

With a respectful *"Voscenza benadica,"* Pepi Tignuso took leave of his masters. The two Safamitas were astounded at what they had learned, and by the audacity of that last request.

Things went as Pepi Tignuso had foreseen—and even worse. On 11 May 1860, Giuseppe Garibaldi and a few hundred volunteers landed at Marsala. Garibaldi proclaimed himself dictator there to govern in the name of the King of Piedmont, and he promised land to the landless as well as to the men who took up arms with him. After a brilliant guerrilla campaign, he succeeded in defeating the Bourbon army and put an end to their reign in Sicily. There were episodes of ferocious violence; properties owned by those known to be supporters of the Bourbons were sacked and their goods burned. In contrast, the Safamitas suffered relatively minor damage and their holdings remained intact.

Domenico took the family to Malivinnitti in mid-August, when the revolutionaries had already passed by, but with the pretext of his wife's advanced pregnancy he did not visit their other country houses. The Safamitas entrenched themselves in dignified silence, but they gave tangible expression of their gratitude to Pepi Tignuso, who by then had acquired a reputation as a patriot and—far more significant—as an important mafioso. "That evening at the castle," said Domenico to his wife, "I wasn't thinking so much about the Bourbons as about us. The request for a coach is only the beginning. We are no longer the true masters, and we shall remain so only as long as it suits these people. There's no helping it."

Giacomo was born in the autumn of 1860, a healthy, sturdy little boy. His baptism—at which Father Puma officiated—was attended only by close relatives. His birth went all but unnoticed by the people of Sarentini, who were taken up with social and political events and with the plebiscite of 21 October that sanctioned Sicily's annexation by the Kingdom of Piedmont and thus put an end to the islanders' hopes of independence.

11

"Mother love will ne'er deceive you."

Caterina Safamita turns against her own flesh and blood.

Maria Caponetto, Giacomo's wet nurse, and Amalia Cuffaro passed their days with the children, who were two and three years old and made good company. Costanza adored her little brother. When Caterina Safamita spent part of each afternoon with them, she devoted herself exclusively to Giacomo. Costanza sought her mother's caresses and approval, but the baroness deliberately rejected her, ordering the women to amuse her with other games. They obeyed with lowered eyes and did their best, but in vain. Costanza kept going back to her mother, clutching at her skirts, grabbing her hands and covering them with little kisses, offering her sweets and toys—in short, she wanted *her*. The baroness's efforts to drive her away did not succeed. Costanza would call out to her, holding out her arms, and when all this was unavailing, she would burst into tears and stand close, ramrod straight, beside her mother. The wet nurse was unable to console her.

The mere presence of her daughter was enough to make Caterina Safamita irascible and almost ill with irritation. The guilt and shame that then assailed her were swept away by the resentment that roiled within her as soon as she saw the little girl again. When Costanza kept her from enjoying Giacomo in peace, she would treat the little girl harshly, heedless of the women's presence—speaking to her unkindly, shrugging her off, and rudely pushing her away. In front of her relatives she controlled herself.

It happened one afternoon in October 1862. The wet nurses and the children were in the playroom, where the baroness joined them. After giving Costanza a hasty kiss, she took Giacomo from his nurse's arms and told the women to leave. Sitting in an armchair, she kissed him all over and hummed him a nursery rhyme. Costanza, too, held out her arms to be taken up into her lap. She called her mother sweetly, gave her little smiles, clung to her dress, kissed the hem of her shawl—in short tried everything to get what she wanted. The baroness summoned Amalia to take her away.

After some effort, Costanza was persuaded to sit down at the children's work table to make tissue-paper flowers for the garlands used to decorate the rooms for All Souls' Day. The little girl was good with her hands. She folded the petals, sticking them together with a lick of glue and then twining them around the crèpe-paper stem to make a beautiful rose. "It's a present for Mama," she said, and ran to her mother in a flash—Amalia couldn't stop her.

Proudly, Costanza offered her mother the paper rose, drumming her feet in expectation of the "Good girl!" she knew she deserved. Her mother looked at her, and Costanza looked at her mother. Caterina's opaque eyes and Costanza's watchful ones locked together. But they weren't really looking at each other. One pair of eyes was pleading, and the other gave nothing.

Caterina's hand seemed to move on its own, descending from a great height. Her index finger and thumb gripped the petals and, guiding them into her cupped palm, crushed the flower. Caterina glanced first at the paper mashed in her hand, then at Giacomo dozing, and finally she turned her gaze to the window and kept it there.

She freed her other hand and balled up the paper flower as if it were a piece of dough, rubbing one palm against the other in a circular motion. A creamy odour came from the damp warmth of the glue. Costanza's flower became a poor pink-green blob. The diamonds glittered and the hands barely touched each other. The movements were slow, very slow, as if Caterina were in a trance. Costanza and Amalia were hypnotised, as Caterina was hypnotised by the sky—a cloudless sky as bright as the sky above Malivinnitti. Malivinnitti.

"Go to Amalia," said her mother, white as a sheet. She looked down at what remained of the flower and let it fall to the floor. "Go away, go away," she repeated, her voice rising. "Go away, go away," and she pushed the child from her.

Costanza clung to her dress. "Mama, no, no, why did you do that?" she kept repeating, without loosening her grip.

Caterina suddenly rose to her feet. She took Giacomo on her left arm and cradled him firmly against her side. With her other hand she pushed at Costanza, shaking her until she had to let go of her mother's skirts. Costanza's outstretched hands groped to cling to her mother. Frightened, Giacomo burst into tears, and this made Caterina furious. She grabbed Costanza by the arm, just under the shoulder, clamping down in a vicelike grip, her fingers clenched under the little girl's armpit, and lifted her slender frame right off the floor. Costanza screamed wildly as her mother flung her about as if she were a rag doll. The shaking became frenetic. Careful not to let Giacomo slip, Caterina twisted, flexed her legs slightly, and hurled Costanza against the wall. The little girl flopped to the floor.

"You're killing her, you wretched woman! Stop it, you're mad!" cried the nurse, and threw herself on Costanza. Blood was running copiously above the little girl's left eye and down to her lips. "Mama, Mama, Mama," sobbed Costanza, weeping, looking for her mother all round the room. But Caterina Safamita had fled.

Her head in her nurse's lap, Costanza sobbed. Amalia stanched the blood from the wound, covered the child with kisses, stroked the curly hair that was matted in sweat, massaged her, and whispered little words of love. But Costanza wanted her mother and her mother only. Her voice grew fainter, drowned in tears. When she could resist no longer, Costanza lost consciousness and stayed like that, half on the floor and half in the arms of her distressed nurse.

12

"Patience is the servant's lot, prudence the master's."

Pinuzza Belice questions her aunt about the circumstances of her dismissal.

"If you were the marchesa's nurse, why did you end up here on the Montagnazza with me?" Pinuzza was licking her lips after having eaten a sweet, ripe fig.

"Where on earth do you get these ideas?"

"Answer me!"

"The marchesa died and her brother Baron Giacomo, the heir, told me to leave. He was the master."

"Were you expecting that?"

"No, not at the time."

"And another time, did you expect them to send you away?"

"Yes, many years before."

"What happened?"

"It's not a matter for youngsters. When you're grown up I'll tell you." Amalia dried Pinuzza's mouth and put her to bed. Then she began to clean the plates with a rag slightly moistened with water left in the bottom of the jug.

The nurses cleaned the wound with damp cloths. It was not deep, but it would leave a scar on Costanza's forehead. They covered it with cobwebs and bandaged it well. To reduce the bruises they applied chamomile-flower poultices. Then they fed the children and prepared them for bed. That evening the parents did not make an appearance.

Amalia put Costanza to sleep in her bed, not so much to comfort the child as to comfort herself. She was utterly distraught: she had insulted the mistress, and she feared that the baroness would take revenge, accuse her of hurting Costanza, and have her dismissed. For most of the night Amalia could not sleep; she fondled the little girl, covered her with gentle kisses so that she would not awaken, wound her fingers around her own, and watched over her in the pale moonlight that came in through the window.

When fatigue seemed to get the better of her, there came visions and nightmares, one in particular. The young baron and the baroness, grown gigantic, grim and solemn, appeared at the foot of her bed. They wore flowing blood-red cloaks and held their right hands aloft, index fingers pointing at her. They spoke in Italian, in unison, like choristers in the big church: "You are guilty of the three worst sins a wet nurse can commit."

The young baron's deep voice listed the charges. The baroness balled her right fist and accompanied her husband's words by ticking off the sins with her fingers, first the thumb, then the index, then the middle finger, all pointing at Amalia. At each movement of her fingers, her rings glittered like reflections from a sword ready to cut off Amalia's head. The baroness was horrible: she had wicked eyes, and her closed lips wore a cruel half smile that deformed her pale face.

"You failed to teach Costanza that it is right for her mother to spend more time with her male child. Costanza is a girl. This is the first," said the young baron. "But you have committed a second, unpardonable sin: you have treated our daughter like your equal. You dare to love her as if she belonged to you.

"The third is very, very serious indeed. You think you are a peer of the Barons Safamita, but that's not how things are, even today. You dared to raise your voice to your mistress when she justly chastised her daughter. You are a nurse here, and you must respect your masters. I could have you arrested. Instead, I will send you back to your in-laws. I want you to return the wet nurse's wardrobe and jewellery. As for Costanza, you will not see her again so long as you live."

The image of the masters began to fade, and their last words—"so long as you live, so long as you live"—echoed ever more faintly. The room began to spin in a dizzying whirl, lengthening to form a dark, narrow cavern that coiled up on itself like a snake and then, straightening out, plunged into the ground: it had become a bottomless pit. Amalia and all the furniture fell headlong into it, bumping against walls that grew narrower and narrower, down, down, down into an inferno.

The next morning, she found herself hugging Costanza in a pool of sweat. They were both soaked.

The day seemed to go by as if nothing had happened. The atmosphere was oppressive, as if a cataclysm were in the offing. When an old embroideress, come to bring back some work, asked incautiously, "What happened to the little girl?" don Filippo Leccasardi instantly gave her the standard reply: "Nothing. What was supposed to happen?" No one else showed an interest in Costanza's injury, and the masters stayed on the main floor.

In the early afternoon, Amalia put Costanza to bed and went to her room. After taking out her brass hairpins and comb, she settled in the rocking chair and closed her eyes. She had almost dropped off when Gaetano Cucurullo knocked at the door. The baron's orders: Costanza and her women were expected at the castle, and the coach was already waiting. Amalia had just enough time to put up her hair again as best she could, throw a shawl over her shoulders, and dress Costanza, who was half asleep. She called Maddalena and all three went down to the stables.

Waiting for them was the baron's own personal coach, with its crimson upholstery and quilted cushions and spherical gilt clock. Don Vito Pelonero, the coachman, was in his seat. With a crack of his whip, he set the coach and pair in motion. Amalia huddled into her shawl almost as if she hoped it would hide her heart, which, she was certain, could be heard at a distance; it was hopping about inside her like a toad in a trap. Her throat was dry. Fear was eating her alive.

She went into the baron's study, where the Safamita brothers were waiting for her in the middle of the room, standing stiff as statues. They did not speak. Murmuring a "*Voscenza benadica*," she put Costanza down on the floor. The little girl ran towards the men. The young baron bent down to kiss his daughter and busied himself with untying the lace cap that didn't quite cover the bandage.

On bended knees, the two brothers unwrapped the bandage and studied the injury in a silence that was their only sign of shame. Amalia felt superfluous, almost an intruder.

"Mama threw me at the wall and made me bleed, and I cried," said Costanza, her hand on her father's arm.

The young baron stood up with his daughter in his arms and walked slowly to the balcony. He stopped in the middle of the window. Her right arm hooked round his neck, her head on his shoulder, Costanza gazed at him with her deep eyes, as if from that trusting abandon a regenerating reciprocal affection had sprung. Her hair, freed of the bandage, was a cascade of dark gold. The outline of their entwined bodies stood out against the bright blue of the sky. They stayed like that for a long time.

The young baron turned round and gently handed the child to Amalia. "Take the little girl to Maddalena and come back here, alone."

Amalia stood in front of the barons, now seated in two large armchairs, their eyes trained on her. The castle, with its dark, gloomy rooms, always filled her with disquiet. The study was an austere place, filled with stuffed animals, bronze statues, and heavy, solid furniture. On the walls, in the spaces not occupied by bookshelves, hung lugubrious ancestral portraits.

The two men looked at her in silence. She swayed a bit, more and more fearful, like a person accused. The baron's hair was grey by now, and his beard was thicker than his brother's, but except for the difference in age they were alike as two peas, with their prominent aquiline noses, their big hands with bulging veins, their small almond-shaped eyes, and their severe bearing.

Finally the young baron spoke. "I have seen Costanza's injury. The baroness has told me that she was at fault. Costanza confirms this. Have you anything to add?"

"No, your lordship," mumbled Amalia.

"We must avoid this happening again, at all costs," said the baron.

"What do you suggest, Amalia?" The young baron shot her a worried look, as if he were speaking to an equal.

The disarming familiarity stunned her completely. They had to protect Costanza and they were asking her for advice—her, the wet nurse, of all people. Her head was spinning, she felt dizzy. She had a strange feeling—as if she had split in two and her soul had flown away from her embarrassed, flustered body and, like a feather, had floated up to the frescoed ceiling and was looking down at her from on high, waiting for her answer. Amalia heard herself saying, "When milady the baroness comes upstairs to see Giacomo, perhaps I could keep the little girl in the other room."

"Think about it, Amalia. When Costanza hears her mother's voice she wants her and she runs to her. We know that my wife must not be with her. At present she represents a danger." The young baron looked her straight in the eye and repeated, "A danger, Amalia, do you follow me?"

"Yes, your lordship!"

"You must avoid any danger whatsoever that may arise from her mother, do you understand this? You must protect her, protect her from everyone—have I made myself clear?" The young baron had raised his voice, menacingly.

"Amalia," the baron broke in, "you must keep Costanza far from her mother. My daughter is not well, and she won't recover in the near future."

"Yes, your lordship. Yes, yes."

"What are the rooms farthest from Giacomo's?" asked the young baron.

"The service rooms, on the ground floor," replied Amalia in a rush of words.

"Good. Then from now on I permit you to take my daughter to those rooms. I shall speak with don Filippo. He will find a place for her toys and everything she needs. My daughter's safety depends on you." And then, raising his voice again, he added, "On you and me."

"Take this, Amalia." The baron gave her a purse full of coins.

She took it, bewildered, and forgot to thank him as she kissed his hand and asked rather boldly, "Has anyone spoken to milady the baroness about these changes? What if she forbids them?"

"Don't be impertinent, Amalia," the young baron admonished her, reverting to his autocratic tone. "I am the master of Safamita House, and I decide. I let my wife do as she pleases within the boundaries I set, and I expect her to be grateful to me for that." This earned the young baron a sharp glare from his brother, but he ignored it and added, "I speak also on behalf of the baron here. At the castle there will be identical systems. Don Calogero Giordano will explain them to you later. You may go."

She was already in the doorway, about to leave, when he called her again. "Amalia, it goes without saying: not a word to anyone."

13

"Maids must ever be kissed or pinched."

The Safamita brothers briefly lust for the wet nurse Amalia Cuffaro.

Maddalena and Costanza were scattering bread crumbs on the muddy waters of the fish pond. The nurse joined them and bent over to embrace

Costanza. All three set off down the path to the stables, unaware that they were being watched by the masters, who had appeared in the garden too late to say goodbye to Costanza.

Guglielmo and Domenico Safamita stopped by the fish pond and followed them with their eyes. The garden was at the height of its splendour: the succulents were plump with water, the roses in full bloom, the trees laden, the tubs and the borders in flower. Amalia's hips swung as she walked hand in hand with Costanza, trotting along at her side. Maddalena, short and stout, followed unwillingly at a distance, clearly unhappy at having to leave the cool of the garden. As she shuffled along the gravel path she turned her head from right to left, now pausing in front of a drinking fountain shaped like a shell, then touching a statue, now caressing the fleshy, glossy leaves of a ficus, then bending over to smell the oleanders.

The nurse walked on, lost in thought. She let go of Costanza's hand as the little girl slowed her pace; then, realising she had left the child behind, Amalia stopped and turned round, breaking into a broad smile. Costanza hastened to catch up, and they continued on their way, hand in hand. Every so often they would smile at each other.

The Safamita brothers stood there watching. That smile was bright and voluptuous. Amalia was walking with renewed zest, the feeling of mild well-being that spread over her revealing itself in her gait, to which she abandoned herself in confidence that she was protected from indiscreet eyes. Her cotton skirt followed her swinging hips, swaying and rustling against the ferny border that spilled over onto the path; the edges of her ample white nurse's apron, with its large gauzy bow and lacework embellishments, billowed up from her blue dress in rhythm with the nodding of her teardrop coral earrings and the trembling of her chignon, which, half undone, had slipped down and almost covered the nape of her neck. She bent down slightly over Costanza and said something to her. They laughed together and disappeared around the bend in the avenue.

"A handsome woman, the nurse . . . I wonder who enjoys that body," commented the baron.

"Hmm," said his younger brother with a rare look of complicity. "Neither you nor I. Hands off."

"No doubt about it." On their weary faces roguish smiles appeared for the first time on that dreadful day.

14

"Study and care keep ill fortune elsewhere."

Costanza Safamita's new life in the ironing room

Don Filippo Leccasarda, the young baron's majordomo, gave specific instructions for welcoming Costanza to the service rooms. The footmen carried out these orders good-naturedly and without complaining or asking questions. The ironing room, next to the pantry and not far from the service stairs, was big enough to allow them to make a spacious, comfortable area for her closed off by a screen, near the terrace where the laundry was hung out to dry. This modest but pleasant space, adorned by foreign prints showing hunting scenes and an old carpet, was reserved for Costanza. The nurse was satisfied with it, and right away Costanza spent her afternoons there.

For the rest of the day, Costanza and Giacomo mostly kept to their old routines. They slept in their respective bedrooms on the second floor and took their meals in the drawing room, alone; accompanied by the nurses, they would go down to the main floor to greet their parents in the mornings and in the evenings. After "*la conversation*" in French with Madame—given their ages, they mostly played with the elderly Austrian lady—in midmorning they took their daily walk to the castle to see their grandfather and Aunt Assunta. After lunch they would wait for their parents to finish their meal, because sometimes these last wanted to see the children as they took coffee. Then the Safamitas would retire, each separately, for their afternoon siesta. At that hour, the young baron, who did not like to sleep during the day, had Costanza brought to him in the smoking room. It was then that he developed the habit of speaking to her in French, as he did in private with his wife.

The children's afternoon was devoted to games and their mother's visit to the nursery, but now Costanza stayed in the ironing room until dinner, separated from Giacomo and their mother. She missed her little brother, yet accepted his absence docilely when obliged to do so, but she was most unhappy about not seeing her mother and often asked for her. Her rare encounters with Caterina were brief, and always in the presence of her nurse or her father.

Giacomo could not work out why it was that from one moment to the next he had lost his playmate. As he grew, and especially when Costanza told him about what went on in the ironing room and the kitchens, where he wasn't allowed to go, he couldn't understand why he was excluded. And his father did not hide his marked preference for Costanza. Giacomo began to perceive her as a rival and reacted by bullying her and being arrogant. Costanza bore this patiently and indulged him in their games, which only increased his anger and frustration.

About twenty-five people lived and worked in Safamita House, including the footmen, the kitchen staff, caretakers, coachmen, and some devoted old retainers who either had nowhere to go in their old age or simply preferred to end their days in the house they considered their own, making themselves as useful as they could. Other employees, who depended directly on the young baron and did not live in the mansion, included the administrative staff and the private guards whose task was to protect the family and its possessions. The place reserved for their exclusive use was the guard room, where they also took their meals, next to the porter's lodge.

The divisions among the various ranks of the domestic staff were rigid, and the division between males and females equally so. The head cook and don Filippo Leccasarda ate together in the cupboard room, where they were served by Lina Munnizza, the assistant cook, who was rumoured to be the head cook's lover and so jealous that she had chosen to be his maidservant so that she could listen in on their conversations. The footmen and the valets ate in the kitchen, served by the women, who were relegated to the pantry for meals, together with the nurses.

By contrast with the relatively solitary life of the masters, below stairs there was a constant coming and going of people and a stream of well-regulated activities that went on in an atmosphere that might be described as serene and even merry. Pampered by everyone, Costanza was specially welcome in the rooms where the women worked. Sometimes they let her help them. At first, the maids had felt uncomfortable in the presence of a mistress, albeit a tiny one; then, as always happens, they became used to it and even grew fond of her. When the family went to Palermo or to one of the country houses, where it was impossible to create a special space for her in the service rooms, Costanza almost naturally sought out the company of the maids.

Without guidance or maternal example, Costanza instinctively modelled herself on her nurse, copying Amalia's speech and gestures and adopting her tastes. Amalia carved out a specific job for herself in the Safamita household that was well suited to former wet nurses: as a mender. In the Belice home mending had been like daily bread, for the rags that clothed parents and children were held together more by darning thread than by the weave of the cloth. It was therefore a nostalgic return to the activities of her youth and soon became her favourite pastime.

Every afternoon the nurse and Costanza would put their stools in front of the terrace window and settle down to sewing. They discussed what needed doing and then chose from the things piled in the basket: towels, tablecloths, rags, socks, handkerchiefs, white gloves for serving at table, uniforms. They were never short of work, which gave them a comforting sense of security. In addition, unlike embroidery, mending doesn't require one's total attention, so they could chat and amuse themselves by listening to the others. Costanza diligently learned how to do little jobs suited to her age and later became a highly skilled mender. Darning remained her favourite form of needlework. She loved to sing and often, as she worked, she would hum a little refrain under her breath; the nurse would hum along with her.

Apart from Amalia, Costanza found avuncular figures in two elderly retired women who were permanent guests at Safamita House. Maria Teccapiglia had been maid to Costanza's maternal grandmother, Baroness Maria Stella, who had died very young and who, as she lay dying—the old maid loved to tell this—had asked her to watch over her daughter. Maria's husband, Gaetano Tignuso, Pepi Tignuso's brother, had died in his youth following a kick from a mule. Accustomed to life in the castle, Maria hadn't liked staying with her in-laws, and had preferred to leave her children at Malivinnitti while she went back to the Safamitas. Her kinship with Pepi Tignuso, as well as her age, had won Maria the respect of both the masters and her peers. She was particularly pained by the baroness's behaviour towards Costanza, and though she had an explanation for what had happened, she kept it to herself. In the hope that in time the mother would learn to love the little girl, she had taken on the task of sustaining and nourishing Costanza's affection for the baroness. When the little girl longed to see her mother, Maria would distract her by telling her stories about her mother's childhood; this was the only thing that calmed Costanza, and, thanks to Maria Teccapiglia, she got to know her mother better and ended up loving her even more.

Annuzza la Cirara—Annuzza Candlewax—had been the house seamstress to Baroness Maria Stella, and she, too, was a great storyteller. Despite her nickname, she had never worked with candle wax. She had been sewing since the age of six, and her physique was that of a sedentary worker who seldom walks but stays seated and bent over for long periods: she was plump, with broad hips and a flat bottom, and she walked with a stoop, taking little steps. Her mother-in-law left her free to sew, grateful for Annuzza's acquiescent silence about the homosexuality of her husband, Peppi 'u Ciraru—a candlestick-maker by trade—and she took on the household chores herself. When Peppi died a few years later, Annuzza went back to Safamita House rather than stay in a family she didn't feel a part of. There she sewed for the domestic staff: uniforms, aprons, pot holders, tablecloths, and other household linen. She agreed to be treated like a married woman, and she behaved like one: with discretion.

Despite her age, the virginal Annuzza remained a young girl inside—romantic, wholly without malice or rancour, and brimming with chaste imaginings. She would sew and tell Costanza stories, never tiring of the tales with which she comforted the little girl, and which she adapted or made to order depending on the circumstances. She even invented a heroine for Costanza: Princess Babbaluci, the Snail Princess. Annuzza being an inexhaustible source of marvellous stories, Costanza knew that with her she would enter a world in which suffering, patience, generosity, and cleverness were rewarded with love, marriage, justice, and happiness.

In the ironing room, Costanza found herself in a world that was wholly feminine and oral, and in which she felt loved and protected; she wasn't at ease in the presence of men except those who were dearest to her: her father, her brothers, and her grandfather. With her adult uncles and cousins she was extremely shy and retiring, unable to say a word, and she became agitated when she met the men who worked in the mansion. Her nurse attributed this to her fearful memory, perhaps unconscious, of the scorn and derision that people had heaped on her when she was a baby because of her appearance. In time, Costanza grew accustomed to the presence of don Filippo Leccasarda and a few of the other male servants, especially the older ones. Paolo Mercurio and Gaspare Quagliata became a part of her restricted circle. They told her true stories of distant lands and foreign cities.

The summer after Stefano's return from boarding school, the young baron wanted Costanza to spend more time with her older brother. Caterina, accepting her maternal responsibility, swore that she would control herself; her only desire was to be a good wife and mother, and she lived in hopes of learning to love her daughter. Her husband thought about this at length and with great sadness. He watched her. In the end, he decided to give his wife a chance to redeem herself. Marriage had not stifled the uncle's protective and indulgent attitude, and at the same time the desire to possess his wife grew keener, precisely because the complete possession of Caterina was an unattainable goal. This was the secret of their passion and his tolerance.

So Domenico Safamita took it upon himself to encourage Costanza to come to the playroom and the main floor with her brothers. The little girl obeyed, but it was clear that she was anxious and uncomfortable; by now she considered the ironing room her little kingdom, and she would return to it as soon as she could, during her free time, to darn with Amalia and to play games with the servants.

15

"Marriages and bishoprics are made in heaven."

The Princess Babbaluci
Annuzza la Cirara invents for Costanza Safamita a marvellous fairy tale
about the Snail King and a shepherd's daughter.

"Once upon a time there was a shepherd who lived in a little house with his wife and seven sons. His wife wanted a daughter, but a little girl didn't come along. One day, while she was picking capers, a sharp thorn stuck in her finger and made her hand swell up. She sat down on a stone and wept. 'Who will take this cruel thorn out of my finger? Oh, if only I had a little daughter, she would get it out in a twinkling,' she said, and sighed.

"'I can take out the thorn for you,' said a voice, 'and give you a daughter, if you do as I say.' The shepherd's wife looked around, but there wasn't a soul. The voice came from a snail as big as a rock; its shell was dark red, with yellow streaks that shone like gold. 'But first you must promise to give me the daughter who will be born to you.' 'I promise,' said the shepherd's wife. The snail slithered onto her hand and left some slime there: the pain vanished and the thorn had gone.

"After nine months the shepherd's wife gave birth to a daughter. One morning she saw the snail in front of the house, clinging to a prickly plant. 'I have come for the daughter you promised me,' the snail reminded her. 'Be off with you, before I squash you!' she cried, and the snail slithered away.

"Her daughter had skin as white as milk and marvellous chestnut hair; in the sun it became red with golden highlights, like the snail's shell. The shepherd and his wife were very happy.

"One day, as the mother was brushing her daughter's hair, she noticed that two little horns were growing on her head, just like snail's horns. She tried to cover them with the hair, but the horns stood up straight as can be and stuck out among the curls. So the mother put a little cap on her daughter's head, and she kept it on night and day.

"The daughter grew up pretty and sweet and was of an age to marry. 'Who will wed a lass with horns?' the mother said to herself. 'And who will wed my seven sons, with a sister-in-law like this? This one will end up at home with me, another mouth to feed!' In despair, the shepherd's wife gave her daughter a good thrashing. Then she talked with her husband and they decided to abandon the girl in the forest.

"Summer was coming and the shepherd had to transfer his flock to the mountain pastures. He took his daughter with him. They came to a hazel wood, where they stopped to sleep in a cave. The next morning the girl awoke to find neither her father nor the sheep. She looked for him all day, and that evening she fell asleep, weeping. That night, silent as can be, many snails came out and they covered her with slime, which became a cocoon: the poor girl became a snail. They took her to their underground kingdom, where the Snail King reigned; there she was revered as a princess.

"After a while, the girl began to miss her mother. She was a bad woman all right, but still, she was her mother. The daughter wanted to see her very much and suffered because of this. The Snail King gave her permission to return home, on condition that she never take the kerchief off her head and never tell a living soul that she had horns.

"Her parents gave her a horrid welcome; they set her to work and beat her soundly. 'Look and see if she still has snail's horns,' said the shepherd to his wife one day. 'Maybe they've shrivelled up, and we can marry her off.' But the daughter would not let her mother feel her head. In the end, they drove her out. Disconsolate, the poor girl went back to the forest. She lay down in the cave, wishing she would wake up a snail once more, but it wasn't to be. The next day she set to roaming among the trees, hoping to meet the Snail King. Instead, she met a handsome prince in the forest; he, too, was lost. He asked her for something to eat. She took him to the cave and told him to wait for her there. After searching here, there, and everywhere, she found nothing to eat. She was desperate: what would the prince say? From under a stone, slow as can be, the Snail King slithered out. 'You mustn't worry, you're not alone. I am here to look after you,' he told her. 'When you want something to eat, pull off one of your horns.' She did as he told her, and a table appeared laden with all sorts of good things. The prince ate everything happily, and they passed the time talking to each other. Whenever he was hungry, she pulled off one of her horns and food appeared. It hurt her a lot to pull the horns off, but she had to do it. Afterwards, her horns grew in again.

"The prince took her to the palace and told his mother that the girl was the greatest cook in the world, and that he had fallen in love with her. The couple would talk all day long, and the queen grew jealous. She took it out on the poor girl and harassed her terribly. The girl cried, but she said nothing to the prince. In the end, the queen arranged for her son to marry a very rich princess, but he wouldn't hear of it.

"One day the prince told the girl that he wanted her hand in marriage, poor as she was and a cook. But first he wanted to see her in all her beauty: she was to take off her kerchief and show him her hair. The girl could not disobey the Snail King, so she refused. The prince was not accustomed to being gainsaid and he took offence. He went off hunting, and when he returned he didn't even look at her. He exchanged sweet nothings with the princess he was supposed to marry, in front of the poor girl, who suffered terribly. 'Never will my prince love me again! I suffer so at the mere sight of him: he wants me no longer,' she said to herself. In the meantime, the queen was preparing for her son's marriage and she tormented the girl even more.

"On the eve of the wedding, the prince summoned the girl to him and told her that he couldn't get her out of his head; he was prepared to elope, but first he had to see her hair. The girl wanted him so very much that she untied her kerchief.

"She had the most beautiful hair, all chestnut curls with locks of red and gold. The prince wanted to caress it. As soon as he touched it, the girl became covered in slime and disappeared: she had turned into a snail again. Desperate, he called off the wedding and went back to the forest. He found the cave where he had met the girl and fell asleep, weeping. That night, she appeared to him in a dream. 'I shall come back to you if you let yourself be kissed on the mouth by the first one of God's creatures that you see,' she promised him. The prince awoke and looked around. There was no one in sight. He set to roaming through the forest. There was no trace of men or animals. Even the ants were hiding in their nests. The prince walked for a day and a night, and the following morning he fell asleep under a carob tree.

"When he awoke, he saw a big snail at his feet. Ever so slowly, the snail stuck out its horns and its moist foot; it climbed up the prince's boots, made its way up his trousers, reached his shirt, and then slithered onto his neck. The prince was filled with disgust. The slime burned his skin like a nettle, but he thought of his beloved and didn't move. The snail arrived at his chin and slithered onto his mouth. The prince did not throw it off. The snail placed its slimy foot on his lips. It burned awfully, and the prince fainted.

"When he awoke, his beloved was beside him. She was most fair; two little horns protruded from the middle of her curls. They kissed for a long time, and then she told him her story. She said that, as far as she was concerned, her real father was the Snail King; if the prince loved her, he would have to accept her horns and forgive the shepherd and his wife. He agreed. Then a king appeared before them, with a crown on his head. It was the Snail King: a witch had put a spell on him that would be broken only when a young girl loved him like a father and was unashamed of her horns.

"On the day of their wedding the girl's horns fell off. But all the people, who loved her very much, went on calling her the Snail Princess."

16

"Lands uninspected are lands neglected."

The Safamitas holiday at Malivinnitti.

The Safamitas would begin their summer holidays at Malivinnitti in June: harvest time. The sisters and Father Sedita were frequent guests, and the family would stay there longer than necessary just for the pleasure of it. Then they would move to their other country houses: their holdings demanded their presence.

Malivinnitti, an inland estate devoted exclusively to growing wheat, was the largest of the Safamitas' holdings. The farmhouse, surrounded by high walls, stood halfway up a hillside, overlooking other hills. For most of the year the estate seemed to be abandoned by man and beast alike, but this wasn't the case, for Malivinnitti was always under the control of the field overseers. Mounted on their mares and armed with shotguns and pistols, the Tignuso men roamed across it far and wide, watching over the land from secret hiding places, while at the lodge where they lived the women took turns at their chores by the windows, one eye on the farmhouse and the other on the fields. Then Malivinnitti came to life during the seasons of ploughing, sowing, and reaping, when dozens of farmhands trekked up from the neighbouring villages to earn their bread. They, too, were under the control of the Tignusos.

The animals and the peasants lived in the old farm buildings. In the early nineteenth century Baron Safamita had had a new house built for his family, with one side against the old farmhouse, complete with a large inner courtyard. The family quarters filled all four sides of the courtyard on the first floor, and boasted numerous bedrooms, like a monastery dormitory. This simple house, devoid of amenities, was the favourite summer residence of three generations of Safamitas, who preferred it to their other, far more luxurious homes.

Their friends did not understand why: the wheat fields came right up to the walls, and the only pleasant feature consisted of a dozen immense carob trees planted lower down, below the terrace, in an airy part where they kept tables and chairs so as to enjoy the cool of the shade provided by the luxuriant treetops. The monotonous countryside was typical of the estate: an endless succession of hills covered with crops, row upon row of them. Not a tree, not a house, not a road. "Land and sky—there's nothing else at Malivinnitti. What do they see in it?" their friends wondered.

At sunrise the damp shadows of the night withdrew from the deserted hillsides, leaving them streaked with blue; refreshed, the wheat fields rustled and birds fluttered over them in search of food. The sky took on depth and became bright blue, then whitened into incandescence. When the inexorable noonday sun dominated and dazzled everything, the birds, wearied and blinded by the dazzling light, took refuge behind the rocks; the herbs and plants alongside the paths withheld their scent and closed their parched leaves. Then evening's thirsty shadows—long, crisp, red—aroused the insects, birds, and scents of the countryside. The sun set behind the hills in a phantasmagoria of red, yellow, crimson, and violet. Then came the calm. Total darkness descended on Malivinnitti. The first fireflies made their faint appearance.

Night and day the countryside lay still but not infertile; in the silence burnished with the chirruping of cicadas, the wheat grew plump, grain by grain, and rich in starch. The earth, parched by the sun, reenacted this rite of fertility year after year. For millennia. Earth, wheat, and sky. Property. The family. That, *that* was what the Safamitas saw in Malivinnitti. It was their way of celebrating life and their tenacious bond with the land.

The little Safamitas had another reason for loving the holidays at Malivinnitti: the company of their cousins. At Malivinnitti the children felt free, even though they were never alone. They ran about in the fields, they ventured as far as the water trough, they played in the wheat, and, along with one of the Tignusos and under the discreet protection of the guards, they followed the reapers. In the farmhouse there were many other things to do. On their own or with the peasants' children, they would spend the hottest part of the day collecting crumbly stones of different colours and crushing them into fine powders—red, white, grey, yellow, light green. They also modelled wet clay, husked the still-green ears of wheat to eat the moist, sweetish grains, and wove little baskets out of reeds: the simple games of time immemorial.

The boys played with Pepi Tignuso's grandchildren and the sons of the country folk, who were shy at first but then came to enjoy it, proud of their familiarity with the little masters and of the skills they could show off in front of them: blinding kittens, tormenting puppies, chopping the wings off birds and the tails off lizards.

Caterina Safamita was happy at Malivinnitti. In the evenings, she would play cards on the terrace, and chat with both adults and children; she would sing with the other women, and she invited Costanza, who had a very good ear, to join them. The little girl loved that.

Every day, Costanza's father would take a turn around the estate with Pepi Tignuso. Sometimes he returned from those rides in a thoughtful mood and kept his distance from the company. Costanza noticed this and tried to cheer him up. In the evenings, after dinner, he would stay on the terrace watching the weary caravan of donkeys and mules coming back from the water trough laden with the huge water jugs. He seemed worried. Costanza went up to him. Her father laid his hand on her shoulder and held her close. She sensed his sadness and her heart ached for him. Once she talked about this with Stefano; he told her not to bother her head about it, it was men's business.

One morning the nurse and Maria Teccapiglia were sitting on the steps of the barn, keeping an eye on the children. Amalia was sewing the hem of a handkerchief, and Maria was unpicking the basting thread on those that were already done.

"I don't like Malivinnitti," murmured Amalia. "The kids have fun, but I don't understand the masters . . . why do they like it so much?"

"Why? Why? . . . I know why," said Maria without looking up from her work. "There's always an explanation. This is where it all started, twenty-odd years back. I was here, sitting where we are now, watching the young baroness and her Scravaglio and Limuna cousins playing in the fields, just like these children today. Nothing has changed. The young baroness had already lost her mother. Her cousin Stefano Scravaglio had his eye on her, the way Vincenzo Limuna has his on Costanza: a Safamita's dowry is very tempting. But the young baroness didn't enjoy her cousin's games—he'd pull her skirts, jump on her, and was forever provoking her. I couldn't say a word.

"One day young Baron Domenico chanced to pass by the barn, and he stopped. Caterina had climbed way up high, and her cousin was teasing her. 'Help me, Uncle! Stefano won't leave me alone!' she yelled, and, without giving him a chance to answer, she jumped down and landed on him; he had just enough time to catch her under the arms. And I saw what I saw. She had the eyes of a woman. And those eyes were fixed on her uncle. I couldn't see his face, but he was holding her close, and he didn't set her down. My head was spinning.

"'Be careful, Caterina. Play at something less boisterous,'" said he, and he went off without so much as a goodbye. Caterina came and sat by me, and she didn't say a word.

"Years after, I spotted them coming out of the farmhouse early one morning. Quiet as can be, they slipped under a big carob tree, one of the ones where the branches reach down to the ground, and they didn't come out again. That's why the young baron and the baroness come to Malivinnitti and stay here: to remember when they fell in love."

17

"Penny wise and pound foolish"

In Palermo people are different,
and Costanza Safamita doesn't understand them.

Domenico Safamita was thirty-seven when he married his niece. In the family it had been thought that he would remain a bachelor. His sisters were puzzled and surprised by the marriage, and not only because of the kinship. Domenico was a well-travelled socialite who appreciated music and the arts, and he was marrying a fifteen-year-old niece who had been brought up in the provinces. But the sisters did not understand the influence of their niece's governess, Mademoiselle Annie Besser. From her Caterina had also learned to know and love French literature and music; she had become a good pianist and played the arias by Mozart, Donizetti, Bellini, and Rossini that Mademoiselle Besser had brought with her to Sarentini. The governess gave Caterina the scores when, after the engagement, the young baron, embarrassed, told her that her services were no longer required: she understood that Caterina had insisted on this.

After the marriage Domenico and Caterina stayed in Sarentini in the mansion house he built there, which was far more comfortable than the one in Palermo, where they spent only a few weeks together in springtime. Every autumn Caterina would return to Castle Sarentini while her husband went to Palermo or travelled. She knew that he had a mistress and she wasn't jealous. This was not an unusual practice, and wives tolerated it so long as it didn't threaten the stability of the marriage. The young baron had other affairs, too, even with women of his own rank, conducted with discretion and unbeknownst to his wife.

When Stefano was sent to boarding school in Palermo in 1860, things changed. Caterina would accompany her husband on brief visits to Palermo, leaving the younger children in Sarentini, and when Giacomo was older the whole family moved to Palermo for the winter months.

For Costanza, the journey from Sarentini to Palermo was both an exciting and a frightening adventure. They would leave in the coach, their route carefully planned ahead of time to deal with the threat of brigands, whose ranks had swollen with the draft dodgers who had been roaming the mountains ever since the unification of Italy. Sometimes they travelled by mule or, along the most arduous stretches, were borne in litters. The convoy was flanked by guards, with others sent ahead to patrol the route and give warning if need be. Costanza found it comforting to spot them, stationed astride their big sorrels on the hilltops, imposing in their green cloaks, the barrels of their shotguns pointing skywards. From a distance, they seemed to her like warrior guardian angels.

Costanza continued with her studies—Italian, French, arithmetic, music, and singing—but her days took on a new, often surprising rhythm, dictated by the need to cultivate social relations. By now she was accustomed to the apparent monotony of Sarentini, and she missed the comforting ritual of tranquil afternoons spent sewing with her nurse: she needed certainties. Costanza looked forward to the industrious afternoon sessions by the window, accompanied by a murmured refrain begun by one and picked up by the other. She felt free to lose herself in her thoughts or to speak without fear of making mistakes or irritating others. Setting her round embroidery frame on her knees, she would spread out the linen and slot in the wooden ring to block the cloth, then pull the ends to draw it to a uniform tension; she would prepare a length of cotton and thread the needle. When she was ready, she would stick the needle in from the top and pull the thread from below, maintaining the correct tension; then, feeling her way and following the pattern, she would push it back up, pull the thread tight again, and stick the needle back into the cloth, pushing it down with her thimble—the same movements, over and over. Stitch by stitch, the cloth was slowly embellished, and every stitch gave her subtle pleasure. When Costanza came to the point where it seemed right to leave off embroidering, she carefully pinned the thread and put everything back into her basket. In Palermo, however, she settled down to her work anxiously every afternoon and didn't dare look forward to the pleasure of it, so anxious was she about the likelihood of being interrupted to receive visitors or to go out.

She soon learned that this was the way things were in Palermo: cutting a fine figure and friendships were important, the rest less so or not at all. Appearances and elegance—of one's person, one's reception rooms, one's coaches—were of the utmost consideration, as was money, which people spent to excess. And one's friendships were assessed on the basis of class and rank. All this was beyond her comprehension.

The women grumbled about society life, complained of indispositions, professed enormous fatigue, declared that they preferred life at home but were obliged to take part in all the social occasions they would willingly do without. But then they organised receptions and announced social calls only to regret them when the time came; after claiming that they wanted to stay at home, they nonetheless took offence if they didn't receive invitations.

In the afternoons her mother would often meet with her aunts, female cousins, and lady friends of the family. She heard her gossiping, talking of marriages, discussing clothes and jewellery. The women would repeat the same conversations as if they had forgotten them from one day to the next, but no one noticed. She saw that her mother took part in them somewhat reluctantly, and that the other women didn't notice this. At such moments Costanza felt close to her mother, thinking that she, too, missed the afternoons in Sarentini, when she would read, play the piano, or chat with her father, and she wondered if she missed the tortoises. But she never had the courage to talk to Caterina about it.

Even the rhythms of family relations changed in Palermo. Costanza missed the company of the servants: in Palermo she was forbidden to enter their rooms. Giacomo attended the boarding school as a day boy and had his own friends. Her father was very busy and was often out. But her mother had more time for her. Caterina took Costanza with her on duty visits to relatives, urged her to make friends with her female cousins of the same age, and bombarded her with advice on how to behave—but never with the encouragement of a smile or a caress. Aware of her different looks, Costanza was afraid of embarrassing her mother with her Sarentinese accent and her sketchy grasp of Italian. She answered adults' questions in monosyllables and was inhibited with her peers; she blushed at the slightest thing. Her carriage was good, but she hunched her shoulders and lowered her eyes to avoid meeting the gaze of people whom she instinctively sensed were hostile.

Costanza sometimes went shopping with her mother. Hesitantly, she would offer Caterina her hand as they crossed the street, but she was disappointed every time; she could feel her mother's coldness in the way she took her hand, ready to let it go before they even reached the other side of the street. And the shops, or the seamstresses' and milliners' ateliers, were pure torment, for Costanza was not vain. The poor souls who made a living by selling to the rich would try to make compliments on her large eyes, her small face, her height. Costanza would look up at her mother, whose pursed lips, contracted chin, and impenetrable eyes seemed to say, "You can save your breath; this unwanted daughter of mine is ugly, and there's no helping it."

This was a torment for Costanza, and her skin would flush with red blotches. Never did she feel so flustered and awkward as she did when in her mother's charge, yet she did not lose hope that one day she might receive just a little of the love that Caterina lavished on her other children.

18

"Mountains will never join other mountains, but men will confront men."

In Palermo Costanza Safamita gets to know her father and Stefano better.

In Palermo Costanza would see Stefano on his days off from school.

They would ride off in the coach to eat ice cream at the Marina. Stefano talked about everything, as if he were thinking out loud. Since from babyhood Costanza had been a first-class listener, she asked few questions but absorbed what she could and forgot nothing.

In this way, she learned that the aristocracy was divided between those who acclaimed the new rulers of Sicily and Italy and those who regretted the passing of the Bourbons and their king; that there were secret societies plotting to help them return to the throne and others who wanted a government with no king, still others who did not respect the Holy Mother Church, and others again who had even stranger and more mysterious ideas. Stefano also talked of a young person's doubts about things, but, above all, he spoke of his hopes. He had his own ideas: he believed passionately that a new world lay on Sicily's horizon. All that needed to be done was to grasp the opportunities that presented themselves: new farming activities, an increase in horse breeding, tuna fishing, working coral, better navigation and industry.

Costanza did not understand completely, but she didn't ask questions; in any case, she liked those trips in the carriage, sitting proudly beside her elder brother as they bowled along the seafront. The road skirted the calm, limpid sea, whose waters reflected, to the west, Monte Pellegrino, the city's magnificent, protective household god. On one side were the aristocrats' great mansions, with their luxuriant terraces. On the other side the pavement was thronged with people dressed up for the promenade, and the coaches would stop for ice cream at the cafés on the Marina. Waiters came out to serve them in their coach, making their way through the people strolling by and the customers seated at the tables. They balanced their large trays—arms held high to clear the heads of the passersby—laden with water glasses and silver-plated bowls of ice cream filled to the top and smoothly shaved off at the rim, with a crunchy tubular wafer stuck in each one. Costanza was greedy for it all; she savoured even the sweet, refreshing water, which she consumed in little sips after the ice cream.

Her father often lunched at his club and did not keep up the habit of their lovely afternoons together. But now and again he would take her out in the coach, as a surprise. On these trips he would often order Paolo to stop so that he could show her something. The features of Palermo took on fascinatingly different aspects.

One day, on the umpteenth stop, he had her get out of the coach. They clambered up a foul-smelling alleyway lined with hovels crammed with people. They made their way through piles of dung, strays and domestic animals, women, children, and wretched old folk. It was all a buzz of grating, harsh voices. The alley ended at a very high wall, where the stench was awful. "Look," her father said, pointing to the stones at the base of the wall. "These stones have been squared off and piled one on top of the other. Do you see how they filled the gaps with thin bricks, inserted there in between?" He pointed with his cane. Around them a small crowd of children formed—half naked, emaciated, filthy, and now silent. Costanza, tightly clasping her father's gnarled hand, felt that she was being watched. Necks craning, the old people were peering at them from glazed eyes under drooping lids, their faces impassive. The women carried on with their chores, every so often giving them suspicious, fearful glances.

Overcome by the stench and by her fear, Costanza clasped her father's hand even more tightly. He caressed her palm with his fingers and continued: "Here you can read history. These stones belonged to the city wall built almost three thousand years ago by the Phoenicians, the founders of Palermo. They came from Africa, they crossed the sea and then, sailing round the coast of Sicily, they passed Monte Pellegrino. And they saw the plain of Palermo—big, fertile, with lots of water, surrounded by mountains, like the inside of my hand." Her father showed her a hand, fingers flexed to simulate a crown of mountains around the palm; a blowfly landed on it and stayed there, its wings an iridescent green. Fascinated, Costanza thought that it was beautiful. She looked and listened. "They said to themselves, 'This is a fine place. We'll stop and drop anchor here. We'll build a city and raise strong walls around it.' And so these gigantic walls rose up, and the Phoenicians stayed in Palermo for many years. They were an intelligent, inquisitive people. They invented glass.

"Then other people came from far away, and they thought the same thing: This is a fine city, we want it. We'll take it and we'll build even higher walls. They were the Romans, great builders. Do you see those rectangular stones, all the same size, higher up? The Romans put them there, on top of the Phoenician stones. Then others came from Africa, the Muslims, and others from Europe, the Normans, and then still more. All these people liked Palermo, and all of them conquered it. Each one of them added other stones, and the walls became immensely high. Can you see the stones up there on the top, the smaller ones? On top of them you can see a little window with a pointed arch. That was built by the Aragonese. They, too, conquered Palermo. Then others came who built new walls. But no one managed to knock down this piece of old wall.

"We are an ancient Palermitan family. The blood of all these peoples runs in your veins, and you, too, will build walls, on your estates. Remember to build them well, and they will continue to stand for your children and for your children's children."

Often her father would take her outside the city, choosing places that struck his fancy: an ancient church, a bridge, an old building, a market, or a spot in the country on the slopes of the hills around Palermo. When they got to where he wanted to be, they would get out and walk, aimlessly, it seemed, hand in hand, in silence at first. "Let's smell the air," her father told her. "Close your eyes and we can talk afterwards." So Costanza, trusting, would let herself be guided. Her nostrils quivering like a hunting dog's, she would tremble all over in search of the smells: pungent, strong, rotten, mixed with sweat and dirt when they were in town; dusty, delicate, bracing in the country; thick and impregnated with damp in the old buildings.

In Sarentini everyone knew the Safamitas. But in Palermo, outside the places frequented by their peers, they were strangers. "Here we are nobodies," said her father. "Nobodies, you understand? You must make yourself recognised by the way you behave, and you must always behave like a lady, wherever and with whomever you may be."

Costanza adored him, and she resolved from an early age that she would never, ever disobey him.

19

"All that enters God's house remains within."

Costanza Safamita visits the Convent of the Madonna del Soccorso and eats ironed hosts.

One day when Costanza was six, Caterina Safamita had a flash of inspiration: the little girl was obviously cut out for the monastic life. She was meek and silent, she obeyed adults, and she was a slave to her little brother's caprices; she liked domestic tasks and she didn't like books.

Although Costanza was still very small, she had already shown that she wasn't coquettish, and she attached no importance to the acquired feminine traits that, together with the innate ones, end up playing a fundamental role in the relationship between a man and a woman. So Caterina Safamita thought she had found the solution to the vexing problems of that flame-red hair—shorn and hidden by a nun's veils— and of her daughter's very presence. Moreover, a nun's endowment was far less than the dowry for a marriageable daughter, and the family property could then be divided into the traditional unequal parts between her sons alone: the larger part to Stefano, while Giacomo would receive enough to live on more than respectably.

She had Annuzza la Cirara sew nun's habits for Costanza's dolls and she gave them to the child. Exaggerating this embryonic religious vocation, she told Aunt Assunta that the little girl loved to dress up her dollies as nuns. Having obtained her aunt's approval, she spoke to her husband and her father about her plan. Neither of them wanted to commit himself: first Costanza had to grow up, and besides, the government intended to abolish the convents.

But Caterina did not desist and, as was the custom, she ordered Costanza's women to encourage her to play with the dolls dressed as nuns; she even went so far as to take the other dolls away. The women, fearing her ire and further mistreatment for the child, didn't dare tell her that although Costanza played dutifully with her little nuns, she calmly provided them with husbands and children, too.

In the meantime, Aunt Assunta took on the assignment of introducing Costanza to the convents. The little girl was happy to go, which to both mother and aunt seemed to confirm her vocation. She didn't say much on these trips and only when adults spoke to her, so the real reason for her enthusiasm for these visits was not revealed.

Aunt and niece would get out of the austere coach upholstered in dark-blue plush, with a crucifix hanging in place of the clock, together with Aunt Assunta's new maid, Peppinella Radica—she too a *monaca di casa*, a "house nun," and Assunta's inseparable companion. They would be received with great ceremony. The mother superior offered them exquisite sweets, prepared according to ancient secret recipes: marzipan shells filled with pistachios and candied pumpkin and covered with a dusting of sugar that gave off a delicious smell of vanilla; mountains of sweet couscous mixed with chopped pistachios, sugar, and chocolate, and fragrant with cloves and cinnamon; almond biscuits that were crunchy on the outside but soft and moist on the inside. The nuns themselves did not savour these delicacies, even though Assunta invited them to taste at least a few, to keep them company. With a pious gesture of the hand, they indicated their renunciation of the sin of gluttony—which, however, was unfailingly rewarded at the moment of farewell, when the coachman unloaded packets of sugar and sacks of wheat and dried fruit destined to lead the convent cooks into temptation and the reconfirmation of their sacrifice.

But the real delicacy, and the reason for Costanza's enthusiasm, was the holy wafers with sugar prepared specially for her in the Convent of the Madonna del Soccorso, where one of her Lattuca ancestors had been a nun. When the attentive nuns did not offer her any Costanza would overcome her shyness and ask for some. They would take her to the convent ironing room, where the young novices—dressed in grey, their shaved heads covered by simple mob caps—silently ironed the nuns' dark habits and starched white accessories: stomachers, collars, and linen bands. The big, black, heavy irons filled with burning embers gave off a dense vapour that smelled of charcoal and starch—the fragrant odour of cleanliness. A nun whispered something into the ear of a young girl, who left the room almost without a sound and returned with a wicker basket brimming with broken holy wafers.

First she carefully selected pieces of similar size, stacked them up two by two, and set them to one side. Then she covered the ironing table with a clean cloth and laid out two rows of broken wafer pieces on it. She sprinkled the first row with sugar mixed with cinnamon and stacked the second row of wafer pieces on top. Now they were ready for ironing. She blew the embers into a glow, then picked up the red-hot iron and, under Costanza's thrilled gaze, brought it down on the first two little stacks. As if by enchantment, the ironing room filled with the smell of burnt sugar and cinnamon: the hosts were transformed into the lightest of wafers, hot and crunchy, the sugar only barely caramelized. Elsewhere in the room, the novices carried on with their work, heads down, obedient to the rule of silence. A fleeting glance full of longing, a long, subdued intake of breath, an imperceptible pause in the ironing said that for them, too, this was the real aroma of paradise; at least that's what Costanza thought.

On Costanza's seventh birthday, her mother thought the time was right for her first communion; she wanted to introduce the girl to convent life without delay, before the laws against the religious orders spoiled her plans. She entrusted Father Puma with the catechism. He accepted gratefully.

20

"The sins of the fathers are visited upon the sons."

Domenico Safamita decides that his daughter will not be a nun.

In Sarentini every afternoon, after lunch, the young baron had Costanza brought to the smoking room. He would sit in the rocking chair and Costanza would lie down on him as if he were a cushion. Sometimes they chatted, or he would tell her old stories about the family and the adventures he had on his travels as a young man; at other times he would doze off, his arms around Costanza's waist as she stayed motionless, her gaze wandering from the walls to the terrace, where there was always something to see: the movement of the wisteria leaves, the flight of birds, or simply the sky.

During one of these afternoons Costanza was dozing on top of her father, but he couldn't manage to relax. "They made promises, they brought hope. Gone up in smoke, disregarded. Bad. Bad. Bad," said Domenico Safamita to himself. "Poverty was unavoidable. Before. Now it is unbearable. Some independence! Some union between equals! They impose their systems, their officials, their army. This is what they have sent us. And they think they are ruling. This is a state of siege.

"Sicily is ungovernable. More than before. We cannot be of any help. Feudalism is dead. There are only the mafiosi. And the field overseers are turncoats—they want to be part of the whole thing. They are something other—they are others, not aristocrats, *others*. They know what they're about. They're ready. Faithful, faithful. To us? It's power they want. And we have lost it. We have wealth. But for how long? Fields and mines—investment is needed. The modern world. All talk and little action. Investment is needed. To emerge from isolation." Domenico balled his fist tightly and let it fall. "We Safamitas will stay rich, but if things go on like this we won't be rich for long. I'm not happy about these sons of Caterina's. Stefano is inconsistent, impulsive, weak. Giacomo isn't promising, isn't up to much."

Costanza's tousled hair tickled his neck below his beard. "This one is different—she is the best. Costanza's children will be the salvation of her mother's stock." He softened at the thought of his wife. Costanza opened her eyes and looked up at him from below. He was holding her tight, his hands on her belly, and he understood her animal sensitivity to the responses of others—their thoughts, too. From here Safamita blood will run in the veins of men and women of merit, he thought. This girl must control her inheritance, she alone.

"Papa, I don't like to sit in Father Puma's arms. Must I go on doing so in order to go to heaven?" Costanza spoke in such a small voice that it almost seemed as if she were sleeping.

"No, you don't have to. Tell him so," answered her father.

"I have told him, but he says that this is the way you learn to receive the body of Christ. It's a secret. I don't like Father Puma. Must I do it?"

"No, there's no need," replied her father. A new sweat began to trickle down his temples, his forehead, and his nose, slipping warm and salty between his lips. He had to know. "Where does he touch you?"

"Here," said Costanza, pushing his hand with hers—tiny, bony fingers—towards her groin. "He hurts me."

"That's not done. You have your papa's word for that," he replied. "Tell him there's no need to do this for first communion."

"But he says that it *is* done, and that it's a secret. What shall I do tomorrow when he comes?" Costanza had become anxious.

Her father was struggling to control himself, rage making his muscles bulge until they hurt. "Don't you worry, Costanza. You can always tell your secrets to your papa. I won't tell them to anyone, not even to Mama. We'll keep this to ourselves, and that's that. I'll speak to Father Puma. He won't come to the house tomorrow. You're ready for first communion and you don't need catechism anymore, and besides, now we all have to go to Palermo to take Stefano to boarding school."

"When are we leaving?"

"On Monday, don't worry."

"Very well, Papa." He felt her finally relax, lying abandoned on his body. Costanza turned over and brushed his beard with a kiss.

"Costanza, tell me something . . . what present would you like for your first communion?"

"Whatever you wish, Papa . . . no, wait, a pretty dolly, one of those with eyes that blink." She was gazing at him with her serious, deep eyes.

"How would you like her dressed?"

Costanza brought a finger up to the corner of her mouth, pensive. She was always thinking, this trusting daughter of his—his daughter, only his. "In green, like Mama's new dress, with red ribbons."

"And when you get married, how will you dress your children?"

"Let's see," said the little girl. "I want four children—two boys and two girls, so they can keep one another company. Then I'll dress them as they wish, but the servants must have our livery. I really like green."

Her father sketched a smile, half serious, half playful. "Costanza, you must obey your husband, as Mama does. She always does what I tell her. You're going to be very rich. This is important to know. With your money you'll be able to do as you wish, but you must think of your husband and respect him. The livery will be that of his house, not yours. Otherwise, what kind of husband would he be?"

"Very well, Papa, I'll do that," promised Costanza, all serious. "But don't tell Mama what I told you. It's a secret, a mystery of religion, do you see?"

"Of course. Domenico Safamita's word of honour. But you must promise to tell me everything that goes through your head, all the things you want to remain only between us. I shall keep it secret, even from Mama, all right? Don't think about Father Puma's secret anymore. Catechism is over."

"Yes," said Costanza solemnly. "Costanza Safamita's word of honour." And she slipped off her father's knee.

She ran to the balcony and stretched, looking outside: tall and straight on her wiry little legs, naturally elegant, her red hair ablaze. Domenico Safamita got up from his rocking chair and wiped his face with his handkerchief. He tugged on the tassel of the bell and laid his hands on his daughter's shoulders. Costanza absently stroked his fingers.

It was hot, the sky was clear, and everything was still. In the distance, wheeling over the rooftops of the town, a flock of scraggly black crows flapped about, cawing.

21

"Fish start to stink from the head."

*A serious argument between the Safamita brothers
and their elder sister, Donna Assunta*

That afternoon the young baron gave the necessary orders.

He sent word to Father Puma that Costanza's first communion would be brought forwards to Sunday. The priest was not to go to the trouble of returning to the house, he said. Costanza had learned what was necessary, and in any case she was indisposed. Obviously, the priest was invited to take part in the ceremony and the lunch after the mass.

He had his favourite horse saddled, chose the best horsemen from his guards, and went off for a gallop. On his return, he informed the nurse of his decisions and ordered her to watch over Costanza with particular care.

Now his final task awaited him: to speak to his brother, face-to-face. As he dismounted in the castle stables, he was assailed by an enormous weariness that seized him body and soul. Domenico Safamita felt all the burden of his years.

He had expected to find Guglielmo alone, but Assunta was there, too.

"What's going on?" asked his sister, agitated. "Why this hasty first communion? This is no way to go about things! You must take religion seriously, Domenico, and communion is an important sacrament."

"Who told you about this?" he asked brusquely.

"Father Puma came here an hour ago, extremely upset. You have offended him. He says you don't want him at Safamita House. Why?"

"Tell me what happened," ordered Guglielmo.

Domenico got up from his armchair. He turned his back on them, then slowly turned around full circle to face them again, and said in icy tones, "What happened? Now, or before, Guglielmo?"

"What are you talking about?" asked Assunta. "Don't talk in riddles."

"Before what?" Guglielmo went on the attack. "Before you took my daughter?"

Domenico shot him a black look. He slammed a chair to the floor.

"For the love of God, this is a simple first communion! With all the things that are happening to the Holy Mother Church these days, this is all we need!" snivelled Assunta.

Domenico was intensely aware of his brother's anger. He didn't answer. Gripping the chair, he looked outside. Dusk was falling and the pretty-by-nights, their petals folded but on the verge of opening, were beginning to emit their scent. The first moths made their appearance. A gentle gust of wind carrying the scent of the flowers wafted into the drawing room.

"Then let's talk about things as they really are. Finally let's talk about them, now, between us brothers. There are times when the past needs raking over. Guglielmo, this house and garden where we were born has seen it all, and we don't forget. Do you know when your daughter became more than a niece for me, almost a daughter to protect? I'll tell you. The time has come for you both to know." Domenico spoke heatedly, but then he continued in his customary monotone. "Poor Maria Stella had just died."

"You will not speak of my wife, I forbid you!" thundered his brother.

"You can't forbid me anything! I'm talking about my mother-in-law, the mother of your daughter and the grandmother of Caterina's daughter, is that clear? I have brought up Maria Stella's granddaughter as the most precious creature in the world. I protect her, as I protected your daughter after your wife died. Caterina was the same age as my Costanza is now. This has nothing to do with Maria Stella. I'm telling you about you and your daughter when she was only eight, and about me.

"I used to go up to the tower from time to time, to the lumber room where I stored my travelling things."

Assunta, confused, gazed at him as if he were raving: this wasn't the time for reminiscences of bachelor days. Guglielmo was trying to figure him out.

"There was a gazebo on the terrace in those days. You could see into it, but only from above, you understand, from up high. I looked out at the panorama and then down to the terrace, inside the gazebo. You"— and here Domenico adopted the disdainful tone with which one addresses an inferior—"you didn't realise it, but you were having a good look round. Good. Very good. You knew you mustn't be seen. But you didn't look up, because you were sure there was no one in the tower."

"Where's the harm in that?" asked Assunta.

"There's no harm in sitting alone in the gazebo and looking around without looking up," answered Domenico. "From the first floor you can't see anything. It's only from the tower that you can get a full view—full and unobstructed." He extended his arm in Guglielmo's direction, his hand rigid, the index finger pointing. "You, you didn't think about that, you damned scoundrel."

Assunta chuckled in a big-sisterly way. "Stop it, Domenico, there's no need for bad language."

"But he wasn't alone. When he was making sure that no one could discover him and his smutty behaviour, he wasn't alone!"

Assunta thought that Domenico, after all these years, was about to accuse his brother of having importuned some maid. "Domenico, control yourself. Who could there have been of such importance with Guglielmo in the gazebo? You're men, after all."

Domenico let go of the chair and walked towards his brother.

"Who was there? I can see her before me, now and forever. Forever. Who was there of such importance? What were you trying to hide?" He lowered his head. He was shaking; the veins in his neck, on the back of his hands, and on his temples were swollen and blue. The deep bags under his eyes stood out in his ashen face. "She was his daughter."

"Enough! Enough!" Guglielmo stormed out of the room, slamming the door behind him.

"What did he do? What did he do to the girl?" Donna Assunta kept saying over and over.

"Neither of these two men did anything to cause serious, irreparable physical harm. I stepped in then as I had to today. But evil is done when it is done. Father Puma must go. Not right away. And Costanza must take first communion and leave. I shall see to this on our return. I'm warning you, Assunta, Caterina must not know about this!"

Donna Assunta fell back against the chair and stared into space. The moment she had dreaded for so long had finally come. Large, silent tears trickled down her cheeks and dripped onto her dress.

"I'm going. It's dinnertime," said Domenico. "And there is no question of putting Costanza in a convent. She must marry and be happy, is that understood? Say as much to Guglielmo." His sister's head bowed, and she sank deeper in her chair.

Domenico Safamita was getting back into the saddle when up came Gaetano Cucurullo, his brother's valet, panting: "If your lordship pleases, wait. His excellency the baron sends a message." His words came out in a rush. "The communion lunch is to be held in the castle—he'll see to the invitations and all the rest. The baroness mustn't worry about it."

"Tell the baron I thank him." The young baron spurred his sorrel.

At dinner Caterina Safamita noted that her husband nibbled at his *arancine*—rice balls with savoury stuffing—with no enthusiasm.

Suddenly he told her that they had to go to Palermo as soon as possible—that Costanza's first communion would be celebrated on the following Sunday and they would leave the day after. Caterina was stunned, for this wasn't the time to go to Palermo, but she made no objections. When he gave orders, she had no choice but to obey, just like everyone else.

After dinner Domenico Safamita asked his wife to play the piano, and then he spent the night with her.

22

"Look before you leap."

The Seven and a Half Days' Rebellion and the vicissitudes of Stefano Safamita

The Safamitas arrived in Palermo on 9 September 1866. Many relatives and friends had stayed on in their country houses or holiday homes, for in the city rebellion was in the air. General discontent and party political agitation led people to think there would be an insurrection, although it wasn't clear which of the various factions would light the fuse. Only a few weeks before, in early August, someone had blown up the powder magazine near Monte Pellegrino.

Don Antonino Cicero, the Safamitas' majordomo in the Palermo household, had little warning of the family's unexpected arrival. In great haste, he organised a full-scale cleanup: the striped slipcovers were removed from chairs and sofas, the curtains were washed and starched, the furniture waxed, and the carpets brushed. That evening, when the masters, wearied by the trip, had retired for the night and even the women had gone to sleep after finishing the cleaning, don Antonino joined don Gaspare Quagliata and don Paolo Mercurio in the kitchen to enjoy a glass of sweet wine and a chat, the way they usually did on the day of the family's arrival from Sarentini. They brought one another up to date about family matters and the news from Sarentini and Palermo.

Don Paolo Mercurio was complaining about the journey: "We had to go over rough, stony tracks. This government is only good for aping the Bourbon kings and the mess they made—all those promises about roads, land distribution, improvements, and then they do nothing at all."

"You're wrong, Paolì," Gaspare corrected him. "That's not so. This government is doing *worse*. Didn't you spot all those ugly mugs along the way? If it wasn't for our guards, we wouldn't have reached Palermo alive. I could see them lying in wait in the hills. They're cowards, for as soon as our guards showed up they slunk off. It wasn't like that before. Now there are bandits all over the place, and the army, too. Soldiers of the realm they call themselves, but they steer clear of the bandits and only kill the poor wretches who don't want to join up. They shoot *them* all right, and even burn innocent folk in their cottages. But the robbers they leave alone."

"*They* are poor wretches," said don Antonino. "They have no money to buy exemptions from the call-up, like the rich. They're not bad by nature—the government forces them to go on the run, and then they steal to live. And it's going to get worse. They tell us they need men for the war, but who's going to earn the family bread, marry off the sisters, give them dowries or trousseaux? Either they end up swamped by debts or they steal or they don't do their duty as sons and brothers." Antonino knew about these things: he was a man of honour, and so he was allowed to lend money and charge high interest, an activity to which he devoted himself almost full-time, and successfully, during the long periods when the masters were in Sarentini.

"This call-up is worse than the penal colony in Tunis, damn it!" exclaimed Gaspare. "At least there you could hope for the Palermo Almshouse after a couple of years!"

"It's much worse, don't you see that?" don Antonino said heatedly. "We won't even remember the name of the almshouses, not the old ones or the ones of today. Haven't they told you lot in Sarentini that the government is abolishing the monasteries, even closing down the seminaries and selling off all the Church property? There's a bread shortage, people can't find work, they're taking away the boys and sending them off as soldiers. Now they're even taking the coins from us and giving us pieces of paper instead. What's more, the cholera is back. Fact is, things just couldn't be worse," he concluded.

Gaspare didn't like the majordomo's know-it-all air. "Of course I'm aware of all this. The young baron is talking of buying at the auctions—that's why he's here in Palermo."

"I know that." Don Antonino wasn't letting him get away with anything that evening. "And I also know there's no hurry. There was no need to come here at a bad time like this."

Gaspare and don Paolo said nothing more, but went on drinking their Marsala in little sips. Don Antonino changed tactics. "I'm dog-tired, my legs hurt, and we've worked like mules so that the masters would find everything in order here. You have to tell me why the young baron suddenly wanted to come, what with everything that's going on . . . What's up? Is it the baroness?"

"I saw nothing, I heard nothing," said Gaspare.

Don Paolo made no reply, his eyes darting from one to the other.

"Don't tell me that we're going to have another stink like the fuss they kicked up in '58?" Here the majordomo had gone to the heart of the matter—the summer of discord between husband and wife about the question of boarding school, and not only about that.

Gaspare turned down the corners of his mouth, looking doubtful.

Don Antonino pressed his point. "The baroness certainly seemed cross today."

Gaspare and don Paolo picked up their glasses again. Antonino realised he wasn't going to get anything out of these two, not that evening at any rate, and he downed his Marsala.

Don Paolo took the opportunity to ask a few questions. "So, tell me, don Nino, what's to be done about this stinking government?"

Don Antonino had a ready reply: "Things are bad, very bad. Rebellion is coming."

"That's all we need!" exclaimed the coachman. "With the littl'uns in the house! Did the young baron know about this?"

"He should have kept the family in Sarentini," said the other laconically. "Unless there was a very special reason for coming here in such a hurry. But you two don't want to tell me anything, and so d'you know what I say? Let's get some sleep—it's late and we're all tired."

The popular uprising broke out in Palermo exactly one week after the arrival of the Safamitas, and it raged through the city for seven and a half days, from the evening of Saturday 15 September until the afternoon of the following Saturday. It was never clear which party had instigated it and, as no one knew what else to call it, the event went down in history as "the Seven and a Half Days' Rebellion."

Safamita House and its occupants were left unscathed, but Caterina Safamita, who had vivid memories of the 1848 uprising, was traumatised by it. She went through moments of unspeakable anxiety, and it became even more desperate for her when they learned that Stefano, seized by curiosity, had run away from boarding school and was missing. The Safamitas sent their guards and household staff out onto the streets of Palermo with the order to enter sacked buildings, infiltrate the slums, and do the rounds of the dives, shops, even brothels, in search of the boy.

Stefano was found in a hostelry in a slum district, unharmed but drunk. He had taken refuge there, frightened, and had remained as a guest—or had been kidnapped by the host, it wasn't clear which—and had spent all his money. He had pawned his gold watch to pay for lodgings and wine for himself and others. In fact, Stefano had offered drinks to the rabble that frequented the dive—a tactic required, according to him, to keep them quiet and to save his skin. His mother welcomed him home with open arms, grateful to have him back safe and sound. She forgave him the suffering he had caused her and barely scolded him. But Domenico closeted himself with his son in the study, where too many hard words, too many home truths, were spoken. Stefano fought back against this paternal rival, who punished him unjustly and humiliated him as a son and as a man. But Domenico Safamita emerged with his pride intact—and with a sense of shame that tormented him to his dying day.

Palermo was subdued by the Italian Royal Navy, after a ferocious bombardment from the sea that lasted four days. A state of siege was proclaimed, and the finance minister ordered the immediate seizure of the convents and nunneries of Palermo and its entire district. Once again the Italian government sent and maintained an army in Sicily, sowing further discontent and creating fertile soil for the growth of the mafia and other secret societies.

A strange calm descended on the city. The people of Palermo, usually resourceful and full of life, were stunned and wary of returning to normalcy. The young baron decided to take his wife and Giacomo back to Sarentini, leaving Costanza in Bagheria as a guest of his favourite younger sister, Maria Anna Pertusi, Countess of Trasi, so that she might attend the wedding of his niece Maria Antonia to Iero Bentivoglio di Piscitelli. She would return with the Trasis to Sarentini at the end of October for the Safamita family's annual get-together. Stefano, humiliated and hurt, remained in Palermo to finish his final year of school.

Costanza had been bewildered by everything happening around her, and the thought of returning to Sarentini had greatly upset her, so she was relieved to accept her parents' decision to send her to her aunt and uncle's house accompanied only by her nurse. She had been initiated precociously and simultaneously in abuse and in a sacrament from which she could draw no comfort. The night before her first communion, she had had a nightmare: upon contact with her mouth, the host began to bleed. The blood of Christ filled her mouth, forcing her lips apart, spilling down her chin, pouring down her neck, and running down her dress into a red puddle at her feet. After that, Costanza approached communion with a vaguely cannibalistic feeling. The uprising and Stefano's disappearance had struck her as divine punishment.

Costanza decided not to confide any of this to her nurse. But Amalia had sensed something—Costanza noted this from her anxious looks, attentive silences, and loaded questions—so she answered Amalia's questions circumspectly. With time, perhaps, she might have overcome her reserve, but after a conversation with don Paolo Mercurio, she realised that this was no longer possible.

One day, before the rebellion, the children and their nurses were setting off for the Trasis' home in Bagheria. Giacomo had run off into the garden, followed by Amalia and Maria Caponetto, while Costanza stayed in the coach with don Paolo; it wasn't the first time, and she wasn't bothered by it. She liked him and sensed the special, affectionate friendship between him and Amalia. But that morning don Paolo was strangely silent. He looked at her, then at the horses, and seemed ill at ease.

"Costanza," he said suddenly, "you must listen to me. I am your father's man, and your family's man. If anyone does you harm, tell me and I'll kill him; no one must lay a finger on you. Don Paolo's word. Do you understand? Just say the word and Paolo Mercurio will sort out anyone who behaves as he shouldn't with you." At that point the nurses arrived, dragging a bawling Giacomo behind them.

Costanza realised that don Paolo knew. She considered this a betrayal on her nurse's part. She swore that she would never again speak either with her or with others.

23

"A May wife will not see winter blankets."

The Trasi-Bentivoglio wedding and Costanza Safamita's misadventure in the chicken coop

Amalia was orderly, and she became even more so to please Costanza, who was a great lover of order. Even years later, in the cave, she kept count of the days with a pencil mark, and every year she would start from scratch. The numbers became almost illegible, but this was the ritual every evening, before going to sleep.

"Tomorrow is the first of October, a good month for weddings!"

"Why is it good?" asked Pinuzza.

"Because the baby is born when the weather is fine and it doesn't catch cold. And besides, the party is really lovely when it's not hot."

"So did the marchesa get married in October?"

"No, in May. That's what they wanted. You shouldn't marry in May: it's bad luck. But her cousin Maria Antonia married in October, after the Palermo uprising, and that was really marvellous."

"Why is it bad luck to marry in May?"

"My dear Pinuzza, you ask too many questions. Because that's the way it is."

"Did it bring her bad luck?"

"Certainly. What's the use of the old sayings if they're not true?"

In the villa in Bagheria, Uncle Alessandro Trasi's large family was happily busy with preparations for the wedding. Count Trasi had nine children, and they all got on very well. The villa was overflowing with children and grandchildren; there wasn't a moment of boredom, and the rooms echoed with laughter. Maria Antonia was the last daughter to be married, and she was made much of by her parents and her older brothers and sisters. Only just sixteen, she was going to marry a son of Don Baldo Bentivoglio di Piscitelli, a senator of the realm: an arranged marriage, but also a love match.

The countess had assigned everyone a task. The nurse and two maids were to see to the bride's trousseau. They had to take from trunks and boxes dozens of items of personal linen, press them carefully, and then lay out blouses, stockings, bodices, underwear, petticoats, and an infinity of dresses, scarves, jackets, hats (each in its own box), shoes, and cloaks, for display on tables covered with damask cloths in the bedrooms and in the little drawing room. In the large salons, emptied of furniture for the occasion, the gifts were on show: jewellery in a display case and other presents put wherever there was space.

At first, Costanza was confused by the Trasis' noisy informality. Her aunt and uncle weren't as wealthy as the Safamitas, and she noticed this: certain luxuries and comforts she was accustomed to were lacking. The Trasis often talked about their shortage of money—but they seemed to be accustomed to it, and in any case the matter did not affect the family's good humour—as well as all kinds of other topics. Parents, children, and grandchildren discussed everything, arguing and then quickly making up. Even her little cousins did not seem overly respectful of their parents and grandparents, but instead of being scolded they were covered with kisses and hugs as soon as they were within range, and she was, too. In short, they loved one another. The Trasis treated the servants with a familiarity that was unthinkable in the Safamita household.

Costanza liked this experience of another way of living. She was too loyal to her parents to envy the Trasis, but she decided that as an adult she would follow her aunt Maria Anna's example, and she was sure that she would run no risk of paternal disapproval.

In Bagheria, feeling a part of the family and surrounded by affection, Costanza became carefree and enjoyed herself. Every evening, when her nurse was preparing her for bed, she would tell her, all excitement, about the day's events.

On festive occasions, the youngest children were allowed to mingle with the adults. Costanza and her little cousins took advantage of this to circulate among the visitors who, every afternoon for two weeks, thronged the villa to offer the customary good wishes to the bride-to-be and admire the display of gifts. Friends and relatives, heedless of the military occupation, arrived by train and by coach in garrulous, inquisitive swarms. With expert eyes, they estimated the cost of every gift, every item in the trousseau; they scrutinised objects to check if they were new or recycled; they made comparisons; they indulged in lengthy comments on the gifts and who had sent them; they picked up the silverware to assess its weight; and, with varying degrees of discretion, they sought information on the amount of the dowry (it was known that the Trasis were not wealthy), on the provenance of the jewellery, on the store of household linen (the responsibility of the groom's family), on the apartment intended for the young couple in Bentivoglio House; and, as was customary, they made critical remarks in low voices. The future mothers-in-law looked on, pleased and ceremonious.

The guests paid no heed to the children. The little ones followed the comings and goings, all ears, picking up sarcastic comments, memorising incautious gossip and criticisms so as to repeat them to general hilarity among their relatives in the evening, when the family would take lemonade and water and *zammù* on the terrace, caressed by the westerly breeze bearing the fragrance of freshly watered soil mixed with the scents of autumn.

Maria Antonia treated Costanza like a little sister, and she took her along as a chaperone together with her niece Giovanna when—with the permission of her indulgent parents—she went on short, chaste walks with her fiancé under the trees in the garden. Costanza learned about falling in love, which she had only heard about in Annuzza la Cirara's stories. Now it was a reality.

Bemused by their lengthy looks dense with moist promise, by the light touching of hands, and by their fleeting caresses, Costanza vicariously shared in the impatience of the betrothed couple. She would follow them down the garden paths humming a refrain she had overheard in the corridors while her mother sang for her father. Every so often, words would come out—"consolation," "sighs," "sorrow"—and a new warmth would come over her.

She was ecstatic about the wedding ceremony. The weeping of the women—being moved to tears was obligatory at weddings—took nothing away from the joyousness of the occasion. Costanza dreamed of the moment when it would be her turn to marry.

After the wedding, the villa emptied. Costanza stayed on with her aunt and uncle and the family of their eldest son, Giuseppe, as she waited to go back to Sarentini.

Adjacent to the villa stood the yard where the caretakers and their families lived and where they kept a few domestic animals, just enough to have fresh goat's milk, eggs, and poultry. But even so there were not always enough fresh eggs to go round. Costanza was very fond of eggs: she would drink one raw every morning. In her family's country houses she would sometimes slip out of bed and go off to find one for herself, a bit of mischief tolerated by her nurse. In Bagheria, Amalia would go down to the henhouse at dawn, but often someone had got there before her, leaving Costanza without her egg.

One morning the nurse and the other women were awakened by the sound of the caretakers shouting: something terrible had happened to the little Baroness Safamita in the henhouse. They threw on whatever was nearest to hand—shawls and aprons—and raced into the yard. It was full of animals, men, women, and children.

The shouting died down, and everyone stood aside to make way for the nurse, who dashed into the henhouse, a ramshackle wooden construction leaning against an external wall, long and narrow, with a low, sloping roof. The squawking of the frightened hens deafened Amalia, while the sour, suffocating stench of the chicken droppings enveloped her. Costanza was lying huddled in the back, where the roof almost touched the ground, with her head on her breast, motionless. In the gloom, two blotches of colour stood out: the white of her nightdress and the tousled red mass of hair hanging free. The caretaker's wife, squatting beside the little girl, seemed like a statue in a manger scene. She hadn't dared even to touch her.

Almost bent double, the nurse approached Costanza. She had fainted, and her forehead was bleeding. Amalia picked her up, her head and legs dangling, and, still bent over, reached the doorway, taking care that the girl's hair and feet did not brush the dung. When she straightened up in the courtyard, she spotted a viscous yellow egg stain on Costanza's breast and a needle stuck in the front of her nightdress.

They laid her out on the table in the pantry. She had two cuts on her forehead and one on her forearm, where the blood had already clotted. They reconstructed the event: at dawn, a stable boy had gone to steal eggs, and in the back of the henhouse he had seen a strange creature dressed in white, its face half hidden by red hair—Costanza, sitting perched on a stone, her head bowed as she started to drink the egg she had pierced with her needle. He took her for a creature of evil, a spirit of the night, a devil. He shouted obscenities, then incantations, but the creature neither replied nor vanished. And so the boy had snatched up some stones and thrown them at her. Costanza, bent over in the corner to pierce the egg and drink it, had fallen forwards.

Count Trasi sent for a doctor, who arrived at the double. He cleaned the wounds and prescribed rest. Costanza, followed by the retinue of dismayed serving women, was taken back to her bed. Her aunt assured her that the stable boy would be dismissed immediately and that she had nothing to fear: she would get better soon. They gave her chamomile tea, and she dozed off. Amalia stayed with her. But the little girl soon grew delirious and saw imagined attackers everywhere—hiding behind the door, concealed under the furniture, gazing at her malevolently from between the slats of the shutters and giving her no peace. The daylight upset her; she wanted to stay in the dark. Costanza's fever rose, and she refused to eat or drink. The hallucinations grew worse. The next day she begged her aunt to take her to the sirocco room, the one below ground level that had no windows. The request became an obsession, so they humoured her. The sirocco room was musty and stank of damp—it was unsuitable for an invalid—but Costanza seemed to grow calm there, and she drank some broth. Then, almost immediately, she became delirious again. Her aunt and uncle, worried about her physical and mental health, decided to tell the Safamitas without further delay.

The young baron soundlessly entered the sirocco room with his sister and his brother-in-law. It was night. Costanza was dozing. Her nurse, sitting on a stool with her head propped on her arm, was holding the little girl's hand; she, too, was sleeping. When Amalia realised who was in the room, she hastily gathered her things and withdrew to a corner to tidy herself up. Costanza opened her eyes. With a weary smile she said to her father, "Lie down here with me." The young baron brushed her cheek with a kiss and stretched out on the bed, bracing himself on one leg. He gestured at the others to leave them alone.

The next morning Domenico Safamita emerged from the sirocco room with his daughter in his arms. He took her back to her room. Two days later they returned to Sarentini.

24

"Sit you down, daughter, sit you down, for good fortune is coming."

Costanza Safamita grows well, thanks to a little affection from her mother.

Caterina Safamita didn't want to know why Father Puma had been transferred to the seminary, but she was not displeased by this. The priest's presence had become superfluous; his devotion made her feel uncomfortable, and his corpulent, slovenly look made her nauseous. Moreover, she had far more important things to worry about: Stefano's nasty experience during the uprising had shocked her deeply. She suffered at the thought of her son at the boarding school, mocked by his classmates and wounded by his father's scolding. She would have liked to be near him, to cosset him.

When Caterina saw Costanza on her return from Bagheria, she was moved. The girl was in a truly pitiable state, with her shoulders and face bruised, the cut on her forehead still open, and an expression of frightened bewilderment. So Caterina lavished on her all the tenderness she felt for Stefano and, for the first time, loved her. She put her to sleep in the room next to hers and looked after her; unwittingly, she began to speak to Costanza in French, as she did with her father, and in that tongue she used endearments for her daughter that she had never used before. She gave her presents. Costanza accepted the change in her mother as if she had been expecting it and responded to it naturally yet with a certain reserve. Instinctively—and not mistakenly—she felt that it would not last.

Costanza began to play the piano again. Her mother gave her some new sheet music, and every so often she would make an appearance during lessons with Madame, staying to listen to Costanza and to offer encouragement. Sometimes Caterina invited her daughter into her drawing room in the afternoons when she played for her husband. Costanza would sit beside her. Slumped in his armchair facing the piano, Domenico Safamita kept his eyes closed, but he did not sleep: his hand caressed the fringes of the armrest and moved to the rhythm of the music. Sometimes he would look at Caterina intently, pensively, and there would be a sudden glow of light, as if a beam had issued from his pupils to penetrate his wife's eyes. Costanza turned to her mother, whose chestnut eyes, bright and gentle, responded with enormous sweetness. Her fingers flew over the keys, and everything was music. It was then that Costanza understood that the love between her parents was different from that of her newly married cousin; it was stronger, and she was proud to be their daughter.

Caterina Safamita was possessive about her tortoises. She kept them on the terrace of her bedroom and did not like her children to disturb them.

One day she showed some freshly hatched baby tortoises to Costanza, who was fascinated by them. The little girl soon learned to handle them with care; she recognised them individually, and like her mother she had an instinctive affinity with the silent reptiles. There were scores of them; the colony on the terrace had to be culled regularly and some of the creatures taken to the castle gardens. Costanza helped her mother make the selection, and together they settled the tortoises in their new abode. Despite this unusual familiarity, they never talked of their feelings, as if they feared them. Costanza didn't know anyone who loved tortoises as her mother did, and she would have liked to know more about this, but she didn't ask; she simply helped her mother feed them. Sometimes Caterina had tears in her eyes. Costanza didn't dare go to her at such moments—an inheritance from the past—nor did Caterina seek comfort from her.

One day, when she was mending with her women, Costanza asked Maria Teccapiglia, "Why is Mama so fond of tortoises?"

"It's a very long story," said Maria. "It all began when she was a little girl. Her father gave her a puppy, black and white—a beauty. She hugged it as if it were a little baby. Then the puppy fell ill and died. The baron gave her another one. After a few months that one died, too. Well, all the pets she got died on her. I said it would be much better if they gave her a kitten. Cats are different—they have nine lives. But she didn't like cats.

"Then what happened, happened, and Baroness Maria Stella died, God rest her soul. Father and daughter were desperate. They clung to each other like two snails. Then the young baron came and said this wouldn't do. He took the little girl and he asked her if she wanted a puppy or maybe a pair of doves. She said no to everything. Then he thought to ask her why, and she said—blunt as you like—that she didn't want any animals because they all upped and died on her. She only wanted a pet that wouldn't die.

"'Very well,' said her uncle, 'let me think it over.' Well, he thought and he thought, and then he had an idea. He showed up with a big box, and inside were two tortoises. 'These won't die until your children have grown old,' he told her. And the little baroness accepted the gift.

"People started looking for tortoises to bring to her. So lots and lots of them arrived at the castle. She could understand them, tortoises. And they recognised her. Sometimes I would find her in the garden with all the tortoises around her. She would look at them one by one as if she was talking to them. Once I asked her, 'What do you like about these creatures?' 'When they want to be left in peace, they go into their shells and no one can hurt them,' she answered. 'And besides, they don't talk. You can say what you like to them and they don't repeat it to anyone.' And that's why your mama has so many tortoises."

And Costanza thought that she understood her mother better.

The family did not return to Palermo except for short visits. In time, Costanza reacquired a certain self-confidence, but only in the protective womb of the mansion house in Sarentini. She did not read for amusement, she grew up isolated from her peers and from her social class, and her Italian was stilted. She was ill at ease with relatives she did not see regularly, she felt her cousins from Palermo were different from her, and she had no friends of her own age: she refused to call on other little girls, and she did not like visitors coming to the house.

Her father was worried: if she carried on like this she would find herself alone as an adult, and this bothered him. He talked about it with his wife, but she didn't share his anxiety. On the contrary, she pointed out that other parents were not so smothering. Caterina became jealous of Costanza, and as her jealousy grew, it checked the rapprochement between mother and daughter. Domenico decided on what he thought he should do: Costanza must spend more time with Madame, and she should be at his side when there were visitors or when he received townspeople or workers on the properties that would one day be hers. Costanza didn't object to this. But although she was loyal to her father's wishes, she couldn't wait to get back to the ironing room; she became very quiet and had little appetite.

The young baron had to agree that it was risky to impose further changes on her, since at this point they might have a devastating effect—Costanza needed to sustain her ingrained habits and her deepest bonds of affection, even if they were forged with people who lacked culture and were almost illiterate—so he concurred with his wife: they didn't have to dig in their heels over transforming their daughter into a lady, nor did they have to make her accept a culture that would be of no use to her. Costanza was by nature sweet and obedient, she played well and had a fine voice, she spoke fluent French and conducted herself with dignity. In addition, she was rich: she would make a good match, and everything led them to believe that she would have a good life.

Costanza spent the last years of her childhood in relative serenity, well protected in her domestic cocoon. But she was not without anxieties about the future. She knew that it was considered unseemly to frequent the servants' quarters, and that sooner or later her friendships in the ironing room would be ruled out. But she was ingenious and farsighted: she set up a working area in a corner of her bedroom where, following the example set by Aunt Assunta, she could darn and embroider together with her women and her nurse, but instead of reciting Rosaries and litanies they would listen to Annuzza la Cirara's love stories.

Costanza wanted to have children, and she was sure that one day she, too, would marry. Marriages were arranged by families, in accordance with the size of the bridal dowry and the social and economic status of the two young people: a custom followed by rich and poor alike. She understood that after her fifteenth birthday there would be no lack of marriage proposals. Her father had told her repeatedly that he would not force a husband upon her and wanted Costanza to take part in the decision; she decided that hers would be a love match. She knew something about how girls met young men and found husbands when marriages were not arranged. In Palermo young people met one another in the salons, at the theatre, and at balls—occasions that constituted a first opportunity to get to know one another. The families would then either flatly oppose or encourage their children's inclinations, always keeping in mind the final goal: a suitable marriage. All this alarmed Costanza, who envied the girls destined for arranged marriages.

But things did not go the way her parents had foreseen. Costanza lived almost exclusively in Sarentini, with brief visits to Palermo, and until she was twenty there was no talk of marrying her off.

25

"He who fails to grasp a favourable opportunity will find no absolution."

The abolition laws and the gossip about
Donna Assunta Safamita's not having become a nun

The Safamita brothers were greedy for property. The chance to acquire assets that had been confiscated following the suppression of the religious orders excited them. The aristocracy had not taken part in the auctions—either for lack of money and for fear of the papal excommunication that many people maintained would fall upon the buyers; or out of respect for the Holy Mother Church, as was said by the aristocrats themselves, who supported the pro-Bourbon clerical party, which had a remarkable following in Sicily at that time.

But Guglielmo and Domenico Safamita found out about the properties that were on sale, chose ones that interested them—of which there was a profusion, since more than a thousand convents and monasteries had been suppressed in Sicily—studied ways and means to buy them at the lowest price, planned their strategies for the auctions, and arranged financing for their purchases. It became something of a contest between the brothers, a treasure hunt, and it kept them busy full-time. In the end, they came out on top, among the biggest landowners on the island.

Donna Assunta, who had been horrified by this latest outrage committed by the government, wanted to do no less than her brothers. She, too, bought properties, either in her own name or as a nominee on behalf of convents, and sold them back to the religious bodies at the same price; then, caught up in her eagerness not to miss a bargain, she went on buying on her own account, and she, too, amassed a fortune. Moreover, thanks to these philanthropic activities she managed to save herself and her brothers from excommunication.

Donna Assunta made a study of the abolition laws, and could repeat their articles and clauses as if they were litanies. She conducted her personal opposition to the government with her usual determination. She saved the Convent of Portulano from expropriation by having the mother superior take advantage of exceptions permitted by the law—of which the ingenuous nun was unaware—and paid the costs of the appeal to the prefect; then, having saved the convent, she kept the number of nuns above six, in compliance with the regulations for avoiding expropriation, and provided an endowment for potential novices. In the Convent of Portulano, vocations were no longer in short supply.

The mother superior lost no time in informing the other communities of Donna Assunta's charitable deed. These nunneries quickly followed her example and turned to Assunta for advice and help; in this way, many religious orders managed to keep their convents from being taken over by the state. In the district, it was soon rumoured that in her youth Donna Assunta Safamita's family had made her give up her vocation to be a nun but that this vocation was still deeply felt, which explained her extraordinary generosity. In the convents, the grateful nuns prayed fervently that the Barons Safamita would grant their sister her deserved, albeit tardy, entry into a religious order.

Baroness Scravaglio came to know of this, and she was alarmed; there was a risk that her hopes of inheriting her share of Assunta's inheritance might go up in smoke. So she rushed to Castle Sarentini to dissuade her sister from taking this rash step. After the customary kisses and even before taking off her cloak, she said without ado, "Assunta, why did you give money to the lawyers of the Convent of Portulano? Is it true that you want to become a nun, at your age?"

"That's my business," her sister replied curtly. "However, I see you are upset and I'll give you an answer because I feel sorry for you. But the next time you interfere in other people's affairs you won't be so lucky. I helped the nuns for two reasons. First of all I don't like this government and the way it has behaved with us Sicilians, and now with the Holy Mother Church. Second, I've become accustomed to the coach trip to Portulano and the delicacies they offer me. There's a magnificent view, and the sweet couscous the nuns prepare is exquisite. At my age it's not easy to give up agreeable habits, the pleasures of the table, and what little beauty there is to see.

"But to tell you the truth, I did it above all to annoy Guglielmo. He had set his eyes on that convent and he was prepared to buy it."

Reassured, as they partook of some chocolate-flavoured Revalenza Arabica—a delicious new variant of the well-known restorative powder—Carolina Scravaglio bombarded Assunta with questions about her brother's plans, but her sister maintained a stubborn silence.

While her sister was busy dipping biscuits in her cup, Assunta stealthily slipped her hand into her bag, rummaged about in it, and then withdrew an ivory statuette of the Virgin, which Baroness Scravaglio had deftly removed from the table where it had stood, together with a crucifix and a statuette of Saint Francis of Assisi.

"Look here, Carolina, one does not steal," she said with reproving severity. "True, if you had asked me to give you this statue I wouldn't have done so, but you must control yourself. It is an object of value. Teach your children not to squander their money and to stay out of debt; this will help you get over your mania for thieving and then selling what you've stolen to rag-and-bone men for a pittance. You solve nothing that way. No one will want to receive you in his home if you carry on like this, myself included. Remember that, and think before you do things. Here's another example: you shouldn't have got upset when you heard it said in the convents that the family kept me from professing my vocation. You should remember that I was the one who didn't want to go into a nunnery. There was nothing to worry about. I'm fine as I am. Let the nuns pray for me. For more than forty years I've thanked the Lord God every evening for not being like them."

When she was left alone, Assunta poured herself another cup of Revalenza Arabica and ate the remaining biscuits, satisfied. Then she joined Peppinella Radica in reciting the Rosary with the other house nuns.

Assunta Safamita had always been very determined. The eldest of Stefano Safamita's and Caterina Lattuca's five children, since early childhood she had shown an enthusiasm for monastic life, and her parents had not opposed this in any way. They found Assunta a suitable place in the Convent of Carmine Maggiore, in Palermo, where she might even have become abbess, thanks to the strong ties between the Safamitas and the Church.

But when Assunta was fourteen she changed her mind; she wanted to stay with the family and to become a house nun—a hybrid of spinster and zealot not unusual in Sicily. Her rapid change of mind was due to a premonitory dream she had had after the uprising of that year.

Baron Stefano Safamita's entire family had found itself in Palermo for a wedding. It was 15 July 1820, the feast day of Santa Rosalia, patron saint of Palermo, and the people were taking part in the usual celebrations. Cries of "Viva Santa Rosalia!" were joined by calls for the restoration of the Sicilian constitution of 1812. In short, there was an uprising, which most thought would be quelled by guards from the garrison, but things didn't work out that way. The guards themselves joined the rioters, attacking shops and buildings, looting left and right, and setting fire to whatever came to hand.

Safamita House, as befitted the home of a family of the minor aristocracy, was not on the main thoroughfare of the Cassaro but in a narrow alley, not far from the procession route. After barring the doors and windows, the family entrenched themselves inside the house, protected by their guards. These last, with great good luck, managed to repulse the attackers. The rebellion was put down, but Palermo was devastated. Many aristocratic mansions had been put to the torch and there had been some deaths.

Stefano Safamita, a wit who as a bachelor had frequented Palermo's salons, had become taciturn and melancholy after his marriage, which required him to live in Sarentini. But sometimes he would regain his good humour and talk again, especially with his children; then you had to keep quiet and listen. At the time of the 1820 rebellion, once the dust had settled Stefano Safamita decided to talk to all his children, the girls included.

"I have been trying to understand what has happened over these past few days, and I have been thinking about our future," he said. "These are difficult and confusing times for everyone. After the defeat of Napoleon, the European powers made agreements among themselves, and we lost importance. The English left Sicily, after being here as masters for almost twenty years—twenty years during which they brought us prosperity, even though they forced the king to abolish our feudal rights. They made him give us a constitution and restore the Kingdom of Sicily. No one likes to do what a stronger party obliges him to do, least of all a king. So when the king went back to Naples he revoked the constitution, and that created discontent among the nobility.

"The aristocracy played no part in this rebellion, either at the beginning or at the end. They didn't even have the foresight to protect their own homes or to get themselves efficient private guards. Many of our friends and relatives will not have the money to rebuild. The middle class has grown rich and they will buy the houses, just as they did with the land. This rebellion marks the end of our class's right to rule. But do not forget that we Safamitas came to Sicily long before the Bourbons, and perhaps we shall remain here longer than they. For the present, we must preserve our family traditions and use the old methods to protect our properties. They still work—and well, too. We must reinforce the guards and keep order on the estates. Remember that so long as the centre of power remains outside Sicily, the state will take no interest in our well-being, nor will it be able to protect us. We have to see to our own protection, by ourselves."

His words confirmed the children's view that there was no place better protected than home, and that they would have to look after themselves because there was no trusting others—including the state. Those words made a profound impression on Assunta, who that very night had her premonitory dream. She was a nun in the Carmine Maggiore convent in Palermo. The nuns were torn from their beds and dragged into the beautiful shady cloister, and there, right under the very columns engraved with the proud arms of their families, they were raped by the rioters, she along with the others. She swore that she would never set foot in Palermo again, and never again leave the safety of Safamita House in Sarentini.

After that, Donna Assunta buried her religious vocation and determined that she would not permit any man to touch her. She lived serenely with her parents and Guglielmo, surrounded by her house nuns, with whom she recited litanies, novenas, and Rosaries and embroidered chasubles, tippets, copes, and other vestments. She never had cause to regret her decision.

26

"*Lamb and sauce and the baptism is over.*"

All Souls' Day at Torre-che-parla
The Ramazza di Limuna family argue and then make up.

The Safamita brothers and sisters were in the habit of spending All Souls' Day together. Every year, at the end of October, a picnic was organised in the olive grove at Torre-che-parla, near Sarentini, followed right after by celebrations in honour of the dead, with the traditional gifts; this was rounded off by a mass in the main church during which their ancestors were commemorated.

The Safamitas attached great importance to good food and enjoyed a reputation as gourmands, which means, on an island where the cult of food and eating is widely respected, that they took gastronomy very seriously indeed. The party also celebrated the end of the olive harvest; the olives ripened early in that area, thanks to the mild climate. Guglielmo Safamita would arrange a separate party for the olive pickers, held at the same time as the masters' celebrations. The two groups had their own special dishes—boiled mutton for the workers, and delicacies prepared by the head cook for the family—but they shared the first course and the ice creams.

Guglielmo had adopted a tradition of the Lattuca family that was considered vulgar and almost embarrassing by his relatives from Palermo. He personally prepared the main dish: a *taganu* large enough to feed a hundred people. This taganu was a traditional dish, typical of Coppolo, the Lattucas' hometown. It was a timbale of macaroni, ragù, and sausages, seasoned with cheese, over which one hundred beaten eggs were poured. It was prepared in an earthenware pot, or *taganu*, from which the dish took its name, as big as two gigantic water jugs, which was used exclusively for this purpose.

Costanza had fun; this was the only occasion on which her grandfather treated the serving women as equals, as she did every day. On that day alone, the women were mistresses of the kitchen together with him—the head cook was exiled to the little kitchen, where he worked with an air of disdainful superiority—and they rose at dawn to begin the preparations: rigatoni as fat as your thumb, taken out of the water when half cooked and set to dry on special cloths, each piece carefully separated; a meat ragù made as it should be, with all the herbs; the sausages pan-sautéed, sprinkled with red wine, and then chopped into little pieces. The less expert women saw to the ingredients that didn't require cooking: the large quantities of grated pecorino cheese, chopped parsley, and beaten eggs. And they sliced the *tuma*, a soft, sweet fresh cheese that the baron brought specially from Muralisci, the estate in the Madonie Mountains whence the Safamitas took their title.

First thing in the morning, the baron, followed by those of his family who wanted to take part in the preparations—most of them very young— and by those unable to refuse his invitation, went down to the kitchen, donned a cook's apron, and set to work. He greased the bottom and sides of the taganu with lard and then began to fill it in accordance with the time-honoured recipe. The bottom was lined with tuma, and he lined the sides, too, as he gradually added the filling. First he put in a layer of rigatoni—being careful not to press them down—which he covered with ragù. Then he sealed the preparation with a mixture of eggs, chopped parsley, and pecorino before adding another layer of rigatoni, which he covered this time with the sausages and their sauce, and over which he poured more beaten eggs, lining the sides of the taganu with more slices of tuma. Thus did the alternating layers proceed—amid general hilarity. Guglielmo Safamita seemed like another person; he was relaxed, he exchanged witticisms with the women, and he handled the ingredients as if he cooked every day. For their part, the women seemed to lose their shyness, and while they did not omit the respectful title of your lordship, they also called him a *babbu*—a simpleton—and criticised his work. In short, they had fun.

That day Costanza noticed that her grandfather seemed tired; he leaned against the edges of the kitchen table, sweating copiously. She realised that he wanted to sit down, but she also knew that he would refuse the offer of a chair. Aunt Carolina Scravaglio was with them, but she seemed unworried by this, so Costanza thought it better not to say anything.

The work proceeded amid the chattering of the women, until the entire earthenware pot was full. At the end, the baron poured the last of the beaten eggs over the taganu and let one of the women cover the huge dish with the final topping of tuma. "So if it breaks up, it's not my fault," he announced, once again half serious, half joking. "Now call the men and have them put it in the oven." The baron had almost finished; there remained only the last, most spectacular part. After the dish was cooked, and while it was still warm, the taganu was carried to the terrace by two men, who set it down on a table near the balustrade so that the peasants assembled in the little square facing the mansion could get a good look at it. And then the baron broke the earthenware pot in the traditional way, with a hammer and chisel, making the pieces of pottery fall away from the sides to reveal the crunchy cheese crust. The timbale towered, magnificent and intact, savoury sauce oozing from cracks in the tuma. The footmen cut a round from the top for the masters, and the rest—the bigger part—was taken down to the courtyard, where the banquet had been prepared for the country folk. They greeted it with applause.

The head cook had been working for weeks on the preparation of ice creams and water ices—tricky dishes to make—using all the ice left in the icehouses. They were like the *masculiata*, the long series of explosions that ended the firework displays in honour of Santa Rosalia, when her festival finished off in grand style with a spectacular display of lights that lit up the night.

Towards evening the party broke up. There were more than fifty people, what with grandparents, children, and grandchildren. Some returned to Sarentini with the Safamitas; others spent the night in the country. The Pertusi di Trasi and Ramazza di Limuna families, as well as Gesuela Scravaglio, Carolina's elder daughter, slept in Torre-che-parla. They were drinking water and *zammù* on the terrace.

"Maria Anna, when is Maria Antonia's baby due?" Vanna Safamita, the Baroness Limuna, asked her sister.

"At the end of November. After that she's moving to Rome, to her in-laws' house."

"You must be terribly sorry to lose her . . . oh, these married daughters who move away!"

"Yes," said Countess Trasi, cut to the quick. "But I know she's happy, and besides, we'll see each other in the summer. Fast ships go to the mainland every day, and soon they'll build a railway, now that Italy is united."

The Limunas still had three unmarried children: Maria Carolina, by now twenty-seven—and hence on the way to spinsterhood—as well as their younger sons, Ferdinando and Vincenzo, both of whom were a little odd. But the true reason for the failure to marry them off was the family's lack of means. Vanna Limuna was envious because the Trasi nieces had made good marriages even though they had received only modest dowries. "Her husband is a handsome man," Vanna Safamita continued. "She must watch out; they tell me that Rome is full of women on the hunt for men, even among respectable people," she added with a knowing air.

"Aunt, such women are everywhere. Iero is in love with his wife." Giuseppe Trasi, Maria Anna's elder son, stepped in to defend his brother-in-law and especially to avoid giving his aunt any satisfaction. All the Trasis knew that Iero already had a mistress, from before his marriage, but in Palermo.

Stefano Trasi, leaning against the balustrade, was listening to his brother, and he winked with his laughing eyes. The conversation was joined by Maria Carolina Limuna: "Cousin, what's the latest from Palermo? I can't wait to be invited! I miss the parties they give in Palermo. You city people certainly know how to have fun and enjoy life, with all those guests from the mainland—royalty, too. At Tafani we are left out. How is Maria Antonia?"

"It seems to me that you amuse yourselves well enough in Tafani," her cousin replied acidly. The Trasis held Aunt Vanna and Maria Carolina in low esteem. It was said that Baroness Limuna had had lovers, apparently with the approval of her husband—a windbag and a slave to drink and pleasure who had squandered his wife's dowry—and that Maria Carolina was no better. No wonder they hadn't been able to find her a suitable husband. With the arrogance typical of penniless aristocrats, the Limunas had rejected all her rich bourgeois suitors—unaware of the girl's reputation—with the result that she was still a spinster and dependent on them.

"If you have cash, you can have fun anywhere—Tafani, Palermo, Rome, even Sarentini, I can assure you of that!" Baron Giovannino Limuna wanted to end the conversation, which he thought was becoming disagreeable. "If I had some cash to hand, I'd have fun, too, and I'm over sixty! Do you want to know how much fun Stefano is having here in Sarentini?" The baron knew a thing or two.

He told them of an appalling affair, which people in the provinces had been gossiping about for some time, but not yet in Palermo—a story confirmed to him, or so he said, by the notary Tuttolomondo no less.

"You know that Mimì is angry with Stefano for what happened in

Palermo during the uprising? Well, he has cut him off altogether; he doesn't even take him to the estates. The young man finds himself in Sarentini—a shithole of a town, with all due respect—with nothing to do and no one to associate with apart from a handful of bourgeois towns-people and commoners. He's loaded with money—Guglielmo sees to that. Stefano had become a woman chaser, and nothing wrong with that at his age. But there's much more! He's fallen for a blacksmith's daughter—except that no one knows who her real father is—a really beautiful woman, everyone agrees. Well, he's made this blacksmith rich—though he's a well-known scoundrel."

"These things happen," said Maria Anna, cutting him off sharply. "He's not the first and he won't be the last."

"Hold on, my dear Maria Anna, before you start pontificating," replied her brother-in-law. "Let me finish. This blacksmith's daughter gave Stefano a son, who died. It seems that Stefano wants another one, you know; he wants to become a member of the blacksmith's family," he added smugly.

Gesuela, sitting a little to one side so as not to be noticed, was all ears. She adored such salacious gossip, which didn't usually go on in the presence of unmarried ladies—even those like her who were getting on—but at that point she couldn't resist exclaiming, "So that's why he told me today that the simple life of the poor has its charms! Now I see what he was driving at!"

"What did this baby die of?" Maria Anna asked with a look of distress.

"I don't know, but I feel it won't be the last," replied her brother-in-law. "He asked the notary about recognising the child. Maybe he's thinking of marrying the beautiful blacksmith's daughter."

At this he was swamped by a chorus of "What?" "Incredible!" "Outrageous!" "Folly!" "For shame!"

Giuseppe Trasi asked his brother, "Do you know anything about this? He used to speak with you."

"No," replied Stefano. "I haven't seen him much since he left boarding school. He used to take me hunting, and he struck me as a bit immature, spoilt, but he's a boy who knows how to behave. I don't believe all this. Stefano is certainly capable of dealing with such a situation correctly. It's probably just gossip."

"Guglielmo and Domenico will see to it that things are sorted out," broke in Count Trasi.

"None of you get the point, do you?" said Giovannino Limuna. "Stefano has kept the matter quiet, so his father knows nothing about it, and neither does Guglielmo." He seemed very well informed.

At that point his wife broke in, agitated. "Given my brothers' economic position, where's the problem? With money, you can sort out anything. Giovannino, you've drunk too much and you're letting your imagination run riot. Stefano can keep this woman and others, and his wife, too. I know plenty of men in the same situation."

"You still don't get it, do you, Vannuzza? But you should, you of all people. You Safamitas, the Palermo branch and the Sarentini branch, are not a homogeneous breed. You are either saints or sinners. There are the pious, God-fearing Safamitas like your aunt Assunta, and there are the Safamitas who think they're the lords of creation and are prepared to outdo the Devil himself to get what they want. Stefano is one of those, and what's more, he's madly in love with this girl. This affair isn't over. Rumour has it that the blacksmith has fallen out with the Safamitas' overseers, and sooner or later they'll kill him. A fine thing, if he becomes the father-in-law of the future master!"

"And Caterina knows nothing of this?" asked Maria Anna.

"Who knows? She never talks," Vanna replied. "My son Ignazio and his family are sleeping at the mansion house. Tomorrow I'll ask Alfonsina to get Costanza to talk."

"Leave Costanza alone! That poor little soul has suffered too much already!" Maria Anna blurted out.

"I wouldn't mind suffering like Costanza, with that dowry!" broke in Maria Carolina. "Aunt Maria Anna, you're exaggerating. You shouldn't feel guilty about that business in Bagheria. Costanza is like her mother—life runs off her like water from a duck's back. She does exactly what she pleases, and Uncle Domenico gives her everything she wants. I'd let people throw rocks at me once a week, just to be as rich as she is."

"You're wrong, Maria Carolina, and at your age you should have more sense," chided her aunt.

"You know what I think? Let's try to find out more tomorrow. My belly's full after all that food—that taganu was like lead, and I feel heavy. Let's go to bed, Giovannino," said Vanna, to avoid an argument.

"When's your brother Guglielmo going to drop this farce of playing the cook? It's unseemly, even once a year. God forbid that Stefano starts to emulate his grandfather's plebeian exploits. Next thing, he'll be shoeing the mules!" Baron Limuna was drunk. "From the window of the big kitchen, this morning, I saw Guglielmo with the women, wearing a cook's apron. His hands were dripping with sauce—not a very dignified sight to say the least, especially these days. When I first met Guglielmo, as a young man, I thought he used to do it so he could feel up the maids' tits and arses, but at his age, and in the condition he's in, I can only think it's an aberration. I'm not surprised that Stefano feels at home in the blacksmith's house. Domenico, on the other hand, is a snob. I'd like to see him in the kitchen surrounded by the women, to keep up a tradition that comes from the Lattucas no less!"

No one paid any attention to him, and it was clear that they disapproved.

At one point Stefano Trasi said, "I have only one thing to say in defence of Uncle Guglielmo. These indecorous scenes, as you call them, Uncle Giovannino, can help to maintain the respect of the servants and the peasants. Nowadays there is no guarantee of tranquillity on most of the estates. But when we come here, we are respected and revered as in the old days. After all, isn't this why we find ourselves all together as guests of our uncles, every year, for these festivities?"

"My dear Stefano, I'll answer you in my name and in that of my wife." Giovannino Limuna was a river in spate. "We come here out of family duty and for their money, which the Safamita brothers don't know how to enjoy, holed up in a town like Sarentini. You'll see everyone's face tomorrow, when Guglielmo's presents are opened. Vanna, tell him the truth—isn't that why you come?"

Vanna spun round like a viper. "You wretch, if you really want to tell the truth, say that we come here on holiday with my brothers because little or nothing is left of your father's fine estates, all mortgaged thanks to you and your vices! We come here to beg for loans and to ask my brothers to guarantee your debts. We come to ask for charity, we do, with children and grandchildren. Now that the mendicant friars are no more, we have the Limunas, the poor relations!" She wrapped her shawl around her shoulders and burst into tears.

With a dignified "Ladies and gentlemen, good night," Baron Limuna stood and beckoned at a footman to accompany him to his room.

The party broke up in silence. Maria Carolina accompanied her mother. When she arrived in her parents' room, she made a hysterical scene, accusing them of being the cause of her misfortunes. Who would ever marry someone like her, with a wastrel father and a mother who humiliated him in front of their relatives from Palermo? Baroness Limuna's only reply was to say that she had heartburn and was feeling most unwell. She unbuttoned her jacket, loosened her blouse, and lay back against the pillows, slackening her corset. Maria Carolina left, slamming the door behind her.

Giovannino Limuna, drunk, leaned against the window, still looking at his wife. It hadn't been their first row, but Vanna had never spoken to him like that in public. Outstretched on the bed, scantily dressed, even at her age she still had an appetising body. This is why he tolerated her infidelities—all of which were committed with people of their own rank, in any case. "Let's go to bed, Vannù," he said to her. "Let's see what you can do to give me a little pleasure. It's not true there's only two kinds of you Safamitas: there's a third, who has a fire down below. You belong to this third type, the whores—luckily for me."

Assunta Safamita attached great importance to the traditional gifts made on All Souls' Day, gifts that brought death closer to life. Guglielmo took advantage of the occasion to have his relatives from the city witness the family's strong bonds with the land and, at the same time, to underline that the Safamitas belonged to the aristocracy of Palermo by birth, rank, and way of life even though they were Sarentinesi by adoption.

They all assembled at the castle the next morning. The children had woken early and had gone to hunt for the presents left during the night by the dead. They found sweets, garlands threaded with little chocolate balls, and biscuits hidden behind sofas, under chairs and cushions, in the corners of rooms, all specially prepared for the feast day—gifts that cemented the bonds between families while simultaneously inculcating respect for those who were no longer with them. Each child also received a sugar baby—one of those gaudily colored sugar statuettes. The important presents were reserved for the afternoon.

In midmorning the Safamitas went to the main church, where their parents and their Lattuca ancestors were buried, for the solemn mass. After the mass, they proceeded to honour the ancestral graves. The local people watched them from a distance; in those troubled and sinister days the Safamitas were a united, God-fearing family who respected their healthy family traditions as few others did.

After lunch Guglielmo offered his sisters and the women of the family some particularly refined presents: exquisitely crafted jewellery of enamel and precious stones, the work of a Florentine jeweller. The youngsters received toys and two large bags of golden coins each.

That night Guglielmo Safamita died in his sleep. He left Villa la Camusa and the land around it to Stefano, Malivinnitti to Costanza, the hunting estate just outside Palermo to Giacomo, and the remainder to his daughter.

27

"No love without jealousy"

*As she irons, Rosa Vinciguerra tells Amalia Cuffaro
the story of Stefano Safamita and his mother.*

It was cleaning day, which was hard for Amalia because she had so little water. She washed Pinuzza's clothes in leftover slops, carefully smoothing them out with her hands to give them a semblance of having been pressed and spreading them on the marl to dry in the breeze with a stone on top of them.

"Oh, how nice it was when we used to do the ironing at the castle!" she said, sighing. "Stefano's shirts were a marvel. Rosa Vinciguerra really cared about them, and they never had any wrinkles."

"But wasn't she his wet nurse? Why did she iron his shirts and not the maid?" asked Pinuzza.

"What's that got to do with it? She always had a thought for him, and she liked ironing. She was good at it, too!"

"And he, was he good?"

"Yes, very good and cheerful, the only one who laughed. The Safamitas were a dour lot. But he was unlucky and ended up desperate. He didn't deserve that, and neither did the baroness. After all, she had a mother's heart."

"So why did he end up like that?"

"You know how it is: everyone has a master, rich and poor alike. The first masters are the father and the mother. He didn't want to obey, but even in the Safamita family that's how it had to be. But he was good, and he loved Costanza."

"And she?"

"She loved him, too—he was her brother. She would let him have his way, always. Respectful of everyone, she was, from the day she was born."

Amalia picked up from the ground a little piece of wood blown in by the wind and started to whittle it carefully. Pinuzza anxiously followed her movements. Sometimes her aunt would cut a wood piece into nothing, a mere stub that could be used only for kindling. But this time Amalia succeeded; with a smile, she showed Pinuzza that she had transformed it into a sort of pointed chisel.

"Now you can have fun drawing," she said, brushing her niece's braids with a kiss.

She set Pinuzza's chair in front of the smooth, crumbly surface of the cave wall and placed the little piece of wood between the girl's finger and thumb. Slowly, she stretched out Pinuzza's arm, watching the girl's silent grimaces until her hand reached the stone. She helped her point the wooden chisel at the wall. "Draw what you like!" she said happily. Pinuzza tried, clenching her mouth, intent on her efforts, driven by her desire to press on the wall and mark it. Her aunt had taught her this, and Pinuzza's little drawings were getting better all the time. Amalia would stand behind her, ready to pick up the little piece of wood if it fell and put it back between Pinuzza's fingers and adjust her grip. Pinuzza drew well that day.

She will get better, no doubt about it, thought Amalia, and she turned round to look at the Montagnazza. The sun was beating down on it and the white stone sparkled, rough in places, smooth in others, its slopes running transversely, parallel, like a heap of freshly ironed sheets that had slipped over to form a slanting pile.

Amalia had liked to watch Rosa Vinciguerra as she ironed. Rosa didn't need to concentrate, because she was so used to the work, and meanwhile she could tell stories. She knew a lot about the Safamitas, and she told Amalia about the events that had led the baroness to fall into melancholy after Costanza's birth. Sitting beside the ironing table with the little girl in her arms, Amalia watched Rosa admiringly as she waited for her tongue to loosen. Rosa would transform sheets stiffened by too much sun, pillowcases with crumpled embroidery, towels with ruffled fringes, and all the rest of the wash into the smoothest linen hot to the touch and impregnated with the scent of lavender released by the steam.

The linen had to be dampened carefully, sprinkled with the water from the basin: too much and you would soak it; too little or unevenly distributed and the ironing would come out with rough, uneven patches. "Dampening the linen is difficult—neither too much nor too little," Rosa would often say. "You have to get the knack of it." Then she would roll up the sheets, folding them well—the embroidered edges in the centre to conserve the dampness—and finally she would set to work on the board, which was padded with thick layers of cotton covered by an old sheet. She fanned the coals in the irons, checking their temperature. When all was ready, she would cross herself, and with a "Jesus, Mary, and Joseph" she would commence. Rosa always began her stories the same way: "You have to know . . ." She didn't welcome questions. She would churn out incredible stories about the household—some lighthearted, many others sad or mysterious, depending on her mood. And these stories became romances.

"You have to know that Stefano was a seven-month baby too, and pretty as a rose. The other male child, Guglielmuzzo, had died three years before. The baroness was going out of her mind; she wanted another son, but they all died inside her, all miscarriages. There was no wise woman she hadn't consulted—though no doctors. The young baron sent her those. She went to the wise women on the sly; he would never have allowed it. But no living children were born. Donna Assunta was desperate, too, and she told the baroness to turn to the Lord. The baroness started praying. She got up at first light for Father Puma's mass at the castle—she didn't miss one. The Lord God heard her, and so Stefano was born.

"They came to tell me that this child she was carrying in her womb looked good and that they needed me. I left my children with my mother-in-law and came here as a wet nurse. How she loved Stefano! She used to look at him, mother naked, and devour him with kisses. She even got her milk back after everyone told her it had dried up, and she tried to nurse him. When the young baron found out, he made such a scene! You can't imagine. They told me he broke a table—when he's in a fury he breaks everything—and the poor soul had to obey. 'Rosa, you must give him all the love I have inside when you feed him,' she used to say, and tears would spring to her eyes. True, she was born a baroness, and baronesses mustn't give their milk to their children, but she had a mother's heart, like us. Listen to me, Amalia, don't you worry about Costanza. Sooner or later her mother will come to love this little poppet—she's her own flesh and blood!"

Rosa folded and refolded the linen tablecloths, ran the iron across them, reduced them to perfect, taut squares, and laid them one on top of the other on a smaller table to her left. "You have to know that Stefano was mad about his mother, as she was about him. The baroness always wanted him near her. I'd spend my days in her room, in the drawing rooms, and on the terrace when she fed her tortoises; she even took me in her coach, sitting facing her with Stefano in my arms. We were always together, and we were all happy.

"But the young baron didn't like this happiness. He wanted his baroness all for himself, and he was jealous. He was even jealous of his own innocent son, and he would have him sent away, sometimes with one excuse, sometimes another. I don't know how often he came into the baroness's parlour—without even knocking—and said to me, 'Off you go, Rosa,' or, 'Take him away.' The baroness would give me a sad look and nod at me to obey. I noticed that she gave her husband a womanly look and smiled at him. They were in love, but only miscarriages came from all that loving—theirs was an unhappy fate."

Rosa paused with a long, satisfied sigh before changing the iron to press the towels of Flanders linen; the ironing room smelled of the light fragrance of cleanness. "She used to play with Stefano as if she was a little girl; she would roll about on the floor with him and they would laugh together. True, he did grow up spoiled, for his mother and his grandfather gave him everything, but they're rich and they can afford it. A bad son would have been ruined, but not Stefano. He grew up respectful and good by nature. He was thoughtful, too—he used to give me presents. The fact is, he was a saint. His father was strict with him but fair, and never raised his hand against him.

"One day, Baron Guglielmo and the young baron, who never had much liking for each other, came to an agreement: Stefano had to go to boarding school on the mainland the following year. The baroness couldn't bear to be separated from her child and she appealed to her father, but he didn't help her that time: Stefano had to go.

"In the end, to meet her halfway, they chose a boarding school in Palermo, but the baroness didn't want that, either. She was in complete despair.

"There was already a governess, Madame, and Stefano was learning French. But that wasn't enough for the Barons Safamita; the boy had to leave home to study. You have to know how pigheaded the Safamitas are, and no one can do anything about that. Stefano didn't want to go to boarding school, but women and children have to obey. They prepared lots of outfits for him—a complete wardrobe for school—as if he was a bride-to-be. Then what happened I don't know, but one day the young baron and the baroness had a furious row. The young baron went off to Palermo then and there. He just went, leaving the baroness alone with Stefano. The poor woman was left there weeping. So her father the baron took her to Malivinnitti for a change of air, and she stayed there all summer. The young baron would come back from Palermo, then set off again, go back to Sarentini . . . to put it bluntly, all hell had broken out between them."

Rosa accompanied her story with noisy slaps as she beat the towels on the edge of the table, unravelling the tangled fringes with each whack and readying them to be combed and then flattened under the steaming iron. "We couldn't understand it at all: one minute they seemed in love, the next they didn't. All this fuss was over Stefano, and he suffered on account of it. At Malivinnitti the baroness became really depressed. Her father worried himself to death about her and tried to distract her.

"He invited his daughter's favourite cousins, and he also set her to work on the paperwork for the mine when the manager was ill. The poor soul had to write letters in French for the clerk at the Corbotta. She obeyed, but she was sad as could be. The holidays came to an end, and the baroness went back to Sarentini, where she got pregnant with Costanza. You have to know that she told me, 'Rosa, I feel this baby is another boy, to make up for my losing Stefano.'

"But I knew it couldn't be a boy. I explained to her that Stefano, at birth, had a caul on the back of his head. The hair says it all: if a baby is born with a caul, the next one will be of the opposite sex, and so she would have a girl. She didn't believe me. And so the little red-haired baroness came along, and now her mother doesn't want her. It's hard to understand. The rich are used to doing and getting what they want. It never entered the baroness's head that sometimes we are all equal. That's the way it is with nature: the caul speaks true."

Pinuzza had drawn a shaky sort of flower, with two little leaves sprouting from the stem, and she tried to catch her aunt's attention. "Do you like it?"

"It's pretty! That's a good girl!" replied Amalia, still lost in thought.

"What were you thinking about?"

"About Stefano when he was a boy."

"What did he do?"

"Stefano used to go riding. He liked to go hunting with the baron, and to talk with the country people. It was a black day when he met that young thing and fell in love with her."

"Is it bad for someone to fall in love?"

"It is indeed, for the nobility must stay with the nobility. But he wanted her, he wanted her very much, and he got it into his head to marry her. And you don't do that."

"Why, isn't it nice to marry the person you love? Couldn't she have become a baroness?"

"No, we must all stay with our own folk—that's the way it is."

"And what did the young baron say?"

"He said plenty, and he did even more. He threw Stefano out of the house—his own blood and his firstborn son! Stefano didn't want to give up his woman, and he went off to Camusa, which he had inherited from his grandfather Baron Guglielmo, God rest his soul, and he had children with that hussy, outside holy matrimony. He married her, afterwards, but it was too late."

"And what happened?"

"Nothing happened, because nothing could happen. That's how it is."

Pinuzza was falling asleep. Amalia carried her back inside the cave.

28

"He who knows no measure in youth, will know poverty in old age."

Costanza Safamita realises something is wrong at home and suffers on this account.

Costanza realised that something was wrong between her parents. She understood—by looks, gestures, sighs—that it concerned Stefano, who had become moody. She was used to being kept in the dark about many things and she didn't want to ask the servants, but they were always in the know.

Stefano had left the boarding school. He had no intention of continuing his studies, and he wanted to go back to Sarentini. Costanza was happy about this; they went out for long jaunts in the gig or on horseback, and they often stayed together with their mother. She accepted her mother's overt preference for her brother and it didn't make her jealous, since it had always been that way. But Giacomo was seething inside, and he found her presence intolerable, so he preferred to go elsewhere.

Relations between father and son did not improve. Cold, polite. The father had no time for the son, nor did the son seek out his father. Domenico Safamita was all too busy with administrative duties, yet he gave Stefano no responsibilities of his own; he didn't try to train his son to begin helping him look after the family assets, and he didn't take Stefano with him when he visited the estates, as was customary. The servants and other workers shook their heads in silence. The baroness was upset, but father and son were entrenched in their respective positions and too proud to admit their mistakes; to make up for this, she spoiled Stefano even more. She gave him money, often in secret.

Stefano felt free, and he wanted to discover life. His father didn't stand in his way, for he hoped the boy would change once his youthful passions had cooled. Stefano loved horses, and he went out hunting with friends or simply with the guards and overseers; he attached great importance to his dress, and he spent lots of money. He was generous, sometimes to excess, and he frequented the landowners and the sons of the bourgeois families of Sarentini and the district. He spent little time at home, but he didn't neglect the family. Often, he would dine at the castle.

Strangely—and unlike the other young men—he didn't seem interested in women of easy virtue or in girls of marriageable age. Then he became enamoured of Filomena Carcarozzo, a child of unknown parents who had been taken from the orphanage at Coppolo and set to work as a servant girl with the family of an itinerant blacksmith; Stefano loved her with all the ardour of his eighteen years. Encouraged by the blacksmith, he was seduced by transgression—by his role as protector of the whole family and by the young girl's good looks. Once Filomena overcame her initial hesitation, she gave herself to him wholly, with a passion that quickly became devotion and true love.

As for Stefano, it wasn't clear whether he'd truly fallen in love or had merely seen this as a fling, the first of many. His desire for such a humble woman contained both an element of bravado and a wish to spite his father, as if he wanted to wound the Safamita family pride, but he didn't realise that he was wielding a two-edged sword.

Stefano was also prompted by a desire to side with the weak and the unfortunate, by a rather fuzzy spirit of participation in the aspirations for social change that were in the air for the first time in a united Italy. But he did not act on the basis of an idea that had become opinion; what he felt, he felt, and his actions sprang from this. He lived for the day, following his instincts, and fell easy prey to flatterers. He had an urgent need to be loved and to identify wholly with those who had never been loved, so he threw himself into things body and soul, with no thought for the consequences.

He eventually confided in his mother about Filomena, but in vague terms. In order to avoid losing him, the baroness listened, and he felt encouraged. One day Domenico Safamita said to his wife, "I suppose I should tell you that your son is having an affair with a blacksmith's daughter. We'll have to let him get on with it, for the time being, but keep our eyes open. Where he's concerned, I always expect the worst. Make sure you don't encourage him."

Baron Guglielmo's sudden death put an end to these confidences between mother and son; they were all distraught by the bereavement, especially Stefano. His mother's response was to refuse to speak of the death, as if his grandfather had never existed; so Stefano turned to his beloved for comfort and would sometimes stay on in the blacksmith's house until the early hours of the morning. Whereas at first he had behaved circumspectly, as time went by he became heedless and often left his mare outside the Carcarozzos' modest home where anyone could see it. All Sarentini knew about his passion for the blacksmith's daughter. Accustomed to the whims of the nobility, no one was surprised by it.

29

"Lovers can't be choosers."

*In the kitchens of Safamita House, the talk is of the love affair between
Stefano Safamita and Filomena Carcarozzo.*

It was 1873, and a year had passed since the death of Guglielmo Safamita. In the kitchens of the young baron's mansion house, preparations were under way for important guests: the prefect Ermenegildo Calloni and his wife. The prefect's maternal uncle had been an old friend of the late baron, who had been a guest on his estate in Asti. They were the first people to be invited after the period of deep mourning was over, and the reception rooms on the main floor had been reopened for the visit. The servants removed the palls from the mirrors and chandeliers in the main salons, the brasses were polished, and the staircase once more took on its customary aspect: red carpet, fresh flowers with glossy, fleshy leaves on the landings, lights on the walls. It was to be an intimate dinner, but an elegant one.

Lina Munnizza and Rosa Vinciguerra were practising laying out the table centrepiece: an epergne with six tiers of different sizes, brimming with pistachio-filled sweets, chocolates, and marzipan fruits prepared by the head cook according to the recipes of the nuns in the Martorana convent. They arranged them by flavour, but without neglecting colour and shape. The French porcelain dinner service was taken down from the shelves and set out on the sideboard, covered by a cloth. The head cook was bustling about; he had been told to prepare a Sicilian dinner, but a plain one suited to mainland palates.

Costanza and Maria Teccapiglia were helping the women shell pistachios for other sweets and to decorate the blancmange. The kitchen maids brought out little pots of boiling water into which they had put

115

the nuts, which they then fished out with a strainer; the other women divided them up among themselves to shell immediately, still scalding hot: this was the only way to remove the tough reddish shells. The shelled pistachios shot out of their expert fingers—whole, gleaming, and green, like little beads of malachite.

Don Paolo Mercurio, at the head of the table, idly lent a hand; every now and then he would pop a pistachio into his mouth.

"Don Paolo, sir, you have been to Turin . . . what are these foreigners like?" asked Maria Teccapiglia.

"I travelled all over Italy with Baron Domenico when he was young. Gaspare and I went along to serve him. Turin was bitter cold. The rivers looked like seas; the mountains were as high as Mongerbino, as high as ten Monte Pellegrinos. But the local folk respected us."

"Is that all you have to tell us? What were the women like?" Nora Aiutamicristo had been expecting something spicier.

"Like all the women on the mainland: when foreigners smell of money they love them, when they are poor devils like us they don't even look at them."

"You know the baron well, don Paolo. Tell me, what was he thinking of, inviting the prefect here? The very man who closed the convents and monasteries, who threw all the monks onto the streets, and who also bosses people around as if he were a bishop?" Rosa Vinciguerra had reason to be upset, for the government had taken six of her nephews for military service, leaving her sisters-in-law's families in poverty for the five-year spell of compulsory service. Shaking her head, she flung a handful of shelled pistachios into the bowl. Some fell on the table. Swiftly, two youngsters gathered them up.

"Mind how you go, Rosa," Maria Teccapiglia admonished her. "They're pistachios—what do you think they are, government agents?"

"Think about it, donna Rosa," added Nora Aiutamicristo. "He's powerful and he gives orders left, right, and centre. The baron must get in his good books if he wants to keep on giving orders too." She emptied another bowl of scalding-hot pistachios and added, "In the meantime get to work, all of you—we have to be quick."

". . . and the same man who bought himself the monks' lands!" murmured don Paolo to himself, following Rosa's line of thought.

Rosa was dumbfounded and speechless. She looked around and with a long, loud sigh began shelling the nuts again. Don Paolo observed her for a moment before saying, "The masters must be respected. They invite who they want. And besides, if it's true that this prefect behaves like a bishop and a general run together, then the baron should invite far more of them here. A great number of bishops—good and bad—have passed through Safamita House."

"Donna Assunta wasn't happy when she found out about this invitation," muttered Rosa.

"Listen to me, Rosa, she's not his mother, is she? She's his sister, and she has to keep quiet. And even though it's true you were wet nurse to the young baron's firstborn son, you still have to keep your mouth shut, and if you have to open it, open it with young master Stefano, and tell him to watch the company he keeps," said Maria Teccapiglia, suddenly serious.

"What are you getting at?" Rosa was still angry.

"Nothing, nothing." Maria Teccapiglia frowned and winked: she'd forgotten about the presence of Costanza, sitting in a corner, also busily shelling pistachios. They carried on in silence.

Then Gaspare came to tell Costanza that her mother wanted her upstairs. Maria Teccapiglia picked up the thread of the conversation once the girl had left. "Do you know what they're saying in Sarentini? That every day Stefano goes to the blacksmith's daughter down at the hamlet of Gli Angeli, that he's treating her as if she were his betrothed and showering her with beautiful presents."

"Who says?" asked don Paolo. "You know how many sweethearts Stefano has. I don't believe it. This is men's business . . . When I think of all the presents I took to the young baron's women, in the old days! Where's the harm?"

"Those were women, but the harm is that this one's a young girl. She wasn't wearing the red garter on her leg when he fell for her." Maria Teccapiglia was emphatic.

"But now she *is* wearing this blessed garter, so that's enough!" snapped don Paolo. He was exasperated by Maria Teccapiglia's veiled accusation.

"If she's not wearing it now, she did. Before . . ." was Nora Aiutamicristo's sibylline comment.

Costanza had come back in without making a sound. She was sitting on a stool in a corner of the pantry, listening. Don Paolo changed the subject.

"Tell me something, one of you. How are we supposed to call the prefect?"

"'Your Excellency'—don Filippo says so," came Nora Aiutamicristo's prompt reply.

The conversation continued about the prefect, and about Italians. Everyone agreed about the barbarism of the outsiders who had come to stay.

30

"He wandered the Arca, the Merca, and Pantelleria."

Costanza Safamita likes the Piedmontese prefect Ermenegildo Calloni.

It was the first time that Costanza had dined with people from the mainland, and she was fascinated by the guests. The prefect was tall and elegant. He had a beard and, like her, thick, curly red hair. She had never met anyone face-to-face with hair the same colour as hers. She had glimpsed some redheaded youngsters in Marsala during a visit to her cousins the Limunas, who had sniggered when they pointed the boys out to her as they bowled along the main street in their gig; they called them Nofrios. Alfonsina had explained to her that all the redheads in Marsala were descended from an Englishman, a certain Onofrio, who had sown the city with bastard children. Costanza had blanched and crammed her hat over her head.

"The little baroness reminds me very much of my sister as a young girl!" exclaimed the prefect as soon as he saw her.

Costanza found herself ill at ease conversing with the guests in Italian and was confused by their friendly tone. Her father, amused and benevolent, watched her but at first did not help her out of her difficulties with Italian. Then he came to her aid by speaking to her in French.

The conversation continued at a brisk pace in that tongue. The prefect was being treated as a friend and not as a foreign dignitary, so the atmosphere was one of restrained informality. The talk was of Egypt, which Calloni knew. He talked of the opening of the Suez Canal, of the Pyramids, and of the beauty of Muslim art—traces of which he thought he saw in certain Sicilian churches—and of the customs, traditions, and religion of those people. Costanza realised that the Egyptians were none other than the Turks of don Paolo's and Gaspare's stories; overcoming her shyness, she took part in the conversation and even asked the prefect a few questions.

When they were alone, her mother asked her from whom she had learned so much. The reply—"From Papa's coachman"—puzzled Caterina. That evening Costanza went to bed euphoric and exhausted, filled with a great desire to know the world and plans to travel when she was grown up. She fell asleep remembering Paolo Mercurio's and Gaspare Quagliata's stories, from which she had learned that there are many other ways of living and thinking and that people ought to be able to do things in their own way.

Since don Paolo hailed from Palermo, he felt superior to provincials like the people of Sarentini. He was a great friend of Gaspare's and the two of them liked to poke fun at each other, engage in repartee, refreshing their memory and repeating the same yarns word for word—unwitting heirs to the oral tradition of the old storytellers.

Their tales were for the most part about the sea, since both men belonged to families of emigrants who, out of poverty or gullibility, had been duped by agents of the old galley owners, and had found themselves alongside Muslim slaves at the oars of those same vessels. That is how don Paolo's grandfather had met the blessed Giuseppe Safamita, when they were both prisoners of the Bey of Tunis, waiting to be ransomed.

"My late grandfather," the coachman would say, "offered to serve as valet to Count Vasciterre in hope of payment. They were prisoners in the penal colony of Tunis with the other slaves . . . at night they'd chain them up like dogs and by day they worked them like mules. The count— he was already a saint—sent word to the Redeemer of the Almshouse in Palermo, telling him he had to find enough escudos to ransom both of them, that he wouldn't abandon my grandfather in that hell. The Redeemer travelled back and forth between Palermo and Tunis to bargain with the Turks. He did as he was told, and those two—like brothers they'd become—returned to Palermo together. Then the count was widowed and he became a monk to thank the Good Lord for having freed him from the Turks. And as for us Mercurios," don Paolo concluded proudly, "we remained Safamita men and we never went short of bread."

Gaspare had been in the land of the Turks. As a boy he had been sent off to sea, and his ship had stopped over in Tunis and Algiers—marvellous cities, with huge markets and gardens full of scents, fountains, and beautiful women. These last would cover their faces up to their eyes when they went out. "Eyes black as ravens they had, and they gave certain looks that made the prisoners' hearts glad and set their legs atremble, so beautiful were they." Gaspare then told of the strange customs of the inhabitants: "People took their shoes off to go into the churches. I say 'churches' in a manner of speaking, of course; they didn't even have roofs, not even a cross, not even pews. But they had to leave their shoes outside, and no one stole them. Just as the Turks are thieving dogs who steal from us, so are they honest among themselves when it comes to church business. People would spend a lot of time in there; there was even a fountain for washing your face and hands, and other things I won't mention, before praying. They would go five times a day. There were no bells to call them to mass, so the bell ringer had to shout to everyone when it was time, and he shouted so much that he went hoarse."

"All those times they came here to Sicily to steal everything from us and carry Christians off into slavery, they might have lifted a few old bells while they were at it!" said don Paolo, with a superior smile and a twinkle in his eye.

"But they have their own customs, and that's how they do things," said Gaspare. "In church they throw themselves to the floor and they bend over backwards and forwards. There's no music, not even an altar, and they have no truck with statues of the saints. The women pray at home. Only men go to church, on Fridays. The women don't even go on Sundays, but it's not a mortal sin, because they're Turks. They do everything wrong."

"And wine, our delicious wine, it's a sin to drink it, on pain of excommunication!" added don Paolo. "Still, their paradise is really beautiful. There's no angels and saints—it's like a garden full of all kinds of good things and even pretty girls in search of a sainted soul to comfort!"

Costanza was ready to meet people who were different, and she wasn't afraid of them. On the contrary, she dreamed and dreamed, letting her fancy run free, and the more she dreamed the more she hoped to go beyond the confines of Sarentini.

31

"Love who loves you, answer who calls you."

Stefano Safamita talks to his sister about Filomena Carcarozzo.

Stefano and Costanza went out riding to pick medlar fruit at Camusa, one of their favourite destinations. The place belonged to Stefano, but until he reached twenty-one he was its master in name only. He would have liked to reopen the house as a family holiday home, but his mother opposed this; the pleasant eighteenth-century villa had been uninhabited since the death of his grandmother, and, like his grandfather, she did not want to set foot in it. Stefano and Costanza climbed the trees to pick the tart red fruit of which she was so fond, fruit that seem to grow deliberately on the tips of the highest branches. And as they picked Stefano told her of his plans to restore the villa.

"They were talking about you in the kitchens yesterday. Have you got a sweetheart?" Costanza asked him point-blank.

"People never mind their own business," her brother replied brusquely.

"But I'd like to see her!" exclaimed Costanza enthusiastically.

On the way back Stefano took a steep, stony path that he rarely used. After passing through the peasants' smallholdings, it rejoined the royal highway at the poorest part of the town, the hamlet known as Agli Angeli. Stefano tugged gently on his reins and peered at the crown of the hill. Round a corner a stone wall had collapsed to form a kind of passageway; flattened stubble showed that this was used as a shortcut to the public water trough. They stopped but did not dismount. The horses nibbled at clumps of wild rosemary, and the plants defended themselves by emitting their strong, pungent odour. Stefano wore a distant look, as if he were alone. Costanza waited anxiously: she sensed that this was an important moment. In the silence of the countryside, the chirruping of the cicadas was deafening.

Then came the sound of footfalls: three barefoot young girls came down the lane, dressed in rags, with water jars on their heads. The tallest came last, her head covered with a sky-blue kerchief; she had an oval face and her skin was smooth and golden. Her gait was supple and light, as if she were walking on air. She slowed down as soon as she spotted them. Costanza looked at her tiny, delicate feet.

She turned to her brother. Stefano was radiating desire and happiness as he devoured the girl with his eyes, spellbound. The girl seemed perplexed, looking from one to the other, her brown eyes darting beneath their heavy lids and thick eyelashes. She pursed her small, full lips, which then opened in a brief, luminous smile; two dimples appeared in her cheeks. Then the solemn expression returned to her face, and she caught up with the other girls. The three of them went straight across the path, the jars balanced on their heads, as if Stefano and Costanza did not exist. He followed her with his gaze until she vanished behind a fig tree.

They were close to the castle stables.

"Do you like her?" Stefano asked his sister.

"Yes, she's very beautiful."

"She is my life," he murmured.

32

"He who has youth is never poor."

*Costanza Safamita thinks of love
as she listens to the talk of the servants in the kitchen.*

Costanza became a young lady at thirteen. She was taller than her mother.

Her body had rounded out and her features had softened. She dressed as a young girl and no longer as a child; she needed an entirely new wardrobe. All the domestic staff—her nurse, Maria Teccapiglia, and Annuzza la Cirara included—called her "the baronessina." But when these last spoke to her they would use the pet name *signurì*, a distortion of *vostra signoria*, "your ladyship"—a form of address used only by the retainers who were on intimate terms with her. Sometimes they would slip back into the old "thou," but only rarely.

Costanza's corner in the ironing room was dismantled: she would no longer go to the servants' quarters. She wasn't as unhappy about this as she thought she might be. She made up for the lost conversations in the kitchens by looking after Madame, who was often indisposed, and not only because of the excessive number of liqueurs she downed. But above all she reorganised her room, bringing her grandmother Maria Stella's harp down from the castle—her first step towards her future role as mistress of the house, when, married, she would have a mansion house of her own—and she passed the time there playing the harp and embroidering with her women. She looked to the future with tranquil expectation.

Costanza was very orderly. She would put her things back in the drawers, perfectly folded and organised according to size, colour, shape, and texture. She compared life to an enormous money box subdivided in drawers of different sizes. Some were empty. Others, more capacious, contained the basic necessities, the fundamental elements. Smaller drawers were reserved for the smaller things she had a fondness for, superfluous but important—things that gave flavour and relish to a day lived well. According to Costanza, love was like the frame of a piece of furniture that gives form and solidity to the whole. She prepared her clothes to be put into the drawers and filled them up, but she still didn't have a place for everything; she waited, serenely, for her wedding day. She thought that she, too, would have a marriage like that of her parents: an enduring love that would prevail over disagreements, difficulties, and sorrows. A money box to be kept in perfect order always.

Stefano's relationship lay outside those parameters, and Costanza didn't know what to think about it. On the one hand she thought that love between people from "different families" was an expression of modern times, but on the other hand she realised that little or nothing had changed in Sarentini. She had a premonition that Stefano's love story contained the seeds of tragedy. Like other young people of her class, Costanza was protected from the ugliness of the outside world, yet on thinking it over she recalled certain conversations among the maids, when she was small, whose sense had escaped her then but which had nonetheless stayed in her memory. Now, she mulled over those conversations again.

As a little girl, Costanza used to listen to the chatter of the women engaged in tasks around the table in the pantry: cleaning vegetables, crushing almonds, shelling pistachios, peas and beans, removing grit from the lentils. They would ritually talk about every permissible topic: the Safamitas, "the family," their own kin, jobs to be done and those already done, preparations for going to the summer houses, the gossip in town, even politics. She would sit and listen at her corner of the table, a bowl full of things to clean in her lap. She would focus on her work in silence, so as not to be a nuisance and not to be noticed.

The talk never failed to touch on misfortunes and afflictions, with a wealth of horrifying details. This seemed to arouse in the women not only the inevitable resignation but a certain satisfaction, especially in their accounts of pain, illness, and death. In turn, without interrupting the manual work, they would discuss the deaths of their relatives, describing their unspeakable and "incomparable" sufferings; mention the devastation of the cholera epidemics, still recurrent in Sicily; talk of the killings and slaughter perpetrated by bands of brigands and by the Italian army—in the kitchens of Safamita House as in the rest of Sicily, bandits, soldiers, and the army were considered, not without justice, on a par for their godless actions—and pass on news about murders committed for reasons of punishment, vendetta, or honour. If there had been no recent deaths, they fell back on past events, commemorating them on the anniversaries, or they talked of poor devils who had suffered so greatly that they longed for the liberation of death.

Then they would move on to grief, to the misfortunes that befell their kin when the future seemed devoid of hope. Theirs was a vision of intolerable sadness, yet Costanza realised that the women took comfort in the conversation and work, and once they had finished the chores they rose from the table satisfied and even happy.

Apart from death, the main topic was love. The girls belonged to poor families that gravitated to the wealthy ones on whom they depended for work and protection; they went into service to scrape together the money for a dowry, and that was their main consideration—even though they knew it was not unusual to run up against the lust of the masters, to which they had to yield. They, too, would find husbands; sometimes the masters themselves helped to marry them off.

Costanza was still unaware that this was the way things were. Her father and Stefano took no interest in the maids, and this discouraged the men in the Safamitas' service from making up for this shortcoming on the masters' part—though not completely. The Safamitas' maids cared little about having to accept husbands chosen by their parents: like all girls, they couldn't wait to marry. In the womanly intimacy of the pantry, the young maids encouraged the married women to talk about love and to let slip imprudent comments and salacious stories. Only the married women might discuss risqué topics, but always by way of warnings and allusions.

Nor did they have to be asked twice. They reeled off stories about local people, complete with names and surnames—true stories, but embellished and exaggerated. The protagonists were women who for love had defied the laws of God and man, mothers forgetful of their duties to their children, men bewitched by women of ill repute, sons heedless of their family obligations, shameless widows. They were brutal, gripping stories: passion, betrayal, incest, shame, disgrace, vendettas handed down from father to son, curses and witchcraft. There were other important characters, the avengers: husbands who slew unfaithful wives in front of their children, shameless women who killed the seducers who'd abandoned them, lovers who inflicted ritual mutilations on each other, wicked vindictive mothers-in-law, mothers who dealt cruelly with daughters who had sinned, and parricides who killed in vengeance. The stories always ended in tragedy and death.

The married women, unconsciously carried away by these tales, sublimated the overwhelming passions of those sinful women. But the young girls dreamed of experiencing these passions and, after the usual lively discussions about the events recounted, seemed to come to an agreement. Costanza wasn't quite clear about what, however, because the girls didn't dare express their irreverent and iconoclastic ideas: "Jesus Christ died to save us. The Virgin Mary suffered more than all other women. Life is suffering. Death and misfortune are forever lying in wait and forever victorious. We women are born to suffer, we must content ourselves and enjoy what can be found. Love is beautiful and a great pleasure, but life gives nothing for nothing. The pleasures of the flesh are mortal sins, within and outside wedlock. Everything that is fine and enjoyable costs money, and we maids in the Safamita household have no cash, so in our poverty all we have is love, which costs nothing and gives satisfaction." When their work was finished, the young women would get up from the table murmuring the customary brief phrases pregnant with significance: "Better than nothing." "God is mercy." "This is all that is left to us poor folk." "Life is short." "The Lord Jesus respected Mary Magdalene."

As an adolescent, Costanza sensed a contradiction in that talk, but she couldn't work out what it was. She was privileged; love and happiness would be her lot. That frank, brutal talk was for the poor, who had neither rights nor hopes, yet in it Costanza recognised a universal dilemma and she felt as vulnerable as the other women. She was sure that Stefano was now prey to a passion he couldn't resist, another passion doomed to end in tragedy. She was at once frightened and attracted by this, just like the young maids.

33

"Love heeds not wise counsels."

A love opposed reveals itself ill-fated.

Costanza did not speak again to Stefano about his girl. A certain complicity had developed in their relationship, and she saw him not only as her big brother but also as an impassioned, modern-minded young man. All the things happening in the family on Stefano's account overwhelmed her, and her brother's love affair was foremost in her mind. Costanza neglected herself.

One day, as she was embroidering with her women, the talk was of the betrothal of Gaetano, son of the notary Melchiorre Tuttolomondo.

"He's twenty, like young Baron Stefano," Annuzza la Cirara said to herself. "And he's in love, too." All the women heard her and said nothing in the awkward silence.

"And what are they saying about Stefano's sweetheart?" Costanza seized the chance to ask the question that had been on her mind for some time.

Maria Teccapiglia shot Annuzza a withering glance of reproof. Amalia raised her eyes to heaven and lowered them again in dismay before Costanza noticed and anxiously went back to her sewing. Annuzza, abandoned by the others and overcome by embarrassment, tried hastily to remedy matters. "Men do as they please, and Stefano is young, and a master. I don't know the girl," she said in a faint, obsequious voice.

"Well, I've seen her. She's beautiful," said Costanza loud and clear, looking them all in the eye, one by one.

Devoured by curiosity, the women were greedy for details. Costanza refused to say anything more; she insisted that first they must tell her what they knew. And so the three women set aside caution and reeled off for the young mistress all the gossip gleaned from below stairs and from the town, too. Costanza learned that Stefano had drifted apart from his friends, that his only thought was for his sweetheart. Rumour had it that the girl was pregnant and that he, glad about this, was thinking of installing his child-lover in the lower floors of Villa la Camusa no less, together with the blacksmith and his family.

The blacksmith was a bad person, but the three women either did not know that or wanted to speak of something else. All the workers and staff of the Safamita household hoped Stefano would fall out of love, not to mention the field overseers, who refused to have any dealings with Carcarozzo. These men, who normally took good care of their mares, preferred to have them unshod and lame than shod by him.

It was clear that Stefano had got himself into trouble. Costanza knew, from conversations with her cousins, that their brothers and other young men had had love affairs with "different" women and that sometimes these women got pregnant. In such cases the man felt betrayed, because a pregnancy was not a part of "the bargain," and he would end the relationship. On other occasions the family had to step in and even pay off the women to get rid of them. Costanza's cousins had no doubt that this was better for everyone concerned. The offspring of such matches were not true children, who came only from marriages with the seal of family approval; these were different and did not belong to the family. Besides, such women were all persons of easy virtue.

As she was embroidering, Costanza mulled over her cousins' words. Stefano's sweetheart seemed like a good girl, and his words—"She is my life"—kept running through her head. She couldn't enjoy her work; not even darning satisfied her. She thought about Stefano's child and decided she wanted to embroider for her nephew.

One day she said to Annuzza la Cirara, "Make me a little blouse."

"For whom?"

"Do as I tell you."

Annuzza understood and made her the blouse. Costanza was preparing a little layette, and her women asked no questions. Silent and unwilling, they helped her, until one afternoon Maria Teccapiglia spoke to her in private: "Signurì, there's something I have to get off my chest and

I must speak. My children were raised by my brother-in-law at Malivin-nitti, and the Tignusos are Safamita men. This business will end in tears. It would be better to stop this embroidery. Better for everyone."

"Maria, for now I'm embroidering, and those who want to help me are free to do so. My married cousins have lots of babies and I have embroidered many a layette. If you want to help, fine."

"Yes, your ladyship," she replied. When they chose the embroidery patterns, Costanza took care to avoid the baronial emblems and crown. Maria Teccapiglia noticed this: "Your ladyship is a young girl and you have the Safamitas' hard head, but you are wise," she said.

Costanza didn't have the courage to talk to Stefano about the girl's pregnancy. When she had finished her work she called Rosa Vinciguerra, who—although Stefano had said nothing to her—was in the know just like all the others. Rosa still felt that she was in Stefano's service, and Costanza knew she would find a way to send things to the blacksmith's daughter, as Filomena Carcarozza was now called in the Safamita household.

"Now don't forget, send the things in your name," said Costanza. And so it was.

"Costanza, what's all this business about a layette?" Stefano was annoyed.

"Why, isn't it true about the baby?" replied his sister, reining in her horse. They were in front of Villa la Camusa.

"Yes, but who told you?"

"Stefano, everyone knows. Even Papa and Mama probably know, though they haven't said anything to me. I must tell you something: no one likes this blacksmith, so watch out for him. Don't be weak about this—the baby can live well with its mother. Send her off somewhere far away from her family, and you can always see them from time to time. You have to think of your life." Costanza was surprised by her own boldness, daring to give advice to her older brother.

"Did Father tell you?"

"No. I don't tell lies."

Stefano spurred his horse. "I know what I'm doing, Costanza, and I don't need advice."

She caught up with him and cried, "Promise me that you'll let me meet your sweetheart and the child!"

"Very well," he replied, and they galloped off.

Stefano's affair, which the family initially saw as an almost normal escapade for a nobleman's son, turned into a scandal. Certain things had to be done in accordance with a precise code: relationships and offspring had to be kept hidden without talking about them around town or giving others something to talk about.

At first Stefano had thought to install Filomena and her family in the outbuildings of la Camusa. He couldn't bear the idea of his son growing up in a stinking hovel where men and beasts lived together. In his presumptuous naïveté he thought that once Filomena reached the age of consent he could marry her and they would move into Castle Sarentini. He had heard of other nobles who had married singers, actresses, and commoners, and he was sure that the Safamitas would be won over by Filomena's beauty and virtue.

One afternoon his father summoned him to his offices. It was the first time they had talked in private since the Seven and a Half Days' Rebellion.

"I know you are in love with a beautiful young girl, who I presume was a virgin," said the baron. "I also know she is pregnant. She is the daughter of a scoundrel. Plenty of men have their shotguns pointed at him, and everyone knows he is alive only out of respect for us. This kind of thing cannot continue. I shall provide you with whatever cash you may require. Melchiorre Tuttolomondo has been informed, and he will see to matters in person. I could have this blacksmith thrown in prison, or I could give a free hand to those who want him dead, but there's no need for that."

"She is a foundling," Stefano replied passionately. "Perhaps she was born as noble as we are. She makes me happy. Why will you deny me a happiness like yours? I am the son of an uncle and a niece—your union, too, was forbidden by the Church. Thanks to our influence and to your love, you overcame the obstacles. All I ask you is to meet her. She will look after you like a daughter."

"You have to grow up, Stefano. To understand your parents you have to grow up, become mature." His father seemed to want to say no more. "I understand love, passion. Perhaps I should have talked to you before and put an end to this whole thing. The happiness you speak of won't last long, and you'll tire of her. Problems will arise, and you will feel the difference in class. She is one of the common people. You are not. This blacksmith is a bloodsucker and a dishonest man. You will ruin the family's reputation, and that would spell the end of the Safamitas of Sarentini. Have you thought about that? You would have to leave town and sell off our property, emigrate. Are you up to that? And in any case do you think I would let you do this? Remember, you have a brother and a sister. Leave the girl now—she will be well off and her son will have a good life, and so will you. You will have a wife and children, lovers, whatever you want. There's no reason why you can't stop seeing her if you want to."

"I can't do that," said Stefano in a whisper.

The baron thought Stefano might have been threatened by the blacksmith, and he pressed his point. "Then let me step in. Take a trip. I'll buy you an estate somewhere else. Put simply, I'll help you get rid of her and her family."

"No, I don't want to leave her."

"Think about it. This is your home. If you marry her it will no longer be yours, and you will no longer be welcome here or on Safamita land. I shall do everything possible to keep up the family name and patrimony, but not for you and the children of this girl, good and virtuous as she may be. It is a question of class and individuals, of a system that has endured for centuries and that the Safamitas have always respected. I am prepared to discuss things with a view to solving the problem in the least painful way for everyone. Stefano, I'm doing this for you, and not just for your mother. You must understand: times haven't changed the way you think—not here, at any rate."

Stefano went straight to his mother and made a scene. He extolled Filomena's innocence and accused his father of having slandered the blacksmith and of having incited the field overseers against him. They ended up weeping together.

After that Stefano continued living in Castle Sarentini, but in perennial conflict with his father. They avoided each other and Stefano spent the days and a part of the nights away. He decided, nonetheless, not to take Filomena to Villa la Camusa.

34

"Suffering and bread is no suffering.
Real suffering comes with no bread."

Pepi Tignuso helps the Safamitas and himself, but not the field hands.

In mid-June 1873, the family was at Malivinnitti for the harvest, just as they were every year. Costanza was anxious: the birth of Stefano's child was imminent.

The crop was a good one. Pepi Tignuso asked to speak with the baron. Domenico Safamita received him with Costanza, whom he wanted to encourage to take an interest in her property.

"I need to talk to your lordship alone," said Pepi. "No offence to the young Baroness Costanza, but this is men's business."

"If it's about Malivinnitti and my son Stefano, she must hear it too," said the baron.

"Yes, your lordship," replied Pepi, but he was nonplussed. Then he went on, "Your lordship will remember that in May 1860 I spoke one evening with your lordship and the late lamented Baron Guglielmo at the castle. Now the situation is much worse."

"Go on."

Pepi Tignuso was sweating copiously. "We Tignusos have worked very hard for the Safamita family on your lands, and not only at Malivinnitti. The other overseers and the townsfolk respect us. It's been hard, but we've managed to keep things going the way we did in the old days. The field hands are grumbling, though, and since that talk we had there are far more scoundrels around—like flies, they are. They buzz off and then they come back, and they're the kind that sting. We don't take any notice of the flies, but other people do. If for now we let these stinking flies buzz around, it's because we know they'll fall to the ground dead at the first nip of frost. We've got other really big worries—all the problems that have come up because of this damned flour tax, the farmworkers, the bandits—but if we set our minds to it there won't be a single fly around, Pepi Tignuso's word. When other people listen to the flies, they start losing respect for us. Then we must silence them.

"Emanuele Carcarozzo is one of those rogues, and he talks too much. He's one of a few people who'd have been silenced already if it wasn't for this business of his daughter and the young Baron Stefano. He keeps the worst company. The girl is not for the young baron—Pepi Tignuso's word. Tomorrow I have to go to town for a few days—your lordship knows why. If I hear anything else around town, I'll let you know."

When Pepi Tignuso had gone, Domenico Safamita said to his daughter, "It is my understanding that you know this girl. Do as you wish, but I don't want to know anything."

Costanza didn't have time to think over this conversation before some very serious events occurred at Malivinnitti.

The very next day, the reapers refused to go into the fields. Demanding a raise in their agreed daily wage and more, they broke off the reaping and instead occupied the threshing yard, where they stayed all day long, under the sun. They sent a delegation to talk with the bosses. The baron was very worried. There had been problems of this type and worse on other people's properties, but until now the Safamitas had been spared, thanks to the Tignusos' ruthless, efficient control. The baron ordered the family to stay indoors and to make sure that Giacomo—a possible kidnap victim—was not left alone, and he alerted the guards. He ordered the reapers to be given food and drink, no more and no less than the agreed amount. They stayed in the threshing yard and spent the night there: no one went back to town.

The next morning the men again asked to speak with the baron. He sent no reply while he awaited the return of Pepi Tignuso, who had already been told of the events. It was a muggy day without a breath of wind. The hazy sky weighed heavy upon the land, dense with dire portents. An oppressive calm enveloped the manor house. Farm life went on, but bleakly, and even the animals and the children seemed to be keeping quiet. The masters spent a second day shut up in the house.

Early in the morning of the third day, the baron made his entrance in the threshing yard, from the outer gate. Opposite him, filling the upper end of the yard, were the reapers: dressed in rags, their faces smeared with dirt and sweat, standing motionless, desperate—a compact group made up of ten squads of twelve men each. Domenico Safamita felt like the target of hundreds of black blowpipes, with those dark, slitted eyes— eyes like his—trained on him in anger, bitterness . . . and hunger.

A spokesman for the reapers stepped forwards and presented their claims. The baron listened, impassively, pensively. He let the men who had agreed on the daily rate say their piece. The talks proceeded slowly but loudly, the main characters gesticulating emphatically like actors: Pepi Tignuso had a leading role, sometimes conciliatory, sometimes domineering. For much of the time he was silent, watching the men. Hours went by. The group of reapers broke up and some of them came closer—at times threatening, at times provoking—each of them with his own opinion. No agreement was reached. The sun was reaching its zenith, and the air was sultry. The cobblestones in the yard—rocks the size of goose eggs taken from the riverbed and embedded in the beaten earth—shone whitely. The baron remained standing in the lower part of the yard, together with a dozen of his men, silent and thirsty. Shouts of annoyance, impatient gestures, dismayed faces, sullen, weary looks. The atmosphere was white-hot. Against him stood more than a hundred reapers. He had lost sight of Pepi Tignuso.

Baron Safamita was afraid. He began to look around, and concealed his anxiety by tapping his cane on the ground absentmindedly. Then finally he spotted him: Pepi had withdrawn into a corner where the tools were propped up against the wall, and he had his back to everyone—the baron thought that perhaps he wanted to urinate. He wandered about and every so often would bend down awkwardly, bracing himself against his stick, as if he were picking something up from the ground. His movements were slow, with his thin bandy legs—deformed from a lifetime on horseback—and his prominent belly. Pepi was gathering stones and slipping them into his back pockets; he seemed completely engrossed. The talks dragged on and on, angry circular arguments that always came back to the same point. It was almost noon. The men had been trapped in the yard under the sun as if some enchantment had transformed it into a prison with open gates but no way out for anyone.

"Get off to work, you ruffians!" thundered Pepi Tignuso in dialect. "To work! To work!" He had thrown his stick to the ground and was coming across the yard, throwing stones at the reapers with both hands. He advanced slowly, inexorably. "To work! To work!" Silence fell. The stones did not hit the men—they were too far away—but fell to the ground and rolled down the slope. Heedless, balanced precariously on his unsteady legs, Pepi made his implacable way up the yard. On he came, on and on, his arms tireless. He had emptied his pockets. "To work! To work!" Pepi bent to the ground, craning his neck, his gaze never leaving the men as he groped around for more stones and even tore some from the earth before straightening up and throwing again. Now he was only a few yards from the men. One man against many. He was hitting his targets now. Unfailingly.

Domenico Safamita watched all this. He had ordered the guards to take up positions by the dovecote, and he feared the time had come for them to intervene. Pepi was in danger. In the yard all that could be heard was Pepi's loud yells, his panting, the clump of his hobnailed boots on the cobbles, and the dull thumps of the stones raining down on the reapers. Motionless under this assault, the men who were struck swayed but stood their ground, expressionless, like flagellants in a Good Friday procession.

Pepi stopped in the centre of the yard. He straightened up and said in a loud voice, but without shouting, "I told you lot to get to work. Can you hear me? All of you! Pepi Tignuso is telling you to get to work, and he's not going to tell you again." He braced his feet against two stones, his arms hanging down loosely, his back straight. He looked at them, waiting. The men did not move.

Suddenly the baron saw him bend forwards and rest one hand on the ground. He feared that Pepi was ill. But then the overseer slowly rose, as if after a genuflection, and drawing back his arm hurled yet another stone that he had torn from the earth. In silence, Pepi bent down again and, panting, threw still more stones at the men, one after another. Then a shout: "To work!" And Pepi bent down no longer but stayed straight in front of the men, sweating and breathing heavily. An old man, vulnerable.

It was as if they had been waiting for that moment. Slowly, the reapers turned around and flocked towards the entry to the shed where the harvesting equipment was kept. They went in and came out one by one, each man carrying his own tools, their woven armguards like chains, some with scythes over their shoulders, cane finger guards on their hands, lengths of binding twine hooked to the cords of their trousers, and others with reaping hooks large and small. Heads held high, they gave Pepi a pathetic look and took the side gate, heading for the fields.

Pepi did not move.

The spokesmen for the farmworkers trailed along at the end of the procession—they, too, with scythes over their shoulders. As they went through the gate, they broke the silence: "*S'abbenadica, don Pepi.*"

That afternoon the baron summoned Pepi Tignuso.

"Pepi, I want to thank you. That was a difficult moment."

"Your lordship knows I do what I have to do."

"You are a good and respected man, Pepi."

"Your lordship had faith in me. Without Malivinnitti I would be a nobody."

"Have you any news about that business?"

"Yes. Your lordship must forgive me for what I have to say."

"Go on."

"If a single drop of Safamita blood smells of Carcarozzo I'm a dead man, and the Safamitas will be powerless masters." He paused and added, "Your lordship knows I'm a family man and have to think of my children, just as your lordship does."

"I understand. Pepi, are you talking only of Malivinnitti?"

"Pepi Tignuso is respected on all the Safamita properties and on those of other masters."

"Thank you. I must think about this."

Pepi looked over at Costanza. She was calm, sitting beside her father. "There's another thing, your lordship. I'm sorry to be the first to say it: this morning the blacksmith's daughter gave birth to a baby girl, and they've called her Caterina. Young Baron Stefano wants to marry her before June is out. Good day, your lordship."

35

"The rings fell off, but not the fingers."

*Maria Teccapiglia consoles Costanza Safamita
by telling her the extraordinary story of her mother's birth.*

At dusk the Safamitas and their guests went outdoors together for a leisurely stroll beneath the carob trees. After dinner, the women played listlessly at cards on the terrace while the men smoked. They didn't talk much, and only about trivial matters. Costanza gazed at the starry sky, at the vast peace above her.

In the afternoon her father had announced to the family, "Everything is settled."

Costanza had learned more from Maria Teccapiglia. It had been a bad day for the Safamitas but not for the Tignusos. Yet Costanza was secretly jubilant: another Caterina Safamita had been born. Then she had suddenly felt all alone, as never before, and in the afternoon she had gone to look for Maria in the pantry to ask her to tell the story of her mother's birth. Maria understood and launched into the story, reverting to the intimate form of address she had used with Costanza in the old days.

"Your late lamented grandmother died twenty years before you were born. She always had a smile on her face, and she didn't dare complain even when your mother was born. And to think what a memorable day it was, the twenty-eighth of June 1831. Three days before, on the twenty-fifth, tremors were felt, as if an earthquake was coming. We ran to close the windows, and the chandeliers were swaying. The baroness told me her labour pains had started. Then the tremors stopped, and the labour pains, too.

"And so it went for three days. We women were all going crazy! It was as if the earth and the heavens were controlling her labour: the tremors came and the contractions would begin; the earth would stop trembling and the contractions would stop, too.

"Then, on the fourth day, everything started dancing around in the house, the tremors got stronger, and the contractions started again with only small intervals in between. The air was heavy, gloomy. You could hear long-drawn-out distant sounds, yet there wasn't a cloud in sight. It was as if the bad weather had been collected under a big blue tent covering the whole sky, and behind it a storm was raging. There wasn't even time to call the midwives. The little girl came into the world all by herself, with us married women lending a hand—and we made a better job of it than the midwives."

Maria was short of breath, and she paused, drew herself up in the chair, and intertwined her fingers, leaving them open, palms up, on her lap. She looked around happily. "And then we heard a rumble, far, far away, very special music, and a fit tribute to the little baroness!" Now Maria Teccapiglia was chuckling. Her faded eyes with their heavy, droopy lids quickened with a flash of vivacity as she winked fondly at Costanza.

"This is what happened on that day. But there's more. It was discovered afterwards that in the open sea, off Sciacca, some much more mysterious events took place when the little baroness was about to be born. Baron Guglielmo summoned Captain Francesco Trafiletti to the castle"—and Maria Teccapiglia pronounced each syllable of the captain's name separately in a loud voice: Tra-fil-et-ti—"to hear directly from his own lips what had happened to him, and he ordered all of us in service at the house to come into the drawing room to listen, all of us. Well, this captain was sailing towards Sciacca from Malta. While he was still well offshore, from far, far off he saw a great upheaval in the middle of the waters. He thought some big fish were having a good time there. Good time, my foot! Those fish were dead: they came bobbing up around the ship, floating about in the seaweed. Then he heard a sound and saw a column of water as high as the church belltower shooting up in the middle of that bedlam of maddened waves, and it continued for three days non-stop. He stood off for a bit and stopped to watch.

"On the twenty-eighth of June, when the little baroness was about to be born, pieces of pumice and tuff began to fall from that column of water—in other words, it was raining rocks, like a hailstorm, but much worse—and suddenly an island appeared. It was born of the sea and grew round and hilly, a marvel! For two months that island born of the sea stayed there, big and peaceful; birds nested on it, too. A most beautiful island it was, and newborn, like your mother. But it didn't stay long—such was the wickedness of men that the Lord made it disappear again.

"King Ferdinand's island it was, and the captain called it Ferdinandea. Then came the English, and they stuck their flag on it and said it belonged to them. The French came, stuck in another flag, and also claimed it belonged to them. They were on the point of fighting to see who would be the master of the island. And do you know what it did? Very, very quietly the island slipped back beneath the waters and vanished. Calmly, with no fuss, it returned to the bottom of the sea, and there it stayed, together with the fish and the coral.

"That's how your mother was born, and she was special right from the start. She was walking before twelve months, and she talked and read when she was still very, very small. She learned English and French very quickly from that good soul Mam'selle Besser. She looked after her mother like a grown woman, so deeply did she love her. A strong woman was your mother, like the island of Ferdinandea. She didn't look for trouble, but she knew her own mind. When she saw people fighting, she avoided it and got out of the way."

Costanza looked at the stars. They were her guardian angels, silent bearers of hope. They trembled in the pitch dark. They expected something of her. She was confused, and tears sprang to her eyes.

She pursed her lips and swallowed. Fixing her eyes on the stars, she finally understood: a promise. She, Costanza Safamita, would protect Stefano's daughter: like her grandmother, the little girl was born on a day in which an extraordinary event had occurred and she was destined to be every bit as special.

36

"Two loves are certain:
mother for child, and brother for sister."

*A mother and a favourite son fall out because of Filomena Carcarozzo.
In the meantime, Costanza Safamita thinks of love
and asks Aunt Assunta some awkward questions.*

Caterina Safamita learned of the baby girl's birth from her husband. She immediately bombarded Costanza with questions and was disappointed that she knew so little, that Costanza had seen Filomena only once or twice briefly, in the country. She had liked the sweet, beautiful girl, who was almost her own age. She hoped that her mother would take comfort from her positive description of Filomena, but her report had the opposite effect. Caterina was dismayed, for she would have preferred the girl to be "one of those"; then one could hope that Stefano would fall out of love with her. A good girl represented a danger.

Stefano gave no news. Days went by, and his mother was almost beside herself. One minute she was laying plans to meet the newborn baby behind her husband's back, the next she was plotting to persuade Stefano to abandon both mother and child. She involved and tormented Costanza with her anxieties and dilemmas; when she realised that Costanza knew nothing of Stefano's plans, she was furious and treated her badly.

Costanza understood that as far as her mother was concerned, her role was to be a go-between with Stefano and nothing more. This upset her, but she comforted herself by thinking about the Snail Princess. She was not the only ill-treated daughter, and, like the Snail Princess, she forgave her mother and continued to love her. Annuzza la Cirara had put it well: "She was cruel, but she was still her mother."

Stefano married Filomena Carcarozzo and they moved to Villa la Camusa. He put some rooms on the ground floor at the disposal of the blacksmith's family. On his return to Sarentini the baron gave orders that his son's name was not to be mentioned, and he told his wife that he was prepared to pay off Stefano to leave Sicily, with or without wife and daughter: the important thing was for him to stay far away from the blacksmith and his crowd. He told her that Carcarozzo was in the habit of going around their properties, watching and listening, then talking about what he learned with a family of mafiosi who were enemies of the Tignusos. A power struggle was under way, and by now the Safamitas were no longer in a position to intervene in or resolve it.

Stefano's reaction was to defy his father. His bonds with the Carcarozzos grew even closer, and the result was that his father prohibited him from setting foot on the family properties. Stefano tried to cultivate the land around la Camusa, but he found himself isolated in the village and unable to carry on with his agricultural activities. Then he decided to put his money into new industries, and he tried various investments—all of which failed, the last one being a scheme for the exploitation of the coral beds around Sciacca—suggested or promoted by the blacksmith and his new friends, people who adulated and flattered him in order to swindle him. In this way he squandered his grandfather's inheritance and lost what little credibility and respect people were prepared to grant him. In other words, he became the laughing stock of the village and fell easy prey to those who wanted to take advantage of him. Costanza was kept abreast of these developments by her women, but she didn't dare talk about them with her parents.

———

One day Rosa Vinciguerra told Costanza, in secret, that Stefano wanted to see her: the meeting was to take place in a chapel of the main church. Costanza went with a heavy heart.

Stefano had lost weight, but he seemed healthy enough. "I promised to let you meet my daughter," he said. "Filomena is expecting another . . . Can you still come?"

"You know that Papa has forbidden us to be with her . . . but not to see her from a distance," replied Costanza.

"I thought as much. Take a ride to la Crocca. On the far side of the pistachio grove you'll see an olive tree with a hollow trunk. If you don't wear bright colours, you'll be camouflaged by the leaves. From there you can see the terrace of la Camusa, where they'll be every afternoon. I'll leave a telescope in the hollow. Tell this to our mother."

"Stefano, how can I send presents, money?"

"Presents you can leave, if you wish, with the sexton. He's Father Puma's man. But I don't need money. Things will get better—it's just a matter of time."

"No, Stefano, they won't get better unless you go away. They say that Italy is beautiful. Why don't you think of going there?"

"Mind your own business, Costanza."

After that mother and daughter got into the habit of taking the gig to la Crocca, where they would stay beneath the olive tree, telescope in hand, waiting for Filomena to bring the baby out on the terrace. And, as if she knew where they were hiding, Filomena would take the little girl in her arms and turn her round to face the olive grove.

This was how Baroness Safamita, hidden by olive branches, met her granddaughter from a distance. When mother and daughter turned to leave, Caterina headed to the gig leaning on Costanza's arm, her face ashen, a spent look in her dry eyes. They never saw Stefano: he was behind the shutters, his telescope trained on his mother.

Costanza's heart was aching. She knew that her father and mother were both suffering, and that each considered the other responsible for their son's failings. They kept up their musical afternoons, but now Costanza left them alone: the music took on a consolatory value of such strength and intimacy that it excluded anyone else. Her parents seemed like two unhappy people doomed to be in love with each other.

More and more frequently, Costanza wondered, What is love, really?

She began by asking perhaps the least appropriate person, but the member of the family with whom she was most familiar, Aunt Assunta. Since the death of her grandfather, Costanza often went to Castle Sarentini to call on her aunt. She was convinced that Assunta did not miss her brother much. Showing surprising vitality, she had rearranged the castle interiors, shifting furniture and changing the function of certain rooms, as if she were finally free to satisfy an old longing. From the rooms in daily use she removed all objects with masculine connotations—busts of ancient philosophers, statues in marble and bronze, portraits of men, pictures of saints—and the décor now featured figurines in feminine porcelain, while the walls were hung with still lifes, landscapes, and floral grotesques. Strangely, she kept the pictures and prints from the religious yet wanton eighteenth century.

Donna Assunta moved into rooms on the ground floor once occupied by her brother and her sister-in-law, and she assigned a large room, not far from her own, to Peppinella Radica. Having developed more and more of a sweet tooth, she obliged the nuns to give her their secret recipes so that her cook could keep up the monastic culinary tradition, even that part of it dismantled by the infamous government. She seemed happy.

One day, as they were eating *minne di vergine*, or "virgin's breasts"—sweet pastries that were a speciality of the Convent of the Santissima Annunziata—Costanza asked, "Aunt Assunta, what is love?"

"Love of what?" her aunt asked in her turn, surprised.

"The love of two lovers." Costanza already regretted having spoken.

"Ah, my pretty, that I really don't know, and I never asked myself. I'll tell you one thing, though. It would be right for you to take a husband, because we Safamitas are getting thin on the ground, and our line must continue. But the older I get the more I realise that all this modern talk about love leads to more sorrow than joy. And if you are referring to the love of Our Lord, I've never understood why so many saints have scourged themselves, fasted, worn hair shirts, and prayed for the holy stigmata—not to mention the people who torture themselves during the Good Friday processions. It seems to me that this kind of love means pain. Between you and me, such things are not to my liking, and I'm sure that not even the Good Lord favours them, either. That's why I didn't become a nun."

"So what is love then, Aunt?"

"If you want to know, in my view the love you are talking about boils down to sacrifice and suffering."

Maria Anna Trasi, a guest at the castle, entered the drawing room.

"Costanza is asking me what love is," Assunta told her sister. "You can answer her better than I, Maria Anna."

Costanza blushed.

"My little Costanza, I'll repeat to you what I tell my daughters. Loving is caring for each other and having children," replied her aunt with a sweet, enigmatic smile. "And then the children give the mother and father all the love they need!"

Costanza was preparing for bed, assisted by her nurse.

"Amalia, what is love?" she asked.

Amalia was letting down Costanza's hair. "It's hard to explain," she began. "Life is like a braid. Each strand is important and has a meaning. The first strand is that of duty, which we all have and signifies obedience. The second is that of possessions—those who have them must take care not to be robbed of them, and those who lack them have nothing but hunger and would really like to have them. And the third is that of love. And if a person has three fine, strong strands, then the braid is very beautiful and she will live a happy life. But many women have the first one good and thick while the other two aren't. If they manage to make the braid it won't be beautiful, but it'll hold, and life will go on. But if the love strand is too strong and the duty one too weak, then the braid will not hold and will fall apart. There must be three strands—that's how it is."

Then Amalia began to brush Costanza's hair; after some vigorous strokes she carefully picked off the hairs on the brush and on Costanza's peignoir, twisted them up, and placed them in the special silver casket through the hole in the lid. She then went back to brushing Costanza's hair, this time less forcefully. With each stroke, the girl's hair sprang back curly and fluffy, the varied shades of deep red gleaming in the candlelight.

"Amalia, answer me. What is love, for you?"

As if talking to herself, lost in thought, Amalia murmured, "Love is contentment."

37

"A woman without love is a rose without scent."

Amalia Cuffaro and Pinuzza Belice receive
an unexpected farewell visit from two women neighbours.
Amalia Cuffaro and don Paolo Mercurio fall in love.

Amalia brushed away the crumbs being assaulted by ravenous ants. It had been a lovely surprise visit from her neighbours, whom she had known for some time but only by sight. Their cave was down below, its entry invisible from Amalia's position. The older of the two, a corpulent but still good-looking woman with a fair complexion, stayed outside her cave like a watchdog; the other one showed herself only rarely. Amalia had wondered for what sad, mysterious reason these women—poor but better dressed than the others—had taken refuge on the Montagnazza.

The older one had noticed that Amalia did sewing. One day a boy had come up to ask if Amalia wanted work, for payment. Since then there had been a coming and going of strange items between the two caves: threadbare dresses with plunging necklines, bloomers decorated with multicoloured ribbons, gaudy blankets embellished with silk flowers and drooping petals—all to be sewn and mended. Amalia decided not to wonder too much about this; she wanted to put a little money aside.

That morning Amalia and Pinuzza had heard voices and sounds from down below, coming closer and closer. When the top of a stepladder appeared, a woman's voice shouted out, "Have no fear! It's us, the neighbours you do the mending for. We've come to say goodbye before leaving!" A few seconds later, a tousled head popped over the top of the ladder, followed by the curvaceous figure of the younger woman and then by a boy. The other woman, shouting and sighing in turn, followed behind.

The visitors were as chatty as if they had known Amalia and Pinuzza for a lifetime. After the customary hugs and kisses, they dug into their pockets and took out the kind of good things that Amalia had not seen since her time in Palazzo Sabbiamena: biscuits, caramels, a little bag of sugar, dried figs, needles, black and white thread, and a pair of scissors. Rosa, the younger one, observed Pinuzza with her big black eyes: "What lovely braids you've got! Let me feel them!" The other woman also complimented Pinuzza on her fine, glossy hair, and both of them asked her lots of questions without using Amalia as an intermediary, as everyone else did. Pinuzza lit up with pleasure. Chatting away nineteen to the dozen, they ate the biscuits, leaving the rest for later.

"We're city folk, you understand. But my niece Rosa and I ended up here because of a rash promise she made to a good man with whom she was in love: a socialist, he was, a man who fights for poor folk like us, a real gentleman." Rosa simpered complacently. "He had to become a 'tourist,' but before he went off he gave Rosa some really important papers. The coppers were looking for him all over the country, and we thought to go into hiding here. Now he's back from his 'holiday' and we can leave. The fact is, we came to the Montagnazza hoping it would be a matter of a few months and instead we stayed here for three years, but we're glad about that."

"Why?" asked Pinuzza.

Rosa replied in a low voice, winking at Amalia. "Let's admit it among us women: the truth is that the folk of Riporto and the other villages around here have never seen such two fine, tasty girls as the likes of us. We've even put a little cash aside."

"Who's this boy, your sweetheart?" Pinuzza was asking now.

The older woman laughed. She bent over Pinuzza, all serious. "You could call him a sweetheart. But he's a particular sweetheart, one who will never become a husband. He's not everyone's cup of tea, but he's more than enough for us just the way he is: the kind of lover who makes you content, and that's what matters, contentment."

Amalia changed the subject straight away.

The two women left as cheerfully as they had come.

The next day the police showed up at the Montagnazza, sowing confusion and fear among its inhabitants, some of whom, forewarned, had gone to ground elsewhere, while others had quickly disappeared, leaving behind only old men, women, and children. The police were asking about two women who had been killed in the canebrake at the mouth of the river, presumably by bandits. Amalia swore that she had never seen them. She was an old woman and had eyes only for looking after her invalid niece.

That evening she prayed for the souls of her neighbours, the way Costanza had taught her: "We are all God's children, and we mustn't look down on those who work and earn their bread as best they can." The two women had earned paradise for their goodness: if the Christian heaven didn't welcome them with open arms, then at least the Turkish one would. Goodness knows what the late-lamented don Paolo Mercurio would have thought of them, he who had been so very wise and who wanted to go to the Turkish paradise.

"Aunt, what does it mean to have a sweetheart?" Pinuzza suddenly asked.

Amalia paid her no heed.

"When you got married, were you in love?"

"Your grandfather arranged the marriage with my husband. That's how things are done."

"And then did you fall in love?"

"He was my husband, that's all. That's how it goes."

"So you've never been in love . . . Our neighbour, the woman who gave you sewing to do, was in love. But you never have been. A pity," concluded Pinuzza laconically.

"You shouldn't talk about these things. I used to say the same to my Costanza, when she asked me. Now I'm going out to bring in the washing before it gets damp, and then I'm going to put you to bed."

Amalia collected the handkerchiefs stiffened by the warm wind and carefully folded them in four. The cliffs were bright and shone black as pitch in the slanting rays of the dying sun. They were streaked with long, greenish seaweed that clung like fingers to the rock, beaten to the sweet and sonorous rhythm of the long evening waves.

"Beautiful are the hands of women who have loved; even if they suffered for it, they have known contentment. Falling in love is worth the trouble," she murmured.

Early one spring morning when Costanza was a little girl, she had gone to Castle Sarentini with Maddalena.

Amalia was left to do her mending in the usual place. After a while don Paolo's curly grey head popped up from behind the screen, and she invited him to keep her company. When he sat down beside her, he was strangely silent. As Amalia threaded her needle, she looked up: he seemed sad to her. Don Paolo would brighten up when telling stories, and so, to divert him, she asked him to tell her everything about the affair between King Ferdinand and the Duchess of Floridia, which he had once mentioned in passing; it was a long tale and the little baroness would not return for a good while.

"Amalia, I'll tell you just one thing. I understand King Ferdinand well, the first king who was really ours, King of the Two Sicilies. I understand him better than the others, because my wife, Tanina, is the spitting image of Queen Maria Carolina, an Austrian who never learned her husband's language. Just like Missus Mercurio"—and he stressed the "Missus"— "who instead of speaking the dialect of the Kalsa, where all Mercurios have always lived in Palermo, still uses the dialect of Bagheria.

"So, to get back to the poor king, after the revolution in France those French devils came down as far as Naples. They conquered all of Italy, though not Sicily—they didn't manage to get here. But they went on pursuing the king and queen, who had to escape on an English ship. They spent Christmas on the high seas and got to Palermo the next day. By way of thanks, the king gave this Englishman a whole county, far bigger than all the lands held by the baron and the young baron put together. The king was a good man and rewarded those who helped him.

"But he had barely arrived in Palermo when his wicked queen began plotting against the nobles of Palermo, who disgusted her. Worse than a woman from Bagheria, she was."

"But why did they disgust her? They're all nobles—barons, counts, princes, and king."

"Because people are never content. A count feels he's better than a baron and a marchese feels he's better than a count and a duke feels he's better than a marchese and a prince feels he's better than a duke . . . and a king feels he's better than everyone. But everyone, even a king, needs other people, and those who think they are great and treat folk badly come to a bad end. And that's how it went for the queen. The nobles of Palermo were getting themselves up to their necks in debt to entertain her and the king, what with receptions and hunting parties and all, but all she could think about was getting away.

"You have to know that the late Count Giacomo Safamita di Vasciterre, the young baron's uncle, was a great hunter, and he had an estate just outside Palermo. King Ferdinand wanted to build himself a hunting lodge in that district. Well, the count and the king became friends. And it was precisely the king's favour that led to the arrangement of the marriage between Baron Stefano, the count's second son, and Caterina Lattuca, the young baron's mother, who was filthy rich and a descendant of a notary with the regional court. The Safamita family needed money in those days. And now you know why the Barons Safamita left Palermo for Sarentini.

"My late father, God rest his soul, became a friend of the royal coachmen and grooms, all of whom gossiped much too much about the king's affairs. He remembered all their stories, and then he would tell them to us word for word at home. King Ferdinand was afraid of Queen Maria Carolina. She was so eager to return to her amusements in Naples that she schemed with everybody—even the French, those shameless wretches who'd cut off her sister's head. And, just like my wife, she bossed everyone about as she wished, as if she was the master of the house and not her husband, the king."

Don Paolo gave a sorrowful sigh. Amalia felt guilty about encouraging him to talk. She folded her sheet, pinning it firmly with her needle, and laid a consolatory hand on his knee.

Undaunted, he continued: "Finally, she managed to leave the king and went off to Austria, swearing that she'd never set foot in Sicily again. What was the poor king to do? He had to go back to Naples to keep his wife happy. He was the king, and he didn't have to worry about earning his bread. I, poor wretch that I am, have to earn bread for myself and my family without the company of a wife, while she has her fun back in Palermo." Don Paolo was gesticulating left, right, and centre, and in the heat of the moment he laid his hand on hers. He left it there.

"And now I am condemned to stay here in Sarentini all on my own, dear Amalia." Don Paolo fell silent and looked at her. She was all atingle: the feeling started from that heavy, sweaty, calloused hand glued to hers, then ran up her arm and down inside her. It was a new, delightful sensation.

Don Paolo went back to his story: "We Sicilians are doomed to have a king who doesn't stay in Palermo. But this time fate decreed that he could not stay in Naples, and after a few years he was hunted again by the French and had to ask our help for the second time. The folk of Palermo forgave the queen, and so the royal couple returned to Sicily. We Sicilians are really bighearted." He kept his gaze fixed on the swallows perched on the clothesline on the terrace, and idly toyed with Amalia's fingers in time with the swaying movement of the clothesline. "The king had to flee to Sicily, in winter, like before. The queen didn't want to go with him, as she should have, being his wife, and she stayed in Naples."

Amalia was trembling. Billowing, tender waves of pleasure possessed her, like the rollers that break on the rocks and caress them before ebbing back into the surf.

"He was old, was King Ferdinand—fifty-four, almost like me. He was lonely. The fine embroidered sheets of his bed were cold." He clasped her fingers and began to caress them. "In Palermo the king was very sad, and the Lord took pity on him. He had him meet a Sicilian noblewoman, and little by little they fell in love. My late father used to say she was very beautiful, sweet as sugar—a woman from Siracusa. Her name was Lucia." He turned his gaze on Amalia. "Beautiful like you, a fine buxom lass with round, white arms and dark eyes. Beautiful like you, Amalia." Don Paolo was all afire for her. He lifted her hand from his knee and shifted it purposefully to his inner thigh, making it run along the coarse cloth of his trousers, but he didn't insist, and was ready to stop at the first sign of resistance—which she, Amalia Cuffaro, an honest married woman, could no longer manage to make. What was happening struck her as natural, inevitable. Suddenly he lifted his hand and freed hers, looking at her with pupils dilated. She did not move.

"When the French got to Naples, she, too, like her husband, had to take refuge in Palermo, but a leopard cannot change its spots. In those days the English kept an army in Sicily to protect the king from the French, and they gave money to the king and queen. She took their money and then plotted against them. The king was a gentleman, and he didn't know how to stop her. He was desperate, and if it hadn't been for that good woman from Siracusa he would have died of shame." He laid his hand on Amalia's once more and left it there, heavy.

"The queen made a pact with the French—betraying her husband, the English, the Sicilian people, and her own murdered sister. But this time her scheming was foiled. Lord Bentinck, the English commander in Sicily and a capable man, had her shut up in the Convent of Santa Margherita Belice, all alone and abandoned by everyone. Then he sent her off to exile in her own country, where she died of shame.

"What do you think of all this, Amalia? The woman from Siracusa was a great comfort to the king, and they loved each other. The king married her and made her the Duchess of Floridia."

"Why didn't he make her queen?" she asked.

"Because kings must marry the daughters of princes, and only they can become queens. If they marry other women, the wife doesn't become queen, but she's still a wife." He gripped her hand firmly, gazing at her intensely. "When a woman really loves a man, she becomes the queen of hearts, Amalia. Do you see what I mean?"

"Yes, don Paolo, I see what you mean." From that moment, she was his forever.

"Amalia, if falling in love is good for the king, for us poor folk it's more than good." Don Paolo drew her hand farther up. She could barely feel it through the layers of cloth, breeches, and underpants, but she felt it. "And then, when the king went back to Naples, he took his duchess and lots of other people from Siracusa and they lived happily ever after."

Some of the maids had come into the ironing room, humming a tune, and Amalia went back to her mending.

It's a great thing to fall in love, thought Amalia, and even better to remember it, but it's getting chilly. And she went back inside the cave to do her chores.

38

"The Lord preserve us from evil neighbours and from the rebellion of mild-mannered men."

The mysterious illness of Caterina Safamita
Guglielmo Safamita is presented at Safamita House, and Caterina dies.

During the summer of 1873, Domenico Safamita and his wife had endless arguments about their elder son. In the end, exhausted and brokenhearted, Caterina Safamita accepted and shared her husband's decision: Stefano was to be excluded from the family.

They explained to Giacomo and Costanza that their brother had disobeyed their father and betrayed the family. Stefano's vicissitudes and foolishness had added an extra dash of spice to already savoury gossip, they said, and from now on people would seek them out, asking questions and setting traps to learn more, the better to speak ill of them. It was the Safamitas' duty to bear this humiliation stoically: they had to entrench themselves in proud silence and give no one any satisfaction.

Giacomo, thirteen, was anything but unhappy about the misfortune that had befallen Stefano. Suddenly there lay before him a future that until then had seemed impossible: he would become the heir and master. The envy of an earlier day was replaced by bitterness over the shame his brother had brought upon the family name.

Costanza understood and sympathised. Mindful of Pepi Tignuso's words, she wasn't surprised by her parents' decision, but she missed Stefano, and she suffered for him.

Right from childhood, Caterina Safamita's life had been marked by great, heartrending losses. An only child isolated from her peers, she had suffered terribly over her mother's long illness and death. In their grief, father and daughter had leaned on each other, but tragically that affection had degenerated. The wet nurse who had stood in for her mother had died soon after.

Caterina had avoided becoming fond of individuals, animals, places, and things, and she closed herself up in a world that she thought was immune to affection but where emotions were filtered through music and her indiscriminate but avid reading. She shunned love because she felt unworthy, and she was sure that she would suffer from it and would lose the object of her love. On the other hand, she had hankerings and was precociously sensual. Her uncle had rescued her from this dilemma, and she finally married him. She loved her husband and Stefano, her favourite child, and was loved by them in turn. Had Caterina not met with immense difficulties in giving the Safamitas two male heirs, difficulties that other women would have found insurmountable, she might have described her adult life as satisfying and even happy. But things turned out differently. Gloomy memories of the past never left her, and she disliked her younger children—both Costanza the unwanted daughter and Giacomo the son who was wanted but was so unlike Stefano.

The loss of Stefano left her desperately unhappy. Mother and daughter took consolation, each on her own account, in music. Never had the piano been played so much in Safamita House, and the people of Sarentini would stop to listen, open-mouthed. The notes of the baroness's music would emerge from the main-floor balconies to be hesitantly picked up by Costanza on the floor above. But it was not always like that. Costanza would also sing love songs with great feeling, thinking of Stefano and the blacksmith's daughter, convinced that her brother's love story was a marvellous thing for which he had sacrificed his duty to the family.

Caterina changed: she was hard on her children, severe and haughty with the staff. Madame decided, amid general relief, to go back to Vienna and live with her granddaughter. She was old and drank a lot. Costanza had never liked her much, although recently she had been looking after her.

When Caterina found out the next spring that Filomena was pregnant again—from whom she learned this no one knew, but in some way she heard about everything—she plunged into a deep depression. She seemed to get weaker and complained frequently of abdominal pains. Scandalmongers said that the more the blacksmith's daughter's belly grew, the more the baroness wasted away.

Costanza saw that her mother was suffering and felt sorry for her. She put up with her moods and her coldness, commiserating with her in the knowledge that Caterina depended on her to keep up the slender thread that still bound her to Stefano. They sent presents for the baby girl through Rosa Vinciguerra and redoubled their trips to la Crocca. The baroness followed Filomena's pregnancy in her thoughts, and was convinced that the baby would be a boy. Irrationally, she hoped that in some way her husband and son would become reconciled.

In that period Baron Safamita received a visit from Prefect Calloni and other worthies, including Senator Baldo Bentivoglio. The two men shared a specific goal: to persuade the baron to accept nomination as a senator of the realm.

Caterina—a woman with no love for society life who was normally unwilling to leave Sarentini and, like the rest of the family, supported the clerical Bourbon Party—was enthusiastic about this, and she encouraged her husband to accept: fate had sent them a sign. She convinced herself that the Safamitas would move to Rome, Stefano and his family included, and there they would live in harmony, far from the Carcarozzos. Domenico promised her that he would think it over.

In the end, he told her that he was old and had no desire to take part in the political life of the Kingdom of Piedmont. His announcement had a devastating effect on Caterina; it marked the end of her hopes of a reconciliation with her favourite son. Her health rapidly declined: her stomach swelled as if she, too, were pregnant, and she complained of ailments similar to those of pregnancy. Pina Pissuta examined her and was left stunned; she had felt a lump in the baroness's insides, but it wasn't a child: it was a hard, deadly growth. At that point, Caterina Safamita refused to let a doctor examine her and declared that the malaise was due to the onset of menopause.

Guglielmo Safamita was born in September 1874. On the day of his baptism Baroness Safamita was in bed, indisposed; Costanza sat at her bedside, embroidering. The atmosphere in Safamita House was one of anxious waiting, a slight tension that could not be ascribed to anything in particular but whose cause was known to all. Rumour had it that Father Puma had agreed to return to Sarentini to baptise the newborn baby.

Annuzza la Cirara and Maria Teccapiglia were walking up the main street, arm in arm. Maria's hand emerged from her long, voluminous shawl to slip under Annuzza's so that she could lean slightly on her arm. Their gait—slow, small steps, an imperceptible swaying—was in unison, as if they had been born attached to each other: a mythical creature with two heads and a single body swathed from head to foot in black vestments. On the first Thursday of every month, Annuzza and Maria made this sortie from Safamita House to the Church of the Addolorata to attend the Mass for Saint Lucy, which was packed with old folk afflicted by all kinds of eye ailments. They were accustomed to passing almost unobserved on the street.

Maria spotted something partly furtive and partly curious in the looks of people in the street, something that put her on her guard. The passersby kept on eyeing the old women. They were in front of the little shrine with the Christ crowned with thorns, and they crossed themselves. Maria put off taking Annuzza's arm again; she adjusted the pin that held her shawl under her chin and looked down the road. In the distance she saw a young man in the middle of the street carrying a white bundle in his arms. She strained her eyes. It was Stefano.

She slipped her hand beneath Annuzza's shawl and grasped her wrist firmly. "Hurry up! I must speak with the baron," she whispered, and she piloted Annuzza to the top of the steps, a shortcut to Safamita House. The two women slipped away rapidly down the stone steps without breaking their rhythm.

Stefano reached the main door of Safamita House alone, his sleeping son in his arms, under the gaze of the local people who had followed him at a distance, prolonging their strolls under one pretext or another. Behind every shutter burned the gaze of the women of Sarentini, fascinated and moved by this tall, dignified young man bringing his first son to his father—breaking the rules of conduct among men and begging for the Safamitas to forgive him. An impalpable collective well-wishing enveloped him and had an amazing effect on the gatekeepers and guards of the mansion house: they got to their feet and with a "Good day, Your Excellency" let him pass, disobeying the baron's orders.

Stefano made his way through the vestibule crowded with servants and went straight for the main stairs. They, too, moved aside, whispering *"Voscenza benadica"* and even "Congratulations!" The door opened as soon as Stefano set foot on the landing. Gaspare Quagliata closed it behind him noiselessly. Domenico Safamita was in the entrance hall.

"Father, sir, I have brought you your grandson, Guglielmo Safamita."

"Go away," said the baron in a clear voice. "This is not my grandson, and you are not my son."

The household staff watched Stefano walk away like an automaton, his head held high. Not a nod, not a greeting. Stefano no longer existed.

He retraced his steps back down the street, lengthening his stride as he went, holding his little baby close, a spent look in his eyes. Mules and donkeys moved aside without waiting for a tug on the bridle; young and old alike hastened to make way for him, flattening themselves against the walls of the houses.

At the end of the street he took the lane that led to Agli Angeli. He kept up his resolute pace and stopped only when he reached the blacksmith's hovel, where the others were waiting for him. "Here," he said to his wife, and he handed her the baby. He went into the shack and headed straight for the opposite wall, as if he wanted to walk through it; he grasped two brackets set in the wall and there he stayed, his head hanging down like a flagellant on Good Friday.

In Sarentini they said the baroness had a terrible haemorrhage that very night and continued to bleed for seven days; she knew of Stefano's visit to the mansion house, but she did not speak of it to a living soul. There followed a succession of visits from doctors, relatives, and midwives. Caterina Safamita never left her bed again, and it looked as if she wanted to die. Her children were unable to cheer her up, but with her husband she seemed to find a certain tranquillity. They held each other's hands and they looked into each other's eyes, but she did not smile even for him. On the seventh day, she died in his arms.

Thereafter, the memory of Caterina Safamita was consecrated: a sainted woman, a faultless wife and mother who erred only in loving her son too much and in obeying her husband, if that could ever be considered a sin. The gossip about her indifference to Costanza was out-and-out calumny: she was a deeply loving mother even to that redhead, so much so that her daughter adored her.

As for the baron, the people of Sarentini said only that he was a Safamita and had behaved like a Safamita, putting the pride of his house before his own blood. In making this observation, they glossed over the fact that each of them, had he found himself in a similar situation, would have behaved just as the baron did or worse. Only the Lord could judge whether he was truly guilty of the baroness's death. In their view there was no doubt about the divine verdict.

39

"You don't speak ill of the dead."

The funeral of Baroness Caterina Safamita

Donna Assunta offered to see to the funeral arrangements. She carried out this assignment to perfection, overlooking nothing: from the preparation of the floral wreaths to the decorations in the church, from the choice of music to the direction of the cortège. For a long time, no one knew that Donna Assunta had for years been planning for her own death and beyond; in fact, she cherished a secret ambition to become the first woman of the Safamita line to be beatified. With modesty and caution, she encouraged her house nuns, the mothers superior, the house priests, and other influential personages to consider her worthy of this recognition on the part of the Holy Mother Church, offering them the specifics necessary for the beatification proceedings. She had planned her own funeral—she wanted it to be as splendid as a wedding—down to the tiniest detail.

She paid a great deal of money in advance to the abbesses of the few surviving convents and to the nuns scattered throughout the community so that they would take part in her planned funeral procession. And now she called them in for her niece's funeral. That morning she said to Peppinella, "It's like a dress rehearsal for my own funeral. You must see to mine. Now I'm going to have to carry on giving alms to that lot; otherwise they'll forget all that I have given and when I die they'll stay put. I know nuns well. They do nothing for nothing. I ought to think myself lucky if they have the goodness to say an Ave Maria for my soul."

There was a huge crowd. Relatives, friends, dignitaries—even the prefect—and all Sarentini: hired hands, field overseers, guards, household staff; in other words, an entire populace. Two very long rows of nuns and orphans preceded and flanked the hearse. The people wondered where on earth the Safamitas had mustered so many nuns—they had almost disappeared after the convents were closed—and in such a short time, not to mention the enormous number of orphans. The funeral cortège was so long that the procession was already at the cemetery gates while people were still flocking to join it back at the church.

Pina Pissuta got there late. During the preceding week, she had been involved in much coming and going at Safamita House. She had told the baron straight off, "There's no hope," and the doctors had confirmed this. They had done all they could to keep the baroness from suffering. She did not want anyone to touch her and suffered with dignity. Composed and dry-eyed, Costanza was present at—but took no part in—the dressing of the corpse. Pina and the other women of the household saw to this down to the slightest detail. Costanza did not even want to put the chain with the crucifix around her mother's neck, nor did she kiss her; she was a strange one, that redhaired girl.

Pina listened vaguely to the murmurings of the people.

"She didn't deserve to die so young!"

"They *were* uncle and niece, of course, but they were happy."

"Have you noticed the baron? He's heartbroken."

"If I had to say one word for the dear departed, I'd say 'saint.'"

"Who's going to look after those two children, now that their mother is no more?"

"She had nothing but love for her children."

"A perfect mother."

A single voice said, "She died on account of Stefano. That son of hers broke her heart."

She had courage and stubbornness aplenty, Pina Pissuta was thinking, and as many miscarried babies as a fairground whore. She didn't make a fuss when I had to lay hands on her; plenty of other women would have made a terrific scene. Not even Pina, who had always been Caterina's midwife, could remember the exact tally. Any other wife would have told her husband, "Leave me alone, that's enough." Then I began to understand: the Lord didn't want to grant them the spurt of life that gives a soul to the children they conceive. He just didn't want to, and I told the pair of them, "These are pregnancies destined to go sour on you. You're unlucky, but it happens. After you have one miscarriage, all the other pregnancies end up the same way." But the baroness would not resign herself; she wanted to give her husband sons, to carry on the family name. In the end, whether God willed it or not, she managed. The Safamitas are a stubborn lot, and nothing will stop them from getting what they want.

Pina lined up behind the others and adapted her pace to the slow swaying of the funeral cortège.

40

"He who has money finds relatives."

An unexpected and unwelcome mourning visit
Gaspare Quagliata, an impeccable serving man, falls from grace.

On the afternoon of the day of the funeral, Safamita House was invaded by visitors who came to offer their condolences.

People talked in low voices about the usual things: the details of the death, complaints about the doctors, praise for the deceased, the past, present, and future grief of the relatives. No one dared to mention what weighed heavily on everyone's mind: the absence of Stefano Safamita.

Gaspare Quagliata, the baron's valet for decades, was highly respected and loved by the household staff; a perfect gentleman, almost a copy of his master. But that day he fell short of his own high standards.

Don Filippo Leccasarda came rushing into the green drawing room, where the next of kin were sitting, and whispered something to Count Trasi. The count's expression changed and he got up, beckoning at Donna Assunta to follow him. In silence, they went to the vestibule and looked into the entrance hall through the internal window. It was thronged with families, servants, and the people come to pay their condolences, all of whom moved slowly aside, casting long inquisitive looks at three strangers as they stepped down from a coach.

Assunta Safamita went up to her brother for a rapid exchange of whispers, and the baron, ashen-faced, returned to the clutches of the mourning visitors; then, with an imperceptible gesture, he summoned his three sisters. They had a few words and dispersed. The three newcomers went up the stairs, followed by curious glances.

In the green salon, those offering their condolences moved slowly from one relative to the next. The three new arrivals stood against the wall. No one made a move to welcome them; it was as if they didn't exist. Gaspare was moving around the room keeping an eye on both guests and masters, ready to hasten to the baron at his first gesture. The youngest of the three visitors stopped him and demanded, "Take me to Baron Safamita."

"It took me just one look to work out who it was," Gaspare said to don Paolo Mercurio afterwards. "The spitting image of the late Baron Guglielmo, his uncle. It was really hard for me to disobey someone with Safamita blood in his veins and the spitting image of the late baron into the bargain, but orders are orders. In short, I didn't know what to do." And, indeed, Gaspare was dumbfounded. Knees trembling and legs like jelly, he backed off, retreating until he bumped into the couch that the notary Tuttolomondo had only just vacated. He plonked right into the seat still warm from the notary's bottom, and found himself wedged, thigh to thigh and elbow to elbow, between Mrs. Teodora Tuttolomondo and her daughter Miss Clotilde, both of whom were speechless at the sight of this liveried servant plunging down next to them. Clotilde wordlessly gave a resolute tug at her petticoat, trapped under Gaspare's legs. He remained motionless, wide-eyed.

Dismayed, the two women looked at Gaspare furtively; to affect composure, they struck an even more pronounced expression of grief, their eyes wandering over the people coming into or leaving the green salon. Gaspare was sweating copiously. And the two women began to sweat, too. Embarrassed. No one dared move for fear of breaking up the unusual formation and upsetting the precarious equilibrium that had been created among them.

This was how the notary Tuttolomondo found them: motionless, shining, and clammy like wax dummies, Gaspare's hands on his knees, those of the women resting in their laps, clutching their closed fans. The notary saw only that perverse contact between bodies, and he demanded brusquely that he have his seat back. In vain. Then he made the two women get up and follow him into another salon. All hot and bothered, they went along behind him.

The unknown young man indignantly retraced his steps and only then saw Costanza, who stood out among the other mourners thanks to the red hair glinting beneath her black veil.

The three left without greeting a living soul, just as they had come.

41

"As you make your bed, so must you lie on it."

Protests are made over Donna Teresa Safamita's dowry.
A son weeps for his mother's death.

Maria Teccapiglia prepared a camomile tea. Gaspare, still agitated, was sipping it. "The one who spoke to you must be the son of Baroness Teresa, Baron Stefano's third daughter," Maria was saying to the footmen standing in a circle around her and Gaspare. "She had a harelip, did Teresa, and she was no beauty. They married her off to a bourgeois, Mariano Lo Vallo, who called himself baron after that. I remember that Baron Guglielmo wasn't happy about it, but Teresa's mother really wanted the marriage, because the Lo Vallo family were relatives of hers.

"They agreed on the dowry: exactly the same as those of the other daughters. After the wedding, the Lo Vallo family sent word to say that the mules had brought them less money than they expected: some ducats were missing. But the money was right no matter how often they counted it. Baron Stefano was fuming, but no one got to hear about that. The reason I know is that my father-in-law, don Vito Tignuso, told me the story.

"He and the guards had gone with the mules from the castle to the Lo Vallo place, which wasn't even a real mansion. Baron Stefano calls for Vito and he asks, 'Tell me, Vito, who could have got near the mules carrying the gold?' Vito answers, 'No one, I swear to your lordship on my mother's soul. I slept on top of the bags, and had a bad night, too. The others took turns standing guard, and there wasn't a trace of bandits.'

"When Baron Stefano died, Lo Vallo expected another inheritance. With his father-in-law still nice and warm in his coffin, Teresa's husband said this to Baron Guglielmo, in front of Count Trasi and Baron Scravaglio: 'Now you must give me the rest of the money. I took her ugly because you promised me a bigger dowry than the others.' Baron Guglielmo answered, 'I know nothing about that. We counted the dowry over and over at the time, and you didn't say a word. This is what I have to say to you: my sister is a Safamita and she made you rich by taking you as a husband. That should be enough for you.' So Lo Vallo turns to his brothers-in-law and says they should give him a part of their wives' dowries because they are good-looking and healthy. Well, it was pandemonium, and you could hear them as far away as the stables they were all yelling so loud.

"Then the baron says to his sister, 'Teresa, tell the truth: did our late father promise you a bigger dowry?' She says, 'My husband is right.' So the baron says, 'You have no children, or I'd ask you to swear by them. Swear to this on your father's soul.' Teresa refused and repeated that she was due more money. Then the baron got angry. 'You married a bad man,' he says. 'Come back home, where you'll be a mistress and respected. You can keep Assunta company.' 'I'm not leaving my husband,' says she. 'If that's the way it is,' the baron says to her, 'get out of here and forget you have two brothers and four sisters.' After that they had no truck with each other. Funerals, weddings, baptisms—they went by as if the two of them didn't know each other. Why now? I say that they've frittered away their mother's dowry and now they're left without a bean. They're hoping for another Safamita dowry, and so they've set their sights on Costanza."

Late that evening, in the stables, don Paolo and Gaspare were putting the horses' funeral trappings back in a trunk. The stable lads were sleeping in the alcoves next to the trough.

"You could do with a smoke," said Gaspare, handing the coachman a half-smoked cigar.

"That I could. There are some pretty bad times in store for us." Don Paolo sat down on a stool and lit the cigar. He drew in the smoke with rapt pleasure, using his feet to brush away the straw and wood shavings on the flagstones. "You don't play with fire. All we need is a fire to round off the day."

"Don't go bringing the evil eye upon us," said Gaspare. "Things in the big house will get sorted out."

"A lame horse can't pull the cart. The house of Safamita will never be the way it used to be, ever again."

"You're wrong. The baron is conscientious. He knows perfectly well what his wife died of. He should call for his son and make peace."

"How is he supposed to know, if not even the doctors know?"

"The heart, the baroness's heart was broken. Over Stefano," said Gaspare with unaccustomed heat. Don Paolo flicked the ash into the runnel in the flagstones that drained away the horses' urine and did not reply. "Just between you and me, it was the baron's fault," muttered Gaspare, running the back of his hand over moist eyes, surprised by his own lack of respect.

"Gaspare," said don Paolo curtly, looking his old friend straight in the eye, "no one can know what really happened between the baron and the baroness. But we two know them better than anyone. He's a good man, and he did a great deal for the family. The baroness, God rest her soul, went from girl to woman too soon. And so a girl she stayed, you see what I mean? She was a good person, and she behaved badly only with Costanza. A very complicated business, that was."

Gaspare didn't reply; he was watching the moths. "Did he have to ask that pig Father Puma to baptise his son?" He sighed all of a sudden. "Did he know nothing about what he did to Costanza?"

"I never had any love for Father Puma, but you have to admit he was the only one prepared to help Stefano," said don Paolo. "He did his duty, and I must respect him for that."

"I don't even want to think about these things. Stefano has his blacksmith's daughter now, and she'll have to help him."

"That blacksmith's daughter! She has brought nothing but misfortune upon us! I have liked women ever since I suckled at my mother's breast, but Paolo Mercurio keeps them in their place. Women they are and women they have to stay. As a young man, the baron knew how to treat them!"

Gaspare made a face. "You know what I say? Every time I pass by the chapel in the castle I thank the Lord for making me what I am, and for the fact that I don't have these problems."

"Right you are, Gaspare, there are times when I'd like to be in your shoes! But even as an old man I still like women too much, so let's content ourselves with the way we are."

One of those big moths with black wings that come out at dusk and fly only at night had drawn closer to the little shell-shaped candleholder built into the brickwork high up on the wall. Attracted by the yellowish light, it circled around it, closer and closer, until the flame licked at its wings. In its death throes, the moth flitted about beating its sizzling wings, the shadows on the wall turning them into gigantic fluttering drapes. Then came a crackle, a pungent odour, smoke. The flame flickered. A flash. And all was as it had been before. The snoring of the stable lads filled the stalls.

"Gaspare, did you know that the baron wanted to lay an olive branch on the baroness's body? Early in the morning he said to me, 'Paolo, get me one as quick as you can and leave it in my room.' So, while you were all at the funeral, I went off to la Crocca at a gallop to take a branch from the tree where the baroness used to hide with Costanza to watch the terrace of Camusa."

"Why la Crocca? Aren't there enough olive trees round here?"

"Gaspare, you haven't a clue how lovers' minds work! He wanted a branch from that tree in order to tell the baroness that he had forgiven her for disobeying him!" Don Paolo was bothered, then he shook his head and sighed. "I went to where the baroness used to hide to watch la Camusa. I stayed there a long time on account of what I saw. On the way back I had to stick my spurs into my mare, the poor thing was foaming. La Camusa was locked up, all the windows shuttered. In mourning, you see? I heard a kind of gasping in the distance, like a dog that had fallen into a ravine and hurt itself. It was grieving, unbearable grieving. Then, silence. I grabbed the binoculars. There was a man chopping wood, under the sun, like a soul damned in hell—cutting so much wood it looked as if he had to cook pasta for an army. Then he stopped. As I was getting pistachios, the wailing began again. I looked through the binoculars again. It was Stefano, standing with the axe in his hands resting straight on the ground in front of him like a sword. He was looking at the sun and his face was so wet that it shone. His mouth was open. And from it there came this harsh sound, very loud, in a monotone, which those who have never heard it can't understand. The wailing of a son for his mother."

The flame of the lamp began to flicker, the shell-shaped stone being almost empty.

42

"We are many rivers from the same water."

The draft dodger's song
Costanza Safamita and her nurse refuse to comply
with the oppressive mourning imposed by the baron after his wife's death.

Amalia and Pinuzza were eating bread and cheese. It was a warm evening and the sound of a Jew's harp could be heard, then a voice singing a wagoner's love song. The mournful refrain drifted upwards, modulated and tenuous. Rapt, Amalia listened to it, a hint of a smile on her lips. It was beautiful music, the first she had heard on the Montagnazza.

"Why's that fellow singing?" asked Pinuzza.

"Because he's lonely, and thinking of his sweetheart. He's young. He was at work in his village when the call-up came, and now he's in hiding."

"And where is she?"

"In the village, perhaps."

"If she can't hear him, why is he singing?"

"He's singing for the sake of it, that's all. Costanza used to do that after her mother died. She used to send me to make sure that no one could hear her, and then she would sing and sing."

"Why did she sing in secret?"

"Her father didn't allow singing."

"Why?"

"You ask a lot of questions, Pinuzza. Why this? Why that? They were in mourning for her mother, and the baron didn't want music in the house. Be quiet and enjoy this song."

The young man was singing melancholy songs of resignation. But sometimes the singing would take a different turn and become intense, full of the desire for love, for company.

The sky was red over the enamel-blue water. The draft dodger's solitary song was just like Costanza's after her mother died, thought Amalia. The baron had taken his wife's death badly. His guilt weighed upon him: Caterina hadn't been able to live without Stefano. Mother love is the strongest, far stronger than wifely love; the baron had thought it was the other way round, and he had been wrong.

He ordered mourning so strict that even Donna Assunta found it excessive. But he was the master, and had to be obeyed. The house was rearranged in the proper mode: black bunting over the chandeliers, mirrors, and pictures; windows and main doors half shut. They had to roll up the coloured carpets, cover the gilt furniture, candelabras, and lamps; even the pianos were shrouded.

But this was still not enough for the baron. The shutters were kept closed for the three months of deep mourning; the maids opened them only to clean the balconies. The household staff had to speak in low voices, and the women mopped the floors without being able to murmur so much as an Ave Maria. And that was the way it had to be everywhere, even in the stables.

The baron even wanted mourning cuisine, which was unheard of until then: insipid dishes, eaten in silence. The new head cook almost wished he could return to Palermo. The baron barely picked at his food. He would bitterly cut off the few words that Giacomo let slip at table; as for Costanza, she hardly ate and grew visibly thin.

Not even after the first month of mourning, when condolence calls stop and people go back to normal life, did the baron want to change. Anything beyond silence and immobility disturbed him. It was as if he had decided to die. He would stay holed up in the drawing room, in the half-light, alone or with Costanza, wordless. He would not go out of the mansion house and forbade his children to do so. At home they had to whisper and move as if their legs were tied together. All in black, Costanza was a shadow of herself. Giacomo fretted; he wanted to go out, take a ride on his horse, but his father said no. And so it went for three months: out-and-out hell.

Amalia could see Costanza before her eyes, decked out in her mourning jewellery, thin as a sprat. Like her father, she, too, had lost the desire to live. It was evening and Amalia was helping her undress. In a corner of the room stood the harp, covered by a black cloth. Costanza ran her finger over the strings mechanically, and it was like when rose water is poured drop by drop over marzipan and the aroma suddenly fills the kitchen.

"No, your ladyship, you mustn't . . ." she blurted out.

Costanza looked at her and said, "Quick, go downstairs and see if my father is asleep."

Amalia went downstairs: Gaspare had fallen asleep in the armchair in the antechamber, and she could hear the baron snoring. Costanza plucked at the strings and they responded sweet as honey, with clear, liquid chords echoing out. Costanza's face relaxed; she seemed reborn. She let her hands fall into her lap and hummed a song as melodious as a lullaby. From then on Costanza started playing music again, hidden, at nights, in disobedience to her father.

Giacomo didn't obey his orders, either. He would sneak into the stables and, swallowing his Safamita pride, would have fun with the stable lads—play that degenerated, according to don Paolo, into indecency. As time went by, he set eyes on a scullery maid and consoled himself with her.

The song was over. Amalia and Pinuzza went back into the cave.

"So you helped Costanza disobey her father?"

Amalia was tidying the straw mattress. "What are you saying?"

"I'm talking about when she sang in secret."

"Pinuzza, at times you have to do things like that without feeling guilty."

"When?"

"When enough is enough, and that happens now and then. Now let's get ready for bed."

43

"Every house has its problems."

Domenico's sisters expected, after the three months of deep mourning was over, that he would take his children to Palermo to make suitable matches for them. While as a young man he had been popular in the salons, he had adapted himself to his wife's intractable personality, yet he had needed to socialise and so, until the business of Stefano and the blacksmith's daughter had raised its head, he had always been keen to go to Palermo every year. But as a widower he sank into boundless melancholy and, like Guglielmo, didn't want to leave Sarentini. He continued to look after himself and after the administration of his estate, but as for everything else he was like a living corpse. He spent entire afternoons in the drawing room where Caterina had once played for him. In his hands he would hold an open book, one of those they had read aloud together. Costanza sat in her mother's armchair, her embroidery lying forgotten in her lap. And she, too, would fall into a hornet's nest of thoughts.

Her mother had dozed off, and Costanza was embroidering at the foot of her bed. "You have been a good daughter. I am sorry for not having loved you as you deserve," whispered Caterina. Costanza looked up from her embroidery frame, but her mother seemed to have fallen asleep again. Those words gave her no peace. Why had her mother been unable to love her? She didn't have the courage to talk about this with her father and could find no explanation but that it was her fault, that she was too different, and she couldn't understand why. She was disgusted by her freckled skin, her red hair, her entire body. Revolting. Costanza felt that she was all wrong, born to make people unhappy. Layer upon layer, like sheets of blotting paper, the monotony of the days was steeped in that misery. But Costanza bore up.

Life in Safamita House changed for everybody. After the first year of mourning the baron entertained, out of duty, various dignitaries and especially Prefect Calloni. In the summer he would go to his country houses and struggle to put up with visiting relatives, an obligation he could not avoid. There, too, the master's arrivals were like travelling bereavements. He started to read again, voraciously, so much so that his sight grew weak. He reorganised the family assets to ensure that Stefano would get nothing from his mother's estate.

Costanza became his regular companion. Her sole concern was to satisfy her father's requirements, and little by little she came to adopt her mother's ways and habits. She played the piano, and her father would sit in the armchair to listen. When he spoke, either his talk was a monologue, in which case Costanza simply kept a vigilant presence with him, or it took the form of considerations on life and reminiscences about times past, in which case she was all ears, as though her attentive interest might help him rouse himself. In the ensuing silences, Costanza would give herself over to those visions, to a timid curiosity about and desire for life, only to feel immediately ashamed of this. She went back to her embroidery and withdrew into her shell.

Her cousins no longer took her mind off things. She had deliberately forgotten her thoughts of love, convinced that her mother's death was a consequence of Stefano's passion for Filomena. Aunt Assunta was right: love caused pain and suffering, nothing else. Costanza did not speak or think about the future, and she began to look like a precocious spinster: she took no interest in her dress, and she was aging prematurely. Her women worried about this, but they were the only ones who did.

Giacomo took refuge in the stables, sure that his father would disapprove, but he couldn't help himself. Domenico and Costanza did not notice his restlessness and excluded him from their intimacy. As time went by, he befriended a group of young men—wealthy bourgeois, minor aristocrats—with whom he rode, fenced, and philandered—leading the moderately dissipated life of the sons of moneyed provincials.

No one in the family mentioned Stefano. But Costanza went on sending presents to his children. Her brother's financial situation had worsened after the collapse of the coral business in Sciacca, and she even dared to slip some gold coins in with the gifts for her nephew and niece. They were not returned to her, and she sent more.

44

"He who would judge must listen to both parties."

Two unusual events at the castle
take the father's and daughter's minds off their bereavement.

Father and daughter were on the terrace at Malivinnitti. "You're seventeen," said Domenico. "You must get to know what will belong to you, and you must know how to manage it. You and Giacomo will have everything." Costanza looked at him. "You must learn how to deal with our people, how to invest money; you must learn the ways of this world we must struggle in—society, politics."

"You teach me, Papa," she said, and went back to her sewing.

During that holiday, Domenico Safamita started to ask her more and more often to read him letters and documents, as well as the newspapers that arrived once or twice a week.

Costanza obeyed. And it was a burden for her. It struck her as an intrusion on her father's private life, and her difficulties were compounded by the fact that she had trouble in deciphering the handwriting. One day her father handed her a letter from Ireland, written in French, from a woman. "I don't know who she might be. Read it," he said. The woman was demanding, on behalf of a nephew—in peremptory tones and in poor French—an answer to letters the nephew had sent to Baron Guglielmo that had been ignored. She wanted to know if the baroness had given birth to a boy or a girl. The manager of the Corbotta, she wrote, had promised to tell her. Puzzled, Costanza looked at her father. "That idiot Guglielmo!" he said. "Let's move on to another one."

The second letter was a simple thank-you note from Countess Orsolina Acere. "That's enough," said her father. "Let's have a little water." Then he continued: "Costanza, don't get the idea that husbands have to be faithful. Not even your husband will be. He will always respect his wife, but he will have affairs with loose women, or others. The main thing is that he keep them outside the family." Costanza looked at him in alarm: he had never before talked to her about marriage, and after her mother's death she thought the matter was considered closed. "Orsolina Acere is a great lady and was my friend for years. Her mother-in-law had a long affair with my father. Treat her with respect. She will always help

167

you." From then on, her father would occasionally indulge in reminiscences of this kind, talking of distant loves and the joys of the bachelor life. He never mentioned his wife.

Costanza was eighteen. It was the third year after her mother's death: the beginning of half-mourning.

The baron had kept on the entire staff of Castle Sarentini, a score of people in all, even though the only one still living there was his sister, who, at seventy years of age, was still in excellent health. Donna Assunta Safamita was held up as an example of the well-deserved longevity granted women of sound and pious religious convictions. He simply thought of her as what she was: a stubborn and ambitious old maid who refused to move into her brother's home.

Donna Assunta had become even more devout after Caterina's death. She passed the time with her house nuns, with monks, friars, and preachers—some of dubious repute—who, after the closure of their monasteries, roamed around in search of a role and sustenance. In secret, she continued to make the necessary preparations for her beatification.

The least of her worries was the garden, but it rained heavily in October and the vegetation grew so thick that it blocked the entrance to the underground passage leading to the fountain. It was decided to remove the mud and to clean and dry the passage in order to avoid flooding. The fountain was very large; in the centre of the basin there stood a statue of Diana, from which a tall jet of water had once issued. The mechanism that activated this jet had long been faulty. To make it work, you needed a man who stayed underground—bent double—to turn the handle manually. But that had been in their father's day. For decades, the fountain had served as a mere basin.

The gardeners, their breeches rolled up above the knee, filed into the dark passageway, bent over to keep from banging their heads. Their expedition was immediately transformed into a tumultuous retreat, however, for their feet were being bitten by unknown creatures, perhaps the spirits of the damned. They asked the priest to take a hand. A rumour spread that the souls of exorcised spirits had taken refuge in that very spot. All Sarentini talked of this.

The problem grew out of all proportion, and Donna Assunta was reluctantly obliged to appeal to her brother's authority.

After lengthy negotiations, Domenico got what he wanted, which pleased him. Once the clergy had been placated, he sent his guards to finish the job. These—and the gossips had it that each of them carried two huge pistols in his belt, so fearful were they—advanced with shovels and buckets in their hands and stout boots on their feet. They worked all day long, and eventually emerged carrying buckets full of mud in which tortoises large and small floundered about. They had discovered a colony of the reptiles which, as soon they heard humans approaching, went for their feet like the hunting dogs of Etna, snapping with lightning speed at leather, patches, and human flesh. The baroness's tortoises had been cheerfully proliferating, enjoying that damp and sheltered refuge and the tender, perhaps aphrodisiac, leaves.

The person who saved them from extermination—and in Sarentini there was much discussion about how to get rid of the baleful creatures—was Costanza. She wanted to see them all, one by one, and she decided to keep them—some in the garden, some at Malivinnitti.

Another event obliged the baron to go to the castle and see to other people's business. Maintenance workers had to repair the chapel roof and plaster its exterior, which was crumbling on account of poor ventilation and the damp; the last mass had been held there before Stefano was born. It was discovered that the chapel, apparently well locked up and chained, had been the site of clandestine incursions the traces of which were manifest. In Sarentini, people were quick to identify these as evidence that black masses had been held there. There were scraps of food, forks, even a tin of Revalenza Arabica: everything suggested that the evildoers were members of the household staff.

The mystery deepened when it became known that it was Donna Assunta, and not the majordomo, who held the keys of the chapel. Don Calogero Giordano was the only one who knew where she kept them; he swore that he had once given them to the late baroness before Stefano's birth, and that they were then returned to him immediately. The servants talked of nothing else, but they couldn't find a single suspect among the staff past or present. It was Lina Munnizza who came up with the only plausible suggestion.

In the kitchens it was rumoured that someone had told the baroness about the extremely high number of concentrated parsley potions that Lina periodically swallowed on account of her "devotion" to the head cook. Shortly before her death, Baroness Caterina Safamita had obtained a full confession from the cook and she had fired him, breaking Lina's heart. The informer had been Celestina Vita, but Lina was convinced that the nurse Amalia was the one at fault. In Safamita House everyone knew—but did not say—that Amalia was having an affair on the quiet with don Paolo Mercurio. Very well liked by the staff and even protected by the masters, she had only to ask the young Baroness Costanza and she got whatever she wanted. She was fairly wallowing in intrigues! Heaven knows how many potions *she* had had to swallow, she with a reputation as an honest woman! It must have been Amalia who had been in the chapel. And she had to pay.

When Lina Munnizza learned that the things found in the chapel included an empty tin of Revalenza Arabica, she had the proof she needed to expose Amalia, who—it was known—had asked the young baroness for tins of the powder, which she would then happily sip, dissolved in hot water, like an English milady. Lina went to make confession with Father Inguaggiato, Donna Assunta's confessor, who went straight to Castle Sarentini.

For the second time, Donna Assunta had to appeal to her younger brother. Below stairs, it was whispered that the discussion between the two had been heated: the young baron wanted to protect Amalia. They said that Donna Assunta was very irritated and got so angry with Amalia that she had to go and take confession—she who by then was famous for being virtually incapable of committing so much as a venial sin. But Amalia's reputation in Sarentini went unscathed, and the nurse and the coachman remained in service. In fact, it seemed to Lina that now they took less trouble to conceal their doings, which vexed her beyond measure. She started to gossip about Amalia outside the walls of Safamita House, but this had little effect, because people knew the nurse enjoyed the confidence of the young baroness and it was wiser to say nothing. Lina began to feel uncomfortable in Safamita House, and she decided to go to live with her sister in a nearby village, where she died soon afterwards.

PART TWO

45

"Love hurts, but it warms the heart."

Frightened by the winds on the Montagnazza, Amalia Cuffaro
relives her love affair with don Paolo Mercurio.

In Sicily, the long, burning summer drought is followed by a brief, rainy winter. The rains are a source of collective relief and rejoicing: the heavier the rain, the better. But for the people of the Montagnazza this pelting rain presaged hardships to come, for the Montagnazza became inaccessible when it was swept by the wind and made slippery by the rain; it was transformed into a prison—wet, cold, and cruel. Amalia had taken care to conserve from the feast of All Souls' Day pieces of biscuit, fragments of the sugar babies, a half-full jug of water, candle stubs, matches—all in view of the coming rains. Pinuzza had never known hunger, real hunger, the kind that clutches your guts and gives you hallucinations; her brothers were the last to surrender to the bad weather and the first to defy wind and hail to bring them food and kindling.

It was pouring, and raindrops hammered at the smeared marl. Holed up in the caves, the people awaited the worst moment: when the rain suddenly stopped, driven off by the wind. Then the wind would rage against the rock, penetrating every fissure with sibilant whistles, shattering the shutters of the little windows, throwing doors wide open, swirling on the floors, sucking up everything it found lying about, and leaving a trail of seaweed, gravel, feathers, droppings, leaves, branches, and even dead birds.

Amalia peered out through the slit that served as a window for her cave. The sea was bleak and foamy. The sky was a battlefield where nimbus clouds and winds were duelling; like a sheepdog setting sheep to flight and then herding them together, the wind swept the rain-swollen clouds first to one corner and then to another, piling them one on top of the other, docile sheep with gravid bellies. Amalia had never seen such a riotous country dance in the impotent sky.

She feared she might die, for the cave door looked as if it might give way any moment, even though she had shored it up with what few belongings she had, jugs and pots included. They would be isolated for a long time, with not even a crust of bread. She felt a great longing to nibble at a loaf fresh from the oven. Bread is life, she thought, and I of all people have to die wishing for it—I, with a baker for a son!

It was thanks to the wickedness of Lina Munnizza that Giovannino had gone off to be a baker in America and his mother was now doomed to die of hunger. The baron had sent workers to rebuild the roof of the chapel in the castle. Lina Munnizza, whom Amalia had always respected and for whom she had never had a bad word, had it in for her, and she didn't know why. But so busily had Lina's tongue wagged that the story of Amalia's affair with don Paolo had eventually come to the ears of Amalia's mother-in-law, donna Titta Cuffaro. Donna Titta came to Safamita House and, without even giving Amalia a chance to explain herself, told her that she should consider herself lucky: Diego was a good man and wouldn't kill her as she deserved. But the Cuffaros were leaving Sarentini, never to return. Giovannino would find work in Palermo, and then he would go even farther away, where no one could remind him that his father was a cuckold. She would not see her son again. They had Giovannino's good at heart, but they could still punish her. Shortly afterwards, Amalia's in-laws sold the wine shop; Giovannino, now nineteen, was put to work in a bakery in Palermo, and later he was one of the first to seek his fortune in America.

In Sarentini the gossip mill got under way: what need was there to emigrate for that! The Cuffaros had already made a fortune in Sicily. Someone had given them plenty of money to keep them quiet and to keep poor Diego from doing his duty, which was to kill his unfaithful wife along with her lover. Instead, the Cuffaros bought themselves a little house and lived without fear of going hungry. It was said that when Giovannino left on the steamship for New York he took along enough clothes to fill a whole trunk. Exaggerating as usual, the people of Sarentini maintained that he got even luckier: as soon as he arrived in America, he opened a bakery with the best bread in New York and people came specially from the other side of town to line up to buy his loaves.

No one knew who had paid off the Cuffaros or why. It couldn't have been the Safamitas, that was for sure: it had been amply proven in the past that they wouldn't cough up money even when they were at fault, and it was inconceivable that the amours of a wet nurse and a coachman might interest them. Who else was there? In the end, people reluctantly decided they'd never get to the bottom of it. Someone very rich held the secret and wanted to keep it that way. Better for everyone to lay off; you never know what might happen in life.

Only Amalia continued to wonder about this. She had lost her son for a second time. They hadn't seen each other as much as they would have liked, mother and son, trying to humour the wicked grandmother, who was always at home to serve him. But they did see each other—and they loved each other. Amalia did not confide in or give satisfaction to anyone, but she was sick at heart. Not even don Paolo could comfort her—and to think he was such a special person, her only love.

It happened in the vestry. After he had told Amalia the story of King Ferdinand and the Duchess of Floridia, don Paolo seemed to avoid her. He would say that he had gone to the castle to get a breath of fresh air, or that he felt like an oldster. People told her that he could be seen in the vicinity of the main church, sometimes in the company of Father Puma. She thought he was getting ready to die, and this greatly distressed her. She got to the point where, forgetting her duties, doing her mending reluctantly, even neglecting Costanza, she yearned to see him alone.

One afternoon, don Paolo took the little girl to Castle Sarentini in the young baron's coach along with Amalia and Maddalena Lisca. As he was helping Amalia down from the carriage, he made a whispered rendezvous with her in the garden, when Costanza would be taking milk and biscuits with Donna Assunta. Flustered, Amalia agreed.

They met at the assigned spot, where he gestured at her to follow him in silence. They avoided the paths and instead pushed their way through luxuriantly overgrown flower beds. Amalia was uneasy. Don Paolo led the way, lifting up shrubbery branches or folding them beneath his feet to make way for her. With the aid of his stick, he calmly broke the blackberry canes and went on gesturing at her to follow him. She followed along behind him.

They emerged in front of the chapel. Don Paolo took a big key from his pocket and slotted it into the lock. They entered hastily, looking behind them: there were no curious eyes around. The chapel was dark. There was no odour of incense typical of places of worship; the marble bowl of the stoup was dry. There was a little door behind the altar which don Paolo opened with another, smaller key. In the damp half-light of the vestry, under the stern gaze of the painted saints on the walls, overwhelmed by the dusty holiness of that abandoned place, Amalia could not and would not deny herself to don Paolo, and they loved each other passionately on the ottoman put there by Donna Assunta for the repose of the priests.

Afterwards, Amalia asked him how the sacrilegious idea of using this place had come into his head. Don Paolo replied that a man like himself, with many years of experience, knew a thing or two and Safamita House held no secrets from him. She could trust him: it was the best place.

But Amalia was overcome by religious scruples, and she felt like a sinner. She knew that she had committed a mortal sin of which she would cleanse herself by taking confession. Her confusion arose because don Paolo had described the love story between the king and the Duchess of Floridia, before their marriage, as something chaste and almost sublime. She tried to talk to him about this alone, but he didn't give her the time for it.

One day, as they were watching Costanza chasing her hoop on the ironing-room terrace, she decided to bring it up. "I'm sorry if I sound like a goose, but you must explain something to me. If the queen was still in Palermo and the king was going with the duchess, then they did this in secret, without letting others know about it, right?"

"Of course. Appearances are important."

"So if one of the king's children or a nobleman had found them out, it would have been a scandal? And if the duchess was in love with the king, that made her a woman of easy virtue in the eyes of the queen and the princes, didn't it? And what did the nobles who knew about it think of the duchess?" She reeled off all the questions that had been running round her head.

Don Paolo thought them over, and then he said, "Amalia, there's something important I have to explain to you. In this world there is a law for us poor folk and a law for the rich, and there's another law for the king. We have our God and they have theirs, even though it's always the same Jesus Christ. If the king falls in love with a woman he ennobles her, her husband, and their children, too, and so everyone is happy. It's the same thing for the rich—like Mr. Benjamin Ingham, the Englishman who was the richest of all, and who brought the Duchess of Santa Rosalia, no less, into his home in Palermo even though she was six years older than he. But she was beautiful and an aristocrat.

"You won't believe it, but the Duchess of Santa Rosalia's children were happy—Count Vasciterre told the young baron this in the coach— because Ingham paid their debts every time their mother made cow eyes at him. The nobles vied with one another to invite the couple to their mansions, because he was rich. If he'd been a poor man, he'd have wound up getting killed."

"And her husband?"

"I don't know about him, but judging from the fact that no one talked about him, if he wasn't really dead he might as well have been as far as the others were concerned. A cuckold's horns are a cuckold's horns, but kings, nobles, and the rich have special, handsome, gilded horns, and everybody likes them, even those who wear them. But the horns that poor devils like us have to wear look twisted and they stink, like the horns of a toad, and they must be hidden and denied. Do you know that people die for this?"

Amalia didn't dare mention that she'd confessed to Father Puma. But don Paolo had probably thought of this, because he added, "For me, you are better than the Duchess of Floridia, don Paolo Mercurio's word of honour. But let's make this our secret, even in the confessional. Otherwise they'll kill us."

Amalia was afraid: either donna Titta or her father-in-law was capable of killing her at the drop of a hat.

"Do you know what the nobles used to say about the Duchess of Floridia?" don Paolo asked her. "They held her up as an example of all virtue and beauty. Even if the king's sweetheart is not beautiful, they say that those who look like her are beautiful." He pinched her thigh. "If she has a long, scrawny neck, they say that long, scrawny necks are beautiful; if she has crooked buck teeth like a rabbit, they say that such teeth are beautiful; if she has red hair like the young baroness, they say that women must be redheads to be beautiful."

"What's Costanza got to do with it?" protested Amalia.

"Oh, she's got to do with it all right! To us she seems beautiful because we love her, although she looks ugly to others. But she's rich, is our baroness, and so she becomes beautiful, as beautiful as can be with all the property she owns. But let's get back to us: if people hear that you and I are sweetening our poor lives without harming anyone or causing a scandal, we'll be driven out of the house and made to die of hunger." He took her chin in his hands and whispered, "My beauty, give me a quick kiss while Costanza can't see us. Don't let's think anymore of these sad things, or I'll start wanting to become a socialist!"

Amalia decided there was no longer any need to make confession. She had no reason to regret following don Paolo's advice or embracing his ideas, and she remained grateful and devoted to him for the happiness he gave her.

"Poor Pinuzza, who must die without savouring the love of a man," Amalia said to herself, sighing. She was no longer afraid of the storm.

46

"He who thinks only of himself will never be loved."

Gaspare Quagliata speaks with the master.
Costanza Safamita returns to Mozart,
and her father decides that she is ready for marriage.

Gaspare brought the baron his morning coffee and prepared the shaving things for the barber. He was ill at ease as he bustled about.

"Begging your pardon, my lord, but I have something to say."

"What is it, Gaspare?" The baron was impatient.

"I don't know if don Filippo has spoken to your lordship, but sometimes not even the majordomo knows what's going on in the house."

"Tell me."

"It concerns young Baron Giacomo. He is a boy, but certain things must be done the right way. There is a handsome kitchen maid he likes a lot, and for some time now. A few days ago, a pretty young washerwoman arrived, and he likes her, too. These two girls got each other by the hair, and it ended in a catfight. People are gossiping a lot below stairs, and I wanted to tell your lordship."

"What else are the servants saying?"

"Lina Munnizza is telling everyone that don Paolo Mercurio and the young baroness's nurse are meeting in the castle vestry. I don't like them talking too much about the vestry."

"Is this tale true?" asked the baron. Reference to the vestry put him on his guard.

"Your lordship knows Paolo Mercurio—he had a girl in every village when he was young. For some time now in Sarentini he has contented himself with Amalia Cuffaro, who is a good woman."

"What's her husband like?"

"A blockhead, like his father. The mother-in-law is a crafty bit of work, and they're up to their necks in debt."

"Off you go, Gaspare. I don't need anything more for the time being."

A terrible ill humour weighed heavily on the baron. The number of people he could trust was fast shrinking. Don Filippo Leccasarda, his majordomo for thirty years, was keeping him in the dark about everything. If Gaspare hadn't spoken up, he would not have known about this. Costanza must not lose her nurse. He summoned the notary Tuttolomondo, and they worked out what to do with the Cuffaro family. Then he talked to his majordomo. He told him he had come to know about Giacomo's escapades from other people and this displeased him—not so much the incidents themselves, for such things can happen with young people, but because don Filippo had obviously been unaware of them or he would have informed him immediately, as he had always done in the past, and done well. The baron asked about don Filippo's health, inquiring discreetly if he was worried about anything, and he made no mention of the rest of his conversation with Gaspare. Then he had Giacomo called in, and he reproved his son in the presence of don Filippo: he was the master, and the master he would remain until his dying breath.

The baron was exhausted. His memories tormented him, but above all he was afflicted with a painful feeling of insecurity. After dinner he asked Costanza to play him the beautiful duet from *The Marriage of Figaro*, "Se a caso madama." She went to fetch her mother's well-worn score, which

Mademoiselle Besser had transcribed in her own hand for Caterina on her forced leavetaking from Safamita House, and hesitantly tackled the piece. Her father closed his eyes and saw the opera again as he had seen it on the stage: sparkling, lively, irreverent, profound, with a bitter undertone—sublime.

Annie Besser had taught him to appreciate Mozart when they were young, when, after poor Maria Stella's death, Orsolina Acere had advised Guglielmo to employ her as Caterina's governess. Annie was an original, unconventional character. The illegitimate daughter of a baron killed during the Egyptian campaign, Annie had grown up in Alexandria. She spoke English and French, and worked as a governess for the fanatically pro-English Sicilian aristocracy, which greatly appreciated her and vied for her services. But Mademoiselle Besser had not forgotten her origins, and in the Piscitelli household she had been rather indiscreet, causing a scandal. There was so much gossip about the husband and the governess that Princess Piscitelli wanted her out of Palermo, and so, in due time, Annie Besser was exiled to Sarentini. An excellent governess, she taught Caterina about style and culture. She had been the one to suggest to Domenico that they meet in the vestry. She told him she could love only one man in each house and the castle was reserved for his brother. When they realised that Paolo was spying on them from his perch on the mulberry tree, she laughed about it: "I was expecting it, it's the ideal place for a voyeur. I find it *très excitant*." After Domenico and Caterina married, Caterina confessed to him that she, too, had climbed the mulberry tree to spy on them. It had been her precocious introduction to the *ars amatoria*.

Although Costanza was so different from her mother, she reminded the baron of his late wife at that moment. She took out another score from *The Marriage of Figaro* and ran through it, concentrating. This time she was going to sing—she often sang for her father—her voice blossoming in the smooth, sensual aria, ever more flowing, animated and impassioned, as if she were rediscovering and celebrating her youth. *Porgi, amor, qualche ristoro*. Costanza sang oblivious to everything, her long neck arching, then flexing, supple and free, her face serene, a bloom in her cheeks: she was a woman ready to burst into life and love. Domenico suddenly saw that he had compelled her to live the life of a recluse, crushed by duty and oppressed by the selfish widower father he had become. He had treated her like a person without desires or sexuality, transferring his own state of mind and all the weariness of his sixty-nine years onto her. Costanza—a "child of love," as Father Sedita had called her—hid from herself and from others the deeply passionate nature she had inherited from her mother. Costanza's clear and modulated voice soared up: she was all there, in Mozart's music. It was up to him to give her the chance to discover and enjoy love.

That evening, after dinner, he asked her, "Costanza, have you thought about getting married?"

She blushed. "I thought that was a dead letter, Papa. I'm fine as I am, I like living with you in Sarentini. I'd rather not." She remained silent and sad for the whole evening.

In the days that followed, Domenico Safamita noticed that his daughter was rather preoccupied; she jumped when he spoke to her, and she seemed constantly worried. He had spoken on impulse, but now he resolved not to raise the subject again and simply to observe her; it wouldn't be easy to persuade her to come out of her shell. But as soon as she touched the keys of the piano, that plea for "comfort" that Costanza was unconsciously making to love echoed over and over in the rooms of Safamita House and in her father's heart.

47

"A bird in the hand is worth two in the bush."

*Costanza Safamita meets her brother Stefano and
decides that there is no need for her to marry.*

Costanza knew that her father, like her, did not talk without thinking, and she understood his desire to set her up with a husband. At heart it was every girl's dream, and at one time she, too, had desired it—but no more. She was tired of the emotional excesses—and the family conflict she had witnessed at first hand—that were caused by love, and the subject all but disgusted her. Society life unnerved her, and the idea of living far away from her father, from Sarentini, and from her own staff struck her as intolerable. Conversely, she liked her life divided among running the house, sewing, conversations with her father, her dearly beloved music, and looking after the castle gardens. Her devotion to her father fulfilled her; in the future she would enjoy Giacomo's children. Why disrupt this hard-won serenity? Costanza had been convinced that she was unsuited for marriage, and now her father had put her in a state of anxious uncertainty.

To these problems was added, a few weeks later, serious concern over little Caterina's health. Stefano was living in poverty. Costanza had offered to pay for his family's medical expenses, but he said that he would not accept money from the Safamitas unless they recognised his right to his mother's inheritance, which—not incorrectly—he maintained had been stolen from him, thanks to his father's scheming in favour of his other children. Costanza was distressed by this, and her eyes were often red.

"Amalia, what is worrying my daughter these days?" Baron Safamita asked the nurse.

"Your lordship mustn't ask me that," said she, agitated.

"Tell me, Amalia, it's an order."

Amalia burst into tears.

"Control yourself and speak."

"It's on account of your son's baby daughter!"

"Get to the point!" The baron was losing patience.

Between sobs and sighs, the nurse told him the story.

"How is your brother's daughter?" The baron's voice was hoarse.

"Unwell. I'm very concerned."

"I know, your nurse told me."

"Papa, did I do wrong to offer him help?"

Her father thought this over, then said, "No. I would expect it of you, and of your mother, too, if she were alive. And I would say to her what I say to you now: act according to your conscience, but let no one know about it."

Costanza went on embroidering. Once she had threaded her needle again, she looked up. "Stefano is not the man he was, they say. I must help his children, but I have to tread softly. I'm sure Caterina has some ailment, but I suspect the Carcarozzos are exaggerating. They need money. To be sure that there is a real emergency, we'd have to send a trusted doctor to examine her. I would feel better that way. What do you say?"

"There's no turning back, Costanza. He and his children are no longer part of the family, but that doesn't mean you cannot help a sick person. One does this for strangers, but as strangers. I trust your judgement. You have obeyed my orders, which I know has been upsetting for you, but it is necessary for the Safamitas of Sarentini, and you know why. Send the doctor and have the girl taken to Palermo. If you and Stefano find yourselves in town together, I shan't keep you from seeing the little girl, but I'd rather not know about it if you meet her parents. If you decide to do so, and for the future, I want payments to be made through the notary Tuttolomondo, with the most absolute discretion. Keep up your correspondence with your brother as if nothing had changed. And when you receive news keep it to yourself."

"Thank you, Papa." Costanza rose to kiss his hand.

"We'll be going to Palermo next month for Giovanna Trasi's wedding," he continued brusquely. "We could go earlier, if you like." And here he paused. "You know that when you are married you will be able to do as you wish with regard to your brother?"

"I know, and I have thought about it. I prefer to stay in Safamita House. I would like to follow Aunt Assunta's example—a life as a house nun would please me. Must I really marry? If you order me to do so, I shall obey."

Caterina Safamita grew healthy and strong. During her convalescence in Palermo, Costanza saw her and got to know her other nephews and nieces. She did not meet Stefano, out of respect for her father, but she saw her sister-in-law again. Filomena had changed—her once radiant beauty was marred by worry—but she spoke to Costanza in a dignified, practical way. She told her that Villa la Camusa had almost no furniture, silverware, or household goods, since everything had been sold to keep the family. Filomena, who was after all illiterate, wanted to have her children educated in proper schools, but Stefano, hounded by creditors, had taken to drink and refused to send the children to the schools for the poor, where they would have studied alongside the children of the Safamitas' workers.

Costanza was torn between two worlds, and she felt that she belonged to neither of them. In Palermo, her relatives were busy with wedding preparations; they talked of nothing but jewels, clothes, presents, the trousseau, parties, and invitations, as if they were matters of the greatest importance. The Trasis spent money and went into debt in order to look good. Costanza's affection for her aunt and uncle and their children led her to slip into what became an act, feigning the good humour of the old days and joining discussions about topics that she found vacuous, while her heart ached for Stefano's family. She could not stop thinking about their wretched situation.

In addition, she suspected that her father had let the family know of his intention to marry her off and that her cousins were trying to persuade her to follow Giovanna's example. Her placid life plunged into disorder and insecurity. Only one thing was certain: she was and would remain rich, and at times this, too, felt like an unbearable burden.

Costanza decided that she had to meet with Stefano, whom she hadn't seen since before their mother's death, and persuade him to accept her offer to help at least with his children. Her father agreed. Stefano chose to have the rendezvous in a café on the seafront, where they used to go as youngsters, and at an hour when it was empty, or at least when the aristocrats wouldn't be there. She slept at Countess Orsolina Acere's house the night before, so that her movements wouldn't arouse the suspicions of the Safamitas' household staff; the plan was for the countess to take her to the Marina and pick her up again in the coach.

"What's happened to you? Are you ill?" Stefano was very upset by his sister's appearance: rail-thin, pale, and still dressed in half-mourning.

"No, I'm fine. And you?"

Stefano avoided questions and did not admit defeats. Costanza looked him over, and was captivated. At twenty-seven, he was a mature man. He had only a few small wrinkles at his temples, and his eyes, which had lost the laughing look that had so bewitched her, had taken on depth and charm.

They didn't have much time, and Stefano needed to talk about his mother at length. He also asked for news of Giacomo, of the old retainers, and of their relatives; he still considered himself heir to the Safamita line and behaved as such, not neglecting to play the role of the big brother. He told her about his new plans for making money, for investments, for exploiting advantageous opportunities—he had lost touch with reality.

When she finally got a word in, Costanza had forgotten the little speech she had prepared. "After Papa, you are my nearest and dearest," she began. "I have promised to take care of your children as if I were their grandmother. I have money—actually, you're entitled to some of it. But you refused my offers until Caterina fell ill. I understand pride, but not when it makes children suffer. Then it is egotism and folly. Yet you sent word to me that you didn't want charity. I'm not free to give you what you are entitled to—I cannot. Our father will not allow it, and I must obey him. But he has allowed me to use my income to help the children, to keep them in school so that they grow up healthy and well educated, worthy of their father and the name they bear. Will you allow me to do this?"

Stefano was listening to her, but absently. Costanza went on: "If you want me to transfer directly to you what is morally as much yours as mine, I have no option but to marry, which will give me freedom of action. But I don't want a husband; I'm fine at home, and I hope to avoid this. If you refuse, I'll take whatever husband I find. But I don't want any repetitions of what happened to Caterina: the doctor in Palermo saved her. Your children are innocents who must be protected. Filomena would be happy about this. I haven't forgotten what you said of her when I first saw her—'She is my life.' Be kind to your life, and to those you have created together."

Stefano took her hand resting on the marble table and squeezed it. "Very well, Costanza, and I promise you I shall do the same for you and your children." They spent their last minutes together recalling their strolls along the seafront—and simply smiling at each other.

In the coach Countess Acere commented, "You looked like two lovers, hand in hand in a café, eyes wet, oblivious to what was going on around you. Is he your favourite brother?"

"Stefano was our mother's favourite son. For me he was all you could wish for in a brother," Costanza replied, then bit her lip for having said too much. She looked at the flat, infinite sea glittering in the morning sunlight. The Marina was beginning to fill up with strolling passersby. She straightened up against the back of the seat, relieved. There was no longer a need to take a husband; what little life offered her would suffice.

48

"Marry young or marry never."

Costanza Safamita reluctantly looks for a husband in Palermo.

In February 1880, an unhappy Costanza, still not twenty-one, went to Palermo with a heavy heart. She had a specific task: to find a husband.

The previous year, her father had taken her with him to Naples—her first long trip. "You've never been to the theatre," he said to her. They were performing *Lucia di Lammermoor*. "Donizetti composed it in this very place," her father reminded her, "almost fifty years ago. Please wear the dress your aunt Maria Anna bought for you."

The conductor raised his baton and music filled the theatre. Costanza was all ears, her gaze fixed on the red velvet curtain, very high and opulent with its gold braid and embroidery. A slight tremor made the folds of the curtain sway. Costanza waited with bated breath. When the curtain rose, a forest was revealed of a kind she would never have imagined: the flats on either side of the stage were trees with tall, mighty trunks and luxuriant foliage in various shades of dark green, shading off in perspective and guiding Costanza's gaze towards the backdrop—the forest of Ravenswood. The light, at first faint, increased steadily, and the chorus—lined up between the flats and in front of the immense backdrop, camouflaged in costumes the same colour as the tree trunks—gradually became visible, their faces pale as fireflies in the moonlight. The sounds from the orchestra pit rose up and blended with the voices of the singers onstage. Costanza leaned forwards and stayed at the edge of her seat, ecstatic: it was another world, the world of the marvellous.

During the interval they mixed with the other theatregoers in the foyer, though neither of them was interested in observing the elegant opulence of the ladies or the giltwork and stuccoes of the theatre itself. Costanza slipped through the crowd on her father's arm. Her bearing was completely new to him: shoulders back and head high, a sparkle in her eyes, cheeks pink, full lips half open in a smile—she reminded him of Caterina at the same age. She was attractive, for the peacock blue of her evening dress and her auburn hair enhanced her milky complexion, and she received curious, admiring glances. But she didn't notice this; she had the stage in her mind's eye, and she was humming the music. Her father realised that men were looking at him, too, and he was irritated: they obviously didn't think she was his daughter. Costanza was entranced, inebriated by the music and wholly wrapped up in the story of Lucia di Lammermoor. The eternal war between Edgardo and Enrico, Lucia's anguish, Enrico's duty. *Verranno a te sull'aure i miei sospiri ardenti*—she repeated the theme of the last duet to herself, sotto voce.

"Would you like something to drink?" her father asked her.

"No, no, I'm fine." Costanza returned to reality, unwillingly.

"Do you like it?"

"Yes, very much," she murmured, distant once more.

"It's a really sad love story."

"But it is very beautiful, Papa. I was happy."

Every so often her father would point out something to her and receive no reply. Costanza heard him, but she wasn't listening; she saw, but she didn't look.

During the second interval, her father did not try to sustain even the semblance of a conversation. They strolled in silence: two unknowns in the crowd. Domenico Safamita had a strange, uneasy feeling. *Appressati Lucia.* What if the marriage he wanted for his daughter did not bring her happiness? *Per poco tra le tenebre sparì la vostra stella.* He had crushed her with his grief. *Io la farò risorgere più fulgida, più bella.* He was seized by the furious, visceral jealousy of a man who would possess his daughter. He glowered at her. Costanza, with a dreamy look in her eyes, was swaying her head to some inner music. Caterina had also sung silently to herself at the opera.

"Costanza, how do you imagine a sweetheart?" he asked her abruptly.

"*Comme toi, mon papa*," she murmured. "I'd like to marry a man like you."

He felt the colour rushing to his face. He reeled, then reverted to the appropriate indolent stroll, but he was crushing his spectacles in his fist. Costanza sensed that something was wrong, but she didn't know what it was and didn't worry about it; all she wanted was for the third act to start. Impatiently, she squeezed her father's arm to quicken their pace, her shoulder and bosom brushing lightly against him. "Easy does it, Caterina, it's only the first call," he said. Costanza didn't hear him. "*Per te d'immenso giubilo tutto s'avviva intorno,"* sang the chorus, and she was with them at the reception to welcome Arturo.

Baron Safamita took Costanza to the opera a second time, on her express request, but he decided to go back to Sicily earlier than planned.

In Sarentini, the household was in an uproar. Maria Teccapiglia did not mince her words when she quickly brought Costanza up to date: Giacomo had behaved very badly during his father's absence, lording it over everyone as if Safamita House were in his charge. Some of the maids had even left service, the guards were restless, and the workers in the administrative office were unhappy. She added, looking right at Costanza, that Filomena's father had disappeared. Costanza realised that the Tignusos surely had a hand in this last piece of news. "He got what he deserved," said Maria, "but your ladyship didn't tell me that you were paying for the children's school . . . I don't care what the others think—I say you did well."

Her father had to take up the reins again. Domenico did not like his younger son, yet Giacomo was the only one who would pass on the Safamita name. The baron would have to pacify and discipline as necessary. Giacomo was a problem: a shrewd countryman, but of limited intelligence. And the Safamita traits he displayed were the ones least suited to modern times: he was a small-town Casanova who upset the maids. Also, since he shunned the company of people from Palermo, he would not make a good marriage. The right woman for him would come from among the dubious minor local aristocrats who annoyed the Safamitas so much. On the other hand, a daughter-in-law of this kind would bow to the wishes and tastes of her husband, thus ensuring domestic stability, and so it was necessary to find her quickly. But first Costanza had to be married off.

Domenico knew that Giacomo harboured an aversion towards him—and that he was surely in part responsible for this; he was also certain that Giacomo felt the same aversion for his sister, and that after their father was gone this would become overt. Giacomo was not likely to treat Costanza with the deference the Safamita brothers had shown Assunta, nor would he oblige his wife to do so. Instead of being the mistress, Costanza would be a guest, an awkward presence tolerated in expectation of her inheritance. Submissive as she was, Costanza would suffer in silence.

Costanza would have to marry an aristocrat and live in Palermo—going to the theatre, travelling, meeting her peers. It was good that the nobility of Palermo was going through a period of revival then, showing a greater sense of improved education and civic responsibility.

Her father talked to her about marriage in straightforward terms: "You are rich and you will be the mistress. I want an arranged marriage for you, one that will suit you, so that you will be as happy as I was with your mother." So that she might choose, he would take her to Palermo to meet some young noblemen. He was very clear: this had to take place soon, because he wanted to die certain that she was settled. Costanza, to whom the verb "choose" sounded obscure and menacing, had to obey and so she agreed.

Word was sent out that the Baroness Safamita, provided with a substantial dowry, was ready to wed. The Trasi relatives were in charge of introducing her to Palermo society. They decided that first of all they would have to refurbish her wardrobe and make her prettier. Costanza went shopping with her cousins and resigned herself to endless fittings for clothes, hats, and shoes. Since she was painfully thin, the dressmakers padded her bodices and thought up other ploys to make her more fetching. Nothing strange about that: from veils to gloves, from shades of colour to the least accessory, the show of femininity—the very show from which she had gradually withdrawn—was in play. Dutifully, Costanza put on the new clothes that were chosen for her, but she missed her simple mourning clothes.

In the salons of Palermo, which she began to frequent, she was introduced to possible good matches—and to their mothers. She found these occasions horribly humiliating. There were evenings when she would fall asleep weeping and dream of snails coming out from under the floor by night to climb up the legs of the bed, slipping between the sheets and enveloping her in a cocoon to take her back to Sarentini. The next day would bring another stroll along the Marina and the endless, inexorable round of social calls: she was at once goods and client. At such moments, one particular memory of her trip to Naples would insistently come to mind.

She had gone with her father to a racehorse auction. The horses were groomed to perfection, so that their handsome musculature stood out. Each animal had a groom standing on its left who controlled it with the bit. Under the critical gaze of the purchasers, they had to go round a little platform at a brisk trot, with their heads up, while the strident voice of the auctioneer extolled their qualities. The best were sold off after only a few turns, but others were condemned to the carousel for much longer, until they were sold or suffered the ignominy of being withdrawn. These horses, dazed and disoriented by the shouting and continuously running round in circles, often tried to rear up, foaming at the mouth and lowering their heads, only to yield to the grip of the sharp bit. Then, defeated, they resumed the proud bearing the occasion required, but their eyes were full of resentment.

Costanza compared herself to these unfortunate beasts. "Straighten up!" squawked her cousins. "Don't make that mournful face!" "Smile every now and then!" "Eyes up, eyes up!" She did try, but shyness inevitably got the better of her and she would make her entrance into the salons with lowered head and bowed shoulders, like those poor horses left on the carousel. As they mingled with the guests, her cousins would give her nods to indicate the chosen young men and their families. An intuitive observer, Costanza realised when she was under scrutiny and understood why those horses had tried to resist. She lowered her eyes, but it was as if she could hear her auctioneers inveigling the families: "The holdings of Mezzeterre, Zirretta, Malivinnitti, Canziati, more than five and a half thousand acres of farmland in the Madonie, cash in the bank, all her mother's jewels, and more still . . ." Costanza wished she could be reduced to a little pile of ashes.

She was afraid—indeed she was almost certain—that she was unattractive and that, consequently, all encounters and conversations were doomed to fail.

49

"True love warms the heart better than any straw or blanket."

Costanza Safamita chances to meet the Marchese Pietro Patella di Sabbiamena and falls head over heels in love with him.

She met him by chance, in the sewing room in the house of Baroness Annina Finocchiaro di Lannificchiati, one February afternoon. She fell in love at first sight, as the saying goes. Costanza and her aunt Maria

Anna Trasi had called on the elderly baroness to do some typical woman's work: over a table placed by the window to catch the light, they were choosing from the sewing basket the colours needed to embroider a cope for the oratory of the Compagnia dei Bianchi.

The baroness had been living in straitened circumstances since her husband's death. The warmth given off by the brazier was insufficient. The room was affected by the damp cold that spreads through old houses in winter, when the walls seem to have gone mad, inexorably releasing the dampness they have absorbed, stone by stone, over centuries of neglect—a dampness that the suffocating summer heat never manages to dry out—instead of protecting those who live inside them. The baroness held a portable heater in her lap and, like Countess Trasi, her shoulders were covered by a voluminous double-crocheted shawl. Costanza had wrapped herself in a wide scarf of very fine wool, dark blue with a coppery pattern.

They were engrossed in choosing suitable colours from the profusion of little skeins and did not hear a gentle knocking at the door. Without waiting for permission, the footman opened it abruptly, standing aside to give way to the new arrival. Flattened against the door, he announced, "The Marchese Sabbiamena."

To Costanza, it seemed that as he entered the room the young man suddenly swept away the stuffy air and the acrid odour of the glowing coals. He was very handsome, with a dark complexion, elegant and relaxed. She felt her heart leap, and she blushed. With the bearing of one who is certain of a warm welcome, the newcomer slowed his pace and bent over to kiss his aunt the baroness on the hand and cheek; his lips barely brushed the hand of Countess Trasi, and then, before bowing to Costanza, he hesitated for a moment, aware that he had made a good impression and giving his aunt time to introduce the unknown young lady: "Dear Costanza, allow me to introduce my nephew Pietro Patella, the marchese of Sabbiamena."

After a rapid "Pleased to make your acquaintance, Donna Costanza," Pietro spoke to the baroness: "Dear aunt, I beg your pardon for interrupting an afternoon of work. I came to remind you that I always think of you and haven't forgotten you." Jovially and slightly ironically, he added, "You're choosing embroidery thread . . . what work is in store for these dainty little fingers?" Then he cheerfully joined the women. Sitting between the baroness and Costanza, he handled the skeins with the expert competence of a woman, commented on the various shades like a connoisseur, and went on chatting with his aunt, touching her arms and hands with affectionate and respectful familiarity, as if he wanted to caress them. She fairly lit up with pleasure.

"I apologise to you all again for this interruption," he said as he got to his feet. "But this week my aunt had been all alone without my usual little visit, so I came to set that right. Yesterday my mare gave birth to an exceptional colt—I feel like a proud father—and it will be a splendid horse. Now I must get back to the stables, and so I'll leave you to your work." As he said goodbye to Costanza he bent down and lifted up one end of her scarf, then stroked it at length, running his outstretched hand back and forth in the most sensual way. "A magnificent scarf," he murmured before hurrying off as quickly as he had come, leaving Costanza dazzled. His playful respect for his aunt, his exquisite taste in the choice of colours, his love of animals, the veiled reference to the joys of paternity, and then that reawakening of the senses conveyed by the scarf—everything told her that she had found the man she was destined to love.

The two other women didn't notice Costanza's agitation, for she was silent as usual, and they began chatting again about this and that. And in the coach Costanza didn't have the courage to speak of her feelings. Her aunt merely observed that Pietro Patella di Sabbiamena always behaved like that: he was unreliable and made only the briefest of calls at inconvenient times, yet the baroness, his only maternal aunt, had been a mother to him after his own mother had died very young. It was clear that she did not approve of the marchese.

Costanza saw him again at the Marina promenade, where, with her aunt or a married cousin, as is the custom for young ladies in search of a husband, she would take the customary drive in the glossy blue-black Safamita coach, with the Safamita arms polished to a brilliant shine. He was on foot, with some other men. He would doff his hat in greeting and follow her with his eyes. One day Costanza thought she recognised a respectfully tender look. She burned with love like a bonfire on the feast of the Assumption.

50

"If the thunder lingers, the rain must fall."

*Costanza Safamita is stubbornly determined to marry Pietro Patella di Sabbiamena
and no one else.
A forced engagement, but not too much so*

Costanza did not tell her cousins about meeting Pietro Sabbiamena. But she thought of nothing else and desired him with all her being. All she had to do was see him from a distance and she was thrown into turmoil. She wanted to know more about her beloved and managed to find out something with a question, posed casually but mulled over at length, that she put to Stefano Trasi, an easygoing fellow and her favourite cousin: "But if Baroness Lannificchiati is a distant relative of yours, aren't you related to the Patella family, too?"

"No, we're not related. Poor Pietro—since he was born he has known only trouble: his father's death, then his mother's, and debts, debts, debts. I'm surprised that he never complains, but he's always in a good humour." These words reinforced Costanza's determined desire for him: she would give him the affection and the financial resources he lacked.

She went out willingly in the hope of meeting him, and together with this hope came memories of her first holiday at Gazzola, when she was eleven. The Safamitas had inaugurated their new country house there, and the Limunas were their guests.

Late one September afternoon, the vacationers went in the gig to watch the treading of the grapes. The mournful singing of the grape treaders could be heard from a distance. The air was still, and it was oppressively hot; the barn stank of the acrid odour of must and the rancid smell of grape dregs piled in a corner and covered with swarms of flies and wasps.

The women gathered beneath a mulberry tree to watch, while the men lined up next to the large wine troughs. Costanza stood beside her father. Three peasants were stripping the leaves and stalks from bunches of grapes, preparing them for the next stage, where they were put into the troughs to be mashed. Their breeches rolled up, the treaders crushed the grapes. Some were crooning the monotonous, plaintive work song, lifting weary knees in unison; others, exhausted, followed their own slow and solitary rhythm. The troughs bubbled and foamed. Swarms of wasps buzzed above, scarcely touching the grapes but settling on the men's clothes, necks, faces, hands, and resisting all attempts to brush them off, alighting in clouds on their legs, whirling dizzily around their heads, and obscuring their vision.

The men ceaselessly trampled the grapes, filing in a regular pattern from one end of the trough to the other like metal toys strung out on a wire, their sweat-soaked shirts clinging to their shoulders and chests, covered with splashes of must like drops of blood—leg up, foot down, over and over, waving their arms and bobbing their heads to drive off the wasps, which they sometimes grabbed and crushed in their hands before throwing into the vat. Still buzzing, the wasps were mixed in with the grape pulp and became must, too. Costanza stood there watching in her cool, flowery muslin dress, with her straw hat and her open parasol, attracted by that theatre of martyrs. She felt ashamed of this.

"Let's go, Costanza. The wasps might sting you." Her father's voice shook her out of it.

On the way back home, Alfonsina Limuna whispered to her, "He looked like a Greek statue. I think you really liked that grape treader." Costanza didn't understand what her cousin—already a woman of thirteen—was talking about, and she burst into tears. Alfonsina gave her a hug and explained that, when girls grew up, they looked at men with a different eye: she, too, had liked that well-formed and muscular young man.

Costanza could not stop thinking about the grape treading. She wanted to do something to improve the treaders' working conditions, and spoke about this with Stefano.

Her brother, eighteen by then and his mind set on quite different matters, shrugged and suggested that she talk to their father, who, after all, was the master. Her father listened to her seriously, and patiently explained that there were even worse jobs, but that this was a way people could earn their bread. Life was hard for everyone in one way or another. She had to be strong and accept this. "Costanza, you must understand that those who work for us are luckier than those who have no work," he told her. "Remember this when you are your own mistress and a married woman."

The party at Gazzola went back to the barn a second time. Alfonsina immediately pointed out the young man, and Costanza stared at him. It was windy, and the wasps were clinging to the grape baskets; the men trampled and sang, their arms on each other's shoulders as if they were dancing. But the young man was treading on his own—all pulsating muscles—breeches and shirt clinging to his sweating body as if he were naked. He trampled with a controlled, urgent rhythm, sometimes energetically, sometimes languidly, thrusting his feet powerfully to the bottom of the mass of crushed grapes. Costanza didn't take her eyes off him. She liked him. He did not deign to so much as glance at her, but he knew. Protected by her veil, she continued to stare at him. She liked him.

Now it sufficed to see Pietro Sabbiamena, to follow his indolent, manly strut, to arouse a similar but stronger feeling in Costanza. She lived only to meet him again; she went out gladly and accepted all invitations, and her eye swept over the groups of men in the salons and the gentlemen on horseback on the promenade, all in hopes of seeing him again. By then she had no doubt that with him she would find happiness, and that they would do good deeds together.

Now more than ever, Costanza refused all matches proposed to her. She hoped the name of the Marchese of Sabbiamena would be suggested, but in vain.

One day, as they were out walking, she found the courage to speak to her father about it.

"Papa, I like the Marchese of Sabbiamena. Why hasn't anyone suggested his name?"

"He is not the man for you, Costanza. He has squandered what little his father left him. He is a gambler—and a loser . . . you deserve better."

"But I am rich, and you tell me that I must look after my property. I won't let it be ruined."

"I'm not sure that he would make you happy."

"Papa, he is the only one I want. If you don't like him, I won't marry him, but then permit me not to have any other husband. I'm happy at home, you know."

"I promise you, I'll think it over, and I'll let you know" was her father's reply.

Most reluctantly, Domenico Safamita decided to indulge his daughter. He had someone speak with the man of her choice, certain that he would receive a grateful and positive response. But Prince Chisicussi, the young man's uncle, who had been entrusted with the task of being the intermediary, took a long time to reply. Baron Safamita's pride was wounded; he even feared a refusal, something hitherto unthinkable. And he cursed his firstborn son yet again, the wretch whose behaviour had besmirched the Safamita name. Still, Costanza's dowry ought to be sufficient to blot out Stefano's shame. After all, the Safamitas were not the first to suffer that kind of dishonour.

Then Baroness Lannificchiati took a hand. She invited her nephew to dinner and asked him point-blank why he didn't want to marry the young Baroness Safamita, a virtuous girl with a highly respectable dowry.

"I don't like her."

"But you have only spoken to her once! You have no idea how good and obedient she is . . . a treasure. What more do you want from a wife, and rich, too! This girl will get you out of debt, she will enable you to go on having fun; you'll be rich, and so will your children. Your mother would have been happy about this."

"She's terribly thin, Aunt."

"I'll fatten her up with cakes for you, if she doesn't get plump for joy at marrying you, you silly thing!" exclaimed his aunt in exasperation. "Soon you will be strangled by debt. I have helped you as much as I can, and I'm not giving you any more until you have repaid what you owe me. But I'll keep quiet and wait while your other creditors itch to get their hands on you—they'll eat you alive!"

"I don't like her!" repeated Pietro.

"You'll like her afterwards. You have to get to know her. She plays and sings extremely well, and she speaks French like a lady from Paris. And besides, she's not exactly repugnant!"

"She is a bit to me, Aunt."

"Don't make me laugh! Actually, you must be a little attracted to her if you're always staring at her. They tell me that's what you do when you see her on the promenade. From a distance you like her. From close up, she'll be even better. You don't have to like a wife. I don't have to tell you that—a wife is not a lover. As for lovers, you can carry on having those, with all her money. I'm talking to you about a wife—the mother of your children, the woman who will make sure that your line will continue and, in this case, who will keep it for you, too. Why have you looked at her so much on the promenade? You're the one who has upset this blessed girl, and now you don't want her. One doesn't do that," said Baroness Lannificchiati, vexed.

Pietro was dumbfounded. "I was admiring her horses!"

"Then think about the horses, the coaches, and all the fine things you will be able to afford. Costanza Safamita has a fortune in land and cash. Think about it carefully; she is your salvation. It's now or never."

Pietro Sabbiamena asked for the hand of Costanza Safamita in March 1880. The wedding was to be held in June, three months later.

The betrothed couple had few opportunities to see each other, but the encounters confirmed Costanza's belief that Pietro was the man for her: his behaviour towards her was irreproachably gallant, with a dash of familiarity. The fact that he didn't even try to steal a kiss she put down to his refined manners. Every time Pietro touched Costanza's arm, kissed her hand, or stroked her hair—gestures he made almost instinctively— her love for him grew. They both loved the same opera arias; Pietro would ask her to sing and play for him, and Costanza happily obliged. She put all her feeling into those songs. He appreciated her talent and told her so. Costanza forgot about her own insecurity, became confident that her marriage would be a success, and was determined to do every-thing to win over Pietro and make him happy.

After Easter, when the Safamitas returned to Sarentini to see to the wedding arrangements, Pietro sent her prosaic letters that had nothing romantic about them. Prepared as she was to find noble explanations for any apparent shortcomings on her beloved's part, Costanza convinced herself that he was restraining himself so as to conform with her own lit-tle notes, written in her basic, limited Italian. But one anxiety increased hugely as the nuptials drew near: she feared conjugal relations and sensed that her fiancé was not physically attracted to her, and not just because of her hair. These worries were compounded by the genuine sor-row she felt at the prospect of leaving her father and Sarentini, taking with her only Amalia and her personal maid.

In Sarentini, rather than blooming anew Costanza began to pine. The baron was aware of her sadness. Although he disapproved of this marriage, he couldn't wait for it to be celebrated, hoping that conjugal life itself would cheer her up. And so he decided to speed things up: the wedding would be held in May.

51

"Nobody's perfect."

Baron Domenico Safamita commits an impure act
on the day after his beloved daughter's wedding.

Domenico Safamita stayed on to entertain his guests for only a little while before retiring for the night, leaving the newlyweds to carry on in his place. His advanced age, seventy-two, made this apparent but necessary discourtesy pardonable: he was exhausted. The marriage was not to his liking—and now more than ever. Costanza had struck him as being like a lamb led to the slaughter, pale and worn-out: she had trembled all through the ceremony, and he had worried that she might faint. This pleasure-loving husband from the big city was not for her, though nothing could shake Costanza's determination. Right up to the last minute, he had told her that she still had time to change her mind and he could tell the Sabbiamenas personally that the wedding was off. What a pleasure that would have been! It had come to his attention that Pietro had made no preparations to welcome the bride to the family home at Cacaci, where they would live for the present, given that Palazzo Sabbiamena, in Palermo, was in very poor condition and partly rented out. Reliable sources had also informed him that the groom was counting on his wife to support him. Domenico hoped Costanza would show herself to be a wise manager, able to keep her husband in check, but above all he hoped she would make a fine family. He had a secret foreboding that things would not work out that way, and now he regretted having urged her to marry. He missed his Caterina more than ever. What an ill-starred family they had reared, and what a price they had both paid!

On the following day the baron awoke at dawn. He decided to take coffee on the balcony, and there he brightened up in a way. A light mist was lifting as the air grew warmer. The hills sloping down to the sea were covered in dew. The moon was just about to set. Despite a terrible night he felt fit, and he thought of all the things he could still do: travel, see old friends again, go to the club in Palermo. The first rays of the sun caressed the hills. Much of the land he could see from the balcony was his, and a part of it would go to Costanza: his daughter and his future grandchildren would have a secure future. He thought of the newlyweds' first night. It must have been very different from his and Caterina's, which had been all fire and passion. Every man does things in his own way, he thought, but at least this Patella has a sound reputation as a stallion, and he smiled. Drawing in a deep breath of fresh air, he went back inside.

From the terrace of the mansion house, the small crowd of relatives and friends noisily bade farewell to the line of coaches leaving town on their way to Malivinnitti. The baron was in their midst, his face ashen. Maria Anna Trasi took him by the arm. "Stop making that face!" she said to her brother. "Let's take a stroll. Marrying off a daughter is a very emotional moment . . . my late husband suffered dreadfully each time."

"Did you see how worn-out Costanza looked this morning?" he asked her bluntly.

"Yes, but don't worry. It happens to all women the first time. Then she'll like it." Maria Anna chuckled, her light-coloured eyes twinkling. A flutter of her eyelashes, and she composed herself anew.

"It's not about 'first time'! She wasn't well, don't you see? She was very, very unhappy."

"You're becoming a hysteric in your old age. Don't worry about it. They're young and they'll work things out in their own way. We old ones should be worrying about our aches and pains, not about their lives." She grasped him firmly by the arm and lengthened her stride. Brother and sister moved off, she chattering away from beneath the veil of her hat and he listening reluctantly. As the baron's gait relaxed, Maria Anna Trasi allowed herself the pleasure of looking beyond the balustrade, enjoying the view across the plains.

Pina Pissuta was preparing a parsley potion for a client. She still worked hard and took pleasure in it, even though she was well on the wrong side of fifty. Her profession brought her into contact with joy and suffering, hope and disappointment. She knew Sarentini's most intimate secrets, and she was respected. She had stayed until dawn at the house of the chemist, who had had his first baby girl after three sons; he had almost hugged her for joy. Pina always had so much work, and it was always urgent, and now the job was to turn a big bunch of parsley into an effective potion for the woman who, curiously enough, lived across the road from the chemist. This lady had a large brood of children—boys and girls— and in her home they had no need of other mouths to feed. God willing, after Pina's secret visit to her, that afternoon she would take a few hours off to rest.

One of Baron Safamita's guards appeared at the door. "The lord baron sends his greetings. He has invited you to taste the sweets made for the young baroness's wedding, and he expects you this morning."

Well, there's a fine thing, thought Pina to herself, This is the first time I've been summoned to Safamita House just to eat something.

Resigned to getting no sleep that morning, she gave the parsley decoction a stir and left it to simmer, then took a ladleful of water to wash her face and hands before giving herself a quick once-over. When she had finished with her client, she would rush off to Safamita House: the baron had to be obeyed.

Domenico Safamita was waiting for her impatiently in his study. He was in a hurry; he had to join his guests at the castle, where they would take lunch in the garden. Apart from brief greetings in the street, he hadn't seen Pina Pissuta since Caterina's funeral.

"I have need of you. My daughter has me worried, and her husband even more so. Go to the kitchens, speak to everyone, listen, get them to talk. I want to know what happened last night between Costanza and that man. Understood?"

"Yes, your lordship, I'll do what I can." She, too, was of few words.

It wasn't an easy request to fulfil, though Pina stayed in the mansion house until the afternoon and managed to talk with almost all the servants. The servants were more than willing to talk. They were all excited: as if reborn after so many years of austerity, celebrations and gossip had finally returned to Safamita House in grand style. Pina had to endure interminable descriptions of the wedding arrangements, the baroness's trousseau, and the time-consuming search, all over Sicily, for the rarest and costliest ingredients for the wedding breakfast and reception. Then the talk moved on to the newlyweds. Pina enjoyed everyone's trust, since almost everyone had reason to thank her for one thing or another, and while the personal servants of the bride and groom had gone off with them, she got even their accounts at second or third hand.

Pina assessed them one by one. She ascertained that after the dinner the marchese had gone with Costanza to the bridal chamber, after which he had returned to the guests: they had been together too briefly to have "done anything." Rosa Nascimbene, Costanza's maid, had helped her to undress and prepare for the night. "Milady the marchesa didn't even want to let her hair down, she was that tired," Rosa had said.

The staff were standing around the big kitchen table, laden with left-overs from the day before and other delicacies lovingly prepared by the head cook. They were eating and drinking together, relaxed at last. Pina sat among the men, which was her privilege. The conversation veered to the salacious side, and though nothing definitive emerged, impressions and chance remarks gradually became clues.

"That's not how things are done. Women have to let their hair down to please a man," thundered the head cook, hero of the day. And this set off a whirl of gossip the essence of which only Pina Pissuta could grasp.

"Yes, if she wants to please him. But did the rest of you take a look at the young baroness? It seems she doesn't want to please anyone, judging by the state she's in. Thin as a wire she's become, all but invisible!"

"She wasn't well. She hardly ate, and then she was all in a muddle and the heart went out of her. She looked like a walking corpse at the wedding."

"But he liked her. Otherwise why did he take her?"

"He took her because her name is Safamita and she has enough money to cover every flagstone in the main street of Sarentini, stone by stone."

"Come on, are you trying to say that there aren't any rich women with a bit more flesh on their bones than the baroness?"

"This marchese is up to his neck in debt. His valet told me he can't even manage to pay him for the full month."

After lunch Pina closeted herself with the key people—the women of the house, all except Amalia Cuffaro, who would never talk—to get to the heart of the matter. And thus she discovered that Rosa hadn't had a wink of sleep all night long; she had told the others the bride had fallen asleep in tears, all alone. Rosa had stayed in the next room to help Costanza if need be before her husband came: for a few weeks Costanza had been waking in the middle of the night and vomiting. Then she had heard the marchese arrive—drunk. Baron Giacomo had had to accompany him to the upper floor, where he handed him over to Baldassare Cacopardo, the valet, who, in no way concerned or surprised by the state his master was in, undressed him and left him staggering about in front of the door to the bridal chamber. Rosa swore that she had heard sounds followed by the blurred voice of the marchese saying, "What a bag of bones!" Then silence. Finally, the lightest of footsteps: Costanza had gone to her dressing room. Rosa pushed the door ajar and saw her lying on the couch there, covered by a shawl. She was weeping silently and went on weeping while Rosa dozed off in her armchair in the antechamber. In the morning, the marchese rose early and went into the dressing room. As soon as he saw his wife still asleep there, he shouted repeatedly for Rosa. On the carpet in front of the couch there was a pool of stinking vomit. Costanza was distraught. The couple washed, assisted by their own servants. They took breakfast and went downstairs together; they both looked worn-out, but certainly not with happiness.

Pina dropped in on the laundry, where she admired the fine silk sheet, the night shirt, the underwear. She observed the bridal linen—clean, barely wrinkled. There were two yellowish stains on the side on which Costanza had slept. She sniffed at them: traces of sour vomit.

In the afternoon, Pina Pissuta presented herself once more in the baron's study. At the back of the room, below the window, stood the imposing writing desk, in front of which were two simple straight chairs. At the other end of the room was a table surrounded by large walnut chairs upholstered in brown leather with carved armrests. The walls were covered with massive bookshelves; the only picture, a pastel drawing of the baroness as a child, hung on the wall behind the baron.

Domenico Safamita was anxious. The thought of his Costanza had become, even more than before, a fixation that tormented him ceaselessly. Sitting behind the desk, his back held well away from the chair, he was on edge, as if ready to spring. Pina Pissuta stood in front of him.

"Well?"

"I have spoken with everyone, and I have seen what there was to see. The servants of the lord marchese and his lady wife have left, but I learned certain things from others."

"I know, I know. Well? Tell me."

"The young baroness is exactly as she was when she emerged from her late lamented mother's womb."

Domenico Safamita turned scarlet. He was sweating and trembling, his balled fists resting on the desk. His eyes were dry, but his flesh wept. He stared at Pina Pissuta. He grasped his walking stick with both hands and held it horizontally, still staring at her. Slowly, with an almost hieratic gesture, he began to bend it; then, with a surge of menacing strength, he bore down on the wood with both thumbs close together and snapped it in two.

Pina was perhaps the only person who knew the intensity of the baron's suffering. It had fallen to her, over the years, to tell him about his wife's recurrent miscarriages, and she had witnessed his inner turmoil: the smashed chairs and the shattered vases. But until that moment she had never feared him.

Although they were separated by the desk, Pina was afraid of this old man. The baron's eyes had widened—his eyes seemed pulled into the hollows of their sockets—and looked as if they would burst; and they were trained on her, black, desperate.

He leapt to his feet, still holding the two pieces of wood. He shoved the chair back and, slowly, went round the desk to reach Pina. The order issued from the depths of his throat. "Hang on to the back of that chair!"

Pina didn't understand.

"The chair, the chair—the heavy one, damn it!" Fearing that he would beat her, Pina did not obey.

His face was inscrutable and terrible. "Turn round and spread your legs," he said in a low voice.

Then Pina had a feeling of disgusted relief. She moved her bag full of the food to take home, to keep it out of harm's way; she grabbed one of the heavy chairs and set it in the centre of the room. She leaned against the arms, hanging on to the grinning dragon's heads, to check its stability. Then Pina straightened, quickly lifted her underskirt and pulled it over her head, loosened the tight cord around her waist that held her bloomers together, then bent forwards against the back of the chair and grasped the arms. With a sense of embarrassment, she realised that in her haste she had scarcely washed.

Domenico Safamita penetrated her with a single thrust, pumping into her harder and then harder still, such was the strength unleashed by his desperation. In a frenzy of anguish, the weeping baron sodomized Pina Pissuta.

"You may go, Pina. Thank you."

Pina was rearranging her clothing, without daring to turn round, when she saw a purse full of coins fall at her feet. She picked it up, her arms still aching, then turned towards him to thank him.

The baron was once more behind his desk, standing with his back to her, his belly flattened against the bookshelves, his head hanging forwards with his brow against the wall, his arms high and his hands gripping the frame of his wife's picture.

"Go, go," he repeated bleakly.

Pina had an impulse to offer him some words of consolation, but she could hear his subdued sobbing, and in such cases men are best left alone. She collected her things and departed.

But the baron's sobs were sobs no more. Once by himself, he began to howl in a loud, high-pitched wail. Or at least that's how it seemed to Pina Pissutta, who paused as she left, then moved slowly away from the closed door of the baron's study.

52

"Marry for love, repent at leisure."

A very strange kind of love

The coach was ready in the courtyard, in front of the masters' apartments, waiting for the marchesa. The peasant women thronged around Costanza to give her farewell hugs. "My marchesa doesn't want to leave Malivinnitti, and now I understand why," said the Marchese Sabbiamena affably; then, in a tone of kind command, he urged his wife, "Hurry up, Costanza, it's time to leave now."

Obediently, Costanza headed for the coach. Maria Teccapiglia made her way through the women and children, her diminutive figure, black and stooped, standing out against the other women as she advanced.

Costanza retraced her steps and fell into her arms in a last, wordless embrace.

Then the coachman cracked his whip, and the horses headed for the main gate. The coach set off down the lane, flanked by guards on horseback. Costanza leaned out the window. The peasants had followed them and were standing in rows against the outer walls of the farm, women and children on one side of the main gate and men on the other, silent. Maria Teccapiglia was indistinguishable among the other women in black. Costanza gazed once more at those apparently inscrutable faces, suntanned and weather-beaten, and she caught the hint of a smile from the folk of Malivinnitti, along with the fluttering of lashes over dark eyes.

The Tignusos caught up with the coach at a gallop and took up their positions at the head of the convoy. They would accompany the couple all the way across the estate. Costanza leant back against her seat and whispered to her husband, "Pietro, I am proud to be your wife."

"As I am to have my marchesa," he replied, caressing her fingers.

The last two weeks had not been at all as she had imagined them.

They had not consummated their marriage on their wedding night, and that was all her fault, Costanza told herself. In the weeks before the wedding she had been unwell: she had vomited and her periods had stopped. Fear of sexual intercourse had clouded her mind and blighted desire. During that first night she had been sick again and had taken refuge in the dressing room, where she had dozed off in between bouts of retching. The following morning Pietro saw her and understood; he didn't say a word to her about it.

They had arrived in Malivinnitti in the late afternoon, tired, sleepy, haggard, and dusty after the long coach journey. They received the congratulations of the peasants and made a brief appearance at the feast Costanza's father had organised for the local people. Then they went to bed, for the first time together, without embarrassment. Exhausted.

The barking of dogs awoke Costanza in the middle of the night: a pack of them was chasing a bitch in heat. She peeped over at Pietro's side of the bed; he had his back to her and was snoring lightly. She drifted back into a doze. The racket got louder and she brought her hands up to her ears. The pack was hurtling around from one side of the farmyard to the other, their paws—eager, swift, scratching—thumping over the stones. The peasants yelling at them had no effect. Costanza listened, carried away by the hullabaloo: she could see the dogs before her eyes, lusting, panting. She was ashamed. She, a girl of good family, desired to mate with the same urgent drive as those beasts.

"What's going on?" Pietro had jumped out of bed and thrown open the balcony window. Costanza closed her eyes, feigning sleep, then opened them a fraction and saw him, bathed in the soft light of the moon, limned against the window. The room filled with the discordant animal sounds, the barks echoing from wall to wall in a dizzying, sonorous whirligig of noise. Costanza desired Pietro, strongly.

He looked at her for a moment. "It's only dogs, Costanza, don't worry. Let's go back to sleep," he said, and returned to the bed. He was soon snoring again.

Costanza fell into a moist, tumultuous half-sleep, hearing the distant, submissive whimpering of the bitch, the panting of the victorious dog, and the yelps of their mating. Then silence. Consumed by unfulfilled desire, her throat aching and parched, she finally fell asleep.

The next morning, in the company of the Tignusos and a crowd of staff and peasants, Costanza showed the new master round the estate. Pietro was solicitous and gallant with her. He wanted everyone to like him and chatted with informal indulgence, interested in everything. He gladly let himself be taken to see the places that were particularly dear to Costanza. He was carried away with enthusiasm, like a romantic, about the crop-covered hills, enjoyed the steep path down to the water trough, marvelled at the rocky gorges. "Costanza, we have the same tastes," he said to his wife. The marchese also visited the enormous farmhouse—the jewel of the Safamita estate—and had cause to appreciate his wife's dowry in full.

In the afternoon Costanza went to rest, leaving him on the terrace. But his wife's tacit invitation of the night before had not escaped Pietro and, having decided to do his conjugal duty quickly, he followed her shortly afterwards. He felt a certain reluctance: this was the first time he was about to possess a woman for whom he felt no physical attraction.

Costanza felt a hand run over her nightdress, onto her belly, and she opened her eyes. Pietro was lying beside her, leaning on his left arm; he looked at her pensively, then his right hand was moving beneath the sheet, slipping impatiently lower down. Costanza was not ready: in her naïveté she had thought certain things belonged to the night. She started in anxiety. Pietro murmured and gave her a slightly ironic smile. "Costanza, marriage is a sacrament," and he made to roll on top of her. His breath smelt of wine, his hand went lower and lower, and finally it pressed on her.

"Leave me alone—no, don't, no, no!" she cried, and through her cry there came a glow, a distant light. Costanza was as if blinded. She floundered, trying to distinguish something, someone. She no longer knew who was talking to her, close by. In the pitch darkness a mellifluous, threatening voice resounded. "Costanza, do you want this sacrament? This is how you receive the body of Christ. It's a secret . . . a secret." She smelt once more the drunken breath, felt the pressure of that stubby hand, those wormlike, slimy breathless fingers, the penetration, pain, fear, disgust—her vulnerability.

Costanza fainted.

Embarrassed, Pietro was wiping her brow with a damp cloth. She was weeping softly, unable to move or to speak. The valet knocked: the horses were ready, as his lordship the marchese had ordered, for the afternoon ride.

"I'm so sorry, Costanza. I didn't think I would hurt you. I'm going with them, you rest. I'll send Rosa to look after you," said Pietro.

Maria Teccapiglia and Rosa Nascimbene came in together. After a quick glance, Maria sent Rosa away: she would tend to her mistress alone. She sat down on the edge of the bed, laid her hand over Costanza's, and said, "Costanza, I am very old and I will talk to you the way I did when you were just a girl. You must not be afraid. These things happen. Marriage is no bed of roses, but it's good for a woman. Here at Malivinnitti we like this husband of yours very much."

Costanza was still weeping. Maria went to perch on a chair, far from her mistress. She told her rosary beads, repeating the Paternosters and Ave Marias in a murmur like a lullaby, and Costanza dozed. When she awoke, she wanted a glass of water. Maria also had them prepare an egg yolk whipped up with sugar and a spoonful of Marsala, and she persuaded her to drink it: "Take it, it'll give you strength. Do it for your husband."

Propped up against the pillows, Costanza was desolated. She was afraid that she had said too much. Surely Pietro despised her. She was ready for the worst.

"May I speak?" asked Maria, and carried on without waiting for Costanza's feeble "Yes." "I'll tell you what I think and what I know, and I know a whole lot of things about the Safamita household, even when the family doesn't tell me. He won't leave you. Try again, and it'll get better."

"It's different for me, Maria. There's something else."

"I wish the tongues of those who say 'different' would drop out of their mouths!" exclaimed Maria. "We are all the same, remember that. Nothing can happen to you that hasn't happened to other people, and there's nothing new in this old, old world of ours. People don't understand that. Now I'll tell you something that is all mine, something I've told no one in all these years. Before I went into service, when I was still a lass, someone did something to me that was worse than the things that shameless wretch Father Puma used to do to the young girls—and boys, too. And I got married and I gave my late husband three children. Understand?"

Costanza raised her eyes, brimming with tears. She understood: she was not alone. Maria looked at her: the face with its spray of freckles seemed to have grown smaller, so that she was all eyes, frightened, like a calf that has lost its mother.

"Then I'll tell you something else," said Maria. "Before the death of your late lamented mother, when the blacksmith's daughter first appeared on the scene, you asked the women, 'What is love?,' the way the daughters of the rich do. But you didn't ask me, and you made a mistake there. We honest but poor women don't need to ask this, we know it. Love is contenting yourself with what there is, and making your husband happy. If this goes on to become great happiness, then so much the better, but that only happens every now and again. This holds for rich and poor alike. Content yourself with what your husband wants and doesn't want."

"Maria, tell me the truth, who heard me? What did I say?" asked Costanza edgily.

"Nothing to give wagging tongues anything to talk about. Your secret is still your own, and you can do as you wish with it. I would leave it at that. The less talk the better."

That afternoon Costanza was consumed with desire for Pietro. She felt in fine fettle, stronger. She was afraid that he didn't want her anymore, and this was an unbearable thought. She played the piano with impassioned feeling until dinnertime, returning to her favourite aria, "Porgi, amor."

"Would you prefer me to sleep in another room?" Pietro asked her at bedtime.

Costanza saw that he was embarrassed and reserved. "No, on the contrary. I'm sorry for what happened today . . . it won't happen again," she burst out.

During the night she awoke to find Pietro gently caressing her back. It felt delightful. Costanza didn't know how to make him understand this. Pietro sensed her heat and pressed himself against her. She longed for more caresses, kisses, sweet words of love. She wasn't ready. Pietro became more urgent. Costanza closed her eyes and squeezed her eyes tight shut. She could see flashes of light, blades of cold, sharp light that paralysed her. The known and the unknown. This is what she feared. She wanted it and she didn't want it. Hesitantly, Pietro guided her hand onto him. At contact, Costanza tried to pull away, but he continued. She felt trapped; she wanted to get this lustful dog off her back. The dog. I should have become a nun was her sole, insistent thought; it almost escaped her dry lips, like a litany, but she didn't push him away. "I should have become a nun, I should have become a nun," Costanza chanted to herself, abandoned to her fate: this was how it was meant to be, and so it was. "Then it gets better," Maria Teccapiglia had told her, and so she had to put up with it and hope.

The rest was a nightmare. Costanza was rigid. Pietro, alone, gave up.

The next morning he rose early and went hunting, leaving her to sleep. Costanza wept all day. She was sure the fault was hers if his desire had waned, and she was devastated by this. Yet, as the hours went by, the memory of the night faded and she loved him more than ever. Before dinner, Pietro asked her to play the piano.

"Costanza, you play like an angel," he told her. "You are a celestial creature—you belong to another world. You are too good for a sinner like me. I have squandered my inheritance and I enjoy life. I like horses, clothes, wine, gambling, and women. I've had hundreds of them—virgins, too. You are not like them. You are pure, and with you I can't do it. I would defile you. I am unworthy of you, I cannot. This is my fault, and I hope things will change, with time. But for now there's no point in trying again."

Costanza fought for her rights. "That's not true. I am not as you describe me," she said heatedly. She felt no restraint: "I am your wife, and I want to be so in full."

"As I do. I am your husband, and I always shall be."

"So?" Her aggressiveness was ill-concealed.

"Costanza, tell me"—Pietro's tone was severe—"what does a wife who loves her husband wish to do?"

"To make him happy!" she replied in one breath.

"If I tell you I am happy the way things are, do you wish to please me?"

"But . . . children . . ." Costanza spoke in a low voice. She was beginning to understand.

"Costanza, it won't be forever, but for the present I can't do it. You saw this yourself. It is the greatest humiliation for a man, and it's never happened to me before. You are an angel, an unspoilt virgin to be loved in a different way, as you deserve." Pietro fell silent, and she sat there looking at him, speechless. "It's a simple matter: do you want to be a good wife and make your husband happy, or not?"

"Yes, yes," whispered Costanza, choking back her tears. She felt she was dying inside. Her hands slipped from the keyboard. She held them in her lap, wringing them with all her strength. Pietro noticed this, and he took them in his. "So, let's put it this way: we are married, and I am proud and happy about that. You are my marchesa, and I hope to become worthy of you. We shall get to know each other better, and things can change. Besides, we get on well together, as I've already seen. You do know that many marriages start off like this, and many more continue like this and are happy just the same? Think of my aunt Annina Lan-nificchiati: she never had children, and now you know why."

"I didn't imagine . . ." Costanza's voice was barely audible.

"You've lots to learn, my little Costanza, but I, your husband, am here to teach and protect you," said he, stroking her wrist.

They carried on sharing the same bedroom. Pietro filled the days with hunting expeditions and long horseback rides with Costanza, which diverted and tired them both. They would go to bed exhausted.

By day, Pietro lavished attention and tokens of affection upon her. They talked a great deal about their plans: the restoration of Sabbia-mena House in Cacaci, shopping, evenings at the opera, even travel. Rapt, she listened to him and never said anything other than yes. Pietro told her about episodes in his childhood and stories about his family; he tried to let his wife get to know him—and her love grew ever stronger. Costanza, aroused by all these activities, and by the excitement of being with him, listening to him, looking at him, and being seductive with him, often felt a strange contentment during the day—a contentment sepa-rated from the deepest desperation by only a very fine line. The despera-tion belonged to the night.

In bed, in the evenings, close to but not beside her beloved, Costanza suffered so much that she could barely sleep. She didn't dare get up, for fear that Pietro might feel ready to take her and she wouldn't be there. Yet despite this feverish tension she felt free of an immense burden: she no longer had to fear that he didn't like her.

The country folk thought they were happy, but not her women, who would sigh every time they made the couple's bed in the mornings.

The baron was told that the honeymoon had been a success.

53

"He who pays in advance will buy spoiled goods."

Amalia Cuffaro tells her niece about her first day at Sabbiamena House in Cacaci.

Amalia was doing the cleaning. She swept away the dirt, pushing it onto the ledge of the Montagnazza, where the straw, grit, and dust fell over the edge and were borne away by the dancing wind. "It takes only five minutes to clean our home," she said in satisfaction. "In Sabbiamena House it took a good hour to clean just the marchesa's room, it was that big!" she exclaimed.

"What was the marchesa's house like?" asked Pinuzza.

"What was it like and what didn't it become! You had to see it to believe it—that in less than a year she transformed it beyond recognition. With money you get everything done fast, but she should have waited a bit before she gave him everything he wanted," said Amalia. "In any case, without the baron's help we would never have managed. He sent cartloads full of all kinds of good things, and three footmen. I arrived a few days before the newlyweds, with don Paolo, to give the staff of the Patella family a hand. And they really needed a lot of help. I'll say that the baron knew the state the house was in, but Costanza didn't. They hadn't even made up her bed! But they had their marchese's bed all ready, the scoundrels! They apologised, saying they didn't know which sheets to use for their new mistress, and you can believe that if you like. The place was small compared to Safamita House, and very old, abandoned since the death of the late marchesa, God rest her soul, twenty years before, but it must have been ages since any workers had put a hand to it. The plaster was coming away from the walls and painted ceilings; it stank of damp. It was dirty, too, dirtier than any nobleman's house I'd ever seen. The servants lorded it over everyone, and they never cleaned anything." Amalia straightened up on her stool, proudly. "We set to cleaning up, and it was only thanks to us that Costanza was able to sleep in a proper bed!"

"What did the marchesa say when she saw it?" asked Pinuzza.

"Nothing. She was discreet, and far too much in love. 'What a beautiful staircase, Pietro! What fine overdoors!' she would say to him. But he was ashamed, you could see that! She had courage, did Costanza. The next day she went round the rooms and wrote down what needed doing in a little notebook, then she called her husband and they decided. Carpenters, workmen, painters, and mattress-makers began to arrive. She had them fix up everything."

"What did the servants have to say?"

"They weren't ashamed. A bad lot, they were, but she didn't dismiss them, out of respect for her husband. She made it clear to the major-domo, don Carmelo Galifi, that things had to change—and change they did, eventually. But at first she didn't know about what was going on under the surface there. Pandemonium it was." Amalia had talked too much, and she added, "Pinuzza, you know what I say? You take a rest and I'll clean the vegetables outside."

Amalia was in a bad temper as she shelled the peas, her blood boiling at the memory.

She put the pods to one side, having removed the filaments to keep the soup from being stringy, and put the peas in a bowl. They were lovely and tender, good for Pinuzza.

It was don Paolo more than anyone who, during the few days he stayed in Sabbiamena House, had put an end to that disgraceful state of affairs. He had noticed that Assunta Sucameli, a brazen hussy of a maid, took the marchese his morning coffee; the valet would let her into the master's room, and she would stay to perform other services for him. Don Paolo took note of this, but in the kitchens no one wondered where the woman had got to, so evidently it was nothing new. One morning the marchesa waited and waited for her husband in her room, longing to see him. She was nicely dressed, with rice powder on her face—she had made herself pretty for him—and in those days he came to see her unfailingly every morning. She asked Rosa Nascimbene to take a peek in his room to see if he was awake, but luckily the marchese arrived at that very moment.

Rosa mentioned this to don Paolo, and he decided to do something. After all, heaven knows what Rosa, who told the marchesa everything, might have seen and heard if she had knocked at the marchese's door. Don Paolo told don Carmelo that Baron Safamita would not be happy to learn what was going on under his married daughter's roof—and after that it was the marchese's valet, Baldassare Cacopardo, who brought him his morning coffee. But that wasn't the end of it, because Assunta Sucameli remained in service, although she went only rarely to the main floor.

Costanza's sole thought was to make her husband happy. Together they chose new fabrics, wallpaper, furniture, fittings, and chandeliers; they were like two children, they were having so much fun. Amalia was amazed, since Costanza had never liked shopping or going out, and she pointed this out to her. "I'm pulling off my horns, like the Snail Princess, to make my husband happy!" Costanza said with a smile. She was mad about the marchese. Amalia could see this in her looks, by the way she responded when he touched her, and how she grew sad when she waited for him and he didn't come.

After a few weeks, the marchese began to pass less time with his wife. He complained that there was too much work going on, that the dust raised by the workmen got on his nerves. So he left the poor woman to give orders to the many workmen they had called in to fix up his house, and he went off on his own to eat at his club or go shopping with his friends. He and Costanza went to receptions together, but Costanza often returned tired and melancholy. After a while, he almost always stayed out while she stayed at home, all alone, with no complaint. Respectful of her husband, she went on directing the renovation work, but she had to decide about everything on her own. "The marchese wants it done like this," she would say, trying to save his face.

When Pietro was there, he was affectionate with her. His morning visits became brief, but Costanza would bloom anew at the mere sight of him. Then she was unwell: she started vomiting again. Her "monthlies" had not come since she had married, and Amalia, hoping that Costanza was pregnant, asked her about this.

"No, Amalia, and you mustn't ask me again," she said. "You'd be the first I'd tell, you know that."

54

"A good woman is a woman who keeps quiet."

Costanza Safamita returns to Sarentini as a married woman
and feels like a stranger in her own home.

In the autumn of 1880, husband and wife returned to Sarentini to celebrate the marriage of Giacomo Safamita and Adelaide Lattuca, a distant
relative. Giacomo's fiancée was fifteen years old, in the full bloom of
youth, and with a placid temperament. All in all, she seemed agreeably
obtuse.

Although related, the families did not know one another well, meeting mainly at funerals and weddings. Cavaliere Bartolomeo Lattuca was
a landowner of modest means who lived in Bagliscasci, a town with no
history. For his family, this marriage represented an unhoped-for step up
the social ladder.

Yet Baron Safamita had consented to Giacomo's wishes with relief; in
his view, the girl was a suitable wife, and he even thought he had been too
severe about his son's judgement. He never knew what had prompted
Giacomo to choose her, nor did Gaspare have the nerve to tell his master, as he might have done in the past. But he did tell don Paolo that it
had to do with sugared almonds, which Adelaide adored.

During Costanza's wedding reception, Adelaide had surreptitiously
filched some of the dorées from the ornamental epergne. Perhaps she
panicked at the thought that she'd been seen: she stuck them down her
bodice, spoiling her curvaceous décolleté. Then she went to stand on
the sidelines in front of a table fitted with a large mirror, with her back
to the guests. She evidently didn't realise that she was now even more
visible than before, reflected in the mirror, and she gave herself over to
her innocent gluttony, popping the golden almonds into her mouth one
by one, dissolving the hard sugar on the outside, sucking it between her
full lips, chewing the softened almond with voluptuous pleasure, and
happily swallowing. Then she stuck her plump fingers into her décolleté
again and rummaged about for another sweet. Meanwhile, Giacomo,
feeling ill at ease among the guests from Palermo, had caught sight of
that vision of virginal gluttony and wanted her for himself. He was so
taken by Adelaide that he scarcely bothered with going up and talking

to her. Their marriage was harmonious and fruitful: of the fifteen children Adelaide would give Giacomo, ten survived. She proved to be an obedient wife and a very loving and indulgent mother.

Costanza felt like a stranger when she came back to Safamita House, which she hadn't expected. The big guest apartment where she had spent her wedding night was now her and Pietro's bedroom, and it aroused painful and embarrassing memories. She decided to visit the room that she had lived in as a girl, and it saddened her: the cupboards were empty, the tables bare, and the curtains flapped gloomily in the autumnal breeze; even the flowers on the balcony seemed to be languishing. The servants made a fuss over her, but they treated her with a certain detachment and a rather too elaborate respect. Her group of women had broken up: Maria Teccapiglia spent long periods at Malivinnitti, Rosa Vinciguerra had reluctantly returned to her family—it was rumoured that once she lost Costanza's protection Giacomo had harassed her because of her devotion to Stefano—while Annuzza la Cirara suffered from rheumatism and spent a lot of time in bed. Costanza went below stairs once to see the staff, but she felt uncomfortable. The lack of her touch was evident, for her father and don Filippo Leccasarda, both of them old men by now, were no longer supervising the servants.

Giacomo's self-confidence had grown, and he now acted with the brashness of the future master of the house. He invited Pietro to go hunting, and the brothers-in-law would often spend the day in the countryside. Costanza stayed for long hours with her father, as in the old times; and this, too, at first, made her feel awkward: she felt that her father was anxious about her marriage.

They were alone in the drawing room.

"Who plays for you now, Papa?"

"Every now and then the town music teacher pays a visit. He's a good pianist, and he even gives me lessons. At my age, I have started to play again a little—not well like your mother, even less like you. Mostly I don't listen to music; I imagine it inside. That's enough for me. But since you've been here I've enjoyed hearing you play the piano—your husband is a lucky man."

"I play at home, but I haven't had much free time." Costanza spoke hurriedly, and her light tone was forced.

The baron observed his daughter. Pale and still very thin, she was dressed with greater elegance than before, and with a hint of contrived charm. She was wearing Caterina's jewels, which he had given her for her wedding, causing a scandal among his sisters and resentment in Giacomo. These were major jewels, fit for a grande dame, but they did not suit her. Costanza's looks were those of a slightly over-the-hill virgin.

"Does it feel as if you've come home?"

"No, Papa, this is not my home anymore," replied Costanza, flushing. "I didn't expect to feel this way, not so soon, and it rather bothers me. We have the workmen in at Cacaci and the house is a mess, but I've come to feel it's my home."

Domenico Safamita looked this daughter of his straight in the eye. "Tell me just one thing: are you happy with your husband?"

"I wouldn't want to be married to anyone else. We are getting used to living together. Pietro is affectionate, and he respects me." Costanza was patently embarrassed.

"So, is there no news yet?"

"Papa, I am my mother's daughter. We shall have to wait and hope," answered Costanza in a tone that gave him to understand that he would get no more out of her.

"Until now I haven't burdened you with the management of your property, as agreed. But as soon as the work on your house is finished, I will send you two of my best men. And you will have to find an administrator— you will see to that on your own. What will your husband have to say about this?"

"He will be more than happy. He already lets me run things—in fact, he encourages me to. The workers began with the lower floors, and the office will be ready before long. Pietro doesn't own much."

"Beware of your brother," her father warned her with a sigh.

"Which one?"

"'Which one, which one!'" thundered the baron in his strong voice of the old days. "The one we have here at home, Giacomo! He is greedy and grasping, and he still hasn't realised that his wife didn't bring him a dowry worth thinking about. When he does, he will want other properties, cash . . . But what has been given has been given.

"Do not follow his advice. Do not yield to his bullying or to his wife's flattery. He will try to take what is yours away from you, to swindle you— if not now, certainly after my death. You will need people to turn to, and Iero Bentivoglio is the right man. Do not let yourself be influenced by family gossip: Iero may well be an unfaithful husband, but he's a good and trusted businessman. Our people will vote for him. Count on him, but don't get too familiar—he tries with all the women, that one."

Costanza was dismayed, but she answered, "Very well, Papa."

"I am thinking of moving to Palermo. I am buying a modern house near the new opera. The city is growing apace. Will you two be going there this winter?"

"Pietro wants to. I'd prefer to stay in Cacaci to keep an eye on the work, and Palazzo Sabbiamena is in poor shape, but we wouldn't want to have workers in both houses at the same time."

"You're doing the right thing, but don't encourage him to go alone. He has to learn to live like a married man. Does he ask you for money?"

"Papa, he's my husband. We spend together."

"Be careful." The baron paused, then added, "Costanza, this house will belong to Giacomo. Aunt Assunta is doing poorly, and the castle will be empty. Would you like to return to Sarentini?"

"The Sabbiamenas have nothing to do with Sarentini . . . I feel like playing something—what would you like?" she asked him, and she sat down at the piano.

55

"An empty sack cannot stand up straight."

The Marchesa Patella di Sabbiamena seems to accept
that her marriage is not to be consummated.

Costanza thought things over: her father knew about her affairs. There were spies in Sabbiamena House. Her father sent her cartloads of provisions and mules with saddlebags of fruit and vegetables; the clerks of the respective administrative offices were in frequent contact, and then there were relatives who called in. All these people kept an eye out, and told everyone what they saw. It was impossible to identify, much less to send away, those who listened and reported.

The months were very difficult, but Costanza would not have described them as unhappy. Annuzza la Cirara used to say, when telling Costanza stories, "He who hopes cannot be unhappy." And Costanza still had hope. But for how long?

Pietro was an assiduous husband. The other wives said that their husbands would stay away from home for nights on end, under one pretext or another—business commitments or amusements. But Pietro came home every night and nearly every morning would call on Costanza in her room, however briefly. Those moments, their only moments of intimacy, were a joy and a torment for her. Pietro would tell her about all his plans for the day, and they would talk of the work being done on the house and of social calls to be made. Costanza sensed that he liked her company. They chatted about people she had met, and he told her stories about their families—preparing her, as it were, for life in society. Pietro really wanted his wife to make him look good, and, among other things, this meant that she had to be in the know about certain matters, and he wanted those who frequented the salons to judge her a lady worthy of him. Costanza believed that he loved her.

Not a day passed without his making her a present, or praising her, or letting her know that he was glad he'd married her. These weren't false words, she was sure. It was as if the absence of physical intimacy wasn't a problem for him. But still, she thought about it all the time. She knew that marital infidelity was normal and therefore acceptable, but she refused to believe that Pietro was betraying her. He would caress her, resting his hand on her waist as they entered the salons—behaving like a fiancé, really. Costanza could not understand why he didn't try once more to make her his wife in the fullest sense. She even contemplated the possibility that he actually didn't like women—married women alluded to such indecent topics—but she quickly dismissed the idea: after all, he had told her that he had had lots of women. Costanza concluded that it was her fault; she had rejected him and had made him fearful of trying again.

Rather than give in, Pietro should have looked, as any real husband would have, for a way out of what had become a humiliating and painful experience for them both. But she had to admit that Pietro ignored things that didn't come to him easily and pretended—with himself and with others—that problems and difficulties didn't exist. This was how he had squandered his inheritance and got himself so badly in debt. It was up to her to give him self-confidence, to reawaken his desire, to spur him on to do his duty, and to convince him that she was truly ready: that she desired and was capable of enjoying sex. And of loving him.

"Costanza, you are an angel," Pietro would often say to her. Well, then, she had to come down from the pedestal he had put her on and be like other women. Costanza sought out the company of other ladies of her own age—studied them, observed them, imitated them. She attended the salons, played at cards, wore elaborate, opulent clothes, and even changed her hairstyle. What else could she do? How long would she have to wait?

Annuzza la Cirara had told her, "The prince scorned her, for that poor girl would not let him see her hair, and so he made her toil and toil: 'Clean here' and 'Clean there.' 'Bring me up the water jug.' 'Cook me this.' To keep him happy, she pulled off her horns in order to serve him and cook him all the dishes he ordered—so often that her head hurt from the many times her horns had to grow in again. The poor soul got to the point where she wanted to leave the palace and not see him again—that's how badly her head hurt and her heart ached. Unrequited love hurts terribly, but it's even worse to be disgusted by the one who says he loves you. So she really did think about going into service with someone else. Then the prince went hunting and he left her all alone to put up with the queen's persecution of her—which was much better for her, because she couldn't care less about the queen."

Costanza, too, came to wish that Pietro would go to Palermo—or away for a few days with his friends—which would relieve her of her torments. To which now another could be added: that her father knew; and if he did, so did goodness knows how many other people in Sarentini.

"Pietro, may I ask you a question?" asked Costanza as her husband was preparing his tobacco pouch before going down to the stables for his morning gallop.

"Anything for my marchesa!" he replied, in his usual semi-serious, semi-facetious tone.

"Why do you never kiss me?"

"Because I cannot, Costanza."

"But I want you to. I want to have children, Pietro."

"Don't you think that I, too, would like to continue my line? Listen to me, we've already discussed this. We need time." Pietro wanted to put an end to the conversation. "This isn't the moment to discuss this—here in Sarentini, in your father's house."

"What does that mean?"

"Costanza, you promised me you would wait. I am happy like this. It's not easy for a man, but let's wait, please."

"But you manage with other women. You said so yourself."

"This is my sad destiny—that with women of no importance all goes well but not with my marchesa. You are too superior, to them and to me."

"I am like other women, Pietro. I want you, and I want children."

"Give me time."

"My father suspects something. He is asking questions," she added, rather irritated; it was the first time she had expressed her resentment.

Pietro was alarmed. "What has he asked you?"

"He wanted to know when I will have children."

"And how did you answer?"

"That Mama had trouble having children."

"That's how to do it, my clever Costanzina. Giacomo is waiting for me—we'll see each other at lunch and we can talk more then." Pietro kissed his wife's hand and went off, filled with apprehension.

Pietro did not find Giacomo's company disagreeable. Giacomo was a connoisseur of horseflesh, an excellent shot, and a man's man; they would talk about women, the way men do. Giacomo knew about Pietro's reputation and he admired him, trying to learn from and emulate him—or at least so Pietro thought. He took Giacomo for a red-blooded but naïve young man who wanted to experience the high life and hear his tales about the sophisticated brothels of Palermo. But that morning Pietro responded to his brother-in-law's prurient questions in monosyllables, having decided that Giacomo was trying to trap him, to have another weapon to use against him. The Safamitas were a tough breed. They were demanding that he pay the price for Costanza's dowry, and this uncouth, stubborn young man would persecute him until he destroyed his reputation. A law suit to annul the marriage for non-consummation was not out of the question. Pietro had to remedy matters, take action.

After lunch he followed his wife to their rooms. Rosa was making Costanza ready for her afternoon rest in the bedroom. He stayed in the dressing room and peeped through the half-open door in the hope that he might become aroused.

220

Costanza was even thinner than he remembered. She looked like an emaciated penitent. Outside a strong, warm wind was blowing. He came into the room, determined. He opened the window, left the shutters ajar, and slipped into bed. He stretched out his leg, brushed her foot, and waited. Costanza caressed his back. He responded with little moans, she with more caresses. Pleasant. Pietro rolled over, lifted her hand, and began fondling her inner arm. Costanza let the sleeve of her nightdress slip down and bared her whole arm. Pietro covered it with swift little kisses. She responded.

This was a new situation for Pietro, too. He was accustomed to women who were used to arousing him while he remained passive. Costanza could not do that—she didn't know how—but she wanted to. He mustn't stop her. She went on caressing his back, not knowing what else to do. Using his imagination and invigorated by his lunchtime wine, Pietro felt ready. Costanza was making it easier by lifting up her night-dress. At that very moment, a gust of wind shifted the curtain, and in the pitiless, full midday sun Pietro saw her: she was a bag of bones with two little breasts. He fell back onto the mattress, limp.

They dressed again in demure, embarrassed silence.

"I'd really like to see Stefano's children," Costanza said. "May I invite them here, when we have no visitors?"

"It's your home, Costanza. I'd like to meet your brother, and his wife too," said Pietro, then added with a pretend smile, "Remember that you are the mistress in Sabbiamena House. I have complete faith in my wife."

Neither of them ever again mentioned what happened that afternoon.

Costanza left Sarentini with relief. Her father's worried looks, her brother's searching glances, and the questions about a forthcoming maternity coming from relatives and the household women had been a torment, on a level with the false intimacy of her marriage bed.

She longed for the silent nights in her own bedroom, the isolation of Sabbiamena House, the tranquil domesticity of her sewing, and her soli-tary music. Distraught by her husband's incapacity, convinced as she was that there was nothing she could do to attract him, nonetheless she was still deeply in love with him. All she asked was to be close to him, and no more, even if she wasn't his wife in the fullest sense. She feared that Pietro would come to find her presence intolerable and send her back to her father—a humiliating and ignominious repudiation—so she tried almost slavishly to indulge him.

Pietro appreciated the advantages of having a rich and complaisant wife. Her innocence came to arouse a certain tenderness in him, though he found her devotion irritating, since Costanza was not physically attractive to him as a woman. In his ingenuous optimism, Pietro convinced himself that his wife's silence was acquiescence and that she was content with what he offered her: trust, respect, genuine affection, and a complicit friendship.

As time went by, Costanza vaguely realised that Pietro was not unhappy with her and so she set aside her worst fears, but she still felt vulnerable and insecure. The couple devoted themselves to renovating the house, a project he was very keen on. The lower floors were completed, and soon the administrative offices would be full of clerks. Costanza spared no expense in furnishing Pietro's study, which he wanted to be comfortable and luxurious; yet her husband took no interest in his few belongings and ended up letting her manage them on his behalf. The study remained unused.

Without realising it, Costanza had taken on the role of an indulgent mother, which gave Pietro a sense of security and stability. He did not change his behaviour towards her—but those caresses, those kisses on her hand, and those gallant allusions came as second nature to him and he did not reserve them solely for his wife. Costanza did not perceive this.

In addition, she was fulfilled by and proud of her husband's generosity of spirit, for he had allowed her to receive Stefano and his family, and had treated them as honoured guests: this, too, was a sign of affection. Never did Costanza feel prouder to be his wife.

Seeing Costanza grateful and cheerful, Pietro felt fully empowered to enjoy the advantages of her dowry, and without compunction he reverted to his bachelor ways.

56

"He who would live a happy life should steer clear of his relatives."

On the death of Donna Assunta Safamita, the Ramazza di Limuna and Arrassa dello Scravaglio branches of the family behave badly.

Amalia spotted something unusual in the sea: three steam packets, on the edge of the horizon, in convoy. The thick, black smoke from their funnels left a streak in the windy sky that ran almost parallel to their route, like the smoke from a train.

Her first train journey dated back to when the marchesa had had to rush to Sarentini to look after Donna Assunta, in 1883. The marchese stayed on in Palermo, and Donna Alfonsina Limuna—married to Cava-liere Cesare Calliasalata and pregnant again—went with Costanza in the Safamitas' private carriage. The two cousins had seen little of each other after they'd married, and now they renewed their old intimacy. Amalia and Rosa had to conquer their fears in order to wait on their mis-tresses in the train; they hung on to the walls, walking hesitantly with legs wide apart on the wooden floors of the long, narrow carriage divided into compartments, as if it were a cabin in an earthquake. Rosa vomited and collapsed into a chair in the cubbyhole that served as a kitchen, but Amalia soon got used to the swaying of the train and looked after the mistresses, both of whom were reclining in their armchairs as calmly as if they were in a drawing room. She took up a place on one side, by the door, ready for all eventualities.

The train ran along the tracks like a millipede, crossing fields, rivers, and highways under the gaze of sheep and their shepherds scattered across the hillsides. In her corner, Amalia kept the white curtains up the better to see; farmhouses, villages perched on mountainsides, inaccessible cot-tages passed before her eyes and then dwindled into the distance before vanishing as the train came upon other farmhouses, other villages, other cottages. The train rolled on, sometimes picking up speed, sometimes climbing slowly up the slopes, panting noisily. When the railway curved, Amalia could see the engine's black smoke puffing out irregularly and flowing backwards over the roofs of the carriages like a long flag of victory. She felt a part of a marvellous new world, and she exulted in this.

Those were happy times; she was later to tell don Paolo, when they finally saw each other again in Sarentini.

Every so often Amalia would glance at the marchesa to see if she needed her. Donna Alfonsina was stretched out in her seat, hands clasped over her swollen belly, pink lips slightly open, legs slightly apart. She was snoozing beneath a soft woollen shawl: the portrait of a fulfilled woman. Costanza was not looking at the countryside. Her eyes, two dull and desperate black shards, were fixed on her cousin's pregnant belly. Amalia had to struggle to curb her impulse to give the marchesa a hug—since Costanza had married, she avoided her when she was unhappy—and, sick at heart, she went back to gazing out the window.

"Why didn't the marchesa have children?" asked Pinuzza.

Amalia started: sometimes it seemed as if Pinuzza could read her mind. "It happens to women sometimes. Her mother had a very hard time having children."

"What's her mother got to do with it?"

"A pear tree produces pears, that's what. And I'll tell you another thing: you can travel round the world as much as you like and it seems to change, but folk are always the same."

"And I'll tell *you* something, Aunt Amalia. You spent so much time with the nobility you became like them, and only you understand them, but the rest of us don't understand you anymore when you talk. That's what my dad always says," concluded Pinuzza with a yawn.

Costanza stayed in Sarentini for two months, first at the castle with her aunts and cousins, then, after Aunt Assunta's death, in Safamita House, where she kept her father company. He missed his sister badly and was in poor health. For Amalia it was a good period—she renewed her relationship with don Paolo, whom she had been seeing only seldom by then, and she once more found herself among household staff whom she knew and considered almost like family. Pinuzza and her brothers were wrong: Amalia was a poor man's daughter, poor she remained, and that was fine by her. But it was not easy for Costanza, who, apart from the sadness of losing her aunt, had to endure being harassed by her own kin at the worst time: a bereavement.

At Castle Sarentini, they found Baroness Carolina Scravaglio with her unmarried children Gesuela and Stefano, as well as Baron Limuna and his two younger sons, Ferdinando and Vincenzo, likewise unmarried. "It's as if they were trying to marry them off now, of all times!" don Paolo said to Amalia. "Wait and see the stink this lot'll kick up: they smell money, but nothing will come their way, I'm telling you." The castle staff rightly worried about their future, but they didn't have time to think about that, busy as they were looking after poor Donna Assunta while serving and keeping an eye on her relatives. Apart from Baroness Carolina—who missed no chance to nab whatever came to hand—it was the others who gave the majordomo and the servants the biggest problems. The Limunas and the Scravaglios were hunting for Donna Assunta's will and asking all and sundry about it. In front of the Safamitas they played the part of grieving relatives, but as soon as they went back to Castle Sarentini they were off the leash.

Gaetano Cucurullo, the late baron's valet, reported to the other servants that the notary Tuttolomondo had cut down on his visits to the castle to avoid being tormented by questions.

"Assunta had a place in her heart for my Gesuela and for Costanza," said Carolina Scravaglio to the notary. "You will certainly be aware of that, signor Tuttolomondo, and she must have remembered them in her will."

"I was Assunta's favourite sister, wasn't I, signor Tuttolomondo?" Vanna Limuna whispered to him with a charming smile.

"They tell me that my aunt also bought herself certain assets that once belonged to the Church," insinuated Vincenzo Limuna.

"My dear Tuttolomondo, poor Assunta's inheritance will be complicated, since she amassed so much land—a little legacy here, a bequest there, goodness knows what dispositions she must have made for it all!" said Giovanni Limuna, resting his arm on the notary's shoulder as they walked together slowly towards the drawing room.

The servants watched and reported everything below stairs. They all took the side of the notary, a man whose mouth was known to be sewn up with wire, as the saying goes.

Disappointed, the relatives fell back on the indiscretions of the castle's household staff. Ferdinando and Vincenzo Limuna had known the majordomo, don Calogero Giordano, since they were boys, and they took advantage of this. They each called for him separately, and put to him their most urgent questions: Where did their aunt keep her business papers? Which other notaries might she have called in? Who administered her estate? From childhood, they had memories of hiding places and secret drawers, and now they demanded that he help them find and open these. Gesuela Scravaglio roamed the house examining everything—furniture, silverware, ornaments—systematically opening cupboards, linen chests, trunks, and chests of drawers filled with embroidered wall hangings and blankets. She would take out the contents and put them back as if she were making an inventory. Alfonsina Calliasalata went with her to make sure she didn't steal, like her mother. The fact is, with all this to do the Limunas and the Scravaglios had little time to spend with their sick aunt, and it was better so.

Peppinella Radica looked after Donna Assunta like a daughter, interpreting her murmurs and, with Costanza, persuading her to drink what little chicken broth she could manage to get down. Whenever Peppinella left Donna Assunta's room, the two sisters would pounce on her and bombard her with questions. The timid house nun didn't know how to get rid of them, and she would cross herself.

"Pippinedda is a poor soul," said don Paolo. "Heaven only knows how many times she has repented coming to the castle. Donna Assunta will leave her nothing, you'll see, though she really should be rewarded for all she's done—more than most would have troubled with."

When the doctor announced that death was imminent, Peppinella burst into tears. Baroness Limuna embraced her and pulled her into Donna Assunta's study, closing the door behind them. Quiet as a mouse, Gesuela Scravaglio followed them. Santuzza Diodato, Donna Assunta's maid, ran to spy on them at the other study door, and when she had seen enough she slipped off to warn don Calogero.

"It was madness! Baroness Vanna grabbed Pippinedda by the arms and shook her like a rat, talking to her non-stop in a low voice. The poor woman opened a secret drawer set in the round table, the one with a column as a base. I've dusted it many a time, but I never noticed the drawer. The baroness takes out an envelope. Then her niece comes dashing into the room, and she and her aunt start reading what was in it. Then the baroness says, 'Shall we burn it?' and she crumples it up and tosses it into the hearth where the fire was almost out. At that point the marchesa arrives to say that Donna Assunta wants Pippinedda. They all follow her. I went in and picked up the charred bits of paper."

Together with Gaetano Cucurullo, don Calogero tried to put the pages together again. They grasped what they needed to know: it was the will, which named Costanza as heir to three-quarters of Donna Assunta's estate, the other quarter to be divided among the other nieces. The household staff agreed that it was a will that really deserved burning: Donna Assunta had done very badly to exclude the men. It took all of don Paolo's patience to explain things to Amalia, and terrible things they were, too.

It was said in Sarentini that Donna Assunta had died in the odour of sanctity, surrounded by her family united in their grief. "She did well not to leave a will," her sister Baroness Vanna said to visitors paying their condolences. "Assunta loved all her nephews and nieces like her own children, and she was a saint of a woman."

On the day after the funeral, the majordomo asked to speak with the baron. Shortly after Christmas in 1859, Donna Assunta had given him a box to be given to her brother Domenico in the event of her death. Inside was a lock of Costanza's hair and a will.

The will disposed of Assunta's properties one by one, leaving about half to Costanza, a quarter to Stefano, and the remaining quarter to be divided among her other nephews and nieces, born and yet to be born. The sole beneficiary of the rest, and of any assets that she might receive or purchase in the future, was Costanza. Father Sedita had witnessed the document in his own hand.

When the time was right, the baron showed the will to everyone. The relatives were furious. Don Paolo told Amalia about what then happened at the castle, where the only ones left were the Limunas and the Scravaglios. "That lot came to an agreement: the women opened the drawers and took whatever they found there—lacework, embroidery, vestments, linen, ornaments, silver—and stuck it in their suitcases, bags, wherever they could. Then one of the men said he had to go home, and he took the things to his coach. Then he came back again with the suitcases empty. Well, they took everything. And then they put the blame on poor Baroness Carolina Scravaglio. When stuff was vanishing before people's eyes, they would say, 'It must have been her, let her get on with it. When she goes away, we'll find the things in her room and take them away from her. She is grieving so much over her sister that we don't have the heart to stop her.' The maids knew this wasn't true and kept an eye on things as best they could, but the others were the masters, and they had to obey. Don Calogero Giordano told the baron about it, but even he didn't want to do anything.

"Young Baron Giacomo was beside himself and he sent his wife to the castle, but she was no use. Her aunts sat her down and had them bring her a tray of sweets, and she sat there eating happily while the others went on stealing.

"The Limunas found—how or where I don't know—a chest full of boxes of gold coins. The Scravaglios knew nothing of this. When old Baron Limuna left, he wanted to take them with him—and he didn't even trust his own doltish children. With his paunch so big he could hardly move, the old man carried the chest in his own bag, but he tripped on the stairs and took a tumble, the bag opened, and all the gold coins fell out of the boxes and rolled down the steps, chinking. The lads and maids got busy helping to pick them up, and plenty of coins ended up in their pockets—they did well! Baron Giovanni kept saying over and over, 'I've dropped my money, help me! Here, here, pick it all up!'" Don Paolo laughed, then added seriously, "Thieves they are—just like the barons of the Madonie Mountains, no more and no less!"

Costanza came to know of all this and was most displeased, but she let them do as they wished. "Amalia, they're still my relatives, and I don't want any scandal," she said to her nurse. "Aunt Assunta has already left me so much."

Giacomo was extremely unhappy about the will, and he argued with his sister. It must have been a big row, because Costanza told Amalia about it. She was afraid that Giacomo would take his revenge on don Paolo or get rid of her tortoises, in spite, and she wanted Amalia to keep her informed.

When the marchese came to Sarentini to bring his wife back to Cacaci, don Paolo and the tortoises went along with them. Baron Domenico told don Paolo that he was sending him to live with his daughter, who would treat him as he deserved, and he was as good as his word. Costanza lodged don Paolo in a cottage by the garden of Sabbiamena House and had them open up a communicating door for it: the only sign that she knew about Paolo and Amalia and approved. There don Paolo lived happily until his death, and Amalia never regretted spending her savings on helping to make his old age easier.

The tortoises were penned up on a little internal terrace on a lower floor, in front of the marchese's study.

57

"He who holds land will soon find his troubles."

Costanza Safamita resigns herself to the troubled life of the married spinster.

Costanza had been married for three years and was feeling the burden of loneliness. She had left Sarentini bitterly disappointed in her relatives. Only the Trasis had shown themselves neither grudging nor envious of her inheritance. Giacomo proved to be as their father had predicted and worse: greedy, untrustworthy, even cruel. One day he had come into her room in Safamita House and said, straight out, "I shall be Baron Safamita, you do realise that, don't you?"

"Our father is still alive," she pointed out. She was used to her brother's outbursts.

"I want to tell you, if your husband should leave you without giving you children, this will still be your home and you can come back and live here when you wish," he continued unabashed.

"Thank you," murmured Costanza, not knowing how else to reply.

"Aunt Assunta was wrong not to leave me as much as Stefano got. She must have forgotten to change her will after I was born, with all the fuss at the time—and the annexation by Italy," added Giacomo.

Costanza went back to her embroidery, but her brother seemed to have no intention of leaving. "She didn't want to, evidently."

"You're wrong. There was a will, but Aunt Vanna destroyed it."

"How do you know that?" Costanza was fibbing about her ignorance, in obedience to her father's order not to talk of this with her brother.

"It doesn't matter. It doesn't exist anymore."

"Do you know to whom she left her property?"

"To you, you fool, but also to her other nieces. Stefano got nothing," said Giacomo angrily. He did not add that the will had not mentioned him, either.

"But in the will of '59 she left something to the Lo Vallo nephews and nieces . . . why include them and then exclude Stefano?"

"They had insulted us, that's all. But Stefano disobeyed, and went against the family, and dragged our name though the mud—all of us, you too . . . Why can't you understand?" Giacomo was exasperated.

"What do you want from me?"

"I want, in fact I demand, that you give me what is morally my right: a part of the estate as big as the part Stefano got without deserving it. You must take it from your share."

"Why should I?"

"You of all people ask me this? I have a son, an heir, and I shall have other sons. Our father has already given you more than would normally be due to a woman: the Safamita estate, properties that should have come to me and to my sons after me. I want them now, not when you die."

Costanza's eyes flashed.

"Who are you going to leave them to?" barked Giacomo. "Your husband doesn't want to have children with you, everyone knows that!"

Costanza leapt to her feet, her embroidery slipping to the floor, and showed him the door.

Giacomo stepped back. He was surprised, for his bullying had always bent his sister to his will. "Costanza, those lands belong to the Safamitas and to Safamitas they must go!" he shouted, purple in the face. "You are not a Safamita!"

"I am the Marchesa Sabbiamena and proud of it!" She stooped to pick up her embroidery, and with the tone she would have used with a servant caught stealing, she said, "Now get out of here."

There were only two people in the world Costanza could count on: her father and her husband. During the turbulent months in Sarentini, she had thought about Pietro a great deal: she missed his presence, his good humour, the way he kissed her hand, his caresses. She gave herself over to desire, which suffocated her when they were together yet now she could no longer repress. Pietro was solicitous, affectionate, and not at all greedy. "Do as you wish with your own property," he had told her. "If you think it's right to give Giacomo what he is asking for, then do so. You have brought much to the Sabbiamena family, and I enjoy it, but I can't forget that it belongs to you." When he saw her sad and pensive, he gave her new sheet music and stayed to listen to her play; he would dine at home to keep her company and tell her stories to take her mind off things.

In a world where people lived on the income from their constantly dwindling land holdings, and where it was almost inconceivable to practise a profession or engage in business, there were only two ways to get richer: inheritances and marriages. Costanza realised that the inheritance her aunt had left her made even strangers jealous. She received many visits—not only from people who came because of her recent bereavement but also from women prompted by curiosity and envy. Pietro took to joining her in her salon to relieve her of the burden of conversation, and Costanza was grateful.

She noticed, as time passed, that Pietro was always present when Baroness Mariangela Almerico came to call. The baroness was a beautiful blonde for whom a lover was rumoured to have died in a duel before she married an elderly rich widower. During her visits Costanza began to feel vaguely ill at ease. At first she didn't understand why. She was used to her husband's drawing-room manners, but this struck her as different: she noted that Pietro would hover around the baroness, and then, out of the corner of her eye, she began to follow the way their darting glances met, how his lips lingered on the back of her hand, how her fan fluttered more rapidly before her face—a clear hint of furtive smiles. Costanza became jealous, then felt humiliated. She sensed that everyone, both servants and friends, was looking at her with pity and a certain scorn.

The thought of the Snail Princess gave her no comfort. The Snail Princess was torn when the prince talked to another woman, but at least she had known love and she won the prince in the end. Costanza recalled her brother's harsh words, and she wished she could run away. She couldn't wait for June, when she could take refuge in Malivinnitti.

One afternoon, after lunch, before going to take her siesta, Costanza decided to go to feed her tortoises. She went down the spiral stair leading to the internal terrace in front of Pietro's study on the main floor.

The tortoises were hiding behind the large terra-cotta tubs that held the luxuriant white and pink frangipane flowers, whose fleshy petals gave off a subtly sweetish scent. Costanza stood in the middle of the square terrace tearing spinach leaves into pieces and methodically placing them, at evenly spaced points on the tiles, in a circle around her. And then she waited, as her mother had taught her to do. The tortoises stared at her with their weary round eyes and their heavy, drooping lids like those of old men, and shook their heads. They didn't move, but neither did they withdraw into their shells. Costanza waited, patiently. She observed them, one by one, following the imperceptible movements of their necks and stubby feet. Then, slowly as can be, one of the more daring ones moved forwards, looking around cautiously before seizing the tender leaf, holding it down with one foot, and tearing at it voraciously. The others slowly followed suit. Soon Costanza was surrounded by her tortoises.

Suddenly she was distracted by the sound of panting breaths and groans coming from the study where Pietro never went. She had told don Carmelo to keep it locked, but evidently he had not obeyed. Costanza thought that perhaps a clerk or a maid had taken refuge there to get over some indisposition or setback. She went up close and gently opened the slats of the shutters.

The windows were half open, the curtains were slightly to one side, and the room was in darkness. But in the gloom she could see something moving in front of the desk. It looked like two people, a woman sitting on the desk and a man in front of her with his back to the window—and the groans, the cries grew less subdued. It was Pietro, with a woman.

Costanza felt faint. She leant against the shutter. Trying not to swoon, she clenched her fists until they crushed the pieces of spinach and bit her lip until it bled. She closed her eyes and breathed slowly. The scent of the frangipane was suffocating, nauseating. She didn't want to hear what she heard, but she couldn't help it. The veins in her temple throbbed and a stabbing pain radiated out from her eyes and hammered at her skull. She felt as if she might burst, as if she were in a press and every groan was another turn of the screw. She had to see, too, so she stayed where she was, her forehead resting against her clenched fist, the crushed spinach leaves between her hair and the shutter, and she watched. The tortoises had ventured across the terrace to follow her; with heads up and eyes trained on her, they waited hopefully for more greens.

Costanza stayed by the shutter until the pair wordlessly left the study. She threw the spinach down on the tiled floor and rushed back upstairs, taking the steps two at a time. Fearful of meeting Pietro, she didn't know where to hide. She found herself in the drawing room and at the piano, where she began to play the first thing that came into her head, which was spinning as if a swarm of bees was buzzing inside it. Instinctively she played on, sometimes pounding on the keys, at other times barely brushing them with her fingertips, until she stumbled across a sonata that she recognised.

She played and played, bent over the keyboard, arching her spine backwards, playing, suffering, enjoying. Then came a spasm and, finally, peace: the last notes. She stayed there, hands in her lap, her sight blurred.

"This house has suffered without its mistress, and I have, too, without my marchesa's music," said Pietro. Costanza started: she hadn't realised he had pushed open the drawing-room door, against which he was leaning languidly, half hidden by the curtain.

Costanza learnt to recognise the signs: Pietro would eat absently, glance impatiently at the grandfather clock, sketch fleeting smiles like an adolescent itching to get away. Every time she determined to resist the temptation, but every time she gave in to it: furtively she would go down the spiral stairs with her bunch of greens in hand, then wait for the usual sounds and watch, avidly, through the slats of the shutters. Afterwards, all in a turmoil, she would run to her room, throw herself on her bed, and savour her lonely, bitter pleasure.

58

"From the sea springs salt and from woman all evils."

Costanza Safamita attains a certain equilibrium and moves to Palermo,
but she is upset by an argument with her brother Stefano
and by her husband's betrayal.

On the advice of Iero Bentivoglio, who had become a member of parliament, Costanza made good investments in the Banca Nazionale; her inheritance from Aunt Assunta meant that she had more liquid assets at her disposal. She also decided to restore Palazzo Sabbiamena and spend the winter months in Palermo, overcoming her aversion to the social life of the city. There she would see her father, who was no longer comfortable in Sarentini and preferred his new home in Palermo, and the Trasis. She would also have the chance to get to know Stefano's older daughters better—especially her beloved Caterina—both of whom were at the boarding school for girls there. Moreover, Costanza cherished the secret hope that by going to Palermo she might cut Pietro off from his amours with the maids in Cacaci, which had become a torment that she could no longer do without.

The bourgeoisie and those nobles who, like the Safamitas, could afford to were building villas and mansions in the new city. In a climate of expansion and renewal, the aristocracy once more dominated Palermo's social and political life, and it became a destination favoured by the crowned heads of Europe. Proud of his family and sustained by his wife's wealth, Pietro was ready to play an enthusiastic part in the revitalized social life of Palermo and to enjoy all that his city had to offer. He was eager to cut a fine figure and to repay the hospitality of his faithful friends, who in his bachelor days had kept him going with loans and invitations.

Pietro stepped up his morning visits to Costanza's room; they would talk about how the renovation work was going, plan the day, and decide on what needed to be bought. Happy with her husband's presence, Costanza accepted his attentions.

Costanza, now a vicarious participant in another aspect of Pietro's life, became in a strange way closer to him: there was a new intimacy, a secret to which he was not privy. Certain by now that her husband did not pick his lovers from among their peers, she took a more lenient view of his affairs with the lewd, brazen women of the lower classes. She hoped that, far from Cacaci, he would tire of such brutally physical relationships and, in time, turn to her, his wife, and finally give her a son, an heir to the Patella di Sabbiamena line.

Wearing the famous Safamita jewels, she went with him to receptions and to the salons of his friends' wives. She didn't enjoy this or find it easy, but she persevered. The conversations among the married women of Palermo were very different from those of the women in Cacaci. The ladies of the aristocracy in Palermo openly alluded to their lovers in what had become a codified language: "a real gentleman," "generous to a fault," "a truly cultured man," "a great friend of my husband's," "tolerant with that hag of a wife of his," "a great connoisseur." The terms and epithets used to describe betrayed wives were heavy-handed—"ingrate," "egotist," "she humiliates him," "an ignorant, stupid woman," "a squanderer," "she'll be his ruin," "she doesn't understand him," "she has turned his children against him"—and as soon as their backs were turned the gossips let loose. This struck Costanza as a cruel and perverse game, but it was one that she had to get used to in order to please Pietro. At parties, during the promenade along the Marina, anywhere that men and women had the chance to meet, Costanza—a great observer—noted the languid glances, knowing looks, courtships pressed insistently, love affairs—all conducted in accordance with an elegant, centuries-old ritual. She felt different, isolated. But Pietro didn't seem to take part in these activities, though he flirted with them all. On their way home, in the carriage, with disarming innocence and his customary good humour he would comment on the women upon whom he had lavished his charm. Costanza, who only a few minutes before had been suffering the torments of hell, felt comforted.

Pietro immersed himself in preparations for the big party for the inauguration of the main floor of Palazzo Sabbiamena, which had finally been restored. Baron and Baroness Almerico came to it specially from Cacaci and were often house guests.

Costanza noticed that when they were expecting the Almericos Pietro showed the same feverish impatience she had seen in him when he had his sordid encounters with those women in his study. Mariangela wore expensive shawls, flaunted embroidered handkerchiefs, fans, even jewels that betrayed Pietro's refined and particular tastes. Some were even similar to her own. And when Baron Almerico was not in Palermo, Pietro would disappear. Costanza observed all this, devoured by jealousy.

One afternoon Costanza was alone with Maria Antonia Bentivoglio. Her cousin was very upset; her fine grey eyes were sad and her face, once quiet and smiling in youth, was careworn. She was quite carried away telling Costanza about her own husband's infidelity:

"Costanza, I don't have a dowry like yours and I depend on him. I put up with things for love of my children. Iero is influential and powerful; he helps and advises everybody, you included, and if I spoke out people would turn against me. You are rich, you keep your husband, you indulge him as if he were your son . . . I'd like to be like you."

Costanza listened to her in dismay.

"Don't say you don't know! All Palermo is talking about Mariangela Almerico. Her husband is old, and she feels entitled to be unfaithful to him in broad daylight; they even say he goes along with this. And you treat her like a friend! I am forever coming across her here in your home . . . You are really different, Costanza. Don't you have any feelings?"

Costanza invited Stefano and his family to Palazzo Sabbiamena. Since receiving his inheritance from Aunt Assunta, he had been drinking less and had paid off his debts; his family was reasonably comfortable. But

Stefano had thrown himself into a new business with some shady individuals: an ice factory, a venture that Costanza and others had advised him against.

After dinner, Costanza and Stefano were left alone.

"I know you're planning to give a reception. Why haven't you invited us?" her brother asked straight out.

"I can't, Stefano. Our father will be here, if he's well, and the family, and all the nobility."

"Costanza, I want you to invite me. It's up to me to decide whether to come or to bring my wife. Will you invite me or not?"

"I've told you, I can't. You are an honoured guest in our house, but on your own. The others don't want to meet Filomena, and they wouldn't come if they knew they'd meet her. She's a blacksmith's daughter, remember. She isn't an aristocrat, and she isn't even rich. That's how our world is. I don't like it, but I must live in it with my husband, and I must respect him. Aristocrats with aristocrats, blacksmiths with blacksmiths—that is how people must wed," said Costanza with some heat.

"Go on, go on, what are you driving at? Horse with horse, donkey with donkey . . . d'you mean to say that I am a horse and my wife is a donkey? And what about my children, then, are they mules? Say it then, say it!"

"Stefano, it's the way of the world." Costanza was desolate.

"So you are calling my children mules? If you don't invite me, I don't wish to see you again, and I shall forbid my children to have anything to do with you . . . What is your answer?"

"If that's the way you want it, Stefano, do as you will. I do my duty. Remember that I love you, and I love Filomena and your children as if they were my own," replied Costanza, heartsick.

After the success of their party, the Marchese and Marchesa Sabbiamena became fully engaged in Palermo's social whirl. Invitations poured in and were liberally returned. Pietro was enthusiastic about this, and with that feminine touch which made him so appealing to the ladies he showered advice and suggestions on his wife, a meticulous and ladylike mistress of the house but painfully shy and hopelessly inhibited in conversation. Baroness Lannificchiati, who had become Costanza's mentor, described her with a certain accuracy—proof of the scarce consideration in which she held her—as a good, old-fashioned provincial girl who had been dazzled by her nephew since the day she saw him and whose ducats added lustre to the Patella di Sabbiamena name.

People were convinced that the Sabbiamena couple had reached mutually satisfactory arrangements, and at times Costanza would have liked to believe this. Pietro was good, kind, full of life, and exquisitely thoughtful: he was the one who had comforted her after her rows with Giacomo and Stefano, he was the one who worried about her ailments, and he was the one who gave her presents and let her do things her way. But he didn't love her. Still, and despite everything, Costanza could not bear the thought of living without him.

59

"The egg is the best mouthful."

Costanza Safamita has a long conversation with her father and catches
a glimpse of a young Neapolitan.
The whisked egg

The new Safamita House in Palermo was a three-story building on the corner of the square where the new opera house was being built. It had all the modern conveniences.

Costanza and her father were sitting on the terrace, in the late afternoon.

"I am old, and I like the idea of dying in Palermo," Domenico Safamita said. "I'm happy here. This house pleases me. Giacomo will decide what to do with the old house in Sarentini, but I really think he won't want to keep it. Do you want it?"

"What use is it to me? I have lots of houses," replied Costanza.

"Listen to me, Costanza. I want you to have a house of your own in Palermo. I don't trust your husband, and I never have."

"You're wrong, Papa. He is honest," said Costanza, immediately upset, as she was every time someone criticised her husband even indirectly, and then she quickly corrected herself, adding, "in his business dealings."

"Does he love you?"

"Yes, in his own way," she said, blushing.

Her father did not answer, and his attention wandered. He was looking upwards, for the weather was changing. Threatening grey clouds were piling up from above the ring of mountains behind the city, and the sky was leaden. A large cloud covered the sun, and the terrace was cast into sudden gloom. The baron raised his sick eyes and looked at Monte Pellegrino,which he could see, blurred, standing out against the sky in the distance, and it was changing colour. New shades of blue and violet gave it an austere and menacing look. That mountain, with its perfect proportions and solid beauty, was the guardian of the bay: a legendary beast crouching half immersed in the sea—the angular forms of its back and legs above the surface—but ready to shake off its slumbers and rear up against anyone who dared come near the city.

Domenico Safamita loved Palermo with an almost physical passion. "They are destroying monasteries and palaces," he said. "They're gutting whole districts. Never mind if there's no water, if the sewers are rudimentary or nonexistent, if the common people live in hovels and die of hunger and disease: the people of Palermo want a grand new opera house. Palermo is ever more beautiful and ever more abject, and it has never shown better how wonderfully—how smugly!—it continues to be the ultimate courtesan-city. Here, even the stones ooze sensuality."

To the left a wide new road ended at the sea, where night seemed to have fallen and the water was scattered with glittering dots—the first lamps lit by the fishermen. Then the cloud slipped away from the sun and all was as before: the sea a dark stain with no gleam of light, and Monte Pellegrino, slightly pinkened, standing out clear and benign.

"Papa, may I ask you a question?" hazarded Costanza.

"Yes, Costanza."

"Why didn't Mama love me?" Her hair, gathered in a chignon at the nape of her neck, was like a dark red halo, her head was held elegantly on her long neck, her freckled skin was gleaming: Costanza was beautiful.

"Your mother loved me very much, perhaps too much, as a matter of fact." Suddenly the baron felt exhausted.

"I don't understand you, Papa. One can never love one's husband too much."

"You're wrong," said the baron. "Excess is always a mistake, even in love." Then he added softly, "In patience, too, and in tolerance and for-giveness." She listened, trying to understand. "Costanza, I have given you all the love of a father and a mother, since the first time I saw you, since the day you were born."

"I know, Papa."

"And I want you to be happy. You are not. I'll tell you something. I loved your mother deeply, but she was never my great love, not the most important one. That love has still not abandoned me, and it lightens the burden of my years. When it does leave me, it will be time to die."

"What are you saying? I don't understand you today, Papa," Costanza said with a sigh.

"Love for oneself. Respect for oneself. You must love yourself. You must like yourself. Only then will others love you. In your home the best guest is you, before all the others. The others come after."

"And what about duty, which you instilled in me, duty which Stefano hasn't respected?" Costanza was confused.

"Ah, duty, duty . . . It's a dilemma, a choice, which everyone solves as best he can. When I was young I did as I wished, and when I was called back to my duties towards our line, I decided I actually welcomed them. And so it was. It's not always easy, but you can do it, and you live better."

"I shall do so, too. I always try to obey you, Papa."

"You didn't when you married."

"Papa, I promise to obey you from now on, always."

"No, Costanza, you must not. What I want for you is that you do as you wish. Happiness must be sought, built up stone by stone, with the stones at hand, like a house."

"Papa, why do I have red hair?"

"You have been a redhead for twenty-seven years, and now you ask me? Because you are a child of love, beautiful as no other, red as the sun." His voice trembled, and then he collected himself. "Remember that other people will not see you like that unless you've done so first, unless you've thought of yourself before thinking of others. Even your husband will realise, when that happens."

"Why didn't you ever tell me these things before?"

"Now you are a woman. You were an innocent before. And I'll tell you one last thing. Sometimes you seem pale, washed-out. Take a whisked egg with sugar every morning, as little children do, *ma petite*."

At the house entrance, as she was getting into her coach, Costanza spotted a young man who couldn't have been more than twenty years old. He was tall, very thin, and pale. Different. His moustache, beard, and hair were red, while his eyes were chestnut-coloured with very pale lashes, like hers. She started. They looked at each other and recognised their likeness. As the coach rolled away, Costanza thought deeply about that young man. She had to know who he was.

Someone told her that he was from Naples, the son of a worker at the Corbotta, and half English. His father had died recently and he was trying to trace his relatives, enquiring about an uncle who had also been an employee at the mine that had once belonged to the Safamitas. Costanza's grandfather had sold it at highly favourable conditions to a Belgian contractor. No one knew anything about what had happened to the workers there.

The baron was left alone, on the terrace. He called for a blanket and a light; he didn't feel like going back indoors.

It was a sunny day in November 1866. Domenico Safamita was preparing for his visit to the Monastery of Grottavacante, and more reluctantly than usual, because he had to tell Father Sedita about Father Puma's transfer away from Sarentini. Secretly a nonbeliever, the baron had welcomed with a certain satisfaction the House of Savoy's anti-clericalism and their expropriation of Church property at the time of Italy's unification, but he was fond of Gaspare Sedita and had respected the words of his Lattuca uncle: "Remember to make sure that he lacks for nothing, and listen to him—he's got more brains than the average priest."

They drank a glass of sweet wine together.

"I know a bishop who will find me a place in a good monastery in Rome. Thanks be to God and to you Safamitas, I have no financial problems. I hope to die in peace before the Savoys establish themselves in the Holy City—as sooner or later they will. For the present, I shall stay here: I want to send that dolt Father Puma somewhere else." Father Sedita began this way so as to spare the baron the embarrassment of bringing up the inevitable. Then, looking straight at him, he added, "Domenico, I'm really sorry for you. I know you love that girl of yours—more than you care for the boys. And that's a mistake."

"If I may say so, all these sons of ours strike me as somewhat doltish," added the baron with an ironic, collusive half smile.

"Go easy, my son. You are talking to a priest. Love, example, and encouragement make even stunted plants grow, even plants that spring from rotten seed. Stefano and Giacomo are Safamitas."

"Costanza had little or no affection from her mother."

"That's your fault . . . I never told you that before."

"Explain yourself!"

"I am bound by the secrecy of the confessional."

Domenico sat up straight, suddenly angered. "Caterina?"

"Don't be stupid—Caterina didn't talk. You people hold your tongues—though silence is not a virtue, even if people think it is. We Sicilians are full of secret societies; we even have our own homegrown one. A new name for an ancient evil. I am old, and in this mafia I see deadly germs—and not only that. The mafia could help Sicily, but only if it disbanded when it no longer had a reason to exist—when the kingdom becomes a true unitary state that can govern justly and that governs us properly. *Omertà* and violence may be acceptable when we are dominated by outsiders, but they only harm a just and efficient state . . ." Father Sedita's gaze was absent, his mind on other things. He collected himself. "Forgive me, I digress. I want to talk to you about adultery and forgiveness, which have much in common. You have practised them both, and well. Perhaps too well."

"You're talking like a priest."

"Not just as a priest but as a man, too. It is a mortal sin to commit adultery, the Commandments say so. As a priest, I must accept this. Silence is essential in such cases, and the greater sin, it seems to me, is to confess the adultery to the unwitting spouse. I used to impose three times the penitence on adulterers who confessed to the injured party. That is pain inflicted for no reason, and it certainly can destroy a marriage. We all know that many people betray their partners, but in forty years in the priesthood I have never met a person who did so only once. One betrayal leads to another. Betrayal spreads like mint: someone plants a root and it infests everything. It is a universal rule, and we priests know it well." Father Sedita went back to his thoughts, staring into the distance and murmuring, "Like incest, like impure acts with children or with those of the same sex. Families perpetuate these practises—from transgressor to victim. The childhood victim becomes an adult transgressor in turn." He turned back to the baron and added, "Domenico, for your sake, only for your sake"—his voice broke—"because we care deeply for each other, we two, I approve the transfer of Father Puma to the seminary, and of course I know there are children there. Vulnerable. Just so you know that."

Domenico Safamita understood and replied without betraying any emotion, "You mustn't worry. I have made a gift to the curia, and shall pay for six seminarists. Father Puma's lodgings are guaranteed. I shall also help them buy back the old seminary at auction, when the time is right."

His elbow trembling, Father Sedita drank his wine. "Thank you," he murmured, and then went on. "Domenico, when it came to adultery, you did the right thing: you hid it and you did well to do so. I'm not saying this is a merit, but you followed our tradition. But as to forgiveness, you never hid that. You erred in forgiving too much and in silence."

"It's not up to me to remind you of the maxim 'Turn the other cheek.'" Domenico spoke with no trace of irony.

"Leave the Gospels out of this! You erred because you let it be known that you knew and forgave. You must hide forgiveness, as you hide infidelity."

"And that means?"

"Men are different from women. Men confess infidelity to their wives not so much out of a desire for forgiveness as out of complacence: both attitudes are egotistical, arrogant, and harmful. Women rarely confess adultery, and not just to avoid getting themselves killed. If your wife loves you but yields to temptation, and you come to know of this but say nothing, then the situation becomes complicated; she knows she has done wrong and expects to be reproved and punished, but she also needs to explain herself, to show you where you, too, have done wrong. If you punish her too much, she will cast your own sins in your face, because that's the way she saves her dignity and regains both her own respect and yours. This is an important step in all relations based on trust. It makes it easier to restore business relations, to re-establish conjugal love, harmony in the family, equilibrium with the children, and affection for those who are innocent but are living proof of the sin.

"But if the husband who wants his wife for himself accepts her transgression and forgives in silence, then he goes on being unhappy. And worse: it leaves the sinning wife with no chance to redeem herself—in his eyes and her own. It destroys her. People must explain themselves and make peace. Only then is it right to forgive." Father Sedita was getting tired, and his drooping eyes were moist. "All I have to say to you is this: Costanza is strong. She is a love child, and you will continue to give her love. But mark my words"—and he shot Domenico a penetrating, withering glance—"all she has is you, her father."

60

"Every day judges the previous day, and the last day judges all."

Costanza Safamita discovers that her husband has fathered a child, and she is deeply embittered.

Baron Safamita's health deteriorated, and the Sabbiamenas stayed in Palermo all winter and part of the spring. Pietro made a few brief visits to Cacaci, especially after the Almericos returned to town. Costanza thought bitterly that he went to see Mariangela, but by now she had accepted the inevitability of the relationship. In April 1886, when Costanza had to go back to Cacaci on business, Giacomo and Adelaide arrived in Palermo to take their turn at the baron's bedside.

Costanza was sewing quietly with her nurse, happy to be once more in what she considered her true home. She had left Amalia in Cacaci to keep an eye on household affairs and to look after don Paolo, who by now was an invalid, and she had missed her.

"Some big things have been going on here," said Amalia. She seemed embarrassed.

"Tell me, Amalia," Costanza encouraged her, and she laid her sewing on her knee.

Amalia told her that during the winter one of the new kitchen maids had felt sick. At first they thought it was cholera, but it wasn't. Then it was discovered that she was pregnant, but the woman had refused to say anything more. They called for a midwife, but the girl wouldn't have anything to do with her. Don Carmelo wanted to tell the girl's uncle, who had sent her into service, but the girl was sure her family would kill her, made a hysterical scene, and didn't want to hear of leaving Sabbiamena House. And don Carmelo let her stay.

"The baron never did these things," said Amalia. "But don Paolo tells me they happened before in Safamita House, with the menservants, and don Filippo Leccasarda would see to the midwives and to setting things straight, and no one ever knew anything. We could have done with Pina Pissuta, who would have sorted everything out, but they don't make good midwives like her anymore!"

"Does the marchese know about this?" asked Costanza.

"I don't think so. Don Carmelo pretends that nothing has happened, but in the meanwhile she already has a belly, and sooner or later people will notice."

"Don't worry. I shall speak to her, and then we'll see how to help her. Do you know who's to blame?"

"I don't know, but it certainly isn't don Carmelo, according to don Paolo," she replied.

Rura Fecarotta was plump, with dark hair and coarse features. Her pregnancy was not yet obvious. She stood in front of Costanza, frightened.

"How many months pregnant are you?" Costanza asked awkwardly.

The woman didn't reply.

"If you don't want to tell me anything, you will have to leave service here. If you talk, I shall see to it that you and your child are helped," said Costanza firmly.

"Don Carmelo shouldn't have talked. It's his job to sort things out. Your ladyship doesn't come into it," the girl replied, and burst into tears. Costanza offered her a handkerchief, which Rura refused, and went on weeping, her eyes lowered.

Rosa knocked at the door. Costanza leapt to her feet to tell her to stay away, and knocked over the sewing table. Little boxes, embroidery, thimbles, scissors, thread, and needles fell to the carpet, and Rura, on her knees, fussed about picking things up, watering them all with her tears.

Costanza looked at her bleakly, thinking, Perhaps I can arrange a reparatory marriage . . . Rura's skirt had hitched up and Costanza could see the white flesh of her well-turned calves between her stockings and her bloomers. Costanza felt a great pity for the girl. And then she noticed a big dark birthmark on Rura's left leg. She recognised that mark.

A disgusting acidity welled up in her mouth. She swallowed violently. Her head was throbbing, as if she had been struck by a large stone. Thousands of thoughts whirled in her head and assailed her. Then, as if by enchantment, her mind cleared. Mechanically, she gave rapid orders to put the fallen objects back in place and to stand the table back on its feet. When she had finished, Costanza stood right in front of Rura and demanded, "Tell me the truth: who is the father of your child?"

Rura remained silent, glowering at her defiantly.

"Answer me. That's an order."

The woman still kept silent. Her puffy, wet face was inscrutable.

"I'm asking you for the last time. Who is to blame?" Costanza raised her voice. "If you won't talk, I'll tell you who it is!"

The two women looked at each other, each fearing the other.

In a tone of command that brooked no disobedience, Costanza said slowly, "It is the marchese. I want you to confirm that."

"Yes, your ladyship," stammered Rura—then added impetuously, bitterly, her voice filled with hate, "I hope don Carmelo gets murdered. He promises the earth and does next to nothing to help the people he gets into trouble."

"Does the marchese know?" asked Costanza, stunned.

"He knows nothing, and may he continue to know nothing," murmured Rura, bursting into tears once more. "It's all my fault, mine, mine."

"What do you want to do?"

Then Rura lost control. She wrung her hands, slapped them noisily one against the other and then against her hips and thighs, tore at her hair, knocking her uniform cap askew, beat her breast, slapped herself, called on all the saints, and cursed her fate. Costanza let her carry on, meanwhile gathering her thoughts, and after a time Rura calmed down, though she was still weeping.

"I have made a decision. If you don't want this child, I'll take you to Palermo and I'll send you to a convent. When it is born, you will leave it at the wheel. You may continue to work for other people, and I shall find a position for you myself. But if you want to keep the baby I'll find you a place where you can give birth. You cannot stay on in service here. You will always have a means of sustenance. I shall see to your upkeep and that of your child, whom I shall have educated as his father's son deserves, but you will remain what you are: a shamed housemaid. You must behave in an upright manner and devote your life to your child, bringing him up with a mother's heart, do you understand? Think it over and let me know." Costanza realised that she had raised her voice. She was trembling.

Rura had fallen to her knees. She grabbed Costanza's hand and kissed it.

"Now go, and do not utter a word of this to a living soul. If they ask you, say that I wanted to see you this afternoon and that you told me nothing. This evening I shall call for you and we can talk."

At table, Pietro was in a good humour. After dinner Costanza asked him to go into her drawing room because she had something very important to tell him.

"Is your father ill?" he asked solicitously as he followed her.

"No, it's not about my father."

Pietro fell into the armchair facing the smaller one in which Costanza usually sat. Relaxed, he looked around: it was an elegant drawing room, with the touch of womanly intimacy that he loved.

"Today I spoke with one of the kitchen maids, Rura. She was hired by the majordomo when I was in Palermo. She is pregnant with your child."

"Costanza, what are you saying? You're mad! Have you asked Carmelo?"

"There is no need to." Costanza looked at him with her big eyes, without a tear.

Pietro rose and moved over to her. She avoided his touch—for the first time. He put his hand on the armrest of her chair and bent over her. When he spoke his face was close to hers.

"Costanza, I realise you are jealous. Women are often jealous. But you have no reason to be. And then, with a kitchen maid . . . You have always been so wise, but now you're acting on impulse. This isn't like my marchesa. You mustn't get involved with the servants. You should have asked the majordomo first, that's what he's here for. He knows what goes on here when we are away; he would have explained it to you; anyway it is for him to sort out such matters. It must have been a groom, a stable-boy, even a manservant. Servants aren't what they used be. They don't respect us anymore. She must be after money, and she set a trap for you."

"The baby is yours."

"Do you want my oath? What's with you? This isn't like you . . . you've always been so sensible."

Pietro straightened up, and his tone was harsh. She made no reply.

"You worry me," he continued, suddenly reverting to his smooth, suave voice. "Do you feel all right? Would you like a tisane?" He laid a protective hand on her arm, keeping up his stance of superiority.

"Don't touch me," said Costanza, jumping to her feet. "This is your child, I know, and that's that." Her eyes were fixed on him and he reflexively stepped back. "You must accept your responsibilities. We must take decisions, and it's already too late. Five months ago you came here for two weeks." And with a sad little smile, as if talking to herself, she added, "And to think I was tormenting myself over Mariangela Almerico!"

"Jealousy has gone to your head. Lover to that poor thing Almerico! And perhaps to a hundred other ladies and servant girls and little nobodies. Costanza, think about it—the woman may be pregnant, if she truly is, but I have nothing to do with it." Pietro's tone was urbane again, but he was watching her with ill-concealed anxiety.

Costanza was silent. He gave a hint of a smile as he shook his head.

"Enough, Pietro," she said. "I have gone along with things, put up with things, by my own choice. Now we're talking about a child of yours, and I wanted one so badly. We shall see to both mother and baby, and your child will be brought up as befits a Patella."

"Child? I don't have any child!" he blurted out angrily.

"Pietro, don't deny it. Think it over, before you destroy everything we have tried to save of our marriage."

"Deny what, Costanza? You're raving." Pietro was giving it all he had: he took two steps towards her, hands in his pockets, well aware of the power of his allure. "Your mind is muddled. It's jealousy. Jealousy has turned my marchesa's head!"

"No, Pietro, it is your child." Costanza was ice-cold.

"How can you keep on repeating such an outrage?" Now he was furious.

"It suffices that you know I am certain of it."

"You're mad! Mad! Mad!" shouted Pietro.

"I am telling the truth. And I wouldn't like to call myself the Marchesa Sabbiamena if you lied to me. Now go away, please!"

That evening, in the arms of her nurse, Costanza wept as never before and she didn't stop even after she had drunk a whole teapotful of water and bay laurel.

61

"Advance not if you have no stomach for it!"

*Costanza Safamita has a most distressing conversation with her
husband as she is plaiting a length of light-blue silk.*

Costanza did not go to bed; she sat thinking, as she did her mending,
about the enormity of what had happened. She was shaken by her own
audacity in confronting Pietro, bewildered by the situation, and astonished by the speed with which she had acted. She had decided without
reflecting, as if someone else had possessed her and given her a strange
courage. Now she was mulling over the many and profound repercus-
sions on herself, her husband, her family, their whole world, not to mention the mother and child. She knew nothing about Rura.

The first light of dawn brightened the sky. It was another day.
Costanza felt somehow calm and serene with almost no rancour towards
Pietro and the woman: she had become used to it.

Pietro, alarmed by his wife's reaction, didn't go to his club, hoping
that he would see her at dinner, but she didn't appear, complaining of fatigue. Dismayed, he spoke to don Carmelo. He, too, was concerned; for
years he had been procuring willing maids for Pietro, and he wasn't the
only majordomo to pander to his master's tastes in this way. He had
taken advantage of the marchesa's absence when he hired Rura, who
knew the ropes and was therefore a suitable choice. But things hadn't
gone well, and he suspected that that busybody don Paolo Mercurio had
told the marchesa. It was a mess, and now the marchese would have to
sort it out.

Pietro awoke at dawn and considered various confused plans of action. Costanza would give in to his pleas. He would offer a more than
reasonable payment out of his own pocket. But his wife would have to be
persuaded to have nothing to do with the baby. He would allude to the
likelihood of otherwise being ostracised by their peers. He would appeal
to common decency. He would suggest shady reasons for Rura's actions,
and dangle before Costanza's eyes visions of chaos in the household staff,
blackmail, even the hand of the mafia. He would promise to change,
even hint at the possibility of having a child of their own—a prospect he
had rejected only for his own convenience. He would point out that the

scorn of their peers would injure the pride of both the Safamitas and the Sabbiamenas.

At all events the child had to disappear; it didn't belong to him, and even less so to Costanza.

Pietro walked heavily down the corridor to Costanza's room: it was time for his morning visit. She was at her sewing table, unravelling a skein of light-blue silk on the winder. Rosa made herself scarce as soon as she saw him. Yet everything seemed normal.

"I slept badly. How are you feeling?" he asked her.

"I didn't sleep at all, but I'm fine now, thank you," she replied, unsmiling.

"Costanza, I am ashamed, and I ask you to forgive me. I am unworthy of you, I know . . ." he began, and sat down, ill at ease, in his usual chair.

Costanza gazed at him evenly. Her father's warning resounded in her ears: *He is not the man for you . . . you deserve better.* And scraps of their last conversation: *Costanza, what I want for you is that you do as you wish . . . you must love yourself.* She looked at Pietro. His crossed legs, his fashionable suit—that was his shell. He was like an upturned tortoise lying on its back.

Pretending to look around, his fingers spasmodically toying with the fringes of the armrest, Pietro appeared to his wife as what he was: a coward, perhaps convinced of the sincerity of his contrite words. *You deserve better . . .* Costanza said nothing: she would have hurt him too much if she had spoken a word. She turned back to the sewing table. She wound the last of the blue silk from the reel and cut it with a decisive snip of her scissors. She held the ends tight and widened her arms, keeping the soft, gleaming fibres taut as she wound one end round the drawer pull. She brought the skein together and began to smooth it out, making sure it wasn't tangled. Then she divided it into three and started to make a braid.

"Say something to me, Costanza. You cannot ignore me! I am your husband! This is a torment—I can't bear it! I can't stand it anymore!" shouted Pietro, exasperated.

"I wanted a child of yours, and this one is," said Costanza softly, in the monotonous cadence of the Safamitas, without taking her eyes off the silk. "I am not acting on impulse. This child must not suffer the fate of Stefano's children. It doesn't deserve that. If you want a separation from me, you can have one. Then I shall see to the child on my own. I won't make a scandal." She had finished the braid and now she was running her fingers along it, from top to bottom, smoothing it out. She took the scissors and cut the end in one crisp, clean clip. Then she looked at him at last and added, "Your aunt Annina told me that Cavaliere Cuccuzzelli is the son of your great-uncle Prince Chisicussi. So it won't be a first in your family. This is what I want."

Now Pietro was pleading, distraught. "But what about us? And that woman—what will happen? Do you want to leave me? What must I do? Tell me!"

"No need to panic. Nothing is going to happen for now." Costanza stopped and brought one hand up to her cheek before letting it slip slowly down to her bosom. She felt calm and at peace. "I'd like to ask you a question: did you marry me for my dowry?"

Pietro was astounded, and didn't know what to say. "Other women, not as rich as you, would have paid a fortune in dowry to become a marchesa," he said finally. "No, not just for your dowry." He gazed at her levelly.

"Then why?"

"I felt sorry for you, Costanza, if you must really know. You were so much in love," he murmured, and lowered his eyes.

Costanza felt something give way inside her, as if a vase that was already cracked had now shattered into pieces. But she controlled herself, swallowed hard, and said icily, "I must ask you not to have intimate relations with the staff, or with other women, in our home. Outside you may continue to behave as you wish." Pietro kept his eyes down. Then Costanza tried to return to her usual tone, "I'd like to visit my father next week. Is it all right with you if we go back to Palermo?"

He said nothing.

Costanza had a sudden urge to rid herself of her husband's presence, and on impulse she pulled the tassel of the bell.

"What does your ladyship require?" asked Rosa, who came running.

"A whisked egg." And already Costanza felt better.

Costanza set the spoon on the saucer and Rosa took away the tray. She was alone at last. Savouring the sweetness of the soft foam in her mouth, she remained seated, hands clasped together, motionless.

She did not eat all day, nor did she get up from the sewing table. The shadows cast by the setting sun spread across the room; before long, the women would come with the lamps. She had to stir. Not knowing what else to do, Costanza went down to the small terrace in front of the study. It was warm and the tortoises were emerging from hibernation. She spotted one near the sandy earth. They looked at each other. Costanza understood it: somnolent but artful. Seeing no greens in her hands, the creature did not move towards her. Even the tortoises, like everyone else, were interested in her only when they could get what they wanted from her.

Every evening, before going to bed, Costanza would put her sewing table in order. She picked up the braid of blue silk. It hadn't come out very well: the three strands were unequal, but they held; the threads were straight, ready to be pulled out and threaded into a needle. "Life goes on, that's how it is," she murmured to herself, and she remembered that she hadn't played all day. She sat down at the harp—which she kept in her room, as she had done in Sarentini—and brushed its strings.

She played late into the night, but she didn't manage to give voice to a song or even to hum.

62

"One law for the rich, another for the poor"

The death of Baron Domenico Safamita and the rows between his children

The Marchese and Marchesa Sabbiamena went to Palermo earlier than planned: Baron Safamita was ill, and it was feared that he would die. Costanza decided to take her nurse and don Paolo, who wanted to see his master again.

Costanza found her father a prey to anxiety; he quickly told her that he had had a bitter quarrel with Giacomo and had changed his will. He said nothing more. Costanza wondered if the young man with red hair, who had been so like her, wasn't her father's illegitimate child and the real reason for the disagreement with Giacomo.

Her father explained that she would receive, as well as her share, Castle Sarentini and an apartment in the new house in Palermo, and that he intended to leave Pietro six thoroughbred sorrels, and his daughter-in-law his collection of miniatures.

"Why have you given so much to us?" Costanza asked him, curious. "Giacomo won't be happy about this."

"Serves him right. He asked for it," her father replied. "But I'm beginning to think I was too hard on Stefano. If he had been less proud, and if I had taken him the right way, perhaps we might have come to an agreement. We could have moved to Palermo, maybe to the mainland. I should have accepted the nomination to be a senator: your mother was right. But Giacomo will bring the family low, in a slow, steady decline." He broke off and looked towards Monte Pellegrino. "I hope his children will prove better than their father. But he is still a Safamita. Do not trust him."

"Papa, if I don't have any children, to whom should I leave my property?" asked Costanza.

"To whomever you wish. You are young and you belong to the modern world. I am of the older generation, which believes in passing on name and wealth: our tradition and the Safamita name matter more than everything else. It's too late for me to change. For me there is no choice."

"Have you other children apart from us?"

"Costanza, you always surprise me with your questions. No, I have no other children."

"And if you had, would you have loved them as if they were the children of our mother?"

"The one I really loved was you, Costanza. Remember, you are special—you, only you, are a child of love. But I haven't answered your question. Probably, yes, I would have loved them. But the property, no, that must go to those to whom it belongs, and it belongs to the Safamitas."

Her father was moved, and they wept together.

The baron died a few days later. The funeral was held in Sarentini, and the whole town attended. Costanza was distraught, but she could not weep. Standing at her side, Pietro held her up.

They were at the cemetery, after the burial. Costanza had one foot on the step of the coach, ready to get in, when she suddenly stopped, stricken.

"What's the matter?" asked her husband. Costanza's gaze was fixed on a point higher up on the road that came down the hill, where two seminarists and an old priest were watching them, sitting in a gig parked on a wide bend.

"Who are they? Do you know them?" said Pietro. "Do you want to have them come here?"

"No," she said. "Not now."

The Sabbiamenas slept at the castle. The next day Costanza sent a note to Stefano. She dispensed with condolence calls for the whole day and stayed at home waiting for him. When Stefano arrived, he was drunk. His breath stank of wine and his speech was slurred. With him was Guglielmo, his son, a handsome boy whose fiery, sparkling eyes would suddenly become sweet and tender, like his father's. He had never been inside the castle before but felt at ease in it; every so often he would glance around curiously, but with no awkwardness.

"Why did you call for me? You know I want nothing to do with you." Stefano refused to kiss his sister and remained standing.

"Papa died remorseful about having treated you badly."

"It's too late. Once again, you are carrying out his orders. You're the baron's servant, milady the marchesa, even after his death! Listen, Guglielmo, that's what she is," Stefano sniggered, dribbling. "She's the baron's servant."

"No, he did not force me to obey him, it was my choice."

"Why?"

"He was the only person who loved me . . . but let's not talk about that. He has left me this castle, and I want to give it to you. May I?"

"D'you know what Giacomo has done? Don't you know about the fire in the town hall?"

"No, when?"

"Go on, pretend. But the truth will out—lawyers are involved. You, too, will have to appear in court to answer for the misdeeds of the Safamitas. 'Safamita versus Safamita'—that's what it says on the papers. Shamed in front of everyone. This is what all of you wanted, and this is what you'll get. I'm not accepting charity from you, not even for my children. I swear this before my son, the true heir to the Barons Safamita. Even if I were to accept your gift of the castle, I would burn it down, down to the foundations! From you and him I want only my due, with a judge's ruling and all. If my children accept a penny from you after my death, they will be accursed!" Stefano was gesturing wildly and speaking excitedly. Unable to find words, he began to stagger and became incoherent. Guglielmo had to take him away. They refused the offer of a coach.

Costanza watched them from the window. Stefano was stumbling, his hat askew, his jacket in disarray. With the youngster guiding his father's steps, they proceeded slowly down the avenue where once Stefano had run around as master: two beaten men. Costanza took refuge in her room.

Amalia came in silently; she found her mistress prone on the bed and called her softly, "Milady, Baron Giacomo is here. He even wanted to come right into your ladyship's room. He says he must speak to your ladyship!"

And Giacomo indeed burst in. He was purple in the face and shouting. "How dare you let him enter our grandfather's house? You have no respect for the dead! You have been a disgrace to the Safamitas since you were born, and you continue to besmirch our name! What did he tell you? The whole town knows you want to give him the castle! You have no shame!"

Pietro, who had come running when he heard the noise, stopped in the doorway.

"Calm down, calm down," said Costanza. Her brother's words had fallen far short of her; they hadn't even touched her.

"Giacomo, don't speak to your sister that way," said Pietro. "Control yourself."

"Oh, so you're here, too, are you? This one here, the redheaded bitch, wants to destroy my family, just as Stefano did, but I won't let it happen. Our mother died because of his wickedness, not to mention what he said and did against our father!" Then, turning to Costanza, he snapped, "And now you, too, you of all people, want to drag us down? I'll destroy you. I'll kill you, I'll kill you myself, with my own hands!" Giacomo threw himself at Costanza, grasping her by the throat and pushing her back onto the bed. Pietro leapt on him and struck him on the back of his neck. Giacomo let go but managed to land a punch to her stomach. His brother-in-law and some footmen grabbed his arms and pulled him back towards the door.

"Remember, you are not a Safamita, you are a bastard! The red bastard! Bastard! Bastard!" yelled Giacomo, beside himself. He struggled in vain to free himself, and in fury spat at his sister. Then he surrendered to his captors.

63

"The fox will piss on the old dog."

Don Paolo Mercurio and Gaspare Quagliata
have another of their conversations in Castle Sarentini.

Don Paolo Mercurio came panting up the castle driveway. He was in a hurry to tell Gaspare Quagliata what he had seen and heard in town that morning. He was disconcerted to learn that events in the castle were much more interesting than his news.

"I didn't expect this so soon! The children already at one another's throats! The poor soul told me, before he died, 'Paolo, I'm unhappy about my son Giacomo. I no longer know which of the boys is the worse of the two! Look after my daughter—she's a good woman.' Goodness knows what happened between father and son . . . I'd never heard him talk like that about Giacomo before!" said don Paolo, shaking his head.

"I know when things changed," Gaspare interrupted him. "Two weeks ago, Giacomo came to Palermo and went straight to the baron. He was carrying a lot of documents—looked like a notary he did, he had so many of them. From the room next door I could hear everything. Giacomo wanted his father to sign some paper. Land business it was, and it concerned the marchesa, too. The baron refused, and his son starts yelling, 'She doesn't deserve it and she won't have any children. Her husband has never touched her and I can prove it!'

"The baron got mad and told him to leave, but he refused and said, 'I'm staying and you have to listen.' That's how he spoke to his father! He tells the baron that Stefano wanted to go to law over his mother's inheritance and was only waiting for his father to die. That's why he wanted him to sign the document now. He was going on about infringement of rights and suchlike monkey business. He told him he had seen to everything; he had called in certain mafiosi, bad ones Baron Safamita had never had any truck with, and they burnt down the office at the town hall where they kept the certificate of marriage with the blacksmith's daughter, and the children's birth certificates too, so that Stefano became unmarried and his children bastards.

"He was expecting his father to say well done, but instead the baron calls him a few names that even I hadn't heard before. So Giacomo says, and I'll repeat it word for word: 'You never loved me. Why? I've never dis-obeyed you, and I've done as you wished.' The baron didn't answer. So the boy says, 'Maybe it's because I amused myself with the maids when I was a boy. But you certainly did the same yourself, so where's the harm?' The baron doesn't reply. So Giacomo asks him again, 'Where's the harm?'

"'Get out of here, Giacomo,' says his father. 'You are dishonest and you have dealings with crooks. You have a lot already, and you must try not to ruin it. As for the maids, no, I never had anything to do with them when I was young. If you really must know, in those days I was at board-ing school and preferred men.'"

The two men chuckled. "That's a good one," said Gaspare.

"Giacomo goes white and he turns to leave, but before he goes he says between his teeth, 'Swine!' and then he rushes out. I close the door behind him and he turns towards the spittoon, then has second thoughts and lets fly a gob of spit the size of a pigeon shit smack on to the brand-new door of his father's room." Don Paolo was astonished. Gaspare added, "Paolo, that's why the baron changed his will and left the castle to the marchesa. Now let's hear your news."

Don Paolo collected himself, now that he was finally able to tell his story. "As I was coming up to the castle, I saw a crowd in front of the big church. It was Stefano, sitting on the steps like a beggar. Drunk he was, and gabbing on and holding court with the down-and-outs you find around there. A barber was passing by and stopped—that's why Saren-tini doesn't need town criers, since everyone will find out about this right away. Stefano was cursing the marchesa, saying that she'd wanted to give him the castle but he'd turned her down. It was justice he wanted—the property wasn't enough for him. And he was asking those poor devils, 'Tell me, isn't it true that justice comes before property?' He was saying that his brother and his father had forced the mayor—the mayor himself, the notary Tuttolomondo's son—to burn his marriage certificate and his children's birth certificates, and that he was going to sue him, too. Well, he was a terrible sight to see, but his son was even worse: he was gazing at his father with a look in his eye that makes me want to weep to think of it."

Don Paolo got his breath back, then asked, "Gaspare, was Stefano telling the truth?"

"That's what you said. I said what I've said and now my lips are sealed, but between you and me . . ." replied the other—and, with a shrug, winked at his companion.

"Uh-oh," said don Paolo, "things are going to get very ugly."

"Could be! Could be!" commented Gaspare gloomily.

"The law is the law," added don Paolo, and he looked outside. The garden was luxuriant. "The late baron really loved this garden. Our master was a good man," he observed, turning back to Gaspare. "We two will miss him."

The friends fell silent, but the conversation had not ended; it continued to run along the silent threads of affinities, thoughts, and feelings that grow between those who have known each other for years. Every so often a word, a sigh.

"They were beautiful, the carob trees at Malivinnitti," said one.

"He wouldn't let them cut those branches that hung down to the ground!" said the other.

"And that was that!" they said in unison.

"The young baron liked the Russell's wheat," said don Paolo after a while.

"That he did!" added Gaspare.

In between the silences, they recalled: "She liked it, too." "That she did!" "How hot it was!" "Down there among the wheat like the peasants!" "Damn right!" "A nice bit of stuff, the baroness was, God rest her soul!"

That's how Amalia found them: their elbows resting on the table, Baron Safamita's valet and coachman celebrating with hints and veiled allusions the deeds of their late master. Their cheeks were streaked with tears, but they were smiling.

"What's up?" she asked, worried.

"Nothing, nothing," again in unison.

64

"I may bend but I will not break."

Costanza Safamita tries to work out who she really is, and takes comfort in the pantry.

One week after Baron Safamita's funeral, the Sabbiamenas went back to Cacaci. Costanza had not stopped for a minute: she had spoken to the notary and requested an inventory of the estate, organised the staff, and received mourning callers in the castle—thus making Giacomo's estrangement public—and she even found time to call on Father Puma. She was amazed at not being as grief-stricken as she thought she would be, but she believed her father would have approved of her actions. The people of Sarentini said, "She's a strange one, this redhead, she doesn't even seem to be grieving. Is she heartless, or what?"

In Cacaci, Costanza plunged into despondency. She had lost her family: she was an orphan, an insulted sister, a wounded wife. She compared herself to her mother, but Caterina had loved and been loved in return. "Your mother loved me very much, perhaps too much," her father had told her.

For her part, she was a woman of twenty-seven condemned to virginity by her husband. "Love child," her father used to call her, and he had repeated this to the end. Costanza believed him. Why had he preferred her to her brothers? Why did Giacomo insist on insulting her? Why had he called her a "bastard"? Yet Father Puma had confirmed that this was not the case. "You are as much a Safamita as your brothers," he had told her. He, her mother's confessor, would have known.

She wept in her bed. Neither music, nor embroidery, nor the tortoises, nor the garden, nor anything else gave her comfort. She even missed the vicarious thrill of peeping through the shutters of Pietro's study.

You must love yourself, you must like yourself, her father had exhorted her. She would have to let down her hair and remake the braid of life. She had new duties, new needs, new loves. Her father's words buzzed around her head: *What I want for you is that you do as you wish. Happiness must be sought, built up stone by stone . . .*

"But where?" Costanza wondered.

She noticed the smell of the candle on the bedside table. It was pungent and made her nostrils twitch. She remembered other scents, from long ago.

Little Costanza had been in the ironing room, weeping. Maria Tecca-piglia and Amalia were caressing her. Lina Munnizza, a rare visitor to that room, looked at her: "She's a baroness, and yet I feel sorry for the girl. She's in a terrible state." Even at her young age, Costanza was proud, and her head snapped up. Maria intervened: "The less talk, the better. Give me the keys to the pantry, Lina, and be off with you." Then she hugged Costanza and said, "Come with me, I'll take you to a really special place, but not one tear must fall on the flagstones or you'll turn into a snail, and you know what'll happen then!" Maria took her by the hand and led her into the pantry. It was a fascinating new world, all to be explored.

There were three pantries in Safamita House: the first for dry, odour-less goods, the second for confectionery products and fruit to be con-served, and the third for everything else. Maria untied sacks of different legumes and told her, "Touch them, mix them up!" Hesitantly at first, Costanza plunged her hands into those big sacks, took out handfuls, and let them run slowly through her fingers—lentils, broad beans, chickpeas, beans—and back into the open mouths of the sacks. The pattering of lentils slipping through her fingers and falling like rain on roof tiles com-forted her; the sacks gave off a fresh smell of dust and starch blended with the scent of straw and aromatic herbs—the things that are dis-carded when the legumes are cleaned before cooking: the smell of fen-nel, wild flowers, fields, and tracks.

With a mysterious smile, Maria said to her, "Now let's go into the pantry where the sweets are kept. It's like the Snail Princess's cave of wonders in the queen's palace."

The pantry was truly like a cave. Like stalactites, from hooks in the ceiling and walls hung wreaths of dried figs, bunches of sultanas, pome-granate branches laden with fruit, bunches of laurel leaves, wreaths of oranges studded with cloves. The upper shelves were full of bottles of liqueur, cordials, fortified wines, and sacks of all kinds of nuts and dried fruits: almonds, walnuts, hazelnuts, pistachios, prunes, raisins, carobs, apricots, and peaches. Lined up in orderly ranks on the middle shelves stood metal boxes and glass containers of sugar, honey, cornstarch, cocoa, chocolate, coffee, cinnamon, vanilla, cloves, aniseed, dried mint, glacé flowers, candied fruit and fruit under spirits, orange zest, quince and other jams, conserves, *zuccata*, or candied courgettes, and all kinds of bis-cuits. The lower shelves, which even Costanza could reach, were brimming with fruit to be conserved: white and yellow winter melons with wrinkly, scented skins, apples and pears individually wrapped in paper, knobbly quinces, and little Neapolitan medlars red as cherries.

"Smell the wood," Maria told her.

Costanza put her nose to the shelf and inhaled the odour of the wood mixed with the aromas that filled the pantry.

"Close your eyes and don't move. Now see what happens." Little by little, in a kaleidoscope of smells, the scent of every single variety of fruit stored there became distinct and stood out from the others: the sweetness of melon, the strong tartness of quince, the delicacy of apple. She could have stayed there for hours, her little head resting on the shelf, her eyes shut, a hint of a smile on her lips, inebriated.

Maria took her into the last pantry. There were big sections of cheese cylinders: salted pecorino, dry seasoned pecorino, caciocavallo; more cheeses in rounds and ovals; barrels of wine, demijohns of vinegar, jars of oil, barrels of olives in brine, and lots of jugs of fresh water. In one corner, under a trapdoor and covered with straw, was a little icebox. She sniffed the pungent brine, the strong smell of the vinegar, the mellow smell of wine, the rich smell of the olives under oil—covered with olive leaves—the bitter smell of aubergines soused in vinegar and preserved in oil, even the almost imperceptible smell of the water in the big jugs, moist and earthy.

Then Maria took her into the kitchen and prepared for her a simple granita made of sugared lemon juice and crushed snow, with a crunchy biscuit to use as a spoon.

Costanza called Rosa and had her bring an oil lamp. She went down to the kitchens and headed for the pantries, which she had organised like those in Sarentini. Alone, she opened the sacks of provisions, smelling the fruit, the cheeses, the oil, and the wine; years later, she was reliving her initiation into the world of smells.

She returned to her room inebriated by the pantry perfumes. Rosa had been worried and had wakened the nurse. "Your ladyship put us through the pains of hell!" Amalia scolded.

The next morning Costanza went to the terrace where the tortoises were. It had rained during the night, and on the fleshy, bulbous stem of a frangipane she saw a striped snail. Ignoring the reptiles, she stood watching the snail, planted solidly on its foot, its head barely peeping out, not moving. You mustn't worry, you're not alone: I am here to look after you, said the Snail King to the Snail Princess.

65

"The poor marry the poor and beget the very poor."

Amalia Cuffaro reflects upon her estrangement from
Costanza Safamita and fails to understand it.

Amalia ran the comb through Pinuzza's hair. Delousing was a bother-some operation, and Pinuzza complained, but it had to be done properly, once a month, after cleaning her head with ashes.

"A lot of ash comes out," said Amalia. "You need patience. The baroness always used to say to Nora Aiutamicristo, when she was comb-ing her hair—and that really did hurt her, as Nora used to curl her hair with the hot tongs, all but scorching her head—'Carry on, Nora, a woman has to suffer a little in the name of beauty.'"

"Did she clean her hair with ashes?"

"No, sometimes with talc. But they mostly washed with hot water, since they had all the water they wanted."

"Did the marchesa wash her hair that way, too?"

"My Costanza was clean as a whistle. She was beautiful, and she didn't complain."

"As beautiful as her mother?"

"Different. She was thin as a rake."

"Men don't like skinny women," commented Pinuzza laconically. "They must be nice and plump."

"Who tells you these things? My Costanza was beautiful." Amalia hastened to redo Pinuzza's braid.

"When you combed her hair, did you talk the way we do?"

"She didn't like getting her hair combed . . . we would talk when we did the mending together."

"Did she tell you everything, as I do?"

"She did when she was a girl, but then less so."

"Didn't that upset you?"

"I loved her very much, and she loved me, too, lots and lots."

"Didn't you miss Giovannino?"

"Of course, but I was a wet nurse with the Safamitas, and there I stayed."

"You know what I think? This marchesa meant more to you than your own son. That's not right. Whoever sent you to the marchesa put a spell on you!"

It was late May, almost forty years earlier. Amalia's mother-in-law was harassing her, insisting that she go to the big house to make the final arrangements for entering service there. Giovannino was almost seven months old, and a beauty. He gave her sweet little smiles and hung on to her fingers when suckling, as if in his innocence he already understood that his grandparents would tear him away from his mother. She tried desperately to postpone the moment of parting, and she almost came to hope that there would be no need for a wet nurse, yet again, in Safamita House. Losing Giovannino was an unbearable sorrow.

Her mother-in-law promised her that she would bring him every day so that her milk would not dry up as she awaited the birth, and then every week after that, but these promises were not enough for her.

She had to give in. She, Amalia Belice, was wretchedly poor and, like all her family, born to obey. In that state of mind, arm in arm with her mother-in-law, she dragged herself anxiously and reluctantly through the alleys of Sarentini, heading for Safamita House. She hoped she could soon return to her son, and she vainly tried to console herself with the thought of the tasty meat broth she would eat which she'd heard so much about; it was prepared in the kitchens of the big house for everyone—masters, servants, and guests.

She hadn't expected to grow so fond of Costanza so quickly and with such intensity. She felt a common bond with her—the baby rejected by her mother, as she had been by her mother-in-law—and she loved her as if she were Giovannino's sister. Her mother-in-law brought him less and less frequently to the mansion house. On Amalia's afternoon off, when she went home, her in-laws would instantly put her to work, and kept her far from him. The love between mother and son was still alive, and Giovannino respected her—at least until what happened, happened. Then she didn't see him for twenty years, but they still loved each other, so much so that Giovannino invited her to join him in America. Too late. He married, life was hard there, and it wasn't true that he had made a fortune. She would have been another mouth to feed, an old lady to be looked after. She didn't know her daughter-in-law or her grandchildren.

Amalia had offered to look after Pinuzza: it was better that way, for everyone.

Costanza had loved Amalia. She had shown this until her death. But, after the age of seven, she no longer confided in her; she was like a little snail withdrawn into her shell. It had happened after her first communion, for no reason. She thought that Costanza held her responsible for not having protected her, but she was wrong; Costanza had no hard feelings and didn't blame her.

Amalia was bothered by the girl's silence, though. After the baron's death, when Costanza no longer had anyone to confide in, she would gaze at her nurse with those big, pensive eyes. It was clear that she wanted to say something; instead, she would just give Amalia a big hug, like a little girl. She wouldn't open her mouth, as if those hugs were enough to convey her unhappiness. She was married, but that husband of hers was there only in a manner of speaking. Costanza was alone and sad. Why she didn't want to confide in Amalia, her nurse, remained a mystery. But there were many mysteries in Safamita House. Don Paolo recommended that she should not brood about it: "She's a noblewoman, and they're like that," he told her. "Perhaps she might have become like a maid, by keeping your company so much, and that wouldn't have been right."

Every so often, Costanza would let slip remarks that were strange but seemed well thought out. Amalia didn't understand them. It was useless to ask for explanations: Costanza would blush madly, as if ashamed of a weakness, and say not a word more. But she still counted on Amalia on difficult and distressing occasions. She wanted her to go with her to the seminary when she called on Father Puma, for example. In the coach, on the way home, Costanza was distraught. "What a state Father Puma is in!" Amalia said to take her mind off things. "He's gone completely daft. That talk of his made no sense."

Costanza fell back against the seat. "It was enough for me," she said, and nothing more.

66

"A clear sky heralds no thunder."

*Costanza Safamita finds tranquillity in her own home,
but people are gossiping about her.*

Costanza came up with a method all her own to give form to her grief:
she had to fulfil her father's wish that she find peace, if not happiness.

She concentrated on herself with stubborn tenacity. She looked after
her person, indulging in long hot baths; she had Rosa massage her head
and feet, and she kept her hair up in a bun in order to avoid the detested
comb. She decided to enjoy everything she had once denied herself out
of conformism and shyness. She had always envied the simple, comfortable clothes of the common people—corsets without whalebone, ample
petticoats above the ankle—and she had similar garments made for herself in handsome, soft fabrics. She had the hanging garden redone and
scented shrubs planted. She spent entire mornings with the gardener,
giving him a hand without even removing her rings: hoeing, pruning,
and planting like the men. On her feet she wore heavy shoes like those
of the countrywomen. And she would go back into the house tired, dirty,
sweaty, and satisfied.

The household servants were puzzled, and said, "Now, to console
herself over her bereavement, milady the marchesa has taken to playing
the servant: another whim of the rich." Amalia let them talk, but it
wasn't like that. Costanza was looking for something, even though she
didn't know exactly what. She would return to the garden at dusk, when
she was sure she would be alone; then she would care for the plants in
the tubs, snipping off dead leaves and withered flowers, then turning
over the soil and watering it. As she worked, Costanza would review in
her memory the stories she used to listen to in the ironing room. Her real
world would become blurred, lose its form, and recede; only then it
would no longer hurt.

Costanza also devoted herself with renewed energy to the complex
problems regarding her father's estate, a thankless but satisfying task. For
the first time, she was glad to be rich. She needed others to advise her on
business matters. She got closer to her Lo Vallo cousins, whom she had
met during the winding up of Aunt Assunta's estate. Paolo Lo Vallo of-

fered to help her with matters concerning the mafiosi of the Madonie Mountains, from whom she had received warnings and with whom—in this unknown territory—she did not know how to behave. Costanza asked his advice and followed it, finding it sensible and rational.

Her other relatives were unhappy about this: they hadn't forgotten past insults and kept their distance from the Lo Vallos, their social inferiors. It was rumoured that Paolo had allied himself with the most sophisticated tenant farmers and their mafia protectors who controlled the votes, and even that he was involved—like certain other barons in the Madonie—in the brigandage rampant there, from which he had obtained more than a few advantages.

During the period of strict mourning Pietro spent a lot of time at home, but Costanza neither sought out his company nor seemed to appreciate it. He was baffled and worried about this; he felt that he had said all he could say to his wife, and he feared for his future. He was also bored. He wanted to enlarge the stables and breed sorrels, starting with those left him by his father-in-law. But this was a very costly project, and he didn't dare talk about it with Costanza. He had no money for such expenses; other people thought he was the master of his wife's dowry, but this wasn't the case. For some time, an agreeable and dignified custom had been established between them: suppliers sent their bills directly to the administrative office, which paid them promptly; in addition, Costanza would inform him regularly about her income—a tacit invitation to spend. When he felt like it, he would go to the office and withdraw what money he needed. Sometimes Costanza encouraged him to be prudent, reminding him of exactly what he had been spent. It was a comfortable existence, and it would have been hard for him to go back to living for the day as he had in the past. Yet because Costanza no longer talked to him about business, Pietro suspected that she was preparing to blackmail him to make him accept his child, and so he found himself in a quandary.

When they moved to Palermo, Costanza resumed her routine there without mentioning that Rura had given birth to a boy and, together with the baby, had stayed on at the charitable institute run by the Dame del Venticello. Believing the whole matter was resolved, Pietro went back to his bachelor life. He went to clubs, to theatres and brothels, complied with the ban on having domestic affairs, and drew freely on his wife's income. He spent little time at home, and only when they received guests. His morning visits to Costanza's room—the last residues of conjugal intimacy—dwindled almost to nothing. Husband and wife had become two strangers.

"Amalia, get ready. Today we are going to see Rura's baby!" said Costanza to her nurse one morning in January 1887.

"Tell me, your ladyship, is this wise?" asked Amalia in consternation.

"Certainly. She has sent word that she is ready to let me see the child."

On their way home, Costanza did nothing but talk about the baby. "He has the marchese's hair and exactly the same eyebrows. Do you think he will like him? And that smile! You can see that Rura is a good mother."

"Your ladyship must forgive me, but this boy is the son of 'one of those' and doesn't belong to you. The marchese doesn't want to know him, and I wouldn't go back there. It's dangerous."

"Dangerous? Why?" For the first time, Costanza was irritated with Amalia and spoke angrily.

"Dangerous because that woman has to stay with her own folk and your ladyship has to be in the mansion. He isn't your ladyship's son, so he's not a blood relation."

Costanza turned to the window and didn't say another word to her for the rest of the journey.

That evening, as her nurse was brushing her hair, Costanza asked her, "Have you noticed that I have changed since my father's death?"

"Yes, your ladyship, a little."

"And what do the others in the house say?"

"That the masters do as they please. What else are they supposed to say?" Amalia was embarrassed.

"No, I want to know what they say."

"That your ladyship has fun in the kitchen and works a lot, that your ladyship is a good mistress."

"And what do you say?"

"I am happy when I see your ladyship happy."

"Do you think I'm really happy?"

"It seems that way to me."

Costanza took the brush and began to run it through her hair by herself. "Amalia, I try to be happy. In my braid there is no love, and I must content myself with what there is. I shall give love to those who want it from me. I have wished for a child so much—maybe this one will love me."

"But there's plenty of little ones in the family, what with all your ladyship's cousins! They'd jump for joy, and their mothers, too, if your ladyship gave them a smile!"

"Yes, that's true, but only because they're hoping for an inheritance."

"So much the better. Your ladyship will find they will be affectionate until the day you die!"

"And you, Amalia? Don't you love me because I'm rich?"

"Your ladyship was put at my breast, and you suckled my milk."

"Only I can give the marchese's son financial security. And he will have it."

"Be careful. Rura is a woman of easy virtue."

Costanza took umbrage: "Rura was a poor, abused woman. She came for the marchese's amusement and she got pregnant. She has behaved well at the institute, and she will work as a seamstress in her own home. She will keep her son by her work. What harm has she done that the marchese didn't do? You have to respect people and take them as they are. And I'll tell you another thing. I don't know any women of easy virtue, but the menfolk of every family frequent them and no one criticises *them*. These women work, Amalia, and it's difficult, risky work. In fact, it's terrible."

Then she gave Amalia a sad little smile, like her smiles when she was a little girl, and added, "You taught me yourself: you must be content with what you find. You took the contentment you found in Safamita House. Treat Rura for what you see in her and not for what she was. Everyone has a right to respect, and everyone can improve." Costanza noticed that her nurse had blushed, and she decided to say no more.

Family and friends were not surprised that the Sabbiamenas lived separate lives, which was not unusual in their class. That Pietro dallied with other women was more than normal, as was Costanza's indulgence. In other words, they were a couple like many others.

But as time went by Costanza's behaviour became the subject of gossip on the part of other ladies. She declined to go on shopping expeditions, she seemed uninterested in clothes and jewels, and she spent a lot of time at home, by choice; she devoted herself to gardening with even greater enthusiasm than the English ladies who lived in Palermo. During her sewing afternoons, she opened her work basket and took napkins and pillowcases that needed mending and worked away on them with zealous dedication, as if she were embroidering altar cloths. She offered delicious sweets, declaring with satisfaction that she had made them with her own hands. She came to be seen as an eccentric, and this was a bad thing. Her lady cousins also knew about her interest in her husband's illegitimate son, but they didn't dare discuss this in public: that alone would have been enough to ruin Costanza's reputation. But sooner or later it would become common knowledge.

With a wife like that, who would ever have been so bold as to criticise the Marchese of Sabbiamena for discreetly seeking out beautiful, sophisticated mistresses? It was no accident that the marriage had produced no offspring: what kind of example would someone like Costanza have set for her children?

67

"Take it or leave it."

The Marchese and Marchesa of Sabbiamena have a brief but significant conversation during the train journey from Palermo to Cacaci.

After Easter 1887 the Patellas returned to Cacaci by train. Pietro was satisfied; he had had lots of fun in Palermo, which had become a hive of activity in preparation for the National Exposition of 1891. Never before had the choice of amusements been so wide and varied: the loose women of the Albergheria district, the cafés on via Maqueda, new clubs, theatres, luxury shops, antiques dealers, receptions in honour of the European crowned heads who visited the city regularly. After centuries, Palermo was a great Mediterranean metropolis once more.

Costanza was sitting opposite her husband. It had been a long time since they'd found themselves alone, without servants around. Pietro thought of their marriage as stable and serene: Costanza seemed as content as he was with their parallel lives.

The railway skirted the beach. It was a magnificent sunny day, the sea flat as a board, the waves barely visible. All was calm. The view from the window seemed like a picture in two shades: the vibrant, deep blue of the sea and the bright azure of the clear sky.

"I wanted to tell you that Rura has gone back to Cacaci and is now a seamstress there. To help her earn a living in an honest way I shall give her work," Costanza told him bluntly.

"But that's madness!" exclaimed Pietro in surprise. "I thought you'd forgotten about that business!"

"I have seen your son. His name is Antonio. I am not asking you to meet him if you don't want to . . . He looks like you" was her only reply, and she turned her gaze to the sea.

Pietro was uncomfortable when his wife spoke to him in such a composed tone, apparently submissive yet nonetheless determined. His sense of well-being lingered on, however, and he decided to take the initiative. "What if I forbade you to let her set foot in the house?" he asked.

"You can give orders to the Marchesa Sabbiamena, and I shall always try to obey them. But not to Costanza Safamita," she replied tranquilly. "The choice is yours. For now, the two are united in me, but I can separate them; all you need do is say the word and I shall do so."

They both looked out at the sea. Embarrassed, Pietro remained in the same position, his elbows bent, his hands with thumbs and templed fingers touching at the tips. He rocked his hands rhythmically against his legs, up and down: they marked time with his thoughts. Costanza noticed this and watched from the corner of her eye as his hands rocked to and fro. The same hands whose physicality she had felt through the fabric of her scarf that long time ago. She softened at Pietro's almost childish transparency; in falling back instinctively on these Sicilian gestures, with that movement of his hands he gave her the answer she expected, and she enjoyed his good looks without a trace of sorrow. Pietro's harmonious, masculine profile stood out sharply against the blue: aquiline nose, high forehead, and long lashes that seemed like silk. He was very handsome, as his son would be.

Rura Fecarotta lived in a cottage not far from Sabbiamena House, where she went twice a week with her little boy. She would sit and work with the women who sewed in the corner of the ironing room, where there was everything the child needed. Costanza would come below stairs and play with him while his mother sewed. The servants, aware of the situation, behaved as if there was nothing unusual about this. The marchese never met either the mother or the child.

68

"The troubles of the pot are known only to the spoon that stirs it."

In Malivinnitti, Costanza Safamita has problems with the field hands and learns of her brother Stefano's death.

In June 1887, the Marchese and Marchesa Sabbiamena went to Malivinnitti for the grain harvest together with Costanza's Trasi cousins. The Lo Vallos, guests for the first time there, were lodged in the less elegant rooms on the ground floor, to underline the difference between the families.

Costanza was encountering difficulties at Malivinnitti. By now Pepi Tignuso was an arthritic old man, albeit still sprightly, and his eldest son, Lillo, had taken his place, but the one who really counted was Maria Teccapiglia's second son, Mimmo Tignuso. Maria's two sons had made a pact not to marry, and they were men of honour, living in town and occupying themselves with other business connected with the estates and politics. Relations were strained between them and their cousin Lillo—as Costanza, though not outsiders, could see—and their kinship made the tension hard to resolve.

The estate was still intact. But the government was talking about opening up a new road that would cross a farm near the boundary; this did not seem like a serious loss, but it actually constituted a symbolic threat of no mean importance to the power of the Tignusos. At Malivinnitti the Tignusos offered refuge to people hiding from other mafia families and from the state, since the deep ravines dividing the hills towards the interior offered hiding places that were inaccessible to those who didn't know them; herds of rustled cattle were also concealed in the valleys— yet another reason the Tignusos had earned considerable prestige in the area. The Safamitas knew about this from hints and allusions, and it was in their interest to tolerate it.

There were two other options: to oppose the road, in which case there would be war in Malivinnitti and elsewhere, fires, poor harvests, and problems with the field hands, not to mention threats and kidnappings; or to sell, and at a loss. Costanza could afford to do this, but it wasn't worth doing. Her father had advised her to keep a firm grip on her power by asserting herself with authority, seeking dialogue but never yielding completely.

The Tignuso family had another big worry: the estates in the Madonie Mountains were controlled by their own mafia, and this now complicated the situation for Costanza. Her Lo Vallo cousin had suggested some people whom she might rely on there, and the Tignusos were on the alert. They could not lose face with the other mafia families, but neither could they deal with them directly. The ruthless mafiosi in the Madonie region were backed up—and, it was rumoured, organised—by some aristocratic families, thus doubly protected by those in political power.

Costanza was in the office with Lillo Tignuso for their first ritual meeting, the day after her arrival in Malivinnitti.

"Begging your ladyship's pardon, but this year you look far better to me. You've even filled out a little," said Lillo, with the respectful familiarity that only he could use with the mistress.

"Thank you, Lillo. You're looking well, too," replied Costanza. "Your family is growing, I'm glad to see. I know that Nunziatina has had a little girl—I'd like to see this new baby of yours."

"They tell me we might be hearing the patter of tiny feet in Cacaci," said Lillo, sounding out the lay of the land.

"There's always a chance of that when there are men about" was Costanza's laconic reply.

"Your ladyship has invited strangers as guests to Malivinnitti this year. Who are they?" asked Lillo, pretending that he didn't know the Lo Vallo family.

"They're not strangers. He is the son of my aunt Teresa Safamita. You won't remember her, but Pepi will. She was my father's sister."

"Begging your pardon, your ladyship, but these relatives haven't been seen at Malivinnitti since the time of the late Baron Guglielmo and the baron your own father!" he exclaimed, staring at her. "They were wise masters, the kind they don't make anymore! Your ladyship must become like them, and you are already a very good mistress. We Tignusos are here to serve the Sabbiamenas as if they were Safamitas."

"I understand, Lillo, and I thank you. My cousin is only one of the guests. Other Safamita relatives will be coming, too."

"A pity Baron Giacomo won't be here, but that's how it goes. I say that he should realise his sister is only a year older, but when it comes to wisdom, she might be his mother!"

"Let's hope so, Lillo. He is still my brother, though, and I respect him," said Costanza, and she saw him out.

Mimmo Tignuso was more direct, like his mother. He asked to talk to Costanza in the house; she agreed—she had a soft spot for Maria Teccapiglia's children—and she received him in the small drawing room, standing.

"Begging your pardon, your ladyship, but I have bad news for you. My late mother talked to me very often about your ladyship, and you are like a sister for us, but you are still the mistress first and foremost. They tell me that four days ago the young Baron Stefano fell from his horse and died outright. A good death, but your ladyship will surely be grieving; he was a good man. The funeral was held the day before yesterday. He had let it be known that your ladyship was not to be informed if he were to die, and your ladyship knows why. We Tignusos have done our duty, and my brother Gaspare went, and your ladyship knows what a risk he took, but we are Safamita men and we'll remain so." Mimmo stood there, his flat cap in his hand, his eyes lowered. He gave her time to absorb the blow.

"Thank you, Mimmo. I am grateful to you. Do you know how his family is getting on?" asked Costanza with weary sorrow.

"All the children were there, and they were well. His son has become a good young man, though he talks too much."

"Youngsters are like that," said Costanza, hoping that Mimmo would take his leave.

But he didn't go, for he had something else to say. "Nothing happens in Malivinnitti that we don't know about, and the harvest is going well. No one pinches anything here. Folk are asking me if things will remain like this."

Costanza lowered her eyes. "This is how things must remain."

"People talk too much. True, your ladyship is a woman, but you are a Safamita first and a woman second. So please tell us that Malivinnitti will remain as it is and that nothing will change, and if there's any talk of roads, then they're not going to pass through here."

"You're right, Mimmo. This is how Malivinnitti must remain."

"Senator Bentivoglio's wife is with your ladyship . . . He's a good man, and the family respect him."

"I'm glad you feel that way."

"The village folk round here vote for him. In our neck of the woods people know the meaning of respect. But I'm not happy about that lot in the mountains on the other side."

"I know, Mimmo."

"We are always at your disposal to serve the Safamitas, and my brothers and I have many friends—here and all over."

"And, as the mistress, I keep my eyes open, and I never forget that you are the children of Tano Tignuso and Maria Teccapiglia."

Costanza did not tell the others about her brother's death, not even her husband: there was no reason. Stefano—who had squandered Aunt Assunta's bequest in misguided investments, who had been so unhappy—Stefano the alcoholic had finally found the peace that had been denied him on earth.

His misfortune sprang from too much love and too much pride, thought Costanza. As had happened on her father's death, her thoughts turned to her mother, who had loved Stefano so much. Now Costanza was in harmony with Caterina; she understood her. She, too, was consumed with love for Antonio, which is why for the first time she had been reluctant to go to Malivinnitti. The little boy aroused in her sensations and feelings both new and forgotten: the pleasure of kisses and caresses and a boundless love that was free of uncertainty or doubt. A love requited.

It was also a possessive love, violent and all-consuming. Now Costanza understood certain expressions used by lower-class mothers that had once aroused her disdain and revulsion: "I could eat you all up," "You're so pretty I could take a bite out of you," "I could kill you and eat you." But she wasn't his mother, and she had to remember that.

69

"Nothing for nothing"

Costanza Safamita's cousin Paolo Lo Vallo desires her; she is tempted but does not yield.

Costanza was alone on the terrace. The sweet, mellow smell of the ripe wheat filled the fresh early-morning air. Almost furtively, Stefano Trasi's son Sandro and his young wife, Maria Teresa, went out through the main gate. They strolled towards the carob trees, dreamily, almost aimlessly. Costanza was delighted by the affection the couple showed each other, evident in the way the young woman, barely seventeen, abandoned herself on her husband's arm. At twenty-eight, Costanza thought of herself as almost elderly. She followed them with her eyes—it was no accident that they were heading downhill towards the large, majestic carob trees with their glossy dark-green crowns. Wandering from one to another, the newlyweds found themselves before a green curtain of branches laden with carobs. The boughs brushed the ground. The youngsters walked around the tree, slowing their pace as if they wished to increase their desire by putting off the pleasure.

From time to time, Maria Teresa picked a long carob pod and rubbed it between her hands to remove the patina of dust before biting into it, chewing on the sweet skin, then spitting out the seeds and fibrous residue, and picking another. From her vantage point, Costanza observed the young woman's swaying gait and her nephew's manly stride; purposefully, Sandro parted the branches and opened up a passageway. Maria Teresa stooped, lifting up her petticoat, and went within, and he followed her. Costanza smiled without envy: they would reemerge hot, embarrassed, and satisfied.

It's beautiful to be in love! she thought. She looked up, demure, and absently admired the expanses of wheat covering the hills of Malivinnitti, iridescent yellow in the morning breeze.

"You are beautiful, Cousin Costanza, and alone. I would like to take you down there, under one of those carob trees," said a voice, and at the same time a hand fell on Costanza's shoulder. She jumped.

"Paolo!" she exclaimed, shaking off the hand that was caressing the nape of her neck.

Paolo Lo Vallo sat down beside Costanza, leaning towards her, one arm resting on the back of her chair.

"Since the first day I saw you, covered by black veils, in Safamita House, I have done nothing but think of you. You are beautiful, Costanza, and I desire you now as I did then."

"Cousin, your wife is under this roof, and I am a married woman."

"Eleanora is indisposed and asleep. As for Pietro, perhaps you do not know, but he rose at dawn to go hunting. Your husband doesn't know what he is missing, and he doesn't deserve you. I love you, and I have loved you for a long time." He laid his hand on the nape of her neck, caressing it once more.

"I am a married woman," repeated Costanza. "I wouldn't have expected this from you, Cousin, of all people. Safamita blood runs in our veins."

"You're wrong, Costanza; you should have expected this. The Safamitas like one another—so much so that they marry among themselves, as your father did. Costanza, I know you are not indifferent to me, and I love you. Well?"

Rosa arrived with a message for her mistress, and Costanza dashed back indoors.

Costanza spent the morning with her women. At the lunch table her cousin looked at her in a way that struck her as ambiguous. She was nervous as a cat, and every time he spoke to her she jumped. In the afternoon she retired for her siesta, but she couldn't sleep. She felt like a pebble on the beach, confused and contradictory thoughts ebbing and flowing over her like waves. No one had ever told her that he loved her, never mind that she was beautiful. She didn't believe Paolo and suspected that he had an ulterior motive, that he was taking shameful advantage of her hospitality: the Lo Vallos hadn't changed; her grandfather had done well to estrange them from the family. She couldn't think of a pretext for sending him away, but she had been a goose to allow herself to be duped like this.

Yet Paolo was kind, amiable, reliable. She liked him, for he was so much like her father and grandfather, with her father's intense gaze, pale cheeks, and half-closed lips. Perhaps Paolo was right, that Safamita blood attracted Safamita blood. Perturbed by her cousin's boldness and suddenly exhausted, she finally dozed.

Costanza had never had an erotic dream, but that afternoon she had a frightening one. Before her appeared two obscene figures, gigantic, mythical; from their knotty backs and arms carob branches sprouted. The two monsters fought over her and possessed her by turns: one was her father and the other was Pietro. Distant memories thronged her mind, memories deliberately forgotten. Her father leaning back in his armchair while she played and sang for him. "*Porgi, amor, qualche ristoro.* Costanza watching him as he listened, eyes closed, caressing him with her gaze. But then something snapped inside her and she saw him as a man, not as her father. She stopped playing. In the deep silence, her temples throbbed. He opened his eyes—a flashing glance—and quickly squeezed them shut again, his face contorted in a mask of suffering. Then, in confusion, she began to play once more, but she couldn't follow the music. She took a peep at him—she couldn't resist it—and he was watching her through slitted, lustful eyes. Costanza relived her sense of anguished disquiet. Her cousin appeared before her, and she recognised the same features: the narrow eyes, the aquiline Safamita nose, the big hands with the bluish, bulging veins. It was her only chance.

"Adultery is a sin, a sin," she repeated. "A sin." She was assailed by memories of Pietro in the study—his spasmodic panting, the thrusting, his hands clinging to that woman's disordered clothing.

Why couldn't she? She fell back on the pillows, breathing heavily, exhausted.

Then she heard a sound from behind the shutters. On the balcony she found a stone with a sheet of paper tightly wrapped around it and tied with a string: "The wisteria branches are interwoven like a step-ladder. See you tonight." Wisteria, ladder. She had heard this before. Where? When? Gradually, the memory took shape, like a mosaic.

She had been in her grandfather's study in Castle Sarentini after Aunt Assunta's death. She was opening drawers and putting papers in order: personal letters, thank-you notes, job requests, news. Some were addressed to her father, who used that study, after his father's death, when he went to the castle. One letter came from Rome, and, since she was used to reading out loud to her father from his correspondence, she opened it curiously. It was Father Sedita's reply to a letter, and it began with stock banalities about his health, the weather, and visits from Sicilian friends. But then the tone and the subject of the letter suddenly changed. Father Sedita described the confession of a young foreigner who used to visit his beloved by climbing up a wisteria vine to gain her room. The old priest wrote contritely that he had erred in absolving this young man and even the adulteress, neither of whom had shown remorse. At the time, Costanza had concluded that Father Sedita had got into a muddle and had wandered off into a personal recollection that had nothing to do with the Safamitas. She was wrong.

Costanza leaned over the railing and looked down: the wisteria was flourishing, its boughs interwoven like a braid to form steps. She, Costanza, was a love child, and, like her mother, she now wanted and felt able to love and be loved in return. She was stunned, and could not turn away from this line of thought.

Rosa came in to help her dress, for the guests were waiting for her to partake of the afternoon refreshments.

Costanza went from one communicating room to the next. Paolo leapt out from behind a door and embraced her. His beard prickled her cheeks, but she let him continue. He kissed her on the lips: Costanza closed her eyes, passive, apprehensive. She didn't like that moist mouth on hers, but maybe that was how it felt the first time. Suddenly Pietro's face appeared before her eyes, and an irresistible desire for him came over her. Annoyance became disgust. Costanza tried to break free, but her cousin persisted. She couldn't get her breath, and she felt like vomiting. Paolo would not let her go, so she bit him on the lip and fled. She came across Maria Antonia with her niece Maria Teresa and joined them.

When the men went out for their afternoon stroll, she went to her room and repeatedly washed her mouth.

That afternoon Costanza ordered the staff to have barbed wire wound around the trunk of the wisteria. The Tignusos were very worried about this: it was clear that the mistress had no trust in their protection. That meant they would have to curb their demands and keep their heads down for a while. The marchesa was a true Safamita; you could see that her father's blood ran in her veins.

70

"*The pear tree produces pears.*"

*Amalia Cuffaro remembers the launching of a ship, a visit to the
seminary, and that Father Puma had six toes on each foot.*

The summer downpour was over. Amalia was busy filling the big jug
with the rainwater collected in the containers she had lined up outside
when the first drops began to fall: basins, pots, bowls, even a tin box.

"It's rained a lot, so we have water," she said, pleased. "And now I'll
wash you." Taking some flakes of walnut-oil soap, she got to work.

"The baroness took a bath every week, in a tub as big as a coffin," she
said to Pinuzza. "It even had wheels, like a railway wagon. It was so
heavy that it took three of us to push it. The other women opened both
doors to let us through. What a lot of water it took to fill it! Jugs of hot
water, jugs of cold water—the men had to run back and forth with them
while the women mixed them up. Then she would stay alone with Nora
Aiutamicristo, who lathered her all over. Nora told me that she would
undress completely, like a little kid."

"So that means the marchesa took a bath without wearing her petticoat?"

"That she did. But then times changed; she had them put running
water in her house and she took her bath alone, without me. She was
modest, was my Costanza," said Amalia, as she soaped her niece's feet.
"You've got skin like a baby's, nice and smooth," she added with a smile.
Pinuzza liked the slight tickling of her aunt's hands; Amalia knew this
and enjoyed it.

"D'you know, I once had to wash a man's feet? It was when the baron
took it into his head to buy a boat. You have to baptise boats as if they
were people, with a priest and a party and all. It was after Costanza's first
communion, in November of 1866.

"We all went off in the coach to Sciacca, where the boat was moored.
It was really big, like a house. And what a celebration! All the big-wigs
were there, and the bishop, too—and along with them the young baron
and Costanza. He held her hand the whole time, and I stood behind
them. Well, they were all ready to name this boat—us, the bishop, the

dean of Sarentini, Father Puma, and some other priests, who were sitting in the front row.

"The bishop was giving his sermon when the weather turned bad. It wasn't raining yet, but the sea was getting very rough and a big wave came in and drenched the lot of them—shoes, socks, the hems of their cassocks . . . it soaked everything. They were running this way and that, looking for someone to dry their feet. Priests they were, but they were cackling like hens! The young baron was laughing up his sleeve, and Costanza was all eyes. They had them take their seats. Servants and coachmen had to bring shawls and blankets from the coaches to dry the priests and those great feet of theirs. Gaspare went to Father Puma, but he didn't want his feet touched: he was as bashful as a woman. So the baron says to me, 'You go, Amalia!' If it had been anyone else I would have said no, but you couldn't say no to the baron. Father Puma had big, stinking feet—he didn't wash—and what feet they were! He had six toes on each foot—six, I tell you. I dried them for him and I counted them—six on each foot.

"Costanza was following me with her eyes, and when I went back to her she said, 'Father Puma has six toes on each foot.' Her grandfather got cross when he heard her, and he told her not to repeat it. I'm telling you, the baron really liked Father Puma, and that's why he set him up at the seminary rather than kick him out."

"Why should he have been kicked out?"

"That's stuff for grown-ups. Now you're all nice and clean, and I'll give you your food."

Amalia went back outside to tidy up. The sun was shining again and the Montagnazza was almost dry, with only a few small puddles left in the hollows in the stone. Oh, that wretch Father Puma! She would never have suspected him of ogling Costanza, totally innocent, and a little girl in the bargain. Costanza used to tell her that she didn't like Father Puma, but she—the girl's own nurse, of all people—hadn't listened. She'd say, "Costanza, studying isn't for you, but you must learn your catechism!"

Then, one day, the young baron had her understand what had happened and told her that Costanza wasn't to see Father Puma anymore. The little girl didn't want to talk about it, and to think that usually she told Amalia everything. Then she began to drop hints, and Amalia understood better. She was appalled. When she told Paolo about it, his face darkened, he clenched his fists, and he spat on the ground. She didn't know that he bore a grudge against Father Puma—it must have been a serious matter that went back a long time. "He's a bad one. You ought to watch out for him," he told her, and he didn't say another word for the rest of the afternoon. She had never seen him so angry.

The last drops of rain glittered on the clean, white marl—like the marchesa's diamonds. What jewels the marchesa had! They had belonged to her mother, and some were as large as a pigeon's egg. Costanza's father was forever telling her to wear them and never to take off the ring with three diamonds, the engagement ring. The young baron was like that—he doted on that daughter of his. Everyone admired those three diamonds, even Father Puma, numbskull that he was.

Amalia had been very surprised when Costanza saw him again and then wanted to call on him at the seminary. Amalia had never set foot in a seminary; it was a huge building, and from all sides people were coming and going—children, youngsters, and adults, all flapping about like crows in their black cassocks.

Father Puma suffered from gout and kept his feet—covered by a cloth—propped up on a stool. He had aged badly: flabby and obese, his belly almost bursting out of the cassock taut around his midriff, unable even to get up to pay his respects to the marchesa. Amalia thought he was out of his head, he was raving so much, but Costanza wanted to find out for sure whether he was still in his right mind.

"Father, tell me if I am a Safamita."

"You are as much a Safamita as your brothers."

Costanza talked to him about the baron's servants and the old family retainers, mentioning them by name. Sometimes he remembered them, other times he didn't, but then his eyes became glued to the marchesa's ring. Those diamonds frightened him, and they seemed to make him lose his senses. He began to get restless, fidgeting about in his armchair and babbling: "The fingers, the fingers, they glitter, light, shadow, confess, need to confess, temptation, sin, who knows?"

Then he broke off and asked both women, "Do you know? Or you? Is it a sin?" Trembling, he shook his head, answering his own question: "No, it's not a sin, the fingers talk, they suffer, they weep, you are not to blame, and I fell short, Jesus, Jesus, love, love, Lord God, the fingers glitter, confession, comfort, it was His fault, His, the Devil's. Oh, mercy, beautiful, soft, woman's fingers, confession, mercy, penitence, they glitter, they glitter . . ."

He became so worked up that the seminarist looking after him had to calm him with a sip of water, but he went on repeating the same words, and groped for Costanza's hand. Disgusted, she rose to leave. Father Puma called after her, shouting and struggling. The cloth slipped from his feet. At the door, they turned round to take a last look at him. Swollen like the rest of his body, black and stinking as Amalia remembered them, the six-toed feet appeared.

Obscene.

"How many fingers did this Father Puma have?" asked Pinuzza before she fell asleep.

"Five, like everyone else. It was only his feet that were different. We all have something different—some things can be seen, others can't. But in the end we're all the same, God's creatures, and that's that. Rosa Vinciguerra told me that Father Puma hailed from Coppolo, a village where people have six toes on their feet but five fingers on their hands, just like us."

"Then what happened?"

"There was a big feed and we were all happy, except for those poor devils whose cassocks were still wet."

71

"War, hunting, and love:
for one pleasure a thousand sufferings"

Costanza Safamita rereads Father Sedita's letter, and this time she understands it.

. . . Years ago a young Irishman wanted to take confession. He had fallen in love with his master's wife, but he didn't feel he had sinned. This made him unhappy. For six weeks they had been meeting intermittently to work on the translation of certain business documents. She was pregnant.

"It certainly is a sin," I told him. "Think it over well."

"Allow me to explain, Father," he said to me. Prompted partly by curiosity, I let him talk. "I was expecting a haughty old woman. I saw before me a girl of my own age, simple and slender. She was wearing rich clothes, but not a trace of powder or perfume. She did not take care of her looks. I had to translate contracts, write boring and prosaic letters, and she would help me without a smile, a vivacious gesture, or a curious look. Every so often she would look up from the papers and stare at the wall. Her pupils were dull. Wearily, she would whisk the flies away from her face and hair, while sometimes she would let them roam undisturbed over her skin, her clothes, and the papers. It was as if she had lost the desire to live. I cannot say how sorry I felt for her.

"We worked at the desk, side by side. The air was stifling, muggy, and still. We were sweating. A wasp landed on her arm and she looked at it, desolate and powerless. I seized her wrist and shook her arm. She was weeping silently, her wrist lying in my hand like a dead weight. We went back to work, both of us with moist eyes. The next day she apologised to me for her weakness, and added, 'I am so sad.' It was high summer and it was always hot. During a break for a drink of water I thought to tell her about the landscape of my country, so different from the yellow, sun-drenched land in which we found ourselves. She listened to me. This gradually became habitual. She began to ask me simple, direct questions, and through them I caught a glimpse of her soul. She never talked of herself or her life. Except for one time. I was telling her about something and she burst into tears. She asked me, 'Do you mind if I weep? I cannot cry anywhere else, not even in my room. I am not alone even there; the maid in the next room would hear me.' Then everything changed. I don't know how or why, but we fell in love. Completely. At night I would climb up the trunk of the wisteria that led to her balcony—it was my staircase. Her smile returned. We knew that it would all end when we completed the paperwork, and we slowed down.

"I don't feel that I have sinned. It was a great love, innocent, as if we were two young people on our first experience. On the last day, before I returned to the mine, she told me that she had been contemplating suicide and that I had brought her back to life. She thought she was pregnant, and that her husband would accept the child as his own. She told me she loved me and that she loved her husband, too. She said she belonged to him. She said she had given her whole life to her husband and was glad she had put it in his hands. I asked her to let me know the sex of the child in her womb so that I could imagine it in the years to come, to love it at a distance. With a strange smile, she assured me that it would be a boy."

Dear Domenico, as a priest I must admit that I made a mistake: I raised my hand and gave absolution to a man who was unrepentant. I would have done the same for her.

The letter ended there, no salutation but a signature. At the foot of the page, Father Sedita had added a postscript: *Domenico, for your sake, only for your sake, do with this as you think best.*

Costanza had to talk with don Paolo. She found him at the bottom of the garden, sitting in front of the door of his cottage; he was dozing in the sun, a blanket over his legs.

"Paolo, have they told you that my brother died?" asked Costanza.

"Yes, your ladyship. The young Baron Stefano was a good man. Oh, that blacksmith's daughter!" said the old coachman, shaking his head.

"But the baron didn't like my brother."

"Begging your pardon, your ladyship, but I don't follow."

"Paolo, do you know who my real father was?"

Paolo smacked his brow with the palm of his hand, but said nothing. Costanza spotted a flash in his eyes that he'd quickly snuffed out.

"Paolo, I want to know his name."

"I'm sorry, your ladyship, but what put this into your head? The late baron loved you more than his sons. You couldn't ask for a better father, and now you're talking to me about another father?"

"Yes, and also about the father of my brothers."

"Oh mamma mia!" exclaimed Paolo. "What happened at Malivinnitti? Someone has been talking too much, someone bad!"

"My mother met my real father at Malivinnitti," said Costanza with conviction, "but he was not the father of Stefano and Giacomo. This I know."

"I was the young baron's servant, and I don't want to hear such talk . . . I'm an old man."

"Giacomo called me a bastard. I must know if he is one, too."

"Then what do you want to do, go and tell him?" Paolo had grown heated and was having trouble getting his breath.

"Paolo, you know me, and you shouldn't even think such a thing. But I need to know who we are and where we all came from!" Costanza was speaking in a way that he had never heard before, with a desperate urgency about the question, and he had to answer her.

He lowered his head and said, "I swear I have known only one father to your ladyship, and that man was the young baron. I was always at his side in those days, and when the late baroness was at Malivinnitti . . . what she did I do not know."

"And my brothers' father? Who was he?" Costanza insisted, pleading.

Paolo crossed himself. "The young baron, God rest his soul, must forgive me if I speak now for the first time. I have told no one what I know, and I shouldn't now. You three are all different, but you are all Safamitas descended from Baron Stefano. Only little Guglielmo, the firstborn, was the spitting image of his father, as the young baron had been of his. The others died in the womb. The baroness's fate was sad, for she had to give sons to the Safamita line. That's what her father and her husband needed: sons, heirs. And that's why things went the way they did. I will say no more than this, and you have Paolo Mercurio's word." Paolo was weeping. He grasped Costanza's hand and set to kissing it: "Your ladyship was the apple of the young baron's eye. You mustn't take it badly; he loved you so very much!" he said to her, holding on to her hand.

Hypnotised, Costanza was gazing at the glittering diamonds of her mother's ring in the faithful coachman's trembling fingers. All of a sudden she had a flash of insight: she remembered a detail that had eluded her during her visit to Father Puma, and she started. Paolo noticed this, and he thought Costanza was afraid of scandalmongers. "Your ladyship mustn't worry about people. Walls have eyes and ears, and mouths too, but they also know when to shut them. And you have Safamita blood. The baroness was madly in love with the young baron, and she sacrificed so much for the Safamitas."

Costanza wasn't listening to him, for her mind was elsewhere. Father Puma had told her, "You are as much a Safamita as your brothers." A bitter truth, known to him alone.

She had to speak to Amalia before Paolo got there before her.

"Amalia, I wonder what Giacomo's children are like. We have seen only the first two."

"They told me that they're handsome, with blond hair like Baroness Adelaide," Amalia replied.

"I wonder if they have five toes, or six." Costanza let the question fall like a trap.

"What are you thinking of, to ask such a question?" exclaimed Amalia.

"But do you know?"

"I certainly do know. I asked the wet nurse's mother: only one son had six toes, and the surgeon cut off the extra one, the way they did with Giacomo—the poor thing cried and cried, but he was just born, and that toe was tiny as could be," replied Amalia calmly.

"And did they cut a toe off Stefano as well?"

"Rosa Vinciguerra told me that they cut a toe off his foot, too, but he didn't cry like Giacomo. Stefano was a good boy and he never cried when he fell down and hurt himself, not even when he fell from the carob tree and scraped his leg . . ." Chatting away, Amalia told stories about Stefano as a child—they had been repeated so often that they had become a part of the common memory of the wet nurses—and on and on she went, believing the stories had consolatory value. But Costanza wasn't listening to her. Now, only now, did she know the truth. She saw her mother for what she was: a fragile, intense woman who had clung to her husband the way a convolvulus clings to an oak tree, inseparable and dependent. She knew she had sinned, and that was why she hadn't been able to love her daughter. Yet Costanza was a love child, unlike her brothers.

Life was like that: things happen, and not always the way they should.

Costanza thought with tenderness about the young Irishman in Palermo who had tried to find out about her; perhaps he had been the son of the man who had wanted to trace her. Her father. But she didn't think of him as a father and had no wish to meet him. An imperceptible sense of well-being came over her, gradually growing until it became peace. *You must love yourself*, her father had told her. And Costanza—aware of herself and of her diversity—felt the desire to know and love herself take hesitant root. She felt free.

She was terribly sorry for Stefano, who had died without knowing all this. And Giacomo disgusted her, as his true father did.

In the years that followed, her brother made no effort to seek a rapprochement and Costanza left things as they were. Giacomo's children grew up without knowing their only Safamita aunt. On the very rare occasions on which they talked of her at home, they referred to her by her title, so much so that her nephews and their children, and their children's children forgot her name: she was merely a dreadful person, "the marchesa."

72

"Water, advice, and salt unasked for should not be given."

Prince Alvaro Chisicussi gives his cousin an imprudent piece of advice that has unforeseeable consequences.

Pietro Sabbiamena put the palms of his hands down on the card table, satisfied. He shoved back his chair, while the others went on discussing the game. "Who wants to have lunch with me today?" he asked, adding with a smile, "It's on me!"

"I'd be glad to accept, Cousin," said Alvaro Chisicussi. The others shook their heads.

Pietro was in great form, and his win had galvanised him. The talk was all about the forthcoming show at the theatre. He was full of stories and scandalous gossip. Rumour had it that the soprano, not only a gorgeous woman but also "hot," was in search of a "special admirer."

"Pietro," said Alvaro, stirring the spoon in his cup more than was necessary, "I have to say something to you that I find embarrassing."

"Go on."

"After the sale of Canziati, and after this win, too, you might pay something back."

Pietro's face darkened. "What are you getting at about my wife's property?"

"Doesn't Costanza tell you anything? She sold Canziati for a fabulous price, thanks to the mediation of her cousin Bentivoglio, and she's on the lookout for other investments: there's no shortage of cash in the Sabbiamena household, even though you may not have noticed."

"It must have slipped my mind. As for my debts, I pay them." Pietro was offended, but he quickly gave one of his captivating smiles and said, "When they don't slip my mind."

Alvaro made a face. "Well, then, without causing you further offence—I didn't take you for touchy—I'd remind you that you have owed me money since Christmas . . . in hopes that perhaps it will no longer slip your mind, like the other matter, and many others, too." He rose and gave Pietro a pat on the back. "Let me give you some advice, Cousin: keep yourself well informed about your wife's business, and don't forget your debts. See you tomorrow!"

Pietro was upset, but not for long. Others surrounded him, complimenting him on his win. As he was about to leave the club, the secretary came up to him, embarrassed: there were bills to be paid, if the marchese would be so good, please. Vexed by this impertinent request, Pietro decided to take a stroll before going home to change for the afternoon.

It was a warm April day. The streets were almost empty, it being siesta time. A light breeze caressing his beard and moustache refreshed him. Pietro had a sunny disposition, and he soon forgot about things he didn't like; life pleased him. He walked along briskly, without a destination, ready to take his chances and enjoy any surprises. Almost by accident he found himself at his own front door and decided to go in; he could ask Costanza about the sale and make a good impression on his cousin.

Ever since Costanza had told him that she was going to allow Rura, now a seamstress, to work in the mansion at Cacaci and to bring her son there with her, the couple had led separate lives. Pietro would spend the autumn and winter in Palermo, while Costanza stayed on in Cacaci. They spent the spring together in Cacaci but did not meet: they had different hours, and he did not take his meals at home. In summertime, Pietro would often stay with friends as a guest, while Costanza kept up her habit of holidaying in the country, where sometimes she went with relations and at other times on her own. When they attended family festivities and funerals, they travelled in separate coaches. The couple seldom entertained, and when they did they treated each other courteously, like strangers. They weren't the only couple to have a ménage of this kind, and Pietro was not unhappy with it, but he did feel uncomfortable when he had to ask the administration for large sums of money. This was why he had got into debt. He feared his wife's reproaches, even though she never mentioned his borrowing. They communicated through the majordomo and the servants.

Others, especially his aunt Annina Lannificchiati, kept him informed of his wife's eccentricities: that she called on her lady friends wearing simple, austere clothes and spent a lot of time alone in the country. Rumour had it that she conducted her business, and even dealt directly with the Palermo mafia, without using intermediaries and that she did the rounds of her estates on horseback together with the field overseers, as her father had done. Unusually discreet, Baroness Lannificchiati didn't dare tell her nephew that the real source of scandal was Costanza's passion for her husband's bastard child, whom she took to ice-cream and toy shops as if he were her nephew or, worse, her own son.

Absorbed in his own affairs, Pietro hadn't even noticed how much Costanza had changed. And, in any event, he wasn't interested.

73

"A woman who laughs with you is willing."

The Marchese Sabbiamena falls in love with his wife while eating a finger biscuit.

Pietro was told that the marchesa was in the service rooms. He bore her no grudge, even though she had disobeyed him and stubbornly insisted on keeping Rura's son in the house.

Pietro had not set foot in the service rooms since Costanza had forbidden him to. With a tingle of pleasure he remembered his past enjoyable afternoons below the stairs: the servants' one-hour break was an ideal time to seek easy encounters with willing maids and without risk. He slipped silently into the kitchen, closing the door behind him, just as he used to in the old days. The shutters were closed and you could hear flies buzzing against the windowpanes. The balcony doors were half shut, and a ray of light struck the table in the middle of the room, slashing down the marble surface like a luminous sabre and zigzagging across the stone floor, freshly mopped after lunch.

He leant against the side of the dresser, waiting for his eyes to adjust to the darkness, which had been made even deeper by the blinding light that cleft the kitchen in two. He gave himself over to fantasising about the buxom women smelling of lye whom he had so much enjoyed mentally stripping as they bustled about finishing their early-afternoon tasks. When the time was ripe, he would accost the maid of his choice and whisper the right words in her ear. It had all been so easy, smooth as butter—until Costanza stepped in.

He thought he was alone, but the crackling of burning wood made him realise that someone had lit the oven. In the corner diagonally opposite, on the outer wall, was a large woodburning oven like those in the countryside, the upper part shaped like a dome—with an iron hatch set into the mouth—and the lower part used to store firewood. In the gloom he glimpsed a servant woman huddled in front of the firewood, busy choosing and preparing branches to burn.

She must have eyes like a cat's to see in this darkness. I wonder if they're pretty, wondered Pietro, agreeably excited. The maid was taking her time, picking the smallest branches one by one and setting them aside. Then she gathered them into a small bundle and broke them almost soundlessly. Pietro became curious and followed her movements. Suddenly she straightened up and opened the oven door. Red flames lit up the room. She poked the fire, then tamped it down by shifting and crushing the burnt wood to make a bed of embers, which she then brushed into one corner of the oven, rapidly sweeping away the ash to leave the cooking surface clean and uncluttered.

Pietro could just hear the murmur of a Sicilian song. This maid aroused his curiosity more and more.

It was hot. Now she was going to put baking tins into the oven—they were lined up on the table beside the oven. An acrid heat reached Pietro's nostrils. The woman, still with her back to him, had changed her rhythm and task: the baking had begun. She moved quickly, skilfully manipulating the baker's peel and oven brush. Like an acrobat, she used the peel to slip the baking dishes into the oven, turning them, lifting the embers to increase the heat and letting them fall back down on the peel, sweeping away the ash from inside the oven, up and down, right and left—graceful movements of elbows, arms, and back, accompanied by the murmur of that same song, sometimes soft, sometimes louder. The burning olive twigs gave off a dense, oily odour mixed with the smell of biscuits: a rich scent of almonds, lard, and sugar.

The maid closed the oven door and carefully cleaned her hands with a rag, dropped it onto a chair with a languid gesture—like a Venus taking off her peplum, thought Pietro—and headed for the door to the garden. She opened it and stood on the threshold, her silhouette outlined sharply against the light flooding into the kitchen. With a movement that was as energetic as it was graceful, she drew the cord curtain closed to prevent an invasion of insects.

She stayed in the centre of the ray of light, her arms crossed over her bosom. She was wearing a flowing dress, gathered at the waist, and her head was covered by a sky-blue kerchief knotted at the nape of her neck.

Maybe she'll loosen her blouse, thought Pietro, excited.

Instead she put her hands on her hips; her figure stood out against the dangling cords through which he could glimpse the swaying tops of the palm trees and, high up, the intense blue of the sky. How attractive he found this woman! Instinctively, Pietro reverted to his old habits; he flattened himself against the wall, in his old vantage point in the corner, almost hidden, ready to pounce on her from the back at the right moment. She raised her arms and bent them to loosen her kerchief, slowly untying the knots at the nape of her neck. The kerchief billowed up under the thrust of hair no longer compressed, like dough left to rise. The last knot was undone. The point of the triangle now reached her waist. Holding the other two corners one in each hand, she slowly opened them, extending her arms to spread out the kerchief. She stretched, arching her back slightly with a movement that accentuated her slim waist, in an invitation to the caress of the afternoon light. Pietro yearned to see her face, and struggled to keep himself from calling out to her.

She released her grip and the kerchief hung down over her skirt. She picked it up and threw it across one shoulder. Bringing her hands up to her hair, she puffed it up. She began singing the same song again, no longer like a subdued lullaby but like a real song, while a cascade of thick red curls fell down over her shoulders. It was Costanza.

Pietro, most disconcerted, looked at his wife with an almost sacred mixture of reverence and lust: his wife, free, desirable, beyond his reach. Costanza now returned briskly to her work—taking the baking tins from the oven, shifting the biscuits from one side to the other, slipping them back inside, checking the heat, adding more wood. The sumptuous mass of her wavy red hair was streaked in various shades of auburn or even darker, almost crimson. When she pushed it over her shoulder and bent over, it fell to one side—long, snaking flames that framed her hot face and big, gleaming eyes.

The first biscuits were ready. Costanza laid the scalding-hot baking tins to cool on the central table. She turned to the table, facing Pietro, who was still hugging the wall, and with rapid, sure movements she sprinkled vanilla sugar over the biscuits. Her milk-white skin emerged gleaming beneath her unbuttoned blouse, and Pietro glimpsed her small, rounded breasts. He had never known this Costanza. He had always seen her as she had appeared on their wedding day—stooped, bony, gauche, repellent. Now he was mad with desire for her. Instinctively, he came slowly nearer, uncertain and confused.

Costanza jumped. "Pietro, what is it?" She looked at him, her glance still wounded.

"I was looking for you."

"Why? What did you want?" Now it was a normal conversation.

"I wanted to talk to you, and you've made me forget what I wanted to tell you." Pietro came up to the table. "I've forgotten it, Costanza, I've forgotten it."

Costanza hastily buttoned her blouse, hooked up her bodice, and pushed back her hair with her long, white fingers. These movements served only to focus Pietro's gaze on her body, arousing him. Costanza realised this and stopped, amazed, her hands in her hair. They looked at each other.

"What are you doing?" asked Pietro.

"You can see for yourself. I'm making biscuits for Antonio."

"Why you?"

"Why not? I enjoy it."

"What kind of biscuits are they?" Pietro came closer. Costanza began to understand. She looked at him without answering. "Tell me."

Pietro could have listened forever to the list of simple ingredients, for Costanza's words were poetry. He asked her questions about the doughs and fillings as if he were a baker. She answered, reserved but forthright. By now they were holding each other's gaze as if they were speaking in a secret language. Pietro breathed in the odour of clean sweat, mixed with ash, sugar, cinnamon, and aniseed that Costanza's skin gave off. She wiped the sweat from her brow with the edge of her apron, as if she were ashamed of it.

"You're all right."

"Thanks, I'm fine."

"No, I meant to say . . . you're beautiful."

"Thank you," Costanza replied in embarrassment. Then, with her old vulnerable look, she hurriedly asked, "Is there some problem with the office? We sold last year's wheat at a good price. I forgot to tell you, I'm sorry. Do you want something?"

"I want . . . a biscuit."

"Which one?"

"That long one, the finger biscuit."

"They're still hot. I'll bring you one later." And Costanza turned her back to him.

Pietro followed her. She felt awkward in her movements and worked away in silence.

"Why don't you sing some more?"

"Very well." A hint of a half smile, reserved.

Costanza did not go back to the Sicilian lullaby but sang "Mon Dieu," Delilah's song from the Saint-Saëns opera, in a low voice, as if she were singing only for herself, her gaze far from him as she carried on working.

Suddenly she stopped—she was choosing a biscuit. She blew on it and took a nibble: it was ready. Costanza went up to Pietro holding the finger biscuit—long, knobbly, and crunchy. He opened his mouth. Costanza stopped, nonplussed.

She held out her arm and put the biscuit between his lips, not letting it go, with a holy gesture. Pietro took a bite, his eyes glued to hers. Another tiny bite. Then another.

Costanza came even closer, with almost imperceptible small steps. They stood there motionless, facing each other

"Do you want another one?"

"Now you take a little bit." Costanza barely nibbled at the tip, then handed it to him.

Pietro shook his head and laid his hands on her hips. Almost by reflex, Costanza raised her left hand to remove his, but when her hand touched him she left it as it was, on his.

Pietro lifted her other hand and guided her wrist so that she could pop the biscuit into his mouth. He ate it with voracious little bites, chewing slowly, savouring the crumbs and looking her in the eye all the while. Then he covered her fingers with little kisses and started to lick her little finger. Costanza—her eyes fringed with ash fixed on his face—let him continue.

Pietro wound his fingers around hers and brought their hands back to her hips, then thrust strongly against her, pushing. Costanza stiffened but offered no resistance. They were body to body. Pietro bent to kiss her. She twisted her head to one side, avoiding him, but he was already lifting up her hair and covering her neck and her ear with a long trail of feverish kisses. Costanza yielded to him.

"Are my biscuits ready?" Antonio had appeared at the garden door.

74

"Look at who I am now and not at who I was."

The Marchese Sabbiamena sees his wife from another point of view, but she cannot accept that he has changed.

Pietro dashed up the service stairs and reached his room. He gave his face a rinse in the sink and looked at himself in the mirror. He knew that he was a handsome man, and he liked himself. But that day the image reflected in the mirror struck him as unpleasant, obtuse.

Is there another man in her life? What if Costanza denies herself to me? Pietro knew that his wife had dealings with Iero Bentivoglio, a great womaniser, and probably with other businessmen, too, and for the first time he felt the pangs of a blind jealousy he had never felt before, against everyone and no one. "Another man, before me! Intolerable!"

Pietro slammed his fist down on the washbasin. He rushed out and headed for his wife's rooms, but she wasn't there. He looked for her in the drawing rooms, on the terraces. He went to the little dining room where she took her meals: it was empty. The servants had returned to their afternoon chores, and he thought it would be undignified to go down to the kitchens. He remained in the communicating room, waiting for Costanza to return to her bedroom. He could think only of her, could only relive those moments and desire her, perhaps as he had never desired any other woman.

The wait seemed endless, but of Costanza there was no trace. Rosa and some other maids glanced at him furtively as they passed through the drawing room. This irritated Pietro. When don Baldassare came—presumably informed by the maids—to ask him if he wanted anything, he dismissed him and, left alone, paced up and down, repeating, "The marchesa, you fool, that's who I want!"

Costanza was wearing the same green dress, but her shoulders were now covered by a silk shawl embroidered in purple. Her hair was pulled into a fluffy chignon, and it looked all the more auburn for the purple in the shawl.

She was beautiful.

They exchanged a few embarrassed words under the curious eyes of the servants. Pietro asked Costanza to play for him.

"Very well, but only for a little," she said obediently. "I have papers to read."

They were finally alone in Costanza's drawing room.

"What would you like me to play, Pietro?" she asked, once seated at the piano.

"Nothing . . . anything would be fine by me, as long as you sing."

And Costanza sang, but without conviction. He was devouring her with his eyes. Costanza noticed this. She let her hands slip down into her lap and said, "I'm going to my room now."

"May I come?" he asked, moving to the piano.

She looked at him with her innocent, sad eyes. "No, why?"

"How can you ask me that after this afternoon?"

Costanza sighed. "I've become accustomed to living first as a sister and then as a stranger. It hasn't been easy, but I've managed."

"You're still my wife! What must I do to deserve you?" Pietro was at her side, tugging at her arm. She resisted, glued to the piano stool.

Defeated, Pietro kept repeating, "What must I do?" He took a few steps and fell onto the divan in tears.

Costanza had never seen him cry. She sat down on the other end of the divan. "Pietro, I loved you very much, but now I'm not sure. I have changed. You wouldn't recognise me."

"Do you love someone else?" asked Pietro, clearing his throat.

"If I did, I wouldn't need to tell you, just as I don't ask you," she answered calmly, trying to keep her distance.

"You have never forgiven me, that's what it is."

Costanza was about to say something, but she didn't. *Excess is always a mistake, even in forgiveness,* her father had told her. *Think of yourself before you think of others.* Distraught and torn between her father's advice and the feelings for Pietro that welled up powerfully within her, she, too, burst into tears. They wept together for a long time on that divan—chaste, tormented by desire, afraid to reach out a hand and touch each other.

Finally, Pietro pulled himself together. He stood up and held out his hand to help her up. Costanza took it. They moved off warily towards the door.

Before opening it, Pietro said, "Once you asked me why I had never kissed you, do you remember?"

She nodded.

"It's only right that I tell you. Because I wasn't attracted to you. You need attraction, to kiss. Have you ever been kissed by a man?"

"Yes, once." Costanza shuddered at the thought.

He perceived this. "Allow me to give you a kiss, only one."

Costanza's face was inundated with uncontrollable tears, but she looked up and offered it to her husband. They exchanged one interminably long, deep, salty kiss, then both withdrew to their respective rooms.

Costanza had difficulty falling asleep. Then, from somewhere inside her, outside her, a voice that was and yet wasn't hers picked up the dear refrain, *Porgi, amor, qualche ristoro,* and so, listening, she fell into a drowse.

The following morning, Pietro knocked at the door of his wife's bedroom.

"I was hoping you would come," said Costanza. "I'm going to the Trasis in Bagheria. I'll be staying there for a week. At the end of May, I'll be off to Malivinnitti. Naturally you can call on me there, but I'd prefer it if you didn't."

"What do you want me to do?"

"Live your life as usual—that's important. Each of us must live life as usual, and then we'll see. I wanted to tell you that I've sold Canziati to a consortium and there's cash. Drop in at the office, if you want."

Pietro did not go to join her in Bagheria. He sold a gold snuffbox and paid off his debts; he was feeling uneasy about using Costanza's money. He stopped frequenting other women.

When Costanza returned to Palermo, she was serene. Her cousins' company had done her good. She had thought at length. She had done much to make Pietro happy in the past. She had torn many horns from her head, and now, as with the Snail Princess, they hurt. But she loved him. Despite everything. She would have to go carefully, teach him to accept her little horns, talk to him about herself, learn to get to know him better.

Pietro was anxiously waiting for her. He was unable to touch her, even to kiss her hand as usual, nor did Costanza extend her hand, still gloved. They stood there looking at each other. "It's right that we try to find out if we are made for each other," Costanza told him, "to see if we can make a braid together. I'm frightened, and so are you. We are different. We must work out how to get on. Now I am the one to ask you not to be a true husband, and I'm sorry about that. But it's not pique. Antonio also comes into it. I love him, but he belongs to his mother. The man who takes me must accept this love of mine, but not share it. In the meantime, I don't want the servants or anyone else to get wind of anything. I shall carry on living my life as you will live yours, including your flings with other women."

The Marchese and Marchesa Sabbiamena did not return to Cacaci. On the rare occasions on which they found themselves in the company of family and friends, Costanza blushed frequently and Pietro tried to keep up his customary urbane manner, but he lacked his usual nonchalance. They didn't leave Palazzo Sabbiamena together, but they would meet in town and at the Favorita riding track, like two lovers whose families opposed them, and they would talk and talk.

Costanza took him to the places she had visited with her father, to the perfumed gardens and to the Phoenician walls. The feelings she had had as a child—the discovery of beauty through knowledge, the wonders of the historic past, and the generosity of teaching—merged with the feelings she now felt, as a woman. She blossomed into an awareness of herself and of the man she loved. Like a tree that sends down its roots to draw up the moisture of the earth, she was alight and ready to burst into new bud; she and Pietro were the link between past and future, the continuation of life.

Pietro knew that his father-in-law had not liked him—had treated him with contemptuous courtesy—but he didn't dare bring this up with

Costanza. Through her stories he learned to appreciate the late young baron, and he compared him to his own father, whom he had barely known and had not got on with. In turn, Pietro told her about his childhood and adolescence as an orphan, spent between boarding school and holidays as the guest of rich relatives; he had grown up neither with a mentor nor with deep affection, always in search of a role and an identity, and always assailed by financial worries. Costanza began to understand her husband's shallow improvidence: they were the reactions of a weak man faced with a reality he didn't know how to deal with.

Pietro suddenly felt inhibited, and in the evenings, in the solitude of his room, he would write Costanza long, passionate letters. As always, Costanza communicated through music. Apart from Mozart, she played with a renewed passion from some handwritten scores that she had found among her mother's papers. They were English songs, and she imagined they might have been transcribed for Caterina—perhaps even for her—by her real father.

At home, Pietro and Costanza exchanged furtive embraces, fearful of being caught by the servants. They were mad about each other, but it seemed as if they couldn't or wouldn't go farther, as if they were afraid of breaking the spell.

75

"As you play me, so shall I sing you."

Red poppies in the wheat fields of Malivinnitti

Costanza insisted on going to Malivinnitti before Pietro, and alone, as was by now her custom. Only there did she have the courage to confess to him the truth about who her real father was. "That doesn't surprise me," he said. "It happens far more often than you'd think."

With a smaller staff and the big house at their disposal, it would have been easy for them to be together undisturbed, but rather than take advantage of this they avoided staying alone in the house for long. Those walls called up distressing memories and oozed a sensuality that was not theirs. They spoke little, and seemed bemused. Costanza ordered the Tignusos not to accompany them when they left the farmyard, and the Tignusos reluctantly obeyed, thinking this was another way of checking up on their protective capacities and their power on the estate. The couple went for long outings on horseback along the narrow lanes running through the ripe wheat, making their way down into the valleys, skirting the ravines. When they made a stop, they would embrace with inexplicable restraint, and in silence. In the evenings, on the terrace, they would stand at the balustrade and gaze at the hills of Malivinnitti, watching as they turned blue and were swallowed up in the damp darkness of the night. Then and only then would they take each other by the hand and wander in the heavens, consumed by desire.

One afternoon they were riding along the foot of a high hill that was full of poppies. From a distance the scattered clumps of flowers looked like bloodstains, so thick were they in the wheat. From close up the flowers were a marvel, the red of the petals and the green of the stems contrasting with the bright yellow of the wheat and the blue of the open sky. They dismounted to look more closely. The wheat had grown very tall and thick, above their heads. Pietro pushed his way through the wheat and called her: "Come on, Costanza!" Immersed in a sea of wheat, they moved slowly forwards. Pietro guided Costanza, holding her arm tight, and used his riding crop to push the wheat to one side; the stalks would bend and then sinuously close ranks behind them.

Costanza followed him lightly. She felt transported to some forest on the banks of the Amazon. When she was small, her father used to tell her that the natives of that place used little boats with sharp, pointed prows to push their way through the high grass and reach the banks of that immense river with its clear, dark streams that flowed along until they met and merged into one amid a thunder of foam and spray at the rapids. Costanza was ready to know and explore the world and herself. The wheat stalks scratched them, the buzzing of the insects was deafening, and it was baking hot. Suddenly a little patch of poppies appeared before them. Pietro took off his jacket and spread it out on the ground. The sky was dazzling.

"Come on!" he said again.

On a bed of crushed poppies, in the shade of the wheat, Costanza knew her husband over and over, and happiness too, in a time she was unable to measure.

Reluctantly, they got ready to leave. Pietro patiently helped Costanza get dressed. He hooked up the chain of her medallion around her neck and, nibbling at her earlobe, whispered, "You're a great lay!" This surprised her, but she was by no means displeased.

On the way back, Costanza reined in her mare.

"Pietro, I have something important to say to you. I'm not asking you to be faithful to me, but on no account must you bring other women to our house. I wouldn't forgive you, alive or dead!"

"Costanzina, I promise you that will never happen. I will have no other women, ever."

Rosa Nascimbene and Baldassare Cacopardo noticed that the masters' clothes were wrinkled, all dusty and covered with bits of straw and little ants, and they were glad about that.

76

"One rotten apple spoils the whole barrel."

The harmony between husband and wife is greeted with joy by many but not by all.

On the masters' return from their long holiday at Malivinnitti, the atmosphere in Sabbiamena House in Cacaci changed, for placid contentment now mirrored their mood. Rosa and Baldassare were well aware of how things stood: the marchese's sheets were untouched, while Rosa had to change her mistress's sheets every other day, such was the tangled state she found them in every morning and afternoon. Amalia noticed this, too, and was the most pleased of all: she had never seen Costanza so happy. Her mistress made no mention of what had happened, but when she hugged Amalia it was no longer for comfort but to convey her joy.

Pietro and Costanza kept up their custom of moving to Palermo in November. Their relatives awaited them eagerly, for they had been told of the change. The couple did not conceal their feelings for each other, but they behaved with restraint, and soon the news of their rapprochement became yesterday's news. In those years the aristocrats of Palermo had other fish to fry: the mood was one of euphoria and satisfaction. The National Exposition in 1891 had set the seal on Sicilian supremacy regained; the local nobles were known throughout Europe and they dominated life in the city—as bank directors, company chairmen, governors of public bodies, members of parliament and the senate. The Marchese Ugo was once again mayor. The affluent English families and the bourgeois entrepreneurs who controlled the Sicilian economy married into the aristocracy, thus offering the latter a chance to reacquire—through dowries—properties they had lost in the past.

Pietro's friends expected that now, with all the more reason, he would take part in Palermo's festivities and civic life during these glorious years, but instead he went off with his wife on long holidays in the country, alone. This disappointed them. They spoke tactfully and with ill-concealed admiration of the redheaded marchesa's bewitching powers. And indeed Costanza was in full bloom. Tall and sinuous, she had filled out, and she exuded femininity; her face, no longer gaunt, would open into a sweet, enigmatic smile that was reflected in her big hazel and blue-grey eyes, which had also acquired a beauty all their own. Even her hair became the object of admiration; as the years went by the red had grown darker, with a profusion of highlights, and Pietro advised Costanza on which clothes and colours would best enhance the whiteness of her complexion and the rich colour of her hair.

At the club they talked about Pietro's rediscovered domestic bliss, shaking their heads and joking about the fact that he had been so unwilling to do his conjugal duty in the past, while he had fully satisfied the obligations required by high society and by his own rank. Now the situation had been stood on its head: seduced by a woman, Pietro had abandoned his social duties, which happened to lots of men, but in his case, unlike all the others, the woman in question had been his wife for nine years, and was rich, too! The young Prince Chisicussi went so far as to assert paradoxically that his cousin's apparent domestic happiness set the worst kind of example: if every couple behaved like this, the aristocrats would die of boredom, the clubs and brothels would go out of business, and Palermo would plunge into decline.

No one mentioned that Pietro and Costanza were, simply, a couple in love.

77

"*Wives are for husbands and loose women for beasts.*"

Rura Fecarotta is plotting, and in not worrying about this the Marchesa Sabbiamena makes a mistake.

Three years went by. Rura stayed on unwillingly in Cacaci, and she was bored. She sewed for others, looked after her son, and went to Sabbiamena House when ordered to. But she felt that she was at the mercy of a person whom she no longer thought of as a benefactress but as someone making her pay for sins she hadn't committed, a woman, above all, who intended to steal her son from her. Imprisoned in an unwanted motherhood, Rura also came to resent the affection between Antonio and the marchesa. She had believed the promise that he would be rich and that, as a consequence, she, too, would be well taken care of; she had never considered that the couple might have a son who would oust hers. And it was exactly this that was now rumoured in whispers below stairs: an heir would guarantee the continuing employment of the servants and their children, and their children's children.

Rura realised that things were as she feared, and even worse. Costanza persuaded Pietro to meet his son, but the marchese still did not want the little boy to come to the main floor. For his part, Antonio knew that the marchese was his father but didn't say so, showing the reserve that Sicilians imbibe with their mothers' milk. Rura did what she could: she went from one wise woman to another in search of sorcery, and paid dearly to have a curse put on the Sabbiamenas and their love.

Rura studied Costanza's habits, tastes, and gestures and told the wise women about them. They suggested spells, gave her amulets, and made effigies of Costanza out of bread dough, clay, straw, and other ingredients onto which they pasted her own hair, even clots of her menstrual blood, before sticking baleful pins into them. Other objects of witchcraft had to be left on the marchesa's person, and Rura entrusted her son with this task, because sometimes Costanza took him into her room. When she found strange things in her pockets she pretended nothing had happened, because she didn't want the child to be scolded by his mother.

———

"That woman is evil, and your ladyship should get rid of her," Amalia told her.

"Amalia, you who have been loved and loved in return should understand her and have pity on her," Costanza replied. "She has a son who has been rejected by his father, and she has been exploited by men. She can do me no harm."

"You mustn't worry about Antonio's future. He is a Patella, and a Patella he shall remain. I shall look after him whatever happens. You go on being a good mother and you'll be happy with your son," Costanza later said to Rura, who stabbed the needle into the smock she was sewing with such force that she pricked her finger: she hated Costanza.

The wise women's demands for money were bleeding Rura white, but the couple were in love, so people said, and none of the curses worked. She wanted her freedom—she already had a little house and enough money to keep the wolf from the door. Nor did the thought of other men displease her: she wanted a chance to marry and do a job she liked, with other people, rather than sewing alone with that damned needle and thread. She felt like a tuna fish trapped in the nets of the killing fields; the marchesa's every word was like a harpoon thrust into her flesh. She decided to bring things to a head, to have a row with the marchesa, confident that out of love for Antonio the marchesa would give her a nest egg and set her free.

As often happened, the marchesa was telling Antonio a story. They were by a window, not far from where Rura was sewing. Rura said to him, "Help me fold this cloth," and she gave him a very long piece of cotton fabric. Reluctantly, the little boy obeyed, and then he went back to Costanza. "I've dropped the pins," said Rura, "help me find them," and, grumbling, he came to help her pick them out of the folds in the cloth. The marchesa said nothing while this was going on, but she was impatient: she wanted to finish the story. It was a tale about Pitichinunu, Antonio's favourite character, and he kept asking her, "Then what happened? Then what happened?"

Rura knocked over the sewing basket, and the spools scattered all over the floor. "Antonio, help me pick them up!" A most unwelcome task, and this time Antonio paid no attention. Rura got to her feet, angrily grabbed him by the ear, and gave him a whack on the shoulder.

"Get to work! You have to earn your bread, too, you wretch!" she shouted at him, and then she made him pick up everything, standing behind him and giving him no peace until he had collected each and every last spool. "Let me hear the end of the story!" he said, and she slapped him so hard that it left a mark on his cheek. "Have some respect for your mother! You only have one, and no father!" And she went back to her sewing without even looking at Costanza. Antonio burst into tears. Rura heard Costanza talking to him, quietly trying to console him. This was the moment she had been waiting for. She stood up and said, "He is my son, and your ladyship should mind her own business. This boy must respect his mother first, because he has only one mother, not two."

Costanza, too, had risen to her feet. "Go to the kitchen," she said to Antonio, "and say that the marchesa wants you to have three biscuits, and that you may choose them." The whimpering little boy slipped off.

"What are you getting at, Rura?"

"There's too many mothers around here! He's poor, all right, but he's my son, and that's how I want him! Money can't buy everything!"

"Antonio has only one mother, and that's you."

"Oh sure, that's what you say, but you're taking him away from me; you amuse yourself with him as if he was a puppy dog. Then you go off and that's the end of it, and I have to look after a crying child. Then you come back and you want him all nice and ready for you. Maybe what I did before was better for me and for my son!"

"Don't say that, Rura!"

"Then give me a little something so that I can feed him and pay for his schooling, but at my own house. I don't need much, but he must be mine. I've never asked for charity, and I don't want to ask for it now." Rura had gone red in the face; she burst into tears, and her sobs were genuine.

"But Antonio is happy, and you have brought him up well . . . He comes here willingly. It would be a crime to take him away and not educate him; he is a Patella."

"Patella, my foot! He's the son of a woman like his mother! Better a whore for a mother than a dead mother. I am his mother, only me, and I can't stand coming here to prick my fingers anymore. I'm taking him away, and even if we die of hunger it would be better for us. You are a marchesa and a marchesa you'll remain, but you don't have children— the Lord won't give you any."

"I have promised that the rent on your house will always be paid, until you die, and Antonio will go to boarding school at my expense and he will be maintained like a Patella," said Costanza. "But expect nothing else. I am going to forget all the rest."

78

"Evils that pursue you will kill you in the end."

Innocently, the tortoises once more bring great sorrow to Costanza Safamita.

The Marchese and Marchesa Sabbiamena were in Cacaci. The tortoise eggs were ready to hatch. Costanza was waiting for this moment and frequently went down to check on the beasts. She was in the ironing room with Antonio and Rura.

"When will the eggs hatch?" asked Antonio. He was looking from his mother to Costanza, and insistently repeated his question.

Costanza thought the little boy might like to go to check for himself, but Pietro still did not allow the child the freedom of the house. "Don't worry," she assured him. "I'll go every afternoon, I promise you, then I'll let you know."

On the little terrace in front of Pietro's study the earth had been turned, but there was no sign of baby tortoises. Then she found them, small with white carapaces, one beside the other, behind a tub. She was overcome by an immense tenderness: it was a propitious omen for her maternity. She heard a rustling sound, and she went up to the study. She had been encouraging Pietro to look after his business affairs and thought, without his being pressured, that he was already using the room.

Costanza peeped through the window, unworried. Through the holes in the embroidery work of the curtain she saw an unknown figure standing in the middle of the room. It was a woman with smooth, light-coloured skin, a round face, prominent lips, and disturbing eyes. Pietro was at the back of the study, behind the desk, leaning against the bookshelf. Slowly, the woman unbuttoned her bodice and opened her blouse;

she took out her swollen breasts and showed them to Pietro, running her tongue over her lips. Her gaze was divided between the offer of her pointed breasts and Pietro's eyes.

Costanza fled.

"Costanza, what's the matter?" asked Pietro as he came into his wife's room. Costanza was seated, her hands in her lap, pale as could be.

"I saw you."

"Costanza, let me explain." Pietro took her hand.

"Leave me alone," she murmured. Pietro, distraught, clutched her even more firmly. She fainted in his arms.

Costanza fell ill with a high fever, and she became delirious. She rejected her husband; the mere sight of him was enough to give her a relapse. Pietro did not leave the house. He watched her as she slept.

Costanza recovered very slowly. She would let her husband enter her bedroom, but only in the company of others. Gradually she got better and returned to her tasks, but she was like a larva, with no energy. Her skin became as wrinkled as a prune. Pietro seldom went out, and only briefly; husband and wife roamed around the house, apparently absorbed in their business and thoughts, like two earthquake survivors wandering in the wreckage, not knowing where, how, or what to rebuild. It was a torment for them and for those who witnessed them.

One day Pietro asked for a private conversation. She received him in her drawing room.

"Costanza, I must explain . . ."

"Pietro, it's too late. I have thought of all the plausible excuses and none stand up. You have lied to me so many other times. You made a promise, and that was that."

"Costanza, I love you," stammered Pietro.

"I love you, too. But I love myself more than you. I must. You would break my heart if what I saw were repeated. I need certainties more than other people do—order, inner peace. It's over."

Costanza rose and made to leave the drawing room. Pietro followed her. Once more, he found himself with her supine in his arms, unconscious.

79

"Better alone than in bad company"

Costanza realises that people do not mind their own business.

The Patellas spent the autumn of 1892 in Cacaci.

Costanza behaved as if she had erased the previous three happy years from her memory, and she returned to her old ways. Pietro seldom went out in the evenings, and after dinner he often went back to his own rooms, from which he could hear Costanza playing. The music slipped under the doors, a faint portent that Costanza might become his once more. He respected her desire for solitude and had no wish to push her before she was ready, which might ruin everything. But he wrote her many letters; Costanza sent them back unopened.

In December the couple went to Palermo for the winter. Costanza offered to accompany Baroness Lannificchiati and Countess Acere to afternoon performances at the opera, leaving the evening box for her husband. They entertained relatives and a few intimate friends; since their participation in the social rounds had been minimal, Costanza hoped their estrangement would pass unnoticed.

Costanza paid a call on her aunt Maria Anna Trasi, where she was joined by Maria Antonia and Baroness Lannificchiati. Her aunt was very happy about Sandrino Trasi's university career: her "studious nephew" had now become a professor, and she sang the praises of her son-in-law Iero Bentivoglio, who had helped him through his political contacts. Then they chatted about this and that. Her aunt kept giving her anxious, questioning looks, and Costanza felt uncomfortable. When the time came for everyone to leave, her aunt detained her.

"Costanza, you are like a daughter to me . . . what has happened with your husband? Lots of people have asked me about this, and I'm sorry— just when you both seemed so happy together."

Costanza winced. She managed to get out, "Men don't change, I realise that now."

"I'm talking to you about this only because Annina Lannificchiati is making herself ill over it. She is disconsolate and says that Pietro is remorseful. Men are always the same, right to the end. Your uncle, who was a good husband, asked me on his deathbed if I might let him see his last mistress, and he was over eighty!"

"And you, what did you say?" Costanza was very dismayed.

"What can a good wife say? She came, one afternoon. But he died in my arms. I knew I was the one he loved most."

"Aunt, I cannot be sure even of this."

"That's Safamita pride talking. I hoped you had been spared it. Dignity must be maintained, always, but pride does harm."

"I'll think about it, I promise."

Costanza no longer took pleasure in the company of relatives, and she avoided being alone even with the female cousins who were closest to her. She withdrew into her shell.

Costanza had other worries. These were hard times for people. All over Sicily they were forming Fasci, associations not wholly unlike the religious corporations that had been disbanded by the abolition laws. Each was different from the next—some were controlled by mafiosi, several by bourgeois and professionals, and a few even by the nobility—but all of them demanded more social justice. For the first time, field hands and the lower classes joined many of these groups. Like the other great landowners, Costanza was on the alert. Her estates were controlled by mafia overseers, and she had taken care, so as not to worsen her vulnerability, to avoid favouring any one mafia family in particular. But at Malivinnitti the two branches of the Tignuso clan were at loggerheads, and she had to cope as best she could.

Costanza had no relations with Giacomo and his family. She would catch glimpses of them, from a distance, at weddings and funerals. They did not greet each other. Yet she worried terribly about the future of his and Stefano's children. Giacomo was autocratic; he dealt with a mafia family that dominated and controlled his lands, leaving him with a semblance of considerable power. He was not the only feudal landowner to fall back on this method, but in his case it was not prudent. For another influential family lived in Sarentini who were enemies, and the Carcarozzos gravitated to them.

Trusted people kept Costanza informed about Stefano's family, but she knew very little about her nephew and nieces and even less about her beloved Caterina, who had married a junior clerk and moved to another town. Guglielmo, the only boy and the legitimate heir to the title, was an angry young man. He had lost the suit first brought by his father against his aunt and uncle, and he railed against Giacomo, who, it was said, made it hard for him to find work in Sarentini. At twenty years of age, he had nothing to do but associate with troublemakers and foment claims against the uncle he considered a usurper.

The Safamitas were tearing one another to pieces out of pride and greed; uncle and nephew were open enemies. Costanza did not feel different from them, and she understood that her own precarious contentment depended on her wealth. But what good was property to her? And to whom could she leave it? She wondered why she had to put so much effort into taking care of her assets and looking for new investments. Once upon a time she had been satisfied by the simple, innocent joy of spending money and enjoying her husband—but no more. She had hoped that Antonio would take the place of the son she never had, but things had turned out differently. Costanza regretted not having taken her nurse's advice to choose one of her cousins' sons as her heir, as her great-uncle and aunt Lattuca had done with her father.

She could no longer return to her former solitude and love of self. She grew melancholy. Yet she kept up all her occupations and everything proceeded in a regular fashion, in both city and country. She did not think about Pietro. He was the Marchese Sabbiamena, her husband, one more stranger among many.

80

"The vinegar barrel never runs dry."

The festivities in Palazzo Sabbiamena for Stefano Trasi's birthday end badly. A memorable train journey

Baldassare slipped quietly into the room to whisper something into the marchese's ear under the disapproving gaze of don Agostino Porrazzo, the majordomo. At the other end of the table, Costanza was managing guests and footmen as only she knew how. With a few words she began or ended her conversations while following the service out of the corner of her eye: one look was enough to convey an order. She noted the intruder and her face darkened, then she reverted to her expression as mistress of the house.

"Would you like more pigeon pie?" Costanza murmured to Count Acere—and the silver salver was already on the count's left, the gloved hand ready to serve—then let her glance slip to the other guests; there were many of them, relatives and close friends of Stefano Trasi, her favourite cousin. The atmosphere was merry, for they were celebrating his birthday. Some distance away, Costanza could hear the laughter of her aunt Maria Anna, on Pietro's right, and she looked over at her, straining to catch her words. Pietro's eyes fell on her, dark and gloomy. She was peeved by this, and continued her survey of the table.

"Did you go to the Teatro Fenice?" Stefano's wife asked her.

"No, the opera wasn't on in Venice when I was there," she answered, but her cousin was already chuckling with the person next to her.

Pietro began to stare at her again, and again Costanza was vexed. This time she looked straight at him—would you stop that! Pietro's gaze stayed fixed, and bleak.

"Pietro, you must go back to Venice and take your wife to the opera!" Baroness Lannificchiati had been watching them, and in her own way wanted to intervene.

"Yes, Aunt . . ." murmured Pietro with a taut smile, and he lowered his eyes to his plate, busying himself with his knife and fork.

The men were discussing the political and social crisis of the day: the Marchese Notarbartolo, former chairman of the Bank of Sicily, had been assassinated in a train tunnel on the way to Palermo—a crime committed by persons unknown, but the name of the instigator was on everyone's lips—and in the meantime the government, in a test of strength, was involved in violent clashes against the Fasci: there had been some deaths. But the talk was lighthearted, as befits a festive occasion. The women listened and even took part in it—it was a way to find out what was happening—though they preferred the gossip.

Lively conversations were weaving in and out, intertwining, blending. The room was full of chatter, with everyone talking at the same time, not waiting for answers from whoever had been asked a question. Baron Francesco Orata and Count Gioacchino Acere were criticising Iero Bentivoglio's political party: since they were related, this was legitimate.

"But who is governing us, Iero? What kind of Sicilian is he? Thirty years in parliament, a real opportunist! A revolutionary he called himself, and now he's sending us the army—and not for the first time! They treat us like a colony. National unity, my foot! That's politics for you: dirty, very dirty indeed, my dear marchesa," said Acere.

"We talked about this Crispi at your christening, Marchesa Costanza. Those were the days! And what a reception your grandfather put on! The Safamita brothers were real gentlemen and honest men, and they don't make them like that anymore!" exclaimed Baron Orata. Costanza smiled faintly.

"Ah my late brother, God rest his soul! Costanza, your father had a passion for Stefano!" Maria Anna Trasi was happy, and with a satisfied smile she said to the guest of honour, "At Malivinnitti he used to take you on the back of his horse, when you were small! How lovely they were, those holidays at Malivinnitti . . ." Her fellow diners lowered their voices and, smiling, listened to her talk. Countess Trasi was a truly beloved mother and grandmother.

But Pietro was still staring at Costanza, inexorably, sombrely. She shot him a direct, irritated look; he was going to ruin the party if he went on behaving like this. She stopped looking at him, but he went on staring. Her irritation turned to anxiety, then panic. Each of Pietro's looks—and she sensed them all—was the bearer of terrible omens. Faintly, Costanza murmured "True" and "Of course" to those who spoke to her; she moved her head in the direction of one guest or another, but she wasn't understanding what was said. Scraps of phrases came to her, words of one person mixing with those of another and reverberating in her head: sounds that accompanied the blows delivered by Pietro's every glance.

"Bad times are coming! Even the flagellants have shown up in the villages."

"That's what happened before the French Revolution!"

"The milliner ruined the Brussels lace with that awful stitching!"

"They boast about the conquest of Africa, and they can't even subdue those ruffians."

"In Catania they have a socialist for a mayor."

"The Heraldry Commission is the only good thing Crispi has done."

"They're people with no history, and they call themselves nobility?"

"She refused to live in her parents-in-law's house, it's unbelievable!"

"A courtesy title is different, but noble blood is noble blood."

"They create work, yes, but for whom? For their friends and for hangers-on."

"The mafia vote counts, and how!"

"They have some fabulous cashmere scarves at the Emporio Moderno, and they're offering a discount."

"The government is levying less tax on citrus groves."

"But our estates are being taxed to death!"

"Extending the suffrage will be the ruin of local government."

"*Palermo felix!* What a laugh!"

"A commoner for mayor after thirteen years of real gentlemen!"

"Field hands need hands to work with, not pen and paper!"

"That's why we have the Fasci."

"A dowry of four million to call herself princess!"

"Ten lire the vote, that's the price."

"You need four quarterings of nobility to be admitted to the club."

"I don't use the train anymore after what happened to poor Notarbartolo."

"Who said that everyone should be able to read?"

The footmen took away the round trays with the dismembered remains of the "triumph of gluttony," Sicily's famed dessert. Costanza rose from the table, followed by the others.

"Costanza, wait, I must speak to you. There's bad news," said Pietro when the last guest had left. "Stefano's son Guglielmo died last night. In Sarentini."

"Of what?"

"While we were at table someone came from Safamita House; it seems there was an accident like the one that happened to Stefano. Instant death."

"Do you know when the funeral will be?"

"No. Is there anything I can do?"

"Nothing, thank you," she replied, and she slowly left the room.

Pietro heard the tread of hurried steps and the voices of the footmen, then the pawing of horses' hooves: Costanza was going to Sarentini. In a rush he ordered a suitcase prepared, but then, impatiently, he himself began to stuff in what he needed, rumpling the clothes that Baldassare had carefully folded and packed. He had to be with her.

The train was leaving. Pietro, in disarray, was running to catch it and Baldassare, don Agostino, and the coachman were behind him, panting. The guard was about to close the door of the first-class carriage.

"Let me in!"

"Do you have a ticket?"

"I am the Marchese Sabbiamena!" yelled Pietro, and pushed the man aside.

"Wait please, we are with milord the marchese!" shouted the other two. Don Baldassare, all out of breath, ran along on his flat feet.

Pietro did not at first realise that the solitary figure in black, huddled against the window, was really Costanza: she seemed to have shrunk.

"I looked for you all over," Pietro said, and sat down opposite her.

"Oh, thank you," she replied, and went back to looking outside.

At the next stop, a couple with a little boy came into the compartment.

"Mummy, I'm hungry," said the boy, and his mother took some bread and frittata out of her leather bag.

"Who's that?" he asked, pointing at the ticket collector.

"When will we get there?"

"Mummy, the sun's gone away, give me your hand!" he said in the tunnel.

"Mummy, that woman's got red hair like the Devil. She scares me!" he said as he left the compartment, making a sign to ward off the evil eye. Costanza turned and gave him a weary glance, as if to apologise.

It was dark. They were alone. Costanza, dozing, slipped to one side with the jouncing of the carriage. Pietro came and sat beside her. She leant against him, her head in the hollow between his shoulder and chin, the way she used to once upon a time, and slept on. Pietro breathed in the pungent smell of her sweaty hair and, without realising, found himself stroking her cheek. In response to the rhythm of the train, she moved her lips, her breathing quickened and slowed, but she didn't wake up. Pietro was sure that Costanza felt his nearness, that she sensed his body, and he hoped. Their "real" marriage had been simple, normal, as it ought to be. Happy. He wanted her to be his wife again. She opened her eyes and closed them again; her head, abandoned on Pietro's shoulder, became heavier. Suddenly Costanza straightened up and returned to an erect position. They continued on their journey in a heavy, awkward silence.

In the coach and at Castle Sarentini, Costanza took care to avoid him; she spoke to him only when she had to and made no mention of her nephew. The following morning, they went to the funeral together; and even after what happened in church she did not speak to him. She kept up her silence in the castle, in the coach, and on the train back to Palermo.

Sinking into opposite seats in their personal carriage, they avoided eye contact, both oppressed by their own anguish. The train ran through the mountains of the interior. In and out of tunnels. The darkness alternating with the light. Dazzling.

"Did you know how he died yesterday?" asked Costanza. She had turned towards Pietro and was looking straight at him.

"Yes."

"But you didn't tell me when I asked you."

"I didn't want to make you feel any worse."

"You said he had an accident, like Stefano."

Pietro lowered his head.

"Did you know that this wasn't true?"

He made no reply.

"Another lie," said Costanza with a sigh, and she went back to looking at the countryside through the window. The train was nearing Palermo. It was dusk. She looked up at Monte Pellegrino, but it wasn't there anymore—it had vanished, shrouded in mist.

81

"A labourer is worthy of his hire."

As the sirocco blows, Amalia Cuffaro thinks of the sugar babies on All Souls' Day and of the tragic death of Guglielmo Safamita.

The sirocco was blowing fiercely. It was muggy, and the unbreathable air was laden with sand. The wind struck the Montagnazza, scorching and parching the tufts of stunted grass growing here and there in the cracks in the marl. The leaden sky and the sluggish sea were deserted: not a boat, not a bird. The rocks were dry, the seaweed shrivelled; insects, lizards, and even ants hid in the hollows and fissures of the stone veiled with sand. The Montagnazza was superb, enveloped in its gilded cobweb. Its inhabitants, holed up in their caves, waited for the northwest wind.

Amalia had barricaded herself inside; she had used rags to stop up the slit that served as a window. She and Pinuzza sat motionless in the semidarkness; the slightest movement exhausted her. Shafts of dull light came in through chinks and cracks. The floor was covered with slippery, vitreous sand blown in by the inexorable wind; it piled up in waves, as if the sea had become sand and invaded the Montagnazza.

"We won't die of thirst, since we have plenty of water. Your brothers are good to you, and they love you. You're lucky, Pinuzza."

"Why lucky? All brothers must love their sisters, Aunt."

"If only all brothers were like that . . . the world would be a far better place," said Amalia.

"Didn't your marchesa's brothers love her?"

"Stefano did, but then he changed. The other one was born bad, and he never loved Costanza."

"Why?"

"Because he was envious."

"And can't you love and be envious at the same time?"

"No, Pinuzza, envy is a very ugly thing. It brings misfortune to those who have it in them."

"So what is it, a spell?"

"Sort of."

"What did your Costanza do with this bad brother?"

"Nothing. Don't think about it. Drink this up, you'll like it a lot," said Amalia, handing Pinuzza a glass of warm water in which she had dissolved a tiny piece of a sugar baby. Then she drank the remaining drops—exquisite. They fell silent, listening to the whistling of the wind.

Amalia could still taste the sweetness in her mouth, and she counted her blessings—a way all her own for forgetting painful memories: a childhood protected by affection, good health, a good, robust son, the tranquil years sheltered from poverty in Safamita House, the love of don Paolo. She thanked God for what she still had: the beauty of the Montagnazza, the ever-changing sea, the sky free and bright; even the laborious effort of looking after Pinuzza was tempered by her niece's good nature and by the thoughtfulness of her brother's family. The Belice family were very close-knit; when they argued they made up quickly, and they had to help one another against the eternal enemy: poverty.

How Costanza's two brothers had made their sister suffer, right to the end! Wealth does not make for a united family, and to think that she had thought quite the opposite about that honourable house! The affection that united poor families, she thought, was like the sugar babies they used to prepare for All Souls' Day—those statues made from discarded pieces of coarse sugar—painted in front and smooth behind. They lasted a long time, and their taste lingered in the mouth. Every year her mother would buy just one for all the children. The flavour was always the same, but the sugar baby was different each year and the subject of endless discussion: the Knight, the Saint, the King. They would put their sugar baby on the top shelf, far from greedy fingers; all you had to do was look at it and your mouth would begin to water. A lick today and a lick tomorrow until the colours faded and the sugar paste thinned out. The fingers and hands were the first parts to disappear, then the arms became stumps, hats and feathers would dissolve. Bit by bit the sugar baby was consumed. Then, all together, they would put the remains in a tin box. After that her mother would dole out pieces among the little ones by way of reward or consolation, and finally she would empty out all the crumbs from the bottom of the box: they were enough to sweeten a whole jug full of water.

The nobles had no respect for sugar babies. Their children would throw them on the floor and break them, leaving pieces that were barely nibbled. They preferred other, more refined sweets. All families need a sugar baby to keep them united, even the nobility, thought Amalia. True, they have their family name, their property, and their blood, but even that needs to be licked.

Oh, Gugliemo's death! It was as if she had been there herself, in front of the main door of Safamita House. Early one morning the porter found two sacks propped up against the door: they contained the head and the body of Stefano's son, the true Baron Safamita, even though no one called him that because nobles with no money aren't nobles anymore. The people of Sarentini understood immediately, but nobody explained it to the chief of police, a northerner who didn't understand such things: it was a punishment and a warning for the baron Giacomo. It came from men whom he had given to understand that it would be in their interest to rid him of his troublesome nephew, who had been saying so many bad things about him—and the people of Sarentini commented that the young man had only spoken the truth, so this showed precisely why he should have kept his mouth shut—because he would reward whomever did him this favour. But when someone came along ready to do what the baron wanted, he had decided not to pay what was due for the job, since he still thought he was the master of the town. Or perhaps he had had scruples, but by then it was too late: men of honour don't renege on an undertaking, not ever. They left the boy in front of the baron's door, shaming him before the whole town. The Safamitas had to obey the rules, too, just like everyone else.

Costanza wanted to attend the funeral. The household staff at Safamita House had to make preparations in great haste, cleaning the rooms and readying the coach to meet her at the station. At the funeral she and Pietro found themselves among strangers: Stefano had become one of the Carcarozzos. They, respectful of her kinship, moved to one side to let the Sabbiemenas sit in the first row, but Costanza stayed at the back. After the mass, she went up to the family. As she stooped to embrace her sister-in-law, Filomena grabbed her hair and seized her by the throat. Such was the force of her grip that she would have killed Costanza if the others hadn't stopped her. "It's your fault your brother was ruined! You are a marked woman, and nothing but death and disaster comes from you. Get out, before I kill you! You and your brother had them kill this darling son of mine, the only one left to me. Get out, before I kill you!" Amalia was told that the first to restrain her mother had been Caterina, but the girl didn't even give her aunt a glance.

Costanza never mentioned the episode, and she never returned to Sarentini. And Giacomo, rather than take his family to Palermo, as any other man would have done, stayed on there with all his children. But the people of Sarentini had lost their respect for the Safamitas. He lived in isolation in the mansion house, full of resentment and conceit. It was said that from that day he no longer set foot in certain parts of the countryside, those under the control of the men he had offended. The field overseers knew him for a weak man, and they were ready to crush him.

82

"The day of birth is known; that of death is not."

The sudden death of the Marchese Sabbiamena during an innocent visit to Teresina Pastanova

It was a warm afternoon in the late spring of 1895. The Countess Trasi, the guest of her niece in Cacaci, was resting in her room. Costanza was in the kitchen preparing a brioche. In the palm of her hand she crumbled up the flour and butter, then she added sugar and yeast, and finally some whole eggs, one by one. The dough had to be well mixed, and Costanza worked quickly, thumping the dough with straight fingers held close together, like a spatula. The dough loosened up and formed large bubbles. Under her expert hands it was taking on the elastic, tacky consistency that is essential to a well-made brioche. Costanza lifted it off the marble table and let it fall back down, and once again the dough looked like glue, coming away from and then sticking to the marble and her hands as if in some conjuring trick. She was humming the duet between Figaro and Susanna from *The Marriage of Figaro: Cinque . . . dieci . . . venti.* She heard shouting coming from the service rooms. The major-domo and Rosa burst into the room together with a hot, breathless boy who threw himself into a chair, his look a frightened one, repeating: "Milord the marchese . . . come quickly . . ."

Costanza covered her face with her buttery hands, leaving scraps of dough on her temples. Quickly cleaning herself up and covering herself with a shawl that Rosa had just enough time to throw over her shoulders, she dashed off behind the boy, followed by the majordomo and some footmen. They ran through the sleepy streets of the town, behind the mansion house. Careless of appearances—her petticoat pulled up, her stockings showing, her bodice unbuttoned, her chignon in disarray—Costanza ran to Pietro.

The house was nearby, a gift from Pietro for past "services rendered." In the little garden, under the pergola, Pietro's body lay on a mattress. Teresina Pastanova, prostrate with her face on the ground and surrounded by a small crowd, was wailing her grief and praise for the dead man. Costanza fell to her knees beside Pietro. She covered her face again. She saw him, serene and supremely beautiful in the pallor of

317

death, through the spaces between her fingers as if through the slats of a shutter. Overcome, Costanza felt faint. In the distance, faintly, the music of Lucia's last-act aria rose up—and this gave her strength.

The thick crowd of bystanders made way to let Rura and Antonio through. Rura also threw herself down on her knees, wailing. Embarrassed, Antonio looked at the father he barely knew and then slowly edged up to Costanza. It was only then that she fully realised she was not alone. She cast a horror-stricken glance at the two wailing women and got to her feet. Ignoring the bystanders, she clasped Pietro's son in a close embrace. She whispered something to him; the little boy listened seriously and looked at his father. They knelt down one beside the other, and together they repeated the quiet words of a short funeral prayer.

The men arrived to do what was necessary; the crowd broke up, murmuring. Costanza received their condolences and then, impatiently, gave orders in a rush of words. She put Antonio into the care of the majordomo and went up to Teresina, who was kneeling and still wailing.

"I am the marchese's wife. Tell me what happened to my husband."

Teresina—"one of those"—was a middle-aged woman whose looks were still pleasing.

"He had become like a son to me; he would come to take the air here every day, two or three hours. Sitting here he was, and he died just like that, suddenly," she said, and burst into sobs. Costanza laid her hand on Teresina's shoulder, and the woman clung to her. Now Costanza was weeping silently in the other woman's embrace. She swayed.

"Her ladyship the marchesa is unwell! Help me before someone else dies in my arms!"

Rura had stayed alone by the dead body. Not knowing what else to do, she began to howl again. "Go away," the majordomo told her. "We have to take His Excellency the Marchese to his own home," and he shoved her aside.

Sabbiamena House had undergone the metamorphosis of death. Gilded stuccoes and large mirrors were covered by black mourning palls, and the large drawing room was ready to welcome the marchese for the last night that a Patella di Sabbiamena would spend in the home of his forebears. Pietro had been placed in the middle of the room, his head higher than his feet, as is the custom of Palermo, while young nuns stood to one side murmuring prayers. Without a tear, Costanza received condolences and introduced Antonio—whom she wanted at her side—to every visitor. In the back of the room, cleared of furniture, Teresina Pastanova and the other women of the household wept in their assigned places. Rura was not admitted to the main floor, but she had been allowed to stay in the sewing room and there she held her clamorous wake.

"Have you spoken to Stefano?" Aunt Maria Anna timidly asked.

"Yes," replied Costanza.

"Well?"

"Well what?"

"Will you send those women away?"

"No, Aunt, why should I?"

"Costanza"—Maria Anna's hand took her hands—"it's not a good thing for those two to stay in the house, far less that they come to the funeral tomorrow."

"Rura's presence is inevitable. She must stay with her son, for his father has died. I shall send her away as soon as possible, agreed. But the other one, Teresina Pastanova, was fond of him. Pietro talked to me about her, and he died in her house; I think it's my duty to let her take leave of him in this way."

"It's not done, Costanza. Appearances are important. You do so many original things . . . people talk . . ."

"What of it?"

"The norms of conduct should be respected. We all need friends."

"Aunt, what can a good wife do when her husband wishes to see his kept woman? I have learned from you. My husband is dead and Uncle Alessandro was still alive: that is the only difference."

"No, Costanza, you're wrong. Only you and Giuseppe, my eldest son, know that. Certain things must be done in secret, that's how it is," said her aunt, shaking her head. "Let's have some broth and stop thinking about this. But take care tomorrow, at the funeral, not to make a scandal. I'm certain Pietro wouldn't have liked that."

"My father told me to do what I wish, and I feel it is right to follow his advice," replied Costanza, and she dissolved in tears.

83

"The cat's eyes are closed by day but open by night."

*Teresina Pastanova pays a call on the Marchesa Sabbiamena
and talks to her about Rura Fecarotta.*

Costanza went down to the terrace with the tortoises. Countess Trasi and Maria Antonia observed her from the inside window, shaking their heads.

"She worries me," Maria Antonia was saying. "She never stops for a second, yet she does nothing; all she does is go round and round the house and garden. Like a ghost. She doesn't cry, doesn't talk."

Costanza didn't even look at her tortoises. Wandering about restlessly, she caressed the long leaves of the frangipane, sniffed at a flower, detached a dead leaf.

"I don't understand why she lets that woman near the house. Amalia tells me she comes every afternoon to stroll in the garden, with the excuse that after Pietro's death her own frightens her!"

"She's a strange one, this niece of mine, but she's also very unlucky!"

"She's strange, all right. But unfortunate like many others, I'd say. She goes looking for misfortune. Pietro had repented and wanted to get back together with her. She didn't want that. Now she is refusing to receive mourning visitors. People will say that she's not weeping over Pietro's death and goodness knows what else! What's certain is that she seems really disconsolate and she isn't responsive. I've told her in every possible way that visits help, and help a lot; they are a comfort, and they take one's mind off things. But she just roams around the house like a soul in torment."

Costanza roamed from room to room on the main floor, following the same route several times a day. It was as if she were visiting a museum: she would stop briefly in front of the portraits of her forebears and images of saints that were darkened by time and hence not covered with black bunting; her glance would rove from ornaments to glass cases, from furniture to curtains. She touched nothing, she saw nothing; it was if the objects didn't exist. Not even she knew the reason for this wandering around the house.

She had lost her soul. With Pietro's burial she had felt it being ripped out of its place to be replaced by emptiness, a hungry worm that cleaved to her insides and fed on more emptiness but was never sated. She had to feed it, and she found it everywhere in the house. The rooms smelt of emptiness, and she absorbed it to nourish the emptiness inside her, which would quieten it, but not for long. Then she would have to begin again: it was an obsession. Costanza did not think of Pietro. She had no memories. She felt no pain. She felt neither hunger nor sleep nor heat nor cold. She sensed no smells, sounds, or noises. The house in Cacaci, her favourite residence, mirrored its mistress: it, too, was empty and had no soul.

A shutter had been left half open, and a beam of light spread across the floor like a long gilded, closed fan. Costanza cut it with her hand, and observed her shadow on the majolica tiling, surprised that she still had a body.

"Your ladyship, Teresina Pastanova wants to speak to you," announced Rosa. "She is taking the sun in the garden, if your ladyship wishes to go there."

"*Voscenza benadica.* I have something important to tell you, something that no one must hear."

"Go on, Teresina."

"It's about Rura and milord the marchese."

Costanza stiffened. "Must I know this?"

"Yes, your ladyship, you must. Milord the marchese talked to me as if I were his mother, and he asked me for advice. He told me that your ladyship was most upset because he had brought a woman into the house. He told me this really complicated story. She was a woman he had had in the past and whom he hadn't seen for years. This woman sent word to him saying that she had married and that her husband had problems with certain men of honour. Well, she was afraid they would kill him, and she wanted the help of the Malivinnitti mafia.

"That woman was a bad lot. She began to strip in front of him even though he didn't want her to. He was really upset and he told her to go away, but she insisted and in the end he called the majordomo to have her dismissed. Nothing happened between them; he swore this to me many's the time.

"But I only half believed him. That story struck me as odd. But now

I do understand, and that's why I have to tell it to your ladyship. A trust-worthy wise woman told me that that woman has no husband. It was all wickedness. A shameless woman wanted your ladyship to see them to-gether. And so it happened.

"It was Rura's idea. It was Rura who paid the woman to importune the marchese. She went to the wise woman to make you both fall out of love, but for all the wise woman's spells—and she knew what she was about—nothing would work. Rura told the woman everything, and now that the marchese is dead she has had scruples and she came to tell me what Rura did.

"Rura hates your ladyship. Rura knew that your ladyship comes down to the little terrace every afternoon, and she sent that woman at the right time. It's Rura's fault, and hers alone."

Teresina had more to say. "It's true that the marchese was a woman-iser, but since the day things began to work between you he wanted no other woman. And afterwards, when there was all the fuss, he would come to my house to talk to me about your ladyship. But I could do noth-ing for him. He thought only of your ladyship. He died in love with your ladyship."

84

"After happiness comes death."

The death of Costanza Safamita, the Marchesa Sabbiamena

Teresina went away through the service entrance. Costanza was left stand-ing by the rose garden. Amalia and Maria Antonia went on watching her from the window. They knew she liked to stroll in the garden by herself, and they kept an eye on her. Costanza headed straight for the little room where she kept her gardening tools and came out holding some secateurs.

"Let's leave her alone, Amalia," said her cousin. "She'll start embroi-dering again soon, you'll see."

"May the Lord be thanked," murmured the nurse.

Costanza made her way along the rose garden, deadheading the withered blossoms. She gathered them in her hand. She had not wanted to listen to Pietro's explanation; she had snipped their love clean off, not only to protect herself but out of pride, the deadly pride of the Safamitas.

She opened her hand and let the petals fall down the escarpment: on one side, the garden overlooked a steep drop down to the valley from the high plateau on which Cacaci was built. Fields and orchards alternated like a soft chessboard as far as the river in the distance. From there began a broad, gentle slope that ended in rocks with needle-sharp peaks, like irregular sawteeth. The sun set over those blades, and then the shadow of the rocks would reach out over the almond groves and become iridescent blue, purple, and green.

Costanza looked up: the sky above Cacaci was still a bright blue shading into a lighter, almost white hue down towards the valley. The sun had swollen into a fiery orange. In Cacaci, the sun was about to set.

Costanza could see again.

She made her way to the middle of the rose garden. Her nostrils were prickling. One by one, the scents of the garden rose up: the smells of damp earth, manure, grass. Then the fragrant perfume of the roses.

Costanza could smell again.

And she heard a distant voice. "Costanza, I have been looking for you all my life. You have deep, strong roots. I wrap myself around you and together we look at the sky, smile at the sun, and we enjoy life," he used to tell her. She, of all people, had lopped off his branches. The sky above the rocks was turning pink, and the sun was low in the sky. She listened. A voice was singing in the distance. *Porgi, amor . . .* The music and the song grew deeper and more intense. Pietro had loved her until the end, he loved her, he loved her . . . The taste of him was in her mouth, she felt his body, touched his hair, smelt his skin, she explored him all over, deep down. She felt faint, and staggered. She looked around for something to lean on. The convolvulus, climbing up the wall, made a wall of blue trumpet flowers; the freshly watered roses tied to the trellis gave off a subtle scent. Costanza hung on to the stem of a rosebush; the thorns pierced her hands. She felt a pang of something breaking deep inside, quick, clean. She saw Malivinnitti once more, the poppies of Malivinnitti, crushed, red as she was, red as her blood. Costanza was happy,

323

unbearably happy, and she slowly slipped down; her hair, caught by the thorny branches, came free as she went inexorably down.

Rosa was searching for her mistress. She found her lying facedown on the ground, on the damp earth, the light of the sunset on her hair, all agleam. A little snail, aroused by the watering, had ventured onto her hand and was gliding placidly along it.

Rosa leant against the low stone wall that served as a balustrade. In the distance, beyond the mountains, the sun was setting. The sky was a blaze of red.

"Oh, how beautiful is this bitter sun!" she exclaimed as she began to wail.

Costanza Safamita was in her thirty-sixth year. She left all that she possessed to her husband, the Marchese Sabbiamena, and to Antonio Fecarotta, his bastard son, and the rest to the sons—born and yet to be born—of her brother, Baron Giacomo Safamita di Muralisci.

No one was grateful to her.

Acknowledgements

Writing—the business of writing, I mean—is a dangerous scissors: it cuts out other people, albeit temporarily. To all those in my family and among my friends who have been tolerant and—in their own way—interested, I send a collective thanks.

But I wish to formalise other acknowledgements. Three are posthumous: first of all to the marchesa herself, because she really existed, though not as I invented her. I feel duty-bound to thank Luigi Pirandello, for he, too, was fascinated by this woman and wrote about her in his own way, thus arousing in me an urgent need to write about her in mine. Finally, there is Giuseppe Alaimo of Canicattì, a lawyer, eminent bibliophile, and writer whose vast collection of books and newspapers was generously placed at my disposal by his widow, Maria Grazia. Among those papers I found not only the prodigious Revalenza Arabica but also news items and historical events that I was able to weave into the novel so that they peep through here and there.

Among the living, I thank Darshana Boghilal Gupta, my beloved friend who lives in Mumbai. I have always followed her advice. When I was thinking about giving up writing, she was the one who urged me to persevere, she was the one who persuaded me to fix for myself strict deadlines and to stipulate contractual terms, and she was the one who suggested how I might reorganise my family and my professional commitments to make room for the marchesa. Darshana has never read my writings.

For the second time, I thank Alberto Rollo and Giovanna Salvia: they have known this story from the beginning, and they have listened to me and my characters. In so doing, they have understood and accompanied them all the way through, with enthusiasm.

Last but not least, I wish to thank Carlo Feltrinelli for his patience and encouragement.